THE BIOCRIME SPECTRUM

ERIK TABAIN

I0739029

First published in 2019

All characters and events in this publication, other than those clearly in the public domain, are fictitious and any resemblance to real persons, living or dead, is purely coincidental.

All rights reserved.

No part of this publication may be reproduced, stored in a retrieval system, or transmitted, in any form or by any means, without the prior permission in writing of the publisher, nor be otherwise circulated in a form or binding or cover other than that in which it is published and without a similar condition including this condition being imposed on the subsequent purchaser.

Text copyright ©E. Jokovich, ARMEDIA Pty. Ltd. 2019

ISBN: 978-0-6481644-2-5

Typeset by ARMEDIA Pty. Ltd.

Published by ARMEDIA
PO Box 1265, Darlinghurst NSW 1300, Australia
info@armedia.net.au

"The pure present is an ungraspable advance of the past devouring the future. In truth, all sensation is already memory."

—Henri Bergson

BOOK I. IN THE YEAR 3034

CHAPTER I.   RAW POWER

He tried hard to grasp meaning from the images appearing in his mind but he just couldn't solve the riddle. He pieced some of the images together; a sea of abstract plateaus, faces he thought he should know, short explosive flashes, coupled with the echoed voices of panic and muffled screams of newborn babies. Just as his collection of edited thoughts gained momentum and logic, they lost traction and echoed into the ether, disappearing, as if they'd never existed in the first place.

The flashes of imagery terrified Jonathan Katcher, but he didn't know why. His mind was sharp and memory was clear but the recurring momentary hallucinations caused havoc with his synapses. The morning cold was exacerbated by the lack of heating in his small living room and, after deciding a different set of acoustics in this cold room would force away his negative thoughts, he moved his hands towards a small plain, cubed black electronic box and summoned it to play the song in his thoughts.

Soon after the small round green light emitting diodes flashed in reponse to his gesture, the music of "Are 'Friends' Electric?" blasted through the hallway of his small ground-floor apartment, and Katcher felt the wall of sound and the energy of the song permeate through this body. The audio system wirelessly synchronized with his thoughts, the volume controlled by his synapse receptors—Katcher wanted the volume levels even louder, so he motioned his head slightly up, and the volume increased to match his movements.

"Are 'Friends' Electric?" was the song of the moment for Katcher, the dangerous and failed revolutionary who, a decade ago, evaded incarceration through a technicality, and now forced to work as a low-level teacher of history at the local community hub, with a specialist interest in the twentieth century. And with a fragmented memory. His life was a flight under the radar for now, but he wanted to subvert the system that almost destroyed him, before it could destroy him again.

It was the year 3034 and "Are 'Friends' Electric?" was a song reissued and re-credited many times over the past thousand years, now owned and 'performed' by the Eastern Dark Collective with its frontman, lead singer Matthias Asmarov. But, as a man who understood his history, Katcher knew the original song and lyrics were written by Gary Numan from the Tubeway Army, one of the more eccentric new wave performers in late twentieth century pop culture. And, for Katcher, the original was always the best.

Katcher was addicted to his BanPro morning thickshake, a combination of textured sweet insect protein and banana paste—and narcotics—and he entered his kitchenette to empty a small sachet of paste into the top tube of his compact food processor, a modern-day Thermomix-styled microwave appliance that sat in the corner of his kitchen bench and could produce any kind of synthetic food in a matter of minutes.

The paste oozing through the appliance triggered off its machinery and the comforting hum of his food processor persisted despite the over-energized music and, after a few minutes, a subtle low level green light let him know his breakfast was ready, while the other compartment of the food processor prepared his synthetic coffee and dripped into his favorite red mug, just as the lyrics *wondering what I'm doing in a room like this* streamed out from the paper-thin audio speakers.

Katcher's life was always on edge. He opened the two doors of his food processor, the outsides covered with scrapings of left-over food and spilt beverages, and took out the BanPro mixture—a yellow porridge-like mixture prepared in a scratched small white bowl—and the synthetic coffee, and retreated back to his small living room.

He reclined into the lounge chair but just when he started to sip his synthetic coffee, the morning routine was broken by the rapid sound of a high-pitched siren and flashing red lights, a common event in these parts of San Francisco.

He motioned for the levels from the audio speakers to go down and reached for his gun, a reaction to living in this area and to be prepared for the worst. His gun—a standard aluminium CX-44 laser, styled to look like the way personal guns had looked like for millenia—was the common defense weapon of choice and comprised two modes—the default stun mode, where it could send an electronic shock signal to disable a target for five minutes—and kill mode, a mode needing special authorization and decoding, a mode only accessible by less than one per cent of the citizenry. And for good reason: the kill mode had point-and-shoot functions, which could puncture the skin like an old-fashioned lead bullet, and killed if aimed at the head or heart.

Katcher rose up from his lounge to see the commotion outside and looked through a crack in his curtains to see the back of a black security vehicle with its open doors, and saw two darkly-clad security agents and a robocop, closing in on a young woman, forcing her into a corner of the narrow pathway, with several bemused citizens rushing onto the street to record the event on their cell devices. The lush artificial trees and vile stenciled graffiti behind them made the scene resemble two saber-tooth tigers circling a wild beast in an urban savannah, and the small crowd of citizens added to the sense of an imminent capture.

"What's your name fucker!" the security agent screamed towards the woman, an early twenty-something, bare footed with black hair streaming half-way down her back, inappropriately and shabbily dressed for the cold morning air and drizzling rain.

"Fuck you! Fuck off!" the woman screamed back, rattled, now she was cornered with nowhere else to go.

"Okay, looks like we're doing this the hard way," the security agent said, motioning to the robocop to target its digital taser gun, which was just about to release fifty-thousand volts into the woman's body.

"One last time—name?"

"Fuck you! Fuck—"

The robocop fired the digital taser gun, which issued a stunning laser shock into the woman, incapacitated her and left her writhing on the ground, as if she was having an epileptic fit. Within fifteen seconds, she was motionless—but still breathing heavily, and her face dripped with the cold sweat from evading the two security agents and the robocop. She'd run for almost a mile, but the security agents and robocop had the advantage in the chase of being in a small four-wheeled security vehicle, able to move through the back streets rapidly.

The second security officer brought out her cell device, a small wafer-thin screen that could access all the electronic secrets of the universe, as well as able to detect the off-gridders that weren't registered in her security systems.

"That was hard work," the security agent said, "a wild one—can you get the iris scan?"

Her work partner leant over the woman, opened up the woman's eyelids to reveal a deep blue iris and a fluctuating pupil, as well as the look of disdain for her captors. The security agent could see the reflection of her own body suit in the woman's eye: the deep charcoal black with a stunning orange stripe, and the reflected logo words of Biocrime, the biggest and most insidious crime surveillance business in the world. It was early morning, but this woman was their fourth capture of the day, and the agent impatiently scanned her iris with the cell device to complete the job, eager to move to the next chase.

"What's it reading?" asked the security agent.

"Radhika Romanov," her partner said, as she skimmed through the incoming details on the cell device. "Twenty-two years old, went off-grid when she was four. Who knows what she's been doing for the past eighteen years, but she's back into the continuum now."

"Radhika Romanov? What sort of fucking name is that? Sounds uppity. You've got the blood sample too?"

"Yep, hang on. In a minute," her partner said, while she knelt down and extracted blood through a small prick from the limp finger of Radhika Romanov. "Just scanning… and… all done! She's in now," as she gave a thumbs-up signal from a hand wrapped in a stylish thick black protective glove.

"Did you confirm she's with the Movement?"

"What do you think? Of course she's with the Movement! Someone off-grid, runs miles to get away from us, looks like, smells like, and probably thinks like she's from the Movement … and… *confirmed*." The agent's cell device beeped and a green tick appeared in her display to confirm Radhika

Romanov was back into the continuum and a companion of the Movement, the main counter-community subversive tribe that wanted to overthrow the current social order.

She dropped the arm of Radhika Romanov back to the ground and completed the profile on the cell device. The device recorded the blood of Radhika Romanov and re-connected to her Lifebook profile, the main way Biocrime kept tabs on citizens. Going off-grid to bypass its electronic surveillance clutches was easier many years ago but for these security agents, their main task was to get all off-gridders back into system. And to close down any private personal networks, wireless old-technology networks that were difficult to create and detect, but enabled off-gridders to communicate with each other outside of the continuum.

"That's all good—and don't forget to send a thank you to Marine Lestre," the security agent said.

"Of course, never forget the one that brung ya to the dance. Let's go."

"Hey," the security agent said, "my app just sent an alert—this is Jonathan Katcher's patch, and he's watching! I thought I recognized this zone. Shall we go and rough him up a bit?"

"I've got just the right thing for him," her partner said, instructing the robocop to lift its laser gun and point towards Katcher's apartment window.

"*Oi, Jonathan Katcher, cradle snatcher!*" she shouted, as the robocop pulled the trigger, releasing a volley of thin laser bullets, smashing Katcher's window and splaying broken glass onto his living room floor.

"Ha, that will keep him busy. Let's go, get some more off-gridders."

And with that, the two climbed into the security vehicle, pushed the robocop into the trunk, and zoomed away. It was a speedy sleek black four-wheeled vehicle that could also low-level hover, but the most prominent display—the Biocrime logo and its motto: 'Do no evil'—could be easily recognized, regardless of the speed.

The area was all clear now—the incident was a regular occurrence in this neighborhood zone but, today, Katcher had a front-row view of one of his own being tasered, recoded and put back into the continuum. And it was another reminder of why he worked so hard to undermine the Biocrime system in the past, and how he needed to return to his role in changing this system. But, in his usual manner, he was dismissive; he didn't care about Radhika Romanov. She was an individual, and he concerned himself with the bigger picture. She would be mobile again in around three minutes, almost as though nothing had ever happened. She would then wander off, unable to ever join her off-grid tribe, and he would never see her again. And, through the continuum, Biocrime was now able to see each and every one of her movements.

*

The commotion Katcher witnessed epitomized the struggle of the times—between the natural humans; and Technocrats, the human clones, the ones who over a short period of a few centuries, managed to reach a level of cybercontrol that permeated virtually every aspect of life in this modern world, sustained their high privilege and dominance over natural humans, and maintained the social order. And the Movement was the revolutionary cause initiated by natural humans who wanted to overturn this social order of control.

The two security agents were Technocrats and Radhika Romanov, like Katcher, a natural human. It was the faultline of historic and scientific progress, but Katcher was angered by these frequent events and frustrated by the restraints placed on him by Biocrime, and his inability to act. '*If only I could do something*' was his constant subliminal thought, and he kept this thought as he retracted back into his lounge, finishing off his BanPro breakfast and synthetic coffee.

Katcher's apartment block was an unspectacular sight from the outside; twenty-three storeys high with thirty small apartments on each level, and a series of small businesses, cafes and eateries on the ground floor, surrounded by other similarly tall apartment blocks. It was colored with light blue paneling, a color chosen to not offend the brilliance of the stark blue sky but, like many apartment blocks in this zone, it was ragged, dirty, barely functional and aesthetically unpleasing to the eye. The sides of the buildings comprised colorful murals painted by young children many decades ago but, in contrast to the optimism they might have shown when they were first created, these murals were now dank and darkened with pollution and neglect, as forgotten as the rest of community they were trying to uplift.

Constructed cheaply, the apartment block was as solid as a rock but, with a squint of the eye, it resembled a tall prison without barbed wire. There were a few large mechanical relics from the past embedded within the architectural design and displayed near the foyer—a twenty-feet pulley with massive cogs and wheels from the 1800s, beside a more streamlined rusted mechanical machine from the 2100s, used for hauling bricks, cement and other building materials. These relics were supplemented with a video lightshow screened onto the side walls, which outlined the working tales from yesteryear—a group of overalled men loading up wooden pylons onto a horse-driven carriage; women working away on Spinning Jennys, mostly with ecstatic faces which perpetuated the myth of an exhilarated work ethic. These types of lightshows were common architectural features in modern buildings: it was more ironical than anything else, supposedly to claim a nostalgic piece of yesteryear while the rest of the world sped ahead in its maniacal drive towards technological perfection.

Just after Katcher took the last swig of his coffee, his music was interrupted by an incoming datacall, which he accepted with a small motion of moving his four fingers towards himself, like royalty requesting the presence of a guest. The datacall appeared on his small lightscreen—an ultra thin Perspex-like televisual structure linked wirelessly to the continuum—positioned in front of his lounge couch and away from the sunlight that usually populated the room at this time of day. He could choose between screen display or hologram, but decided the hologram display was too intrusive for morning time. A familiar face appeared on the lightscreen.

"Good morning Jonathan, this is Rowena from Biocrime for your daily report."

"Yep, hi Rowena," Katcher said, after an exaggerated pause. "It's me. As you can see, I'm here, behaving like I should be, like I have for the past ten years."

"You can never be too careful can you? What's on your agenda for today."

'Rowena from Biocrime' was a synthetic bot monitoring Katcher's digital house arrest. It was the same call every morning, and at the same time—08:00 hours. She wasn't real, but the questions were. She could see and record all of Katcher's movements and conversations and, if anything seemed unusual or worthy of further investigation, an automatic trigger could be sent to local Biocrime security agents, not dissimilar to the ones that cornered Radhika Romanov, for a follow-up and, if they felt like it, a blow of a baton over Katcher's head, or a fist to the solar plexus, just to show him who was in charge.

The invasive monitoring was primarily to continue Biocrime's ongoing humiliation of Katcher; partially to verify his whereabouts, partially to be a nuisance, but mainly to accrue revenue each day to Biocrime for doing its community service and keeping tabs on Katcher. Biocrime had over thirty-thousand permanent digital house arrests on its books just in San Francisco and it was a lucrative market.

Whenever Katcher received these datacalls, he put his usual arrogance and bravado in check. His terrifying hallucinations were usually triggered by the Biocrime datacalls and after a decade of monitoring, he wanted to reduce their interactions to a bare minimum.

"Just the usual today Ro," Katcher continued, "study, my research, teaching those classes at the community hub that you force me to do. Having breakfast, lunch, and probably dinner too."

"And have you been engaged in any counter-community activities you're aware of?"

"Nee. Nein. Votch. O'hi. Tidak. Nej—"

"Please, in universal English, not one of those dead languages."

"Okay, okay. No, I haven't."

"Okay. And we've recorded you've had the complete sachet of BanPro this morning. Can you confirm?"

"Yes, one BanPro, just like I have every morning."

"That means you have four satchets left. Your monthly batch will be delivered to your apartment tomorrow morning. Thank you Jonathan Katcher, that's it for now. Until tomorrow, enjoy your day!"

"Yes, and fuck you, you holographic fuck," Katcher said under his breath, making sure his anger eluded detection.

Most of the conversation was perfunctory—small data chips inside each sachet of BanPro sent signals to Biocrime once they were opened and consumed, and 'Rowena from Biocrime' had all the information she needed before the conversation commenced, but visual identification and voice recognition added to Katcher's psychological torment and humiliation. Their short conversation was also recorded and stored in Biocrime's data center and transcribed in real time, as well as date-stamped for 08:02. It fulfilled the requirements of Katcher's digital house arrest.

On some days if he was bored or could adequately manage his hallucinations, he'd have a longer conversation with 'Rowena from Biocrime' but the longer these conversations went on, the more he realized the limitations of a holographic bot programmed to do the necessities—ask the questions, get the answers, tick the boxes—and the more he realized the futility of engagement.

The daily BanPro addiction was critical for Biocrime. It was tailored for Katcher's memory matrix and contained a mixture of trace elements of narcotics and assorted deliriants and disassociative substances. His extreme hallucinations were based on the allegations made against him during his crowd trial, and Biocrime created the perfect concoction that would exacerbate negative experiences which were triggered by certain events—such as the morning datacalls from Biocrime—but left the rest of his brain receptors in tact. This combination of drugs was partially experimental but an essential way for Briocrime to ensure the punishment of Katcher continued indefinitely.

Aside from the hallucinations, life was bearable for Katcher now, but it wasn't always this way. He was forty-four and supplemented his low universal yearly income of €10,000—the universal currency unit of the day, known as 'ucas', or simply 'dollars'—by offering historical academic talks, material and information to willing learners at the all-purpose community hub down near the old university town of Berkeley.

He knew enough about his own history to remember he'd been a failed and irresponsible leader of the Movement, even if his narcotic diet meant he couldn't quite piece together the remnants of his experiences, the people involved, or how he even arrived to the position of leadership.

Katcher was passionate about history and this passion belied his tough, rugged look, as a former leader of a revolutionary movement and leading intellectual, the one that beat the system on a software malfunction and a legal technicality, ten years earlier. His life thoughts fluctuated between anxiety of being the failed and irresponsible leader, the mundanity of his current life, and being prepared for opportunities in the future, if they ever presented themselves and, if the opportunities didn't arrive to him personally, he wanted to engage the next generation, and beyond, with future activism.

In his previous life before his digital house arrest, he was a violent, petulant and impatient counter-establishment figure, a leading intellectual of a loose alliance known as 'the Movement', committed to ending the domination of Technocrats and questioning how the social order of the world could be changed and improved. He had a fascination with twentieth-century life: politics, society and the new-wave Marxists, who in the twenty-second century claimed that the best way to achieve pure communism was through a period of unbridled technological capitalism, where the fruits of mechanical labor were shared through universal income to each citizen. Katcher argued for higher distributions of income and more transparency in Biocrime's surveillance operations, but was considered to be too radical and disruptive, mainly because of his widespread agitation to close down human cloning clinics and incubation systems, which would have resulted in smaller Technocrat populations in the future.

Leading up to his arrest a decade ago, and like many other high profile people of his caliber, he had been monitored by crowd-funded citizen surveillance operatives through the continuum—stalkers on the Lifebook platform who liked to watch, surveil, and earn revenue at the same time. His Lifebook account was patched through to an online profile through Biocrime, and citizens lodged 'click-bait' negative reports about his behavior, real or imagined. Once his profile gathered enough 'likes', 'wants' and revenue to justify detention, Biocrime security agents would track Katcher down, detain him for several days but then release him, due to insufficient evidence.

Through this process, Katcher was detained many times for acting against community interests and finally threatened with deportation to a universal penal zone—remote uncivilized and inhospitable empty islands, where people were incarcerated and had to fend for themselves—unless he curtailed his organizing activities and subversion. He would have been sent away to a universal penal zone years ago and probably dead by now, except for technicalities relating to his profile and data management. Biocrime was also certain Katcher, as a revolutionary, had murdered many Technocrats and even some natural humans, and created destructive events such as apartment bombings and releasing anthrax gas in a San Francisco incubator hospital—killing over a hundred late-stage clone fetuses—but their surveillance systems were intercepted by sophisticated hacktivists and Katcher defied Biocrimes legal structures.

Biocrime was never able to resolve how their systems were breached, but assumed it was through a sophisticated hacking process that bypassed the continuum and, because of this suspicion, fast-tracked a number of large-scale surveillance projects that closed digital loopholes and cracks in their coding. For Biocrime, Katcher was seen as the one that got away. But they could still make life as difficult as possible for him.

His digital house arrest was low level for now—but for the first few years, it was different: daily apartment inspections, permanent surveillance, psychological testing, routine bashings and 'visits' from Biocrime agents. But, over time, Katcher was considered 'de-radicalized' and no longer a threat to the community.

Katcher's exterior psychology had changed over the past decade, but none of his interior psychology had been breached by the persistent harassment and digital house arrest, and he saw himself as being 'technically' in hibernation, or even on 'sabbatical'. He was a chancer, a risk-taker with a winner-takes-all mentality but knew when the odds were stacked against him, and they were stacked against him right now. He had curtailed his violence and reluctantly became a non-participant—not that he had a choice—but would jump at a chance if it ever presented itself to him, to again be the revolutionary leader that he thought he was made to be.

Because of his previous existence as a leading intellectual for 'the Movement', Katcher was often contacted by activists, who were often themselves detained or sometimes exported to a universal penal zone in the more extreme cases, to head up a new wave of resistance against the Technocrats. He was regarded as the modern-day 'spiritual leader' of 'the Movement' by many underground revolutionary agents: a movement needed its leader, and that's why they wanted him back.

But Katcher trusted no-one, except for the two people that defended him in his crowd trial—Mike Scanlen and Maria Renalda—but the daily cocktail of narcotics meant his memory of them had become scattered and, on some occasions, he doubted whether they had even ever existed at all.

Scanlen and Renalda were leading members of the Movement and were the ones who masterminded a series of software malfunctions and legal obstacles in Katcher's crowd trial that resulted in him found not guilty of the catalogue of criminal allegations collated by Biocrime, but both disappeared soon after the trial was completed. Scanlen hadn't been seen or heard of for many years, and Renalda reportedly died in suspicious circumstances. But Biocrime realized the psychological connection between Katcher and Scanlen and Renalda and worked over many years to diminish his memory of them, and their strategy of enforced daily BanPro mixtures was the best way of achieving this.

But even while Katcher's memory of the only two people he could trust had almost been completely eradicated, he maintained a deep-seated suspicion of almost everyone else and could never be sure if an activist sent to befriend him was a grand plan of entrapment initiated by Biocrime. He refused all requests from anyone he thought would offer a remote possibility of entrapment, and felt that each contact was a recipe for disaster. He knew becoming engaged with the Movement again had major repercussions and, for the time being, preferred his much lower profile, one where at least his intellectual needs were satisfied.

There hadn't been any negative activity on his Lifebook profile since his arrest and subsequent release ten years earlier. True to his word, he'd curtailed his activities of subversion and acquiesced to the digital house arrest and court-ordered citizen service at the community hub—the only revenue-raising actions he was permitted to engage in—and his profile was only subjected to citizens interested in historical information about him, or general knowledge about his past actions.

He was relatively free for now: Biocrime wanted to maintain the semblance of 'freedom' for the citizenry, but it was a fig-leaf, and most of the population knew it. In reality, Katcher was a prisoner under constant surveillance, and would be detained and sent away forever if he made any false moves.

So, for now, he existed within the general community and, as long as he flew under the radar and kept away from any activism and contact with the Movement, he would be safe. For the time being.

*

LIFEBOOK LIVES LIFE. BIOCRIME PROTECTS LIFE.

'Life. Is Lifebook' was a successful advertising campaign to promote the relationship between Lifebook, the all engaging and all pervasive data collator and aggregator, and Biocrime profiling, when it first became a part of the continuum in the year 2600. Every citizen had a Lifebook account created biologically as soon they were born or created in a incubator—there was no need to register or apply—the Lifebook software automatically and seamlessly produced a life-long account, based on detecting changes in cumulative DNA material, and only that citizen could access the account through DNA matching. And the account remained with that person until they died—or circumvented by citizens that escaped the system and wanted to go off-grid.

Lifebook, of course, was the central part of 'the continuum', a term first used in the 2300s. It sounded fancy, but it was merely a replacement for the 'internet', an electronic system that existed between circa 1980 and the 2300s. The internet was an electronic network of networks that existed between computers, telephony connected through copper and fiber wiring, and mobile cell communications, but became much more than that with the introduction of biotechnology, where networks could be linked through a combination of biological matter, plants, trees, DNA material, molecules and air particles.

It was based on scientific research and development over many years, and the merging of electronics, electricity, the biology of the natural world and human behavior, and was considered to be the 'holy grail' of science until the continuum was finally achieved circa 2300. Through the continuum, all of life's transactions were consolidated and found in the one location: love, education, business—and crime detection.

Lifebook had its many precursors during the technology era between circa 1970 and circa 2200, initially with bulletin boards, chat rooms, the first social media platform known as Six Degrees, following by Facebook, which became a media behemoth in the early 2000s and kept its hegemony for roughly a hundred and fifty years. Media and social management went through a period of entropy where smaller and ineffective systems became prevalent, but through the symbiotic relationship between biology and technology, these smaller networks became redundant and obsolete, resulting in Lifebook becoming the sole system.

Access to Lifebook was through ubiquitous lightscreens—the modern computer of the day—and smaller hand-held cell devices and tablets, miniature versions of the lightscreen. Through convergence technology, lightscreens and cell devices were the avenues of information where every piece of digital bioelectronic data could be accessed and produced—talking, listening, watching, recording and computing.

Over time, Lifebook developed an offshoot called Biocrime, which itself, became the largest corporation in the world, based on surveillance and monitoring, using citizens and crowd funding to do its work.

Biocrime profiling became a key asset of Lifebook and 'Life. Is Lifebook' was the first advertising promotion used to encourage citizens to create Biocrime profiles if they ever saw anyone engaged in crime, or behaved suspiciously or performed counter-community activity. It was a system egged on by vigilante behavior, and encouraged financially by imploring the crowd to donate monies for someone else to act upon the crime, like a conduit between the act of crime and crime enforcement.

For the first time, there was a link between crime, community vigilantes, and profit, and there were immediate rewards for all involved.

The first moments of the thirty-second advertisement, shown on all media avenues, personal screens and public billboards, are arresting: a slick montage of a group of hoods attacking an older woman late at night while she walks her dog, leaving her for dead on the ground. It's a slick cinematic production, and the voiceover and graphics announces: "You can do something. Don't be a bystander". The scene then cuts away to a middle-aged woman summoning up a Biocrime profile on her lightscreen after seeing the incident through surveillance cameras, and within seconds, generates €300 for herself through a number of 'likes' and 'wants'. A Biocrime vehicle apprehends the culprits and another vehicle takes the woman to hospital.

The edit then cuts to a wide shot of a diverse group of concerned citizens, their faces turning to smiles with the final graphic: "Lifebook lives life. Biocrime protects life. See something, do something. Be rewarded".

CHAPTER 2.   THE HUMAN DIVIDE

Katcher was a natural human—and proud of it—but needed to keep his pride in check and show indifference about what he was, and who he was. It was better, for now, if he fitted into the crowd and kept away from trouble. But, like many natural humans, he pondered the world from different vantage points, and at different points of time within human history. What would his life be like if he existed in the year 2514? Or in the year 1389? Or during other calamitous events, such as the second world war of the twentieth century? Sometimes, he drifted in and out of thought, almost like being in a meditative state, meandering towards thinking about what life would be like as a Technocrat, before he snapped himself out of it.

The modern world had two types of people—natural humans and Technocrats, and at the start of the fourth millennium, around seventy per cent of the world's population of eighteen billion was Technocrat. Through the London Convention Agreement in the year 2214, synthetic reproduction of human substance was permitted and resulted in major developments in human cloning and advances in bio-stem cell research. However, chromozonal imbalances that occurred in cloned humans meant almost all Technocrat men were infertile and it was difficult for adult Technocrat women to fall pregnant. Even the few Technocrat embryos that reached full-term and a live birth, were severely malformed, underdeveloped and unviable, born with violent characteristics and some with animal features. Between 2214 and 2300, only two live births from Technocrat women survived past the age of two years, and neither of those survived past the age of four years.

It became impossible for Technocrats to reproduce naturally, and they needed access to the DNA from natural humans for survival. Over several centuries, two segregated classes of peoples developed: natural humans; and Technocrats, the cloned 'synthetic' people. Like the billions of their predecessors throughout, natural humans were born through natural sexual reproduction, but Technocrats could only be cloned or reproduced artificially in birthing clinic incubators from natural human DNA—sold by desperate humans or compulsory acquired by Biocrime.

Cloning clinics and incubations become a high level of business development—technological advances resulted in small incubation kits that contained the materials for full development and realization of a child in a home or personal environment. The first incubation kit in the field—i-Incubate—comprised a small rectangular metallic box with a lightsceen on its side, large enough to encompass a full-term fetus, and a range of sachets including the artificial ovum, sperm, and nutrients to kick-start life, and temperature modulators that provided the optimal conditions for human life to form and develop.

Because of the ease of artificial reproduction of human life, many Technocrat families developed very quickly, some deciding to purchase and develop multiple fetuses concurrently, and the more affluent families outsourced this work to cloning clinics. This lead to the proliferation of Technocrats in a short space of time, and they gradually outnumbered the natural human population, becoming the dominant group around the world. And with dominance, the Technocrats assumed a higher level of social, political and economic control.

The manner of birth also became an important consideration—natural birth, as opposed to the incubator birth—and there were scores of academic debates relating to child attachment theories, and how the lack of mothering in the incubator births caused the low emotional quotients that were pervasive among the Technocrat population.

The human–Technocrat divide had existed for centuries, and was the only class of differentiation that had survived over time: racism wasn't an issue any more, nationalism had dissipated after the gradual removal of state borders, religion had been relegated to the zone of quack theory, English became the *lingua franca*. But human existence thrived over millennia, based on difference and fear of otherness, and once one point of difference was removed, another one would take its place. Societies throughout history depended on eternal and ongoing conflict. The human–Technocrat divide was the last remaining differential between humans and, for the time being, firmly entrenched.

Natural humans wanted to maintain diversity and differences and create better regulated worlds, but were outnumbered by Technocrats who believed a world free of governments, religion, and different peoples would ultimately create a more controlled, efficient and better world—and using technology was the best way to achieve this.

Very few Technocrats worked beyond their €40,000 per year universal income requirements—aside from engaging in crowd-funded surveillance—and would often fill their time reliving historical experiences through inexpensive virtual reality holographs, or attend the more expensive historical sessions provided by historical figures such as Katcher.

Natural humans were at the other end of society's scale, receiving only around a quarter of the individual universal income allocated to Technocrats, and were the workers usually engaged in mundane low-income employment, in poor working conditions. Essentially, they were the exploited workers supporting the economy, while the Technocrats enjoyed the rewards and leisure from this exploitation.

The advantaged world of the Technocrats could only be achieved through more community-based law enforcement and surveillance, with short-term detention centers for minor indiscretions, and deportation to permanent universal penal zones for any citizens deemed to be acting against the interests of the community, whether it was through serious criminal actions, or working towards a change in the social order.

Natural humans were considered the 'higher' life form with full emotional and intellectual potential, while Technocrats, even through they were the wealth accumulators and controlled virtually every aspect of the world, were considered 'inferior', with lesser emotional qualities, and fixated on the here and now of the world, the technical and economic requirements of the world, rather than the inequities of society and those divisions between natural humans and Technocrats.

The natural humans thumbed their noses at such audacious cybercontrol of the world, and were prepared to engage in counter-establishment actions and activities, knowing that all of their actions could be retrieved and used against them, resulting in detentions, or the worst fate of being sent to a universal penal zone, likely to die a horrible death, and certainly never to return. But yet they continued to resist, even though theirs was likely to be a lost cause.

Many worked for 'the Movement', a cause which had it roots in the mid-twenty-fourth century, when Technocrats started to outnumber natural humans, and the general understanding of 'what it meant to be human' changed drastically.

Technocrats were considered to be the 'idiot' class by natural humans. Cold, calculating, almost on auto-pilot, ensuring that every task needed to maintain the law and order of the community was in place. They caused the radical change in social and cultural existence: the end of borders, the end of governments, free passage of citizens and capital, bio-medical advances, with the 'we cannot stand in the way of progress' philosophy. Many Technocrats ridiculed 'the Movement' and all it represented and often queried why the natural humans couldn't accept the good changes they'd implemented over centuries, bemused by resistance that, if successful, could only result in a return to destructive competitive nationalisms, warfare and social chaos.

Katcher saw himself as some kind of internationalist and believer in equality and fraternity amongst all humans, but he was as chauvinistic as the worst. He would never admit it but, subconsciously, he didn't think Technocrats were people at all, even though they'd been created from the DNA of natural humans. He thought Technocrats were like factory chickens, sterile and couldn't be like humans because they couldn't reproduce outside of their incubators. He engaged with these thoughts, but he never attempted to push them away. Internally, he was a hypocrite, one of the enduring and timeless of all human frailties. He accepted his personal hypocrisy, but also believed that purity in thought and action was unattainable and only the impotent were pure and consistent.

How else could he have been responsible for the deaths of so many Technocrats if he believed in equality and fraternity for all?

CHAPTER 3.   THE YEAR 3034

There were very few places to hide in the year 3034. The continuum, genetic memory and lightcapture made sure of that. Every movement, every discussion, every conversation could be retrieved through data scanners and lightscreen devices. Every citizen who wanted to watch the world through the continuum could link through Lifebook or becoming a self-appointed stalker, where anyone could report crime and social misdemeanors through citizen surveillance and updating details on other citizen's Biocrime profiles.

The continuum created a web of linkages between all existing DNA in the world—living and dead—as well as the storage of genetic memory and historical lightcapture, which meant that anyone with a lightscreen could access the experiences of everyone and every event from human history—for a fee. It also meant citizen stalkers could datamine genetic memory and lightcapture—if they had the time and energy—to detect actions and activities by anyone in the past, and to see if there was anything can could be reported or updated on Biocrime profiles. It was a sophisticated system, one which reduced crime to a level where only extremist natural humans or off-gridders were engaged in subversive actions.

Jonathan Katcher knew every move he made and every word he uttered could be retrieved through the continuum.

He was on many surveillance watch lists, and his actions were recorded and uploaded to his Biocrime profile but, mainly, they were only minor blips and nothing of value to any stalkers, and wouldn't be, as long as he maintained his current lifestyle and current level of interests. Biocrime allowed for some leeway in crime monitoring, as it was determined by crowd-sourced material and assessments, so, for now, Katcher was safe.

Regular stalkers could see he held his regular historical and economic lectures, but they were nothing controversial and they could see there were no ucas to retrieve by producing updated reports. He was so low on the radar that he barely warranted an appearance on so many watch lists, and he hoped eventually, he would drop off entirely. This was unlikely, but there was always a hope.

Katcher was a thought machine and a deep thinker— thinking about ways to lead his revolution to the forefront again, and end the domination of the Technocrats. He liked the fact that English was the universal language, with a few variations around the globe, but he often wondered about the dead languages that dropped off—German, French, Arabic, Chinese, Japanese. These were only spoken in a few historical learning and research environments but the advent of automatic real-time translation through the continuum made most languages redundant, and in 2650, English became the universal language.

Language was important but there were many parts of the modern world that Katcher was marveled with. Skin colour, language and cultures averaged out over hundreds of years and, with no controls over human and capital flow after the collapse of state and national boundaries, around ninety-five per cent of people lived in cities and close to water zones.

People lived wherever they wanted to, anywhere in the world, as long as they were prepared to pay for it.

Medical advances had reached a stage where few people were physically or psychologically ill, and medical robots performed all surgical procedures, but natural life expectancy was still only around eighty years and had only marginally increased over the past millennia.

Nanomeds, created by the BioMed industry, the medical equivalent of Biocrime, kept the population well, but they cost a fortune. Medicines had been reduced to three types of nanomeds: regular maintenance nanomeds taken once each year—nano-medical robots that travelled through the circulation system, monitoring core bodily functions and performing nano-biopsies, scaling back built-up cholesterol and other blockages with the body, removing any sign of cancerous growths, clearing blood flow and pulmonary functions, brain health and emitting medical updates to the central BioMed system, which, of course, was linked up to Lifebook through the continuum.

Onset nanomeds were taken as a remedial and preventative response to accidents or wounds and had the ability to repair small-scale damaged tissue. This performed a preliminary triage for a patient, could monitor immediate danger signals and assess whether a BioMed ambulance, equipped with a health robot, would be required to take the injured to a hospital.

Standard nanomeds were the cheapest, the new-wave headache tablets, combining paracetamol, barbituates and an entire range of biochemical and medical substances which the body took and used as needed, depending on the ailment, with remaining and unwanted substances eliminated through the body's urine system. Standard nanomeds were widely available through a wide range a brand names, and were commonly known as 'happy pills'.

Due to the depletion and scarcity of resources and economy of extraction, recycling materials was one of the biggest business activities in the world, second to Biocrime's crime and surveillance business. In the mid-2200s, the world was faced with an environmental catastrophe, and had the choice to continue obtaining metals from more obscure parts of the earth's crust, or put an end to resource wastage, and recycle an already plentiful supply of metal and resources that had already been extracted from the earth. Every material was recycled—metal, plastics, wood, lightscreen parts and pieces, organic materials, food waste, water, cloth—and consumer behaviors changed within a short period of time.

There was no centralized government and all human activity was managed through citizen surveiling. Everything could be scanned and checked, and there were no privacy restrictions or limitations. Genetic recording and lightcapture meant people could be monitored, in the hope they would refrain from any activities considered counter to society's expectations.

Citizens decided how their communities should be built and constructed, through online and technological interactives, but through the evolution of time, many cities and communities around the world had a similar look and feel to them, mainly only differentiated by geographical landmarks and topographical features.

In the world of 3034, citizens were multi-skilled. Through the results of having less working time and less time absorbed by menial tasks, citizens had more skills and personalized interests, and education was based around the ability to learn and acquire new knowledge, rather than provided with core data and facts, which could easily be acquired through other means.

There was a universal income that was generated through super-private entities, where profits and surplus revenues were collated through the continuum and distributed to citizens through Lifebook. Universal income was enough to survive well, but many citizens, especially Technocrats, supplemented their income becoming engaged in any industry of activity they could find. The main source of income and activity for many citizens was crowd-funded surveillance to catch 'criminals', or people engaged in counter-social or counter-economic activities. It was a combination of infotainment, news, work and, if someone was lucky, a supplement to universal income.

Online surveillance stalking relied on two main methods of data access: Lifebook Live was an add-on within the main Lifebook platform and provided live and real-time visual footage from virtually any molecular point from the surface of the earth, with the sound and imagery presented through a lightscreen. It used a combination of lightcapture technology, where any visual vantage point could be accessed—panoramic, aerial view, close-up view, a three-sixty-degree street view, and anything in between.

The second mode of data access was from historical recordings of this lightcapture and genetic sampling material—through an extension of Lifebook Live which recorded and stored genome data into a system known as the world memory bank.

Stalkers accessed and monitored Lifebook Live and the world memory bank to detect counter-establishment activities and, if they saw anything that warranted intervention from Biocrime, posted embellished reports to seek crowd-funded payments and rewards to make an arrest. Posted reports that were found to be false or incorrect were marked down as unreliable sources and if there were too many mark-downs on a stalker's account, they were banned from the system for one month, and serial offenders were barred permanently.

It was a process that required a fine balance between factual and embellishment, but it was a system that weeded out the inexperienced and the sensationalists, and one that rewarded the best.

CHAPTER 4.   THE SNOWFLAKE EFFECT

The morning had turned overcast and the grey of the sky seemed more in tune with the depressing light blue paneling on the outside of Katcher's apartment block. Inside, his apartment was just as drab—a colorless combined living and eating area with bland light grey walls, with a seemingly out-of-the-way toilet and bathroom area tucked in behind his small bedroom door—a rudimentary setup, but at least his living area was enlightened with ornaments from yesteryear positioned in various parts of his apartment.

One ornament was a miniature cat-like figurine from the ancient republic of Egypt—not an original, but a mass-produced artifact—that was housed in the practice rooms of Sigmund Freud, a leading psychoanalyst from the twentieth century. Katcher couldn't quite understand the relationship between ancient Egypt and psychiatry, but he was impressed with the exploration of *psyche*, and keeping a memento with a spurious link to Freud reminded him how the power of one person gave rise to a thousand years of the symbiotic relationship between the mind, the body, and technology.

Katcher looked at his inanimate feline friend from across the room, thought about this relationship between the continuum and synapses, not just in his brain, but everybody's brain. It was a momentary thought before he returned to putting the final touches to his presentation for his weekly one-hour session at the community hub—this one was titled 'Communism and the rise of supraliberalism', to be uploaded to his Lifebook profile.

Although he was a failed revolutionary and still considered by Biocrime and the community to be a threat to the social system, he was still considered to be a leading influencer and thinker among his tribe and, for this presentation, he expected the usual number of around forty in attendance, most of which were humans, and a few semi-interested Technocrats. He would be paid through the continuum, like every other financial transaction in the world economy. Each person attending the session paid what they thought the value was to them—on average, it was around twenty ucas, paid in real time as Katcher spoke. If any of the attendees left early, that was the point they stop paying and that was when Katcher stopped receiving income. And because of this, he needed to entertain his audience like a song and dance man—nobody had time for boring monotones and unimpressive speeches.

Normally for this type of event, Katcher would have his lectures and talks screened through the continuum—he'd probably have another five or six thousand citizens paying up to watch if that was the case—but his Biocrime profile had been restricted under international security guidelines and didn't allow him to webcast to an audience so, for the time being, he provided old-school in-person presentations, only available to a small band of adherents and interested parties.

Katcher was intrigued by *supraliberalism*, the brand of economic philosophy that expanded into all areas of human activity, and had become the only kind of economic system available. It was a term that became prominent in the early 2100s and gave rise to many other functions of human existence. Its antecedents were rooted in the economic philosophies of Freidrich Hayek in the early twentieth century, which developed into neoliberalist thinking from the Chicago school of economists towards the latter part of the century.

The great economic schism that existed for nearly two centuries—the Marxism–*laissez-faire* dichotomy—and led the world to the brink of catastrophe in the mid-twentieth century and the early twenty-first century, largely disappeared towards the mid-2150s, where collectivism and the virtues of organized labor were only discussed in the few historical and societies in existence at the time, and examined as historical curiosities, rather than a serious return to collectivism. Collectivism, and any ideologies relating to communism or socialism were not outlawed or discouraged, but due to the onset of expanded neoliberal ideas (and further into supraliberalism) and the acceptance of these new ideas, their popularity fell away.

Like many current economic thinkers and theorists, Katcher was bemused there was only the one world economic practice that had been prevalent for the past thousands years. He pondered about the dichotomy of economic theories throughout history, and the systems that preceded the onset of communism in the twentieth century—serfdom, the free market and the slave market, where empires were built on the enforced labor of citizens.

As Katcher summoned his lightscreen to complete and check his presentation, he wondered whether the world of today really did have the one economic system or, whether in reality, it had reverted to the economies of old, based on a free market on one side, and a sophisticated form of slavery on the other side.

He made a note about this issue for discussion and added it to his presentation. He flicked his hand towards the lightscreen to approve his presentation and it would soon be available through the continuum, onto Lifebook and through to the forty or so citizens likely to attend his lecture.

He wanted to maintain influence somewhere and somehow through his restricted activities, and influencing the minds of a small gathering at a community hub, however insubstantial, could make a difference. It was only a small contribution into his world of 'snowflake' activism—the belief that it was always the one snowflake that tipped the avalanche into the valleys and crevices below—but it was a contribution, nevertheless.

CHAPTER 5.   I LIKE TO WATCH

A subtle buzz sounded on a lightscreen in the Potrero Hill apartment, a more salubrious and densely populated Technocrat zone, not far from the harbor water. The thirteen-storey block was in the midst of other apartment blocks and surrounded by well-kept recreational zones, complete with enough visual space, greenery and parkland, designed to create a harmony between the inner workings of the mind and the grunge of the modern world.

The lightscreen was in a small untidy room, a stark contrast to the external environment, with a range of smaller disused lightscreens and gadgets and digital storage units: everything had a reason for being there but, for the outside observer, it was a disorganized chaos. Among the chaos was a bank of three personal i-Incubate kits, placed in the corner of the room, almost like a forgotten relic. The small liquid crystal diode numbers on each of kits showed incubation commenced eight weeks ago, and all fetal functions were performing normally. Someone in this apartment was expecting triple clones, but it was difficult to tell who it was going to be.

From her loungeroom chair, Marine Lestre moved towards her standing desk and summoned her lightscreen to display the incoming alert, already signaling a positive message, so she knew it was, more likely, providing news about a recent capture of an off-gridder.

"Fuck-ing fan-tastic!" shouted Lestre, as she read the message on her lightscreen, hoping her partner, Marlon D'Souza, would rouse from his sleep on the couch and share in her news.

"What is it," D'Souza said, sleepily. "Another off-gridder?"

"Yup. Mmm, fancy. Radhika Romanov. Total of twelve-hundred ucas, and six-hundred to the security agents that put her back into the continuum."

Lestre scanned through the visual recording of the capture, a screen within a screen on her lightscreen display. It was a pseudo three-dimensional recording which combined the viscam recorders from the two security agents with the dashcam from the Biocrime vehicle. When combined with the dynamic sen-surround audio recording, Lestre could easily imagine herself at the scene of the chase—a twelve-minute segment which commenced when the security agents and the robocop first detected Radhika Romanov, progressed with the chase through the back streets of San Francisco, and finally where the security agents put her back into the continuum.

The picture was crystal clear, the audio was dynamic and, with the wide-screen cameras and automatic stabilizers, it had the appeal of a Hollywood blockbuster movie. Lestre edited out the top and tail of the visual recording, superimposed a series of information graphics which outlined the details of the capture—the name, date, location, and brief description of the chase—and uploaded the visual to her Lifebook account, under the 'Verité' section.

She allowed thirty-seconds of the visual recording to be freely available, but imposed a €2 fee to watch the remaining eleven minutes. She'll probably have around a thousand paid views for this visual and, all up, this little investigation and capture would earn her around €2500—not bad for a few hour's work.

Lestre was a former Biocrime surveillance officer hounded out after she was incorrectly accused of stealing security secrets. Although she was eventually exonerated by Biocrime, her passion for crime prevention and money outweighed her distaste for the organization that almost crucified her, but she had a constant motivation to be the best in the field, and to prove Biocrime wrong.

She was now an official citizen surveillance stalker, linked in with her tribe of stalkers, a ruthless Technocrat and on the hunt for the sorts of crime that resulted in a big payout. While many other stalkers easily became bored with the whole process and monitored only for around an hour each day, Lestre was obsessed and relentless. The success of Biocrime depended on people like Lestre. She was on the system for around sixteen hours each day, and monitored her cell device from any location and from any situation.

Lestre was one of the best in the field—if not the best. She supplemented her universal income of €40,000 with around €200,000 in stalker fees. Although her partner D'Souza wasn't as active, he still managed to collect around €18,000 each year.

Like many other obsessives, she had been on the system for an eternity, and was always on the lookout for the next big case. Her work resulted in some detentions, and a share in several universal penal zone deportations but, just like a gambling system, she always felt her next big catch was just around the corner.

She knew the ropes: she'd worked inside Biocrime, and moved her way up through the system to become their most senior and sophisticated crime stalker and security agent but, after the accusations of theft, and the realization that she could make many more ucas in the outside world, she decided going 'freelance' gave her the freedom she was after—and still having the inside contacts high up in Biocrime gave her an added advantage over so many citizen stalkers. She was in the top five of stalker reward points and still had security clearance with Biocrime. One of the star performers.

She had partnered up with d'Souza, another citizen surveillance stalker. He wasn't as obsessed as Lestre but, being a Technocrat, was dedicated to the ideals of cyberstalking and reducing or removing subversive elements from society and an easy way to supplement their universal income. And the three incubation kits, albeit in a forgotten part of their surveillance room, showed they were ontrack to perform their civic duties and contribute to the ongoing population dominance of the Technocrats.

Like many other citizen stalkers, Lestre had Jonathan Katcher on her watch list. Her profile and stalking software registered Katcher wasn't doing anything unusual, nothing outside the parameters developed and recorded over the past ten years. She also monitored past records and profiles on Biocrime, such as Jonathan Katcher's, to see if there was any value in pursuit. She last monitored Katcher's profile five years ago—very low activity, but his profile remained on her 'watch list'.

The only natural human within their circle was a local citizen in the neighborhood, Gordon Lumbardo, a crazed messed-up conservative whose only priority was to raise revenue for himself, and the reduction of crime—if it actually happened—was a side benefit. He was one of the few natural humans who socialized and worked with Technocrats—about five per cent of humans existed and lived within the social tribes of Technocrats—it wasn't illegal or frowned upon, just the outcome of social development over many centuries, but was considered to be unusual and not according to the accepted social moirés of the day.

Lumbardo was a brash contrarian, loved the idea of being a human among Technocrats. He was also a surveillance stalker, and a good one, and it was his type that would be despised by activists in the Movement. A turncoat human working against 'the Movement', one who supplemented his income by raining misery upon his fellow kind.

He was only interested in one thing—money—and had worked himself into a system where he made a great supplement through his stalking work, and maximized everything he could through the system: Reward points for detentions above his monthly quota, referrals to other stalkers, he was incentivized to the hilt.

Like many others living in San Francisco—a massive super city of thirty million inhabitants—they lived in small studio apartments. Lumbardo survived in an apartment on level three which, essentially, was a medium-sized room, but Lestre and D'Souza shared a slightly larger three-room apartment on level four; small but spacious enough for all of their technological mod cons and room for their surveillance stalking work. Lestre was obsessed with surveillance and, like many other Technocrats, had an eternal drive towards accumulating more money and wealth from her activities.

Fresh from her success in reclaiming another off-gridder, and after she uploaded a new monetized visual recording, she focused back onto her lightscreen, scanned all of her points of interest, accessed Biocrime profiling and summoned the lightscreen to scroll down, so she could assess any new areas of anti-community activity and crime. The information on the lightscreen scrolled down quickly, and paused when Lestre wanted it to, and sped up when she wanted it. The lightscreen only stopped when there was a distraction—such as when d'Souza, now fully roused and finally launched into the day, decided it was now time for a morning beverage.

"You want a synth Marine?"

"Just the usual."

It was a mechanism not dissimilar to Katcher's food processor—there were over a thousand different types and brands on the market—D'Souza placed two cups in the front tray of the processor, summoned one espresso and one latte, and the low-level hum of the food processor commenced its work and, within two minutes, produced two perfect synthetic coffees, and he passed the latte to Lestre, and kept the espresso for himself.

"Anything else up this morning?"

"No, just the usual low level. It was good to nab that off-gridder, but I'm working on a detention in New York—just need to get some more details on what they're up to. I'll set up a post after I finish my coffee."

Biocrime surveillance was a common way for citizens to supplement their universal income. The process was simple in itself, but required a certain degree of diligence, patience and perseverance. Like all crime monitoring, it was plain boring. But the rewards were great. The great motto of the surveillance process was '*I like to watch*', a motto which became a catch cry after a humorous advertising campaign was released many years ago through public screen displays, person-to-person advertising and citizen announcements.

The process itself was relatively simple: firstly, stalkers would create a personal Biocrime account through the continuum, and link to their Lifebook system and their universal income account. This process automatically retrieved the correct scanning and surveillance tools that could access genetic recording and light storage data systems, and linked to an entire range of citizen surveillance systems around the world. Every corner of the globe, except for universal penal zones, was accessible.

Through aggregator software, 'unusual' activity was detected and lodged, but still required some interpretive analysis and scrutiny as to whether the unusual activity warranted a post.

Posting about 'unusual' activity was all about income and generating thought-bait, attracting the attention of citizens in a specific neighborhood or, if the crime or criminal was more notorious, attracting a wider audience. Posts were linked up to a wide range of crowd funding systems—GoFunder being the largest—and the larger the interest in a case, the more likely citizens were to pledge funds to resolve the crime, and close off the case.

Lestre's data scanning tools picked up activity in the back streets of New York—three hours ahead of the San Francisco time zone—the live surveillance tool enabled her to zoom overhead to a teenage boy who was throwing rocks at a street light. She summoned the lightscreen to display details of the boy and within a second, the details of Miller Drayton appeared, a sixteen-year-old layabout, without any priors. She summoned up another screen that analyzed Miller Drayton's blood levels and showed that he was intoxicated with alcohol and crystalline.

Lestre decided to add Miller Drayton to Biocrime profiling and created a new entry on her lightscreen and spoke into her cell device.

"Young punk smashing street light," Lestre said, as the cell device switched into action, and decided its next move.

The auto-fill function on her lightscreen analyzed Lestre's words and behavior through the continuum and assessed her anticipated course of action. The process was based on a series of complex algorithms and predictive computations. It seemed a little like thought control, but it was the logical extension of rudimentary anticipatory technologies from the 2100s, where around ninety-nine per cent of human behavior was predictable and, once the precedents of an individual's patterns were assessed, it became easy to determine what their next moves were going to be.

Based on Lestre's previous predictive behaviors, the auto-fill generated the text for her entry and completed the description:

We have detected a young man, Miller Drayton near your location in Halleck Street, Hunts Point, New York. Engaging in anti-social behaviour. No prior Biocrime data, but advise short detention as a precautionary measure.

Course of action: One-day detention.

Crowd pledge: €1

Lestre read the generated text on her lightscreen and, after agreeing with the version of events, she summoned the software to approve the text. The post went up immediately, and alerted citizens in this area of New York. If citizens in that area felt it was warranted, they'd summon their cell devices to 'like' the request, and pledge the €1 until detention was completed.

'Likes' were usually prepared by local citizens but, sometimes, citizens from other areas would contribute, for the sake of punishment or, in Lestre's case, a process where she trawled and added names to her crime portfolio, and the possibility that people like Miller Drayton could become more serious criminals in the future.

Bounty hunters in the area were alerted and if there was enough community request to proceed with the detention, they would arrest a fugitive, usually with the assistance of a robocop, in a three-way split between stalker, bounty hunter and the local Biocrime detention unit.

In this case, Miller Drayton was lucky. Lestre's post attracted only four 'likes' and one 'want' for a total of €4 through GoFunder—not enough to attract any bounty hunter. But he now had a Biocrime profile. *An investment for the future*, thought Lestre. This was low-level for someone like Lestre, but best to keep busy during idle time.

D'Souza noted the post on Lestre's tablet.

"Slow day?" he asked.

"So far, it is. Aside from the off-gridder, there's not much this morning—I'll go down to the gym and might catch up with Gordon and see how his leads are going."

"No old activists or subversives to monitor? They don't lay low forever you know."

"There's too many has-beens," Lestre said. "Most of them have been inactive, and most of their monitoring involves toilet visits, showering. No thanks."

"Just have a look," D'Souza said, "it won't hurt. What's Jonathan Katcher up to?"

"Let's see then…"

Lestre summoned her screen to display her Biocrime watch list, which displayed a long list of low-level activity of every potential criminal or high profile activist. But they were all there: Katcher, Chomksy, Smithson, El Guavero, Grayndler; another subgroup list of the members of the Fort Street Seven that destroyed one avenue in Los Angeles in the year 3019—

it was like a list the who's who of counter-subversives in the North America Zone.

Lestre zoomed in on Katcher's profile.

"Yup. He's still there, but not much value."

"How much?"

"Can you believe after ten years, he's got a bounty fee of two-hundred-and-twenty ucas. That is fuck-all, not even enough for a newbie to take interest."

"Well, he must have been doing something for those ten years. You know, breathing, eating, shitting…"

D'Souza reference was to the art exhibition and accompanying program produced by a group of Technocrats of Katcher doing all of his daily routine events, including bathroom and toileting activities, material extracted from the world memory bank. Purely designed to humiliate, the exhibition raised massive crowd funds and set the groundwork for other ex-activists to be humiliated in a similar way.

"I'll just take a look. Hasn't updated since yesterday, but looks like the same old stuff—that weird stuff he makes in his foodie, and those stupid 'historical' lectures he presents at the community hub."

Lestre scanned through Katcher's genetic storage and lightcapture. It appeared on her tablet in low-grade color. It wasn't in real time, but she could scan back to when Katcher was born if she wanted to, but that would be too expensive, even if it was just for personal interest. Besides, if she really wanted to access it, she could probably access it for free through some other convoluted means.

Katcher was now even of less value to stalkers than the average law-abiding citizen. Like many other high profile people with a Biocrime profile, any frivolous or spurious posting of his actions would be knocked down quickly, resulting in stalker accounts being banned for one month, so it was in nobody's interest to make things up or sensationalize. The lectures Katcher presented were seen as innocuous and tolerated, under the figleaf of 'freedom of expression' and 'diversity of opinion' but it was widely understood that too much freedom of expression or diversity of opinion would result in a detention, or worse.

"Must be hard for someone like him to be monitored by so many stalkers. But he deserves it," D'Souza said.

"Sure, but he needs to know that one false move and he's fucked."

*

I LIKE TO WATCH

'I like to watch' was the advertisement of the time and was universally accepted as one of the best.

It was a 30-second promotion, commencing with a team of dancers and a heavy bass-dub soundtrack. With each refrain, it cuts to a different person, each one mouthing 'I like to watch', with a computer-generated view of the Biocrime profiling, and finally focusing on a full screen € symbol. Overall, there are seven different characters, of different ages. It appealed to all groups and was a key reason behind an increase in Biocrime stalker numbers, after a decrease in participants over time. Its minimalism is a key feature—slick, sleek, succinct, with an overlay of footage and imagery of featured offenders and captives over time.

The key task of this advertising campaign was to humanize the process of citizen stalking and surveillance, through humor, slickness, and the use of diverse characters to more readily engage the community. After the campaign, Biocrime revenues soon increased by fifty per cent, and citizen participation rose by twenty-seven percent, a level that that continued up to the present time. Although the campaign was first released in 2822, variations of the advertisement existed in different forms and are still in usage.

CHAPTER 6.   SEEING THE LIGHT

A major technological advancement in the twenty-fourth century was the ability to capture the history of light travel, and recreate and store visual memories from DNA samples. While for many years the idea of travelling through time remained within the realm of science fiction, there had been a long history of experimental theories and research in this field—in the early parts of the twentieth century, the Swiss psychoanalyst Carl Jung believed there was a constant transition of memories from the living to the dead, through intergenerational transfer, commencing *in utero* and continuing through dreams, the human subconscious and the collective unconscious.

From the latter part of the twentieth century onwards, there were many biological and pharmacological experiments relating to sensory deprivation, and towards the end of twenty-second century, the ability to access and capture historical light and experiences was considered to be 'the Holy Grail' of scientific development.

The antecedents of lightcapture arrived in the early twenty-first century, through a technology known as light detection and ranging, or LIDAR, based on a surveying method that measured distance between objects by using pulsed laser light and sensors. This was a process known as Google 'street view' and was used to map urban areas and cities, enabling close-up views of houses and indoor environments: the technology eventually reached its physical limitations, before the merging of electronic and biological data became a possibility.

The first major breakthrough came in the twenty-fifth century through a team lead by the Nigerian scientist, Bennet Omalu, who initially adopted telekinesis technology to enable sampling and recording of historical light data. The first successful experiments were conducted on small microbes replicated in laboratory conditions, and enabled short lightcapture transmissions of around one microsecond. Omalu established a rudimentary device resembling a small solar panel that could access the history of a subject's molecules, and convert electrical and biological signals into viewable material on an old-fashioned television screen. Over the next thirty years, Omalu extended his program to smaller creatures and was able to recover and record the molecular light history of a pharaoh ant for a two-week period.

The second scientific breakthrough was the extraction and digital replication of genome material from organisms, and storing this digital data into a system which became known as the world memory bank, essentially a bank of high storage data units around the world that were accessed through the continuum, and accessed through a wide range of software tools and apps through Lifebook.

Two hundred years later, it was possible to re-create the light history of all living beings, and by the year 2700, any living being, object, or fossilized material could have its light history captured, extracted, analyzed and reproduced visually.

For many years, the most common way to access genetic memory was through screen viewing on a standard television screen or holographic projection, but developments in experiential software and entertainment in the year 2800 resulted in real-life experiences of history.

In 2918, it was announced at the Lagos Conference on Scientific Research that an estimated 94 per cent of all fossilized material had been collected and historical light retrieved, dating back to 4.37 billion years ago. A team led by Danish mathematician Asger Aaboe created a calendar assessment to 4,376,102,086 years—give or take a few million years, due to instability and inconsistencies in carbon data and capture—where it was agreed by the Copenhagen Agreement of 2917, that this was where the earliest recorded life on planet earth existed. The other six per cent of material was considered to have departed through space, or destroyed.

Lightcapture, genetic recording and the creation of the world memory bank were the major developments of the millennium, along with the upgrading of the internet into the continuum, after which, a series of major corporations developed, including Biocrime and other large-scale entertainment industries.

As more leisure time became available due to mechanization and less productive economic output from manual labor employment, virtual reality re-enactments and visualizations became the prominent form of entertainment, and gave rise to a new industry of historical revisionism.

These virtual reality re-enactments were based on genome data extracted from the world memory bank, and recreated into viewable video material accessed through the continuum two modes. 'View' mode, known as VR Watcher, was a simple mode where dates, events and locations could be searched—going back four billion years in time—with the lightcapture data retrieved from the world memory bank and displayed as moving video footage on a lightscreen. Like any other video recording, the visual footage could be scrolled backwards and forwards, and viewed from any perspective.

VR Watcher was a brilliant invention in itself, but the true phantasmagorical experience was through the 'reality' mode, a system known as VR Engage. While the 'view' mode enabled the viewing of historical material extracted from the world memory bank, the 'reality' mode placed the citizen directly into the scene of the action.

The more expensive VR Engage system relied on a cell device app, with a fiber-optics cable connected to the cell device and the other end of the cable wrapped around the upper arm of a citizen, similar to a small blood pressure monitoring machine, wirelessly connected to the continuum. Once the app was activated and locked into a date and location, citizens could nominate the perspective of any being they wanted to experience the event from—human or animal—and then moved into a hallucinogenic state and lived the full experience, as if they were actually there.

The 'reality' mode was popular, although it was the despots of history that citizens mainly wanted to experience: the life of the tyrant Ghengis Khan during the 1200s; German fascist dictator Adolf Hitler during the 1930s; the genocidal Attila the Hun from the 450s. Other virtual realities commonly experienced were the French heroine Jeanne d'Arc burning at the stake in 1431, and the 1066 Battle of Hastings from the perspective of King Harold Godwinson's horse. The mode was also a haven for prehistorical and scientific research, including life from the viewpoint of *homo naledi* and *ramapithecus*, and explorations of dinosauria experiences.

Assassinations of political figures were also commonly sought but the experiences from the former republic of the United States of America were the most popular—still resonating in the North America Zone over a thousand years later—and through historical lightcapture and genome extraction, many conspiracies theories were finally put to rest. The assassination of President John Kennedy in the twentieth century was not by John Harvey Oswald, as was commonly believed. The Warren Commission of 1979 was the first to officially suggest the 'lone gunman' factor in this assassination, and lightcapture technology confirmed that John Krimmer, working as an operative through the Central Intelligence Agency, was paid to kill President Kennedy through radical elements of the Cuban revolutionary guard. The CIA actually called off the assassination, but it was too late.

CHAPTER 7.   MODERNITY IN THE FOURTH MILLENIUM

After her slow start to the day, Lestre decided it was best to head off to the gym—her regular was the twenty-four-hour Anytime Fitness center just three minutes away from her apartment. If anything came up on her Biocrime account, she could easily access the details and any updates through her cell device.

Almost as an afterthought, before leaving her apartment, she checked on the three incubator kits in the corner of her workroom—two months earlier, Lestre and D'Souza decided to embrace their civic duty to bring three more Technocrats into the world—many others were incubating six or seven fetuses, but they felt three was the right number for them at this stage of their lives.

She switched on the lightscreens on the side of each incubator, and flicked between pages of progress numbers and data, and finally onto the image of each eight-week fetus floating in amniotic fluid. She carefully inspected the eyes and the small developing hands and smiled as she switched off the lightscreens.

Lestre was six-feet-two, thirty-six years old, slightly overweight with dark shoulder-length hair, but she didn't look different to any other Technocrat. In the year 3034, six-feet-two was the global average height for men and women—both natural humans and Technocrats. Very few citizens worked in a location away from home and because of this, gyms were the most common physical activity centers, usually filled with rows of treadmill cubicles and cycle blocks for general and standard activity, with more advanced options, such as weightlifting, for those that wanted it. The universally recommended aerobic–cardioid action was one-hour each day and there was no shortage of locations for those that wanted to fulfill this level of activity and exercise.

As soon as Lestre walked into the gym, €2 were eked out of her universal account. It wasn't much and because there was no physical exchange of funds, as had been the case for almost a millennia, she didn't notice it. Depending on what she did at the gym, the extracted amount remained at €2, but if she decided to spend an extra weights session, or finish off her session with a sauna rather than a standard shower, it would cost a total of €3. All seamless and transferred from her universal income account, to the universal income account of the gym owner.

Because it had been a slow day, Lestre decided on a sauna that lasted twenty minutes and, when she finished, she motioned a message to Gordan Lumbardo to meet at their regular haunt, The Old Soviet in the South Beach food zone.

After she completed her gym session, Lestre walked out onto the street and waited for an autobus. The autobus was the common mode of transport in San Francisco, an autonomous vehicle system controlled by passenger intentions and nominated destinations. The system aggregated existing passenger destinations with those waiting for transport on the streets, and indicated the likelihood of the autobus taking a new passenger directly to their destination.

Lestre checked her cell device and a list of numbered nearby autobuses appeared on her screen, with a range of different ratings—64 per cent, 38 per cent, 76 per cent and 94 per cent. A rating of 94 per cent meant the autobus was likely to go through a direct path to her destination, with only a short walk at the end. She summoned her cell device to accept the autobus numbered 4768 and, within minutes, it arrived.

As she boarded, the scanner on the autobus captured her DNA through the continuum—it recognized the messages she'd sent to Lumbardo and the plans to meet at The Old Soviet, calculated the likely travel and automatically deducted the €2.24 fare from her universal income account. If she changed her mind, or decided to go elsewhere, the scanner would re-arrange the fare and deduct the new amount. And all of this happened within a microsecond. Ten minutes later, Lestre alighted the autobus and headed towards The Old Soviet, where she could make out Lumbardo's profile sitting at the back of the café, looking out on the marina and sipping on a synth latte.

Food zones were common in metropolitan areas, usually made up of small cafes and restaurants that sold similar food, but were differentiated by marketing, colors and service types. The Old Soviet had a yellow and red décor with old communist-era block-style lettering from the 1950s in its logo. Very few citizens knew the link, but Lumbardo vaguely recollected the relationship with old-style command economies and reveled in the irony of a café badged up in old Soviet styling, but operating in a supra-capitalist world.

The Old Soviet was typical of many other medium-cost cafes around the world, with a three-point business model seemingly the best approach to maximize revenues and keep down costs—a sophisticated food processing unit that could produce any synthetic meal on the menu, a virtual holographic waiter to accept orders, and a human waiter or robohelper to physically bring out any food or beverage that was ordered to the table.

Clothing hadn't changed much over the more recent centuries, but had become more streamlined and basic, usually differentiated by colors and patterns. Essentially, there were two types of clothing: cheaper branded clothing, and more the expensive unbranded style.

Lumbardo, the natural human in the midst of Technocrats. He loved the irony and he loved the contrariness of his life. He was brash, upfront, and loved all things commercial. And money. He looked like a walking advertising billboard—not only was his clothing cheap, but he generated advertising revenue, or Ad-Rev, with a large advertisement on the back of his T-shirt, and another two smaller advertisements on the front. And another on his cap for good measure. His advertising zones were matt woven screens with revolving messages—they weren't too garish but subtle: advertisers realized long ago their messaging had to be targeted and all about being 'on brand'. There was no time for jingoism, or in-your-face marketing.

His Ad-Rev was based on where he was, who he interacted with, and with how many people—all clocked up on his tablet app which generated income in real time. And that was also how he got his exercise, walking around the streets of San Francisco, 'talking' to people. In his mind, it was an easy pathway to an annual income stream of €29,000, and a nice addition to his €260,000 stalking income.

Lestre walked into The Old Soviet and summoned the virtual waiter for a synth long black. It was €2 if she retrieved it herself from the food processor, or €3 if the waiter brought the beverage out to her. She wanted to impress Lumbardo and requested the waiter bring her order over to the table.

"Gordon, the main man. What's happening?"

"Hello Marine, it's good to see you," Lumbardo said, as he stood up to greet Lestre with a firm hug and a kiss to each side of her face.

Lumbardo's advertising zones registered Lestre had arrived and up splashed a slow video animation of her favorite synth coffee, Amore, and a message to let her know there was a discount only for today at the vendor just fifty yards away, or a twenty-nine second walk. Or if she purchased now and accepted delivery by miniature drone, it would be delivered within the next day.

He'd receive €0.1 just for this animation playing, even if Lestre didn't watch it, and he'd receive five per cent of any purchases she made of Amore coffee over the next week.

Lestre and Lumbardo settled in their tables and got down to business.

"What's happening?" said Lumbardo, throwing the question back to Lestre but, after a slight pause, knew he'd have to continue with a response. "Usual stuff. Some low-rent activity, usually young hoods who should know better. But, you know how it works, they're now in the system, might reap some rewards in the future. Working on a big fish that I might get in a couple of week's time. The usual."

Lestre was humored by Lumbardo, with his ostentatious short stubby look and balding head, but she knew he was good for business and as long as he generated work for her, she could bypass the image of a man that resembled an advertising billboard. She'd never known his age but guessed that by now he must be in his late thirties, and the receding hairline was the giveaway.

They'd known each other ever since Lumbardo moved to the neighborhood fifteen years ago. Lumbardo was a natural human, but his zealotry and dedication to law enforcement and crime prevention attracted her to him. They were friends, almost a love–hate relationship, but never with the full personal trust—it was the balance of tension that was typical of the very few human–Technocrat relationships in the world.

"You're not getting bored with it are you?" asked Lestre.

"Nope, I love it. That and walking around like a billboard— what could be better in life?"

"I'm actually getting sick of the mundane," Lestre said. "I love the surveillance, but it's getting harder to get the more interesting cases. Crime is down overall."

"Well, maybe if you were born through a vagina like me, you'd work out a way of getting more of those big guns."

"Fuck off Gordon. That's such a well worn cliché, I'm sick of it."

"Well, the truth hurts sometimes, doesn't it."

Lestre ignored the teasing from Lumbardo, and started to focus on food. They were both creatures of habit—Lestre ordered the plain meat burger with fries, Lumbardo ordered the fettucine pesto with a side salad—€14 each. From the café kitchen the familiar low hum of the food processor could be heard, and then a soft 'ding', which announced the food was ready for eating.

It wasn't real though—totally synthetic. There was no difference in taste or texture when compared with traditional food, but the food was manufactured in the food processor from an insect-based paste, modified and shaped by the machine. And the paste used by food processors was insect-based for two reasons: environmental crises during the early centuries of the second millennium resulted in many agricultural and harvesting lands disappearing through subtle changes in climate; and edible insects were found to contain high quality protein, vitamins and amino acids for human consumption, as well as creating less greenhouse emissions, and a high food-to-land conversion rate.

The meal was highly nutritious and, at €14, cheap, affordable and convenient. There were upmarket restaurants and cafes in the Downtown area promising 'real food' and the original eating experience but why pay €90 for a burger and fries when you could have the same for a fraction of the price?

The aroma of the food satisfied Lestre—she was hungry but her appetite would soon be sated and the conversation with Lumbardo, more bearable.

"You still thinking of heading back to Biocrime?" asked Lumbardo, in between the scoops of fettucine that smudged his lips with green artificial pesto. "They could probably do with someone like you at the moment."

"No, not seriously," Lestre said. "I only think about it when there's not much going on freelancing. It's always greener back on the other side, until I think about the reasons why I left in the first place. Treated like shit, accused of being a traitor, fucked around by bosses—in more ways than one. No, I'll only go back there in a fit of desperation. Or if they come to me, licking my boots."

"Well, I heard a rumor," Lumbardo said, "that some Biocrime secrets are being traded out to the Movement, and they don't know how. They might come back to you and lick your boots."

"Everyone has heard those rumors, but it's probably Biocrime pushing it out just to keep a level of fear among the citizenry. That's the business model. That's what it was like when I was in there."

"Possible. My rumors also say there's a bigger underground network of the Movement—somewhere—but they've managed to avoid detection and is totally off-grid."

"I've heard those rumors too, but there's a whole level of garbage out there on the continuum. The citizens know it's garbage too, but keep wanting to believe. Just like flying saucers and spaceships from alien galaxies."

"Maybe." Lumbardo was onto his final scoop of fettucine, and moved on to sip from his synth coffee. "Keep a lookout for Katcher. It's just a hunch but someone like that can't lay dormant forever."

"We'll see," Lestre said, signaling to Lumbardo that it was time to go.

As they both got up from their tables, Lumbardo's shirt advertising showed a new animated advertisement: 'See something. Report something'. He won't receive a fee for this one. It was a community service promotion, but as the ultimate beneficiary of crime reporting and monitoring, he wasn't too fussed to give up valuable advertising space for something that he would benefit from in the long term.

As they left The Old Soviet café, they didn't receive a bill, but they knew it was €22 each, including gratuities. The amounts were taken away from their universal income accounts and deposited to The Old Soviet account, for a total of €44. The transaction was split into all of its components and distributed immediately. The human waiter instantly received their €4 payment, an amortized rental of €4 was paid to the landlord, €2 to the energy supplier, €4 to the company that maintained the footpath and walkway to the café, €8 to the supplier of the food paste, €2 to the synth coffee supplier and so on, to all the various suppliers. And €14 to the owners of The Old Soviet. Every transaction was sliced into its small portions and distributed automatically and instantly through the continuum. It was the modern way.

CHAPTER 8.   THE MOVEMENT IS COMING

'The Movement' was a term first used in the early part of the twenty-first century to co-ordinate a lose alliance of extreme populists and economic nationalists in the America and Europe zones, but it was a short-lived experiment at the time and its influence waned and dissipated towards the end of the 2020s. By the mid-2400s, but there was debate about the antecedents and original meaning of 'the Movement', and its use by nationalists had been largely forgotten about. Essentially, the new iteration of the Movement had no relationship at all with the original invention and the name was adopted around the time Technocrats first started to outnumber natural humans, only two-hundred years after Technocrats first started being cloned.

Technocrats first appeared after the 2214 London Convention, where it was agreed human cloning was ethical and, therefore, permitted, and legalizing the practice was partially to standardize an underground and illegal market. Humans had been cloned since 2050, where radical experiments carried in the late twentieth century on animals were first performed on sheep and then, chimpanzees. There was much resistance to concepts about human cloning and stem cell research and development, essentially from religious figures and conservative political leaders, but as religion became less reliable as a basis for human ethics, and religious and theological thought less influential in social life, science became the clear replacement, and there was a common belief that the clearest pathway to existentialism and theories about the existence of Gods and other celestial beings was through science and technology.

The practice of cloning had its roots in the successful clone of a sea urchin by Hans Driesch, a biologist from Germany in the Europe Zone in 1885, but then moved onto more sophisticated molecular structures, through research developed by geneticist John Haldane, in the 1950s in the republic of England in the Northern Europe Zone. The first successful clone of a sheep occurred in 1996, followed cloning of a monkey in the year 2018 and by 2100, there was trade in human cloning, mainly from citizens that saw it as a process where their lives would be prolonged through a replica of their own image, albeit with a different and unique consciousness.

After legalization, clones became known as 'Technocrats', mainly to differentiate from science fiction and popular cultural depictions of clones as rampant robotic creatures. Technocrats were seen as a novelty initially, regarded as the future of humanity: cloned humans that had their own thoughts, their own free will, and were created, essentially, equal. But they had less emotional thought than natural humans, almost to a psychopathic level, and were fully subscribed to the notion of technological advancement, science and introduction of whatever means were available to implement this. Attachment theories developed over many centuries determined that full emotional capacities were only achieved in the mother's womb: a human developed in an incubator, no matter how closely science tried to replicate the uterus in an artificial environment, was no match for the emotional powers created by the attachment relationship between mother and child.

Over time, Technocrats were considered to have too much control over the direction of humanity, and numerically, they had a significant advantage, eventually making up almost seventy per cent of the world population.

Natural humans relied on the emotion of yesteryear, bringing up the hot ethical debates from the 2000s and 2100s, where there were many concerns about cloning and stem cell research, culminating in the 2149 two-week international symposium: *What Does It Mean To Be Human?* Although this symposium mainly dealt with the negative consequences of cloning, it was seen as the turning point for human cloning and accelerated the acceptance of this practice.

What Does It Mean To Be Human? also explored robotics, androids and artificial intelligence. Robotics had already been in development for some time, mainly as 'human helpers' and law enforcers, but to achieve the type of advancement robotics needed to fully replicate human life would take thousands of years and, besides, the technology to clone humans was already available.

Robotics reached its final level of advancement in the early 2500s, where robotic androids shaped like sophisticated mechanical humans were able to respond to voice instructions and follow rudimentary but essential tasks. They became commonly used as robot police officers, or 'robocops', and robot service officers, or 'robohelpers' but never reached a level of advancement where they could act independently or take on intricate actions, and usually functioned under the command of a human instructor.

Physically, robocops were slender versions of the popular culture representations of androids in the late twentieth-century, popularized by the franchised *RoboCop* movies. Modern robocops were usually a dark color or black, helmeted and made from a combination of hard-plastics, computerized machinery and robotic gadgetry. They were acquired and manufactured by Biocrime, and operated on a relatively sophisticated level but, unlike their representations in historical popular culture, where they were depicted as autonomous and high-functioning killing machines, in reality, they simply operated as an adjunct service in law enforcement and surveillance.

Robohelpers, due to the nature of their service support work, were clad in a less threatening manner, usually in neutral or lighter colors, and tended to be slightly smaller than the more prevalent robocops.

The common scientific understanding was that artificial intelligence could only develop fully through a symbiotic link between biology and biochemistry, and these concepts from the *What Does It Mean To Be Human?* symposium led to future developments such as the continuum, genetic recording and lightcapture. Which, eventually, led to creation of Biocrime.

Natural humans generally moved towards communitarian ethics and values, whereas Technocrats followed free thought, radical libertarianism and free markets and supracapitalism. By the mid-2400s, there was a view among natural humans that the question of *What Does It Mean To Be Human?* had lost its meaning and relevance, where scientific development and technological change happened too rapidly, and communitarianism was on the way out.

Radical libertarianism meant new ideas and thoughts about humanity were introduced, adopted or dispensed with, modified, discarded at too fast a pace, and the only ones who could cope seamlessly were Technocrats, or the few like-minded natural humans. It was the dialectic method on hyperspeed, where opposites engaged with each other to produce new theories of existence.

And now, with Technocrats making up around seventy per cent of the world's population, the mid-millennial fears about their rise were well-founded.

Natural humans wanted to reclaim 'what it meant to be human', and this reclamation was considered to be the basis of 'the Movement'. The Movement started off and remained as an underground collective, in most cases literally, to avoid future surveillance methods, and at the time, was considered by nearly all Technocrats and most humans to be a radical counter-establishment movement. But, over time, as natural human populations decreased relative to the Technocrat population numbers, the Movement became more of an accepted resistance by natural humans, with 'the Movement is coming', becoming a clarion call for a return to human values and providing the answer to the question of 'what it meant to be human'.

The main considerations in the contemporary world were: Technocrats had become too powerful, social and technological change had become too extreme, and there was no turning back. But there was a belief that 'the Movement was coming', and that it would only be a matter of time—whether it be fifty, five-hundred, or a thousand years, the times would suit them at some point in the future.

CHAPTER 9.   THE AFFAIR THAT CROSSED THE DIVIDE

Sunrays were beaming through the window of the small ground-floor apartment, lapping the edge of the bed where Greta Banda slept. She preferred to wake to the natural light, rather than anything assisted by technology, as if she was paying homage to her fallen predecessors and resisting the relentless push of the Technocrats. She knew it was only a weak resistance but, like so many other members of the Movement, subscribed to the theory of 'snowflake' activism—every act of resistance contributed to 'the Movement', and Banda started off every day in this way. Her apartment was like many others in this area of South San Francisco populated by natural humans—small, but large enough for one person to carry out their regular life and business, and hers was one of a hundred and forty-four in this block—arranged according to Fibonacci mathematics and golden ratios, an architectural style that was repopularized in the late 2600s.

She was an idealistic on a mission, obsessed with and committed to 'the Movement'. She held the underlying belief that to take on any existing order based on injustice, five committed adherents were needed to create the 'Shining Path' and she was one of the self-appointed group known as the Revolution Five. There were currently four members: she was number two, and number one was reserved for their highest priority—the recruitment of Jonathan Katcher.

Like many other obsessives, she knew about the work and the history of Katcher's work, his detentions and experience of almost being sent to a universal penal zone, but she wanted to meet Katcher and re-recruit him to the Movement. She was a leader within her tribe, and believed she had access to the right people that could infiltrate and bypass Biocrime, which would lead to a reunification with Katcher and overthrow the world of Technocrats.

Banda was fit, active, thirty-five years old and trained in weaponry use and explosive handling. Her serious looks were only occasionally peppered with laughter, and her piercing blue eyes and deep black hair portrayed a cynic on a quest for justice and retribution.

She was also a high-level scientist and engineer, a quick thinker able to sweet-talk her way out of anything, with grand intentions. For as long as she could remember, she had always been committed to the Movement. She was a radical, an upcoming intellectual for the Movement and a technological wannabe, was well connected with a number of tribes and subculture groups, but clever enough to avoid registering any links to a Biocrime profile. She was highly ambitious and believed the return of the Movement was a non-negotiable outcome, if the world was to break away from the shackles of a citizen-based police state. But, like many activists for the Movement, although she was highly radicalized, she was also impatient and naïve. She despised Technocrats and, because they were cloned, she didn't consider them to be human and didn't rank their intellect. She was potentially violent and was prepared to do whatever it took for the Movement.

Her parents were active in 'the Movement'—too active for their own good, but now gone. According to Banda, they were victims of Technocrat neglect, denied access to the BioMed system and nanomeds, even though they could afford them. It was the typical hypocritical way of the Technocrat world—'do no evil' on the surface but behind the veneer, a hardline passive method that achieved the opposite result—it put natural humans in their place, especially the radicals and troublemakers.

Although she was born off-grid—and wanted to remain that way—through a range of fabricated Lifebook accounts, she managed to trace her lineage to the South Asia Zone, the former republic of Indonesia, in the small earthquake-prone area of Banda Acheh. In her research, she was surprised to learn the area was nominated as a potential universal penal zone after it was removed of all citizens in the year 2750, but was considered to be too close to other heavily populated areas in the South Asia Zone. As part of the free movement of human resources in the late 2100s, Banda's ancestors moved to the America Zone, and into the San Francisco region in the 2800s.

As part of their activism, Banda's parents always emphasized it was important to be 'off-the-grid', to avoid scrutiny, and lay low. For Banda and others like her, living outside of the continuum—as well as Lifebook, Biocrime profiling, the lightcapture system and the world memory bank—was critical. She was part of an underground resistance movement with around a thousand hardline activists, spread out across a number of different cells in different zones around the world, with access to different facilities and different networks. Lightcapture technology couldn't access subterranean or submarinal areas, so, underground was the best way to work.

Biocrime's reputation among citizens was one of infallibility, a system where every move and every action could be recorded, stored, and used against counter-community activists and recidivists. But Banda knew this was not the case—there were software glitches within Biocrime—and with the help of a Technocrat insider, she worked the system. The rumors Gordon Lumbardo talked about with Marine Lestre were actually true.

The sunrays were now encroaching on Banda's eyes; she could feel the warmth on her cheeks, and she woke once this warmth reached her eyelids. Banda never slept deeply, and when she opened her eyes, she still needed to remind herself of her surroundings, her small and sparse apartment room, with a naked male body next to her.

In her bed, Banda leaned over to the male's ear and whispered: "Michael, it's time to go."

"Just a few more minutes…"

She reached under the bed sheets and over Michael Kransich's slightly aroused body. The sex was mechanical and it was what Banda expected from a Technocrat man but, ultimately, it was a pleasurable action that enabled her to engage her mind for the day ahead. Three minutes later and it was all over.

"You've got to go," Banda said, finally encompassing the aroma of whisky on Kransich's breath after seeing the empty bottle lying on the floor. It was the only item out of place in an otherwise impeccably arranged bedroom.

"It's okay, there's no rush today. I'm not expected at Biocrime until eight-thirty." Kransich searched the side cupboard for a standard nanomed—he had a splitting headache but once the paracetamol and barbituates sunk into his synapses, his pain would be gone and he would feel totally refreshed, as if last night's late-night drinking session never happened.

"Oh, and the documents?" enquired Banda, seeking the exchange of secret documents Kransich usually delivered from Biocrime.

"Sure. I'll transfer from my cell—there's some interesting stuff in there. Tech, malware, phishing software, schedules for underground inspections. Should keep you busy for a while."

The sounds of a bathroom shower followed, the slither of Kransich's clothes onto his body, a passionate kiss and then he was gone. There was a bypass serum in Kransich's bloodstream—a serum injected by Biocrime which deactivated and removed his DNA from the continuum—which meant he was invisible to genetic memory recording, lightcapture, and Lifebook. Unless someone actually witnessed him in motion, no-one would ever find out about his relationship with Banda. Or his sale of Biocrime secrets to the Movement.

And, in addition to this, Banda used decoder software attached to her cell device, a system developed by the Movement with secrets extracted from Biocrime, a system which allowed her to deceive genetic memory capture and avoid Lifebook detection.

Banda's highly surreptitious affair with Kransich had been going on for three years—relationships between Technocrats and natural humans weren't frowned upon, but they were unusual and could potentially raise interest from Biocrime. Because of this, and the ineffectiveness of genetic recording in subterranean areas, Banda had initially instructed Kransich to use a narrow tubed pathway tunnel which had been excavated between Banda's ground floor apartment and the back end of a nearby autotram tunnel—his movements couldn't be traced easily by Biocrime, but it had to work both ways. Banda didn't want his movements or the relationship to be known by natural humans either. But over time, and growing in the confidence the chances of being discovered were negligible, Kransich avoided the tunnel after dark and only used it during daylight hours.

After Kransich left, Banda washed herself down with a long ten-minute shower. She didn't hate the Technocrat man that was in her midst, but she didn't like the thought of having remnants of him left on her body either.

Michael Kransich was a muscular dark-haired Technocrat, coming up to his thirty-fifth year since inception. He was an outsider in life, but he was different to most Technocrats—he queried the meaning of life; his life, and the life of natural humans, and their question of 'what does it mean to be human'. He was perplexed about how his life was created in the incubator in a hospital, rather than inside the womb of a mother and how and why his psychometry was different to natural humans, and many other Technocrats.

He was 'recruited' by Banda through sex and bribery when she considered it was possible to bypass Biocrime surveillance. She didn't know how, but surmised the best way to find out was to get the information directly from Biocrime. Her plan was high-risk but after six months of research and engaging with different affairs with Technocrat men and women, she seduced Kransich at The Alchemist, a popular late night bar in the Castro District. After a bout of audacious and drunken sex in a darkened laneway, Kransich ended up in Banda's apartment, and the access through a hidden tunnel to reach the destination added to the mystique and the intrigue of their assignation. Having never had anything to do with natural humans before, Kransich was opened up to a completely new world by Banda, a world he found seductive.

Officially, he was senior 'project satisfaction' manager at Biocrime, but in reality, he was a high-level security officer and, like many of his other fellow managers, had high-level access to data, if he ever wanted it. He was a part of the trusted upper echelon and was one of only around two hundred people on the planet that had been injected with bypass serum. He had been at Biocrime for a decade and it was his job to ensure everyone in profile data management was analyzing and working to their full capacities. And, supposedly, maintaining their work enthusiasm.

It was critical, but nevertheless boring work and Kransich preferred to do this, rather than just receive his basic universal income. During his idle times, he would access his own genetic data and access *The Lineage Code*, a popular entertainment app where citizens could access the lineage of anyone on the planet, provided they were in the continuum and in Lifebook.

Kransich had scoped his lineage through the America Zone and back through the Europe Zone, and through to the German republic and Serbian empire of the thirteen-hundreds. Of course, every citizen linked back to a collection of common human cells of around seven million years ago, going back through *homo sapien*, Cro-Magnon Man, *homo habilis* and *ramapithecus* but, for Kransich, the thirteen-hundreds era was the time he found most fascinating. After accessing his genetic history through the world memory bank, he discovered that his predecessor, Marko Kranzić, was first cloned in the year 2280, and had been reproduced 17,345 times in the past 1,054 years.

He was bored, liked doing something different and lived close to the edge, as well as being a bit crooked too. He was one of the slowly growing band of Technocrats that had become more like natural humans in character and desire, adopting the philosophical and existential questions of 'what does it mean to be human'. He wasn't dissatisfied with his life but, unlike many Technocrats, he wanted to believe there was more to existence than just profiling miscreants and undesirables, detaining them to 're-educate' them or, in the more extreme cases, sending them away to die.

He'd been selling Biocrime technical and software material to Banda over the past three years and realized that with his DNA deactivated, he would never be discovered and, as a Technocrat, he'd never be suspected either. Since his relationship with Banda started, he earned the equivalent of around €800,000 in black market crypto-currency: it was undetectable and able to get him most of the things in life he'd ever wanted. And the great sex he was having with Banda was an added bonus.

The crypto-sphere was always just that one step ahead of Biocrime. If one avenue to black market currencies was closed down, another one would pop up elsewhere, like a cat-and-mouse game. Sometimes, crypto-gangs would create bypasses and software patches that would send Biocrime teams into technical cul-de-sacs, taking months before they could detect they'd been deceived. They'd eventually almost catch up, but never quite, which meant crypto-currencies were always part of a buoyant market, with a host of willing traders, buyers and sellers.

Banda's role was to provide these data secrets and software plans to her underground technical team, in exchange for the black market cryto-currencies. Although she despised Technocrats, she was pragmatic and always scheming to work out ways of accessing knowledge and information valuable to the Movement.

She discovered Michael Kransich—he had the right access, and had the psychometry that suggested he could be recruited with the right incentives. For her, initially, Kransich was a tolerable fool, even though he was highly credentialed and highly intelligent. As the emotional barriers between them came down, she was unsure if she had feelings for him, but she convinced herself that because he was a Technocrat, she couldn't be in love with him.

Kransich also provided details for bypass access to Lifebook, where Banda matched up details and blood samples of off-gridders that had died—either through accidents, or natural causes—to create a bank of plausible Lifebook accounts, where Biocrime was deceived into thinking their own security officers had added lost off-gridders to the system, when in fact, Banda used her own fabricated credentials to create working Lifebook accounts.

Although his information and material was invaluable to the Movement, Kransich was always going to be a fall guy, dispensed with after Banda got what she needed from him, but it seemed like there was always more Biocrime information she could gain from Kransich—for the right price—and he seemed like good company.

CHAPTER 10.   GOING UNDERGROUND

The continuum, Lifebook and all associated surveillance recording technology were less effective in subterranean and submarinal areas. Biocrime knew this, but was not prepared to apply expensive resources to research and develop new technological systems that could change this. As far as Biocrime was concerned, nobody worth pursuing could survive in an underwater community, and certainly not be able to sustain themselves for long enough to be a threat. Very little was known about the sea and oceans, except for underwater topography. Even though submarinal exploration commenced well over a thousand years ago, only around three per cent of the ocean floors had been explored, and remained a deep dark secret. And, with Biocrime existing as a vast amoral corporate business venture, there was no need to invest large amounts of financial resources into something that was not going to generate profits.

Going underground was a slightly different matter—while the continuum was ineffective underground, making it difficult to extract genetic recording in these areas, Biocrime determined it was best to be vigilant for any possible human counter-community activity. It performed irregular and random geological scanning to compare physical underground structures—where newly created and illegal underground caverns could be investigated and, if necessary, destroyed. Biocrime tolerated smaller cells of activism, and accepted they were always going to exist. The only issue of interest to them was the large-scale resistance, and they were certain they had removed the larger cells and existing networks.

For this reason, existing caves, natural tunnels, or disused mine and train shafts presented the best opportunity for the Movement to organize its resistance. The development and sustainability of this network was a slow and painstaking process developed over many years and these underground cells were connected to the outside world through old style hyper-fiber-optic cabling and food supply chains, where food and nourishments were transferred through a complex link of underground passages, some up to five miles long.

There was a good reason why subterranean and submarinal human endeavor had moved at a glacial pace over the past millennia. While there had been a fascination of the underground and what lay beneath the oceans through literature and popular culture, there were physical limitations to what could be accessed and what could be achieved in these areas. Aside from the extraction of a diminishing supply of metals, no-one ever went underground for any kind of useful purpose.

But the Movement was a step ahead in their thinking of practical application, which meant a resistance group such as the Movement always had a good chance to succeed in the underground. This most recent underground establishment was located in the outskirts of San Francisco, a city with a network of thousands of disused underground tunnels, and this one was located not far from Banda's apartment.

While most of these tunnels and networks had been catalogued by Biocrime, there were several that had been used to illegally dump nuclear waste products, sealed in the 2300s with protective sealants and considered too dangerous for human activity, let alone for anyone to live down there. The original exploration of urban tunnels began in the 1970s with a group known as the Suicide Club, a secret society credited as the first extreme urban exploration society, also known for anarchic and anti-establishment activities. This speleological fad continued for around four hundred years in the San Francisco area, before it become too dangerous and remained in the realm of a few diehards and misfits.

The Movement used the Suicide Club as an inspiration for its subterranean activity and constructed 'Anika-6', its most recent underground location, created almost a decade ago. It was named 'Anika' after the famous scientist from the 2400s—Anika Serafian—and the 'six' referred to the sixth underground location created by the Movement in San Francisco—established soon after Banda commenced her relationship with Kransich, and technological advances made it possible for natural humans to exist in this type of subterranean zone.

And the Movement had two good reasons to feel secure in this zone. Firstly, inside information provided by Kransich showed Biocrime had written off this zone as an area of interest, due to the understanding the tunnel area was radioactive and dangerous, and although the waste materials were over a thousand years old, Biocrime knew there was enough radioactivity to create dangerous conditions and had the belief that no-one could survive there for a long period of time.

Secondly, through their own speleological research, the Movement uncovered a branch of smaller caverns beneath this tunnel that was not easily detectable by above-ground scanners and sonar, due to its depth and the presence of radioactive material, and a layer of lead-plutonium had seeped into the area, which shielded the continuum from passing through.

Kransich's documents outlining Biocrime's secret technological research and developments had advanced the Movement by many decades, where they were able to adapt Biocrime's technological advances into their own research and systems, creating a range of products and technologies that could bypass the continuum and avoid detection by Lifebook and Biocrime.

There were two software developments at the pinnacle of achievement by the Movement—the decoder, and the emulator—both created by Maverick Weller, a software genius and one of the Revolution Five who predominantly resided in Anika-6 and was responsible for counter-surveillance and software interception. Theoretically, hackers like Weller knew it was possible to bypass Biocrime, but even with their team of expert hacktivists and computer scientists, they hadn't been able to get close to cracking the code. Having access to Kransich changed this.

He had sold the secret data to Banda for the sum of €200,000, and Weller and his team then spent another six months coding, recoding and testing—and achieved the major breakthrough for the Movement which enabled them to develop and design decoding and emulation apps that scattered genetic light material, and made it bypass the continuum and the world memory bank.

The decoder was an app uploaded into a cell device, synchronized to individual DNA, and once installed, could scatter and disperse that person's genetic recording. It exuded a combined ferric and plutonium three-yard zone and was based on Biocrime's DNA bypass serum but had the advantage of avoiding an injection and being able to be switched on or off at whim.

The other software creation was the emulator, also an app uploaded into a cell device, which manipulated realtime surveillance cameras into creating false visual footage for display to the outside world through the continuum and Lifebook Live. It was visually seamless and as soon as the emulator app was activated, it would suspend the Lifebook Live footage for that person's account from real life material, and transition to fabricated video footage created by algorithms programmed to insert innocuous daily life scenes. When Banda was linked up to the emulator app, it meant she could be cloaked from the continuum and out of the purview of Lifebook Live, and whenever she met with Kransich or descended to the underground, surveillance stalkers that happened to spy on her would only see fabricated images of her in her apartment, even if she wasn't there.

*

Banda patched the latest batch of data from Kransich into her cell device, and prepared herself to go underground. As part of her preparation, she wore light clothing, tough but lightweight boots, and covered herself with a thin plastic protective suit to avoid the grime from the tunnel on the way to Anika-6.

She switched on the emulator app on her cell device, which intercepted and scattered her genetic data, and if anyone was to retrieve data from the world memory bank, or surveil her in real time on Lifebook Live, all they would see was the fabricated video of Banda in her apartment, going about her daily activities.

Banda took her cell device and lightpen, exited through the floordoor in the laundry and slithered through the lead tubing that provided access to the autotram tunnel. After a few yards, there was a junction point that provided two options: continuing along the tunnel leading to the back of the autotram station, and another smaller point that took her down to Anika-6.

After she reached the junction point, she went through another slender lead tubing. It wasn't quite commando style, and wasn't totally comfortable, but was a five-minute crouch walk to a larger tunnel: another tunnel wide enough for two people to walk through. The walls at this level were covered by a thin lead–plutonium layer, an amalgam that deflected sonar tracer movements from above the ground. It wasn't a hundred per cent foolproof on its own, but it deflected enough genetic recording and lightcapture to avoid any detection through the continuum or Biocrime surveillance. The lead–plutonium was another remedy direct from Biocrime, thanks to the work of Michael Kransich. The cost for this information was €50,000 but the value to the Movement was priceless.

A thirty-minute walk through this small circular tunnel led to a larger cavern, and the location of Anika-6. The key underground environment for the Movement, it was a network of well-connected small natural tunnels and caverns—housing around fifty hacktivists working across four smaller caverns. There were around six hundred in other areas dispersed in autonomous cells of roughly the same size in more remote areas around the North America Zone, but Anika-6 was seen as the central cell, although each cell was designed to allow the others to carry on with their work, in case one cell was destroyed or detected by Biocrime.

The caverns in Anika-6 were not massive—the larger caverns were the ones that could attract interest from above-ground Biocrime scanners, but the smaller seemingly disconnected ones were more difficult to scan, and along with the higher levels of radioactivity, it was easier for this underground crew to remain anonymous.

By the time Banda reached her destination, she was four-hundred yards underground. She reached a thick control door made of tungsten and titanium, designed to withstand external explosions and land movements, genetically locked and synchronized with Biocrime profiles—another technological benefit gained from Kransich—so anyone with DNA coding matched to Biocrime profiling couldn't deactivate the lock. Banda was off-grid, so she used her finger to deactivate the genetic lock and, after passing through the entrance, moved into a vestibule that separated the circular tunnel and the main part of Anika-6. Banda then deactivated the vestibule door and entered the cavern, and closed the doors behind her.

In this cavern, there was a team of twelve tech-heads led by Maverick Weller—he wasn't the best in the field, but he more than made up for it with his zealotry and fierce dedication to the Movement. Weller was intense and always cut to the chase quickly: he had no time for losers or people not committed to the movement.

Weller looked the part in his role as a hacktivist—long swirling dark hair, a five-day growth, with a maniacal stare and permanent smile that almost resembled a Guy Fawkes mask—all housed in a black hoodie with a skull logo on the left crest.

"Got some more of the good data for me?" an impatient Weller asked, as Banda handed over her cell device to him.

"I haven't had time to check, but there's always something we can use."

Weller connected Banda's cell device to his lightscreen and started the slow data transfer to extract the contents.

"We haven't the same data speed as upstairs you know, so it will take a few minutes," Weller said, apologetically.

Banda surveyed the cavern and saw a row of light panels among the circus-tent structures, against the backdrop of stalactites and stalagmites. It was a busy scene, with the teams of hacktivists and programmers gesturing and summoning towards their lightscreens, casually and calmly issuing coding instructions to produce computations for the vast range of projects they were working on.

"What are they up to?" asked Banda. It was partially idle chit-chat, but she wanted to make sure they were on task and 'on message'.

"Just the usual about-ground surveillance," Weller said, "keeping one step ahead of Biocrime. Lachie over there picked up some chatter about a routine underground surveillance coming this way, but we're not sure when."

Underground surveillance by Biocrime was something the Movement needed to keep a track of. As well as low-level detection for subversive underground activity, Biocrime prepared random high-grade inspections, on average, every four years and, as the Anika-6 area was last scanned four years ago, the area was due for another inspection soon.

Weller and Banda assessed the latest batch of data from Kransich, motioning and summoning a range of documents on the large lightscreen, and looking for any data that could either be useful for above-ground monitoring or protection of the crew.

"It's mainly the usual admin crap, but look at this one," Weller said, pointing to the Biocrime maintenance routine for subterranean scanning. "Looks like we've got low-grade scanner coming through soon. Details about when and how many Biocrime people are involved. Small, just four or five officers."

"Does this mean we have to get out of here?"

"No, not for a low-grade scan. High-grade is what we have to look out for—that's when they actually drill and come down to have a look. It's a hassle, but we can move everything to a lower cavern. It will take maybe a day to move, but we have to do it. You should be able to get Kransich to provide the date of the high-grade scan."

The task of high-grade Biocrime specialist officers was to go underground and physically assess locations they thought might be areas of counter-establishment activity—known as targeted assessments—and then compare with previously recorded sonar scans. In this case, Anika-6 hadn't been scanned or assessed for four years—they didn't have to leave the area pristine for a targeted assessment, but couldn't leave one part of any technical material behind. If anything was left behind and raised suspicions, they'd be subjected to further and ongoing targeted assessments, and that would mean capture and a total shut down of Anika-6 or, if they were lucky enough to evade capture, needing to relocate to a new site.

"Is the information we're getting from Kransich still useful to us?" asked Banda.

"This batch is. But some is good, some isn't. But the genetic coding stuff he gave us a few years ago, that was the big one. Even if we don't get anything more useful from Kransich, having the material that led to us developing the decoder and the emulator was the big one."

Banda had the need to be assured that all of her actions and motivations were worthwhile and contributing to the Movement. Weller's affirmation to her made the difference. The 'genetic coding stuff' Weller referred to was the key data provided by Kransich the Movement used to circumvent genetic recording and the world memory bank, the central platform of Biocrime.

After a year of testing, Weller was certain that his systems could bypass Biocrime. He assured Banda that it was clear to use these systems on the one they really wanted back into the fold. Jonathan Katcher.

CHAPTER II.   SCANNERS

Four-hundred yards above the Anika-6 cavern, where Weller, Banda and the team of hacktivists were plotting the return of the Movement, a small Biocrime surveillance team arrived. Two women and four men exited a blue large vehicle marked with the large white letters 'USM'—underground surveillance and monitoring. It was a sleek and sophisticated vehicle, fifty-thousand pounds of mechanical and technological sophistication with a presence that commanded fear and respect. It had room for ten people, and four robohelpers but, for today, the internal cabin had a less-than-full feel to it.

The six Technocrats were dressed in the standard black Biocrime protective suits with orange and white trimmings, with laser guns in holsters ready for use. They were dressed to withstand anything that could be thrown at them and, although they weren't wearing them, their heavy-duty helmets at their sides gave out the collective 'we-mean-business' appearance.

It was a small parkland on the edge of suburban Paradise Valley, surrounded by apartments and a healthy collection of large redwood trees—one of the few remaining green zones in this poorer part of the city—but it provided the best access point to the underground.

The vehicle had been physically secured to the ground and, from beneath its chassis, a one-inch tube started screwing into the ground. It was a soft machine, akin to the sound of a dentist's drill but its softness belied the strength and power of the machinery. At the end of the tube, just above the tungsten and diamond drilling bit, was a scanning camera and a collection of mini-sonar detectors, and it drilled quickly and efficiently to the depth of twenty feet within two minutes.

After the drilling ceased, the camera and sonars scanned to the depth of one mile, and the surrounding one square mile. The technology for underground scanning hadn't progressed much over the past millennia, and it was a process still dependent on reflective seismographic techniques.

Georgia the Biocrime security manager, was one of the thousand field agents engaged by Biocrime to perform and manage underground surveillance. It was routine work and required a combination of patience, physical fitness, dare and bravado, and the ability to go to areas no-one else wanted to go to. She was a tough *mujer firme* and she summoned her team to the lightscreen on the side of the vehicle.

"Let's see if we can dig up some dirt," she said as she waved the lightscreen to retrieve the app to enable subterraneal scanning data. "Dig up dirt… and in more ways than one."

"Such a joker aren't you," her male security operator said, while he extracted and interpreted the onscreen data. "I'm laughing on the inside, really hard."

"Okay, I'll cut the crap. We want a deep scan now, and compare to previous recordings. What's the data on that?"

"Rome wasn't built in a day you know. I'll get it up soon." A few more seconds passed while the scans and previous data recordings were retrieved and compared with the current information.

"Previous recording, just over four years ago. I'll assess any change or movement," the security operator said.

"Haven't done this area before, I think it's before my time. The closest one I've done around here was Devil's Slide Bunker down on the coast. What's down here?"

"Looks like a series of caves and tunnels, but the scans aren't showing any change over the past four years. Looks clean—oh, hang on…"

On the lightscreen, the operator could see what seemed to be a morass of cabling—but was difficult to discern through the grainy seismological scans.

"Not sure what this shit is—could be some kind of cabling. You get rats that bring this sort of stuff down underground, but not this far. It's probably nothing, because everything else is clean."

"Seems like it would be a good place for those fuckers to do no-good down there."

"No, don't think so—the scans are coming up with a lot of radioactivity. One of those no-go zones. But it's close to apartments, and we're in a human zone, so maybe."

"Well, we're due for a targeted assessment in this area. Sure, it will cost a lot of money and resources for Biocrime, but we're due for one. Plus we'll get a bonus for the radioactivity. Let's put this one down for a heavy-scan and inspection on June the seventh."

The lightscreen listened and understood the intention of Georgia the security manager, and scheduled the date of June 7, 3034. It then accessed the Biocrime system through the continuum and scheduled the time, and the human personal and resources required to perform the targeted assessment, which involved drilling a hole three feet in diameter, four-hundred yards below the surface. A special Biocrime USM with a stronger drill bit and extraction unit was scheduled and, on the day, it would be the second targeted assessment, to commence at 08:00.

The Biocrime team was nonchalant as they finished off this job, and closed the twenty-feet hole they had just created with a solid rubber sealing glue. It was business as usual and they calmly and professionally cleared away their work, and left behind the smallest footprint possible, as if they had never actually been there.

They weren't expecting their targeted assessment on the seventh of June to be any different to the hundreds of others they'd performed in the past. It was likely to be a comfortable cool day of around seventy degrees Fahrenheit, perhaps with a small amount of precipitation. But, as they would discover when they returned to this site, their targeted assessment would prove to be nothing like the others in the past.

CHAPTER 12.   THE MEETING WITH KATCHER

Greta Banda had never met Jonathan Katcher but, like many others in the Movement, felt like she knew him intimately. She looked up Katcher on Lifebook through her own fabricated profile and could see his next session at the Optimus Center in the San Francisco Community Hub was next Wednesday, at 14:00; a ninety-minute session titled '*Communism and the rise of supraliberalism*'. There were data notes, historical references, essays and video recordings to support the session but they were usually not accessed by many—the few people that did arrive at Katcher's sessions were mainly those who needed to attend for community participation obligations so they could continue receiving their universal income, a few genuine historians, and others who wanted to see a legendary figure close up.

These sessions were classic 'old-school'—just like the people going to the theater to imagine how the Shakespearian world appeared, or to see in real life, the amazing skill of actors on stage being able to recite verbatim, two hours of prose. In this case, it was the spectacle of seeing a failed historical revolutionary who provided his interpretations of history. Katcher still had some social and cultural cache, even if he was on the periphery.

Banda scanned through the 'Also by...' and 'You might be interested in...' sections of Katcher's Lifebook page and saw a list of other lecture topics: '*Supracapitalism and how it failed the citizenry*'; '*Revisiting 2149: What Does It Mean To Be Human?*'; '*The Rise of Technocratic Power: 2500–2700*'; '*Capital class and labor class systems of the future*'... She had read them all, and it was pure academia—well-written articles with succinct ideas, but almost too perfect because no-one really spoke like that anymore. There were no hidden messages in these lecture notes calling for an uprising of labor class people, or for revolution. For Banda, and many others in the Movement, the articles and lecture topics were a disappointment. There was no mistake about the articles as excellent literature but, for those in the Movement, to see their hero and potential leader of the future revolution in this forum was akin to watching an old toothless tiger paraded in a zoological garden; no longer the king of the jungle, but withering away, catching any small fry for a meal, and waiting to die.

She flicked the lightscreen over to the attendance region and clicked on 'Attend', followed by an 'Are you sure?' prompt, which she confirmed and motioned forward to view the 'Also attending will be' screen, which provided a list of the other thirty-one profiles attending. They were as meaningless to her as her own Lifebook alias—DynaMiteMax—was to others: DogPig499, SplodgerNess, DavidM22, DangerFieldTribe. They were all linked to real and easily identifiable people, but Banda's profile was linked to Moira Harding, a natural human who died last fall, in a hovercar accident on the outskirts of San Francisco. It was one of the account names provided by Kransich and Maverick Weller was able to intercept the closure of the account through a virus code he sent from Anika-6 through his private personal network. It would be several weeks before this Lifebook account was correctly closed down by the trawling bots navigating their way around the continuum but, in the meantime, Banda was going to use it for her own surveillance.

*

It was a cool Wednesday afternoon, typical of the San Franciscan winter, the sun barely breaking through the clouds as the temperature nudged its way past fifty degrees.

The community hub was housed in a multi-function polis in the old University of California grounds in Berkeley, a combination of older sandstone buildings that had survived for over a thousand years, and newer apartment-style buildings that were earmarked as 'educational places of learning', although, in most cases, they were filled with bored people that had nothing better to do with their time.

It was close to 14:00 when Banda arrived at the community hub, dressed to fit in with the crowd of metrosexual men, street rats and unisexed women. Culturally and socially, these were not her people but she decided it was best not to be too try-hard and selected a deep grey new wave Gore-Tex thinsulate jacket, with matching pants, and a woven beanie to keep out the cold.

The Optimus Center in the hub was an oppressive twenty-five storeyed building and, although it was built in the year 2826, it used a quasi-brutalist architectural style from the late-twentieth century common in communist countries but, for unknown reasons, was applied to many educational buildings at the time, as if to suppress creative and educational thinking in a time of cultural liberalization. Optimus was a large company in the America Zone that was engaged in the dual businesses of electricity and education, and building a educational center in a community environment assuaged some of its guilt for fleecing its customers in all of its other business activities.

The building was not in a state of disrepair, but it was obvious that it had not been maintained for some time and, along with many other buildings provided by Optimus for educational purposes, was largely forgotten about.

After entering at the ground level, the elevator zoomed Banda up through the interior of the building and stopped at level seventeen; she exited and found her way to the lecture room. There were a few late bookings, and class numbers were up to forty-three. Banda was there with her decoder app, so she was invisible and impermeable to Biocrime's genetic data recording and lightcapture systems. Although she enrolled in the session, her profile, DynamiteMax, would be recorded as a 'no-show' and because it was a large session, Katcher wouldn't notice the difference: not that he would care.

Banda's mission for today was to obtain a piece of Katcher's genetic material—a strand of hair, or skin scraping—synchronize it with another decoder app, and relay the material to Weller in the underground Anika-6. Weller's team had created a seamless 'cut-in' and 'cut-out' technique producing perfect cloaking where from the point the decoder was switched on, actual genetic data and light recording for that person would cease, and not reappear until the decoder was switched off.

The 'on-off' process alone would have caused a problem, as there would be a retrieval gap—if a person was being monitored through Lifebook and then instantly disappeared from the lightscreen, this could raise suspicions with Biocrime.

Weller's solution was to produce an algorithm based on the first end point of light recording when the decoder was switched on, and the beginning point when the decoder was switched off. The algorithm would average out the two points, and fill in the sequences in between. It had been checked in their simulation zones and in the field—thanks to the material provide by Kransich, and through the work of Banda, Weller's software and coding team created a system that could bypass Biocrime.

The lecture room at the community hub was just a standard room, one of the old style rooms—just the way Katcher wanted it—and there was a combination of seats, desks, beanbags, and the large lightboard, ready for Katcher's presentation.

At the stroke of 14:00, Katcher walked into the room to the sounds of 'Another Brick In The Wall' and the name 'Pink Floyd – 1979' on the lightboard—it was a copyright infringement and Katcher would automatically be deducted a small penalty fee—the song was re-issued recently and attributed to Indigo Bluemen, a manufactured 'concept' musical group. The common belief was that Indigo Bluemen created the song, but as Katcher despised the trading and repurchasing of song titles—a big business in the 3000s—he insisted on the original attribution, even if he was penalized for it.

It was the first time Banda had seen Katcher in real life. To be sure, she had seen all of his videograms and holographs, but seeing him live in the flesh was radically different. She was not overawed, as she saw herself as an equal in the Movement. Katcher was the spiritual leader, even if he didn't see this himself in this way, but she was one of the Revolution Five, and what she needed to do today was just a part of business.

Katcher was a tall man, but didn't seem to have the presence that he had televisually, but when he spoke, he spoke in a manner that commanded authority, respect and attention. He could talk the legs off chairs, and ad-libbing his words was no problem at all for him. He was familiar with the time when governments existed, the long filibustering sessions in the American Congress during the twentieth century, and the especially long eighteen-hour speeches at the United Nations forum by Fidel Castro in the 1960s, the leading figure of Marxist politics in the former republic of Cuba. For Katcher, a ninety-minute session about politics was barely clearing his throat.

"Welcome to Communism and the rise of supraliberalism, I know it's not as fashionable as it used to be…" The standard for real-life presentation was still the same as it had been for millennia. The introduction. The jest. The eye engagement with the audience. The quick flip over to audiovisual material on the lightboard. Stylish graphics and stark typefaces. Then a switch to moving imagery, of leading figures of communism in the twentieth century; the economic figures behind the commanding heights of the supraliberalism movements of the twenty-first and twenty-second centuries.

Banda could tell Katcher was enjoying himself. He might be the toothless tiger parading through the plains in search of the small meal, but this serious and charismatic character needed some outlet, and this venue provided it.

Banda had heard this presentation many times before, and read it so often that she almost knew it verbatim, like most of his other presentations. But this was partially surreal, partially like witnessing a magician perform on stage, with wild gesticulation, summoning on the screen, engaging his audience. But it was a small audience.

By the end of the session, twenty-nine citizens, including Banda, remained—the others decided they'd had enough, their interest wasn't sustained enough by their short attention spans, or had to be elsewhere.

Several attendees chatted with Katcher, now seated, and surrounded the area where he provided his presentation. Banda knew that humans shed around a hundred strands of hair every day and Katcher, with his full head of dark hair, would have shed about six or seven strands, and they'd be somewhere on the floor. Although he was animated, Katcher was only moving within around one square yard of the scabby dirty floor, made up of recycled parquetry.

Banda tried to maintain discretion—to avoid the appearance of some weird person looking for hair follicles—and she fluctuated between looking engaged with the small crowd around Katcher and the floor. As if trying to get a closer look at the information on the lightboard, she moved to the area where Katcher had been standing and could see three or four dark strands of hair. She nonchalantly dropped her handkerchief on the floor, as if by accident, and scooped up the strands.

That was the first part of her work. Casually, she went to the restroom of the community hub, scanned the hair strands and sent the genetic code through to Weller, via her personal private network. Although she was invisible to genetic capture and light recording, she couldn't talk and sent her message to Weller through text recognition, for fear of being overheard by someone else, or scanned through other personal private networks.

Weller's team was fast and dedicated and they matched up Katcher's DNA from the hair strands to the decoder, activated the app, and then relayed the data through to Katcher's cell device in the next room. Their revolutionary leader was now in their system, and they could now exclude him from lightcapture and genetic recording. All they had to do now was convince him to come back to the Movement, that the Movement was coming, and that they now had the technology to support his return.

When Banda returned to the room, Katcher was alone and started packing up his small datacard system and digitally disconnected it from the lightboard. While the ninety-minute presentation wasn't overly onerous, today he was tired, he hadn't had lunch and he wanted to get away in a hurry. When he saw Banda appear in the corner of his eye, he was disgruntled—not too much, in case she wanted to mark him down for poor customer relationship service—but enough to let her know he was on the move.

"Jonathan? I'm DynaMiteMax."

"Oh, hi—I noticed you in the presentation, but DynaMiteMax came up as a 'no-show'. That's odd."

"Might be a glitch in the system, it does sometimes happen. I just wanted to chat about—"

"—look, I'm actually in a hurry—and hungry, so maybe next time?"

"Well, it's three-fifty now—what about a quick bite? A few nice places around the corner—Gloria Jean's?"

Katcher sometimes had the hardline groupies come to his lectures; the ones that had read all of his essays; the ones that had his posters on their wall, next to the silkscreened posters of Che Guavara, even though they had no idea of his role as a revolutionary in the twentieth century; the ones who were part of sub-culture 'Jonathan Katcher' reading groups, able to recite all of his works—even his new material—word for word. But they were usually much younger, and Katcher estimated 'DynaMiteMax' was mid-to-late thirties, so perhaps there was something else going on.

Katcher agreed to a visit to Gloria Jean's, but only because he was hungry—and could probably do with a different type of company.

"What's your real name then, *DynaMiteMax*?"

"I'll tell you when we get to Gloria's."

*

Gloria Jean's was only a five-minute walk from the community hub, in the middle of a bustling food area and shopping precinct. Katcher wanted a spot closer to where other people were seated—he didn't wanted this to be seen as a romantic interlude—but Banda wanted seats in a quiet zone, away from other people.

They summoned for a burger and fries for Katcher, and a synth latte each—and Banda indicated she would have a sweet cake treat afterwards. Banda had already activated Katcher's decoder app when they were at the community hub—whatever either of them did or said wouldn't be collated by the world memory bank—but Banda didn't want to arouse any suspicion by being overheard by some alert Technocrat or, even worse, a do-gooder human who couldn't tell the difference between right and wrong.

"So, what's your real name then?" asked Katcher.

"Greta. Greta Banda. I've been reading your work and really fascinated with it."

Katcher had heard all of this small talk before. '*Love your work…*'; '*…been reading your stuff for a long time…*', '*…really fascinated with it…*', but Banda was striking up the friendship and relationship first, building up the trust. Katcher had the feeling that this meeting was something different—listening to Banda talk about the ideas from his presentations sounded like she was in a lot deeper than she was letting on.

But Katcher was on guard—after all, he knew Biocrime was in the practice of framing people like him through entrapment—it had security officers like Banda, claiming they'd developed some type of device that bypassed the continuum and the world memory bank. Entrapment was one of their key strategies for sending high-profile people off to the universal penal zone, under the banner of 'crimes against the citizenry', and he had to be careful.

"Why *DynaMiteMax*?" asked Katcher, seemingly disinterested in talking about his work.

"Just a Lifebook alias. Nothing special, nothing significant. I wanted to change it from the number I was given at birth, just like everyone else does, and DynaMiteMax just seemed like the right name at the time."

"When was that?"

"When I was eight—it's okay. The privacy settings aren't that high, so people can easily dig a little bit deeper and find out who I really am."

'DynaMiteMax' thought Katcher. He was a serious man, demur and liked to go straight to the point—his Lifebook profile was *'Jonathan.Katcher.3290'*. Bland, straightforward, and what-you-see-is-what-you-get. He'd had other groupies in the past—assuming Banda was a groupie—with far more ludicrous names: *PixelPunkPink, Juice_Lucy_Dime, Snapper_Dampering*. So DynaMiteMax was tolerable.

They exchanged mental notes about the future of the capital class, the labor class and universal income, and what it meant for the future direction of the citizenry. Katcher was engaged: '*She knows her material*', he thought. They continued for another thirty-minutes or so, exchanged pleasantries and automatically picked up their respective tabs.

"See you next week…"

"Sure. Next week's talk is an old one—The Decline of Organised Governments: 2200. Should be a good one."

"OK, I'll see you then."

After he departed from her vision, Banda deactivated Katcher's decoder app and, without his knowledge, he merged through the continuum seamlessly back into the realm of Biocrime. Nothing from their meeting was recorded by the world memory bank, as though the meeting had never occurred.

*

Back in his apartment, Katcher lazed on his couch and motioned his lightscreen to provide visual entertainment on his YouTube account. He scanned through the list of 'watched' visual programs, but saw nothing of note. He preferred 'old' entertainment, rather than 'new', but he was spoiled for choice. The system comprised billions of different programs and projects—traditional movies, computer-generated and crafted blockbusters, citizen-uploaded programs and snippets of the mundane—real-life activities from the household, or action material where citizens superimposed themselves in famous movies or scenes from history—a fabricated document looking like they were actually there.

Katcher liked to go back through history to see what people thought about the future, and the advanced life they perceived for themselves in a hundred or a thousand years away. Humanity always considered itself to be at the apex of civilization at any given time, but there was always the anticipation the future would be far more sophisticated, and far more advanced. And far better. While there had been many technological advances over millennia, Katcher wondered if human thinking had changed in the years since the Greek philosophies of Plato and Aristotle in the third-century BCE.

He'd always felt all humans today existed from the influence of others throughout history—the good and the bad—the product of millions of years of time and evolution, and the driving force for humanity had been the belief in the virtues of optimism, the idea that the future would always be better.

He continued to scan through the list of visual programs, until he came across one that piqued his interest—*The Time Tunnel*. He had watched some of these episodes before—an old-fashioned American television series produced in the 1960s, where a team of scientists travelled back and forth in time and found themselves in impossible situations, only to be rescued by their home base at the last possible moment.

He summoned the lightscreen to play the episode 'One Way to the Moon'. The opening credits appeared on his lightscreen and showed a glimpse into the future—flying saucers, hovercrafts, technological sophistication—all of which Katcher assumed were the clichés of what the future world would look like—and the final graphic in the opening scene faded up on the screen announcing the year of this future world—'1978'. He scanned through the production credits and noted the program was produced in 1966, only twelve years before. For Katcher, it was a classic case of 'future optimism', where the producers of this episode imagined life would be so advanced in a decade or so, humans would be transported in flying saucers and quickly travelling to the moon and planet Mars.

They had no fucking idea, Katcher thought to himself. The future was nothing like the one anticipated by his predecessors. There were no flights to planet Mars, no flying saucers, no telekinesis where unusual boxes could teleport people over long distances. But it was the optimism that provided the future direction for humanity: the ridiculous ideas of Leonardo da Vinci, the imaginations of Jules Verne, the future according to H.G. Wells, or even the predictions of Nostradamus. All ambitious ideas that provided a roadmap for future technologies. The modern world of 3034 was highly advanced, especially in surveillance and small-scale gadgets, but the old ideas of the future were positively retro and humorous to Katcher. The world turned out differently.

The heroes of *The Time Tunnel* were stuck on the moon, a gunfight between the four scientists ensued, and they were quickly running out of oxygen. The images from the lightscreen played in the background as Katcher faded in and out of the program, thinking about his day, his lecture and what he needed to prepare for his next performance. And he was also thinking about Greta Banda—he had many 'fans' come up to him after his lectures, but there was something different about her.

'One Way to the Moon' ended with the heroes rescued by the time machine before they ran out of oxygen and the villains hijacking the spacecraft, continuing on their way to planet Mars. Katcher wondered if they would ever make it.

***

BOOK 2. HUMANS UNCHAINED

"Humans are born free yet everywhere they are in chains."

—Jean-Jacques Rousseau

CHAPTER 13.   THE BORDERLESS WORLD

"L'homme est né libre, et partout il est dans les fers" is the opening line of *The Social Contract*, written in 1762 by a French philosopher, Jean–Jacques Rousseau, a treatise on the best way for communities to organize themselves politically, in the face of a more sophisticated commercial world. It was a collection of words that guided Jonathan Katcher's thinking throughout his life and directed his revolutionary actions. He was agitated by Rousseau's commentary that people everywhere were inherently born with freedom, yet everywhere they were shackled by oppression, and a world directed by inequity.

Katcher modeled himself on two great philosophers from the French republic—Rousseau's philosophies that gave rise to the Enlightenment throughout the Europe Zone and the French Revolution of 1789—and Pierre-Joseph Proudhon, the original anarchist who lived in the nineteenth century, with the one lasting notion that all ownership of property should be regarded as theft from the working classes by capitalists. These ideas were over twelve-hundred years old, but Katcher found they were more relevant than ever.

For Katcher, the direction of the world was caught between this bind of freedom and justice, where he felt too much freedom resulted in too many inequities and injustices, a world controlled by Technocrats and large corporations such as Biocrime.

For many centuries, it was the neoliberalist dream to put an end to state and national borders and allow for the free global movement of capital through globalization of trade and commodities. But part of this dream of wanting unbridled capital flow, was the conundrum of wanting to restrict the movement of peoples, to the point where during the early parts of the twenty-first century, citizens moving past different borders without identification documents, such as passports and visas and, in most cases, escaping from violent wars or economic hardship, were incarcerated in island jails as deterrents to others.

This was in contrast with the ideals of international socialism, which suggested citizens should be free to geographically move to wherever they wanted to, but confined to localized and restricted areas of finance and capital. The battle between *laissez-faire* and centrally-controlled communitarian economics was a battle waged over many centuries, and resulted in four main waves of globalization.

The first period was between 1492 and 1800, where the world started to move away from serfdom and subsistence and towards industrialization, through the globalization of countries and economies. This period was initiated by the physical exploration to different parts of the globe and the realization the world wasn't flat after all. While this was motivated by imperialist grandstanding and the quest for competitive world domination by England, France, Holland and the Iberian Zone, the result was a greater level of trade between the Europe Zone and the Orient.

The second period was between 1800 and 2000, where growing trade and interaction between these countries gave rise to the globalization of companies, and the rise of corporations in England and the North America Zone. This period was marked by a combination of industrialization, religion, nationalism, and a Europe Zone that had sprouted from the Century of Lights during the 1700s, and the development of primitive machinery, such as the steam engine, and developments such as the manufacture of steel through the Bessemer process of blowing oxygen through molten pig iron to burn off the impurities, resulting in solid high quality steel.

Although this second wave of globalization was also coupled with the corporatization of war and the development of the arms industry, especially during the twentieth century, it was a period of high innovation and investment in mechanization and computerized technology. Virtually every sector of the economy was revolutionized during this period, with improvements in farming and food production, health, education, shipping, building and personalized travel such as automobiles and motorbikes.

This period then gave rise to the globalization of the individual from 2000 to 2300 and the extension of the philosophy that capital was created, not just through human labor, but through human thought and intellect and, it followed from this thinking that individuals should have the same level of freedom as capital movement.

This period became known as the era of supraliberalism.

More frequent people movements, especially as a result of wars and politically-motivated famine in the Africa and Middle East Zones during the early parts of the twenty-first century, gave rise to limited fascism in the Europe Zone and hostile receptions to people coming from other zones, and after a fifty-year period of violent reactions to individual people movements, as sociologists had predicted, people movement became more acceptable throughout the world, once the links between free global citizen movement and economic benefit became more obvious.

Many intractable conflicts in the Middle East and Africa zones were resolved in the mid-twenty-second century. The republic of China became the international powerhouse in the early-to-mid 2000s, using its financial power to oust the republic of United States as the key influencer in many political pressure points and hot-zones throughout the world.

Chinese diplomacy resolved the erstwhile Palestine–Israel conflict through increased economic support and development for both regions and through a one-hundred-year moratorium, with an expectation that through further economic development, and technological and political changes over the long term, the conflict would be resolved permanently—which proved to be correct. Known as 'Road to Renewal Plans', or *fuxing zhi lu*, these models were appropriated and applied to other problems zones around the world—the schism between north and south on the Korean Peninsular and the demilitarized zone; Georgia–Abkhazia and Nagorno-Karabakh in the Russia Zone; Kashmir in the Northern Asia Zone; Cyprus; Rwanda–Burundi; Serbia–Croatia–Bosnia.

The rise of China occurred for two reasons: firstly, the United States gradually vacated its involvement in international conflicts and zones, and Chinese diplomacy advanced the notion that the political and financial relationship between the United States and Israel had poisoned the entire Middle East region, and removing Israel from the political equation could produce a reverse domino effect.

Secondly, China matched its population size with its economic and military might, as it had during the time of subsistence economies before the first phase of globalization in the fifteenth century. Its economic might was based on fast capital movements, and a strong belief in removing the barriers to people movement, and this thinking gave rise to the ideas of supraliberalism in the mid-twenty-first century.

For the supraliberalist, capital flow had to be merged with human flow, and this provided the answers to the questions posed by neoliberalists and international socialists and merged the dichotomy that existed between these two philosophies. There was an economic school of thought that suggested the combined opening up of human and capital flow would create short-term violence between different nations as they moved to different locations around the world, but the removal of national borders would increase international domestic product, create further economic opportunities, and lift millions out of poverty.

The theories combined to pronounce that restricting human flow and traffic was the antithesis of democratic and free economies and, over time, because of the domination of international supraliberalist ideals and technological change, borders were opened up and the world moved towards a universal currency, free of tariffs and subsidies, and free movement of all citizens anywhere in the world.

The major migration clampdowns and draconian measures that largely existed during the twentieth and twenty-first centuries were considered 'against the human spirit' and against the principles of supraliberalism and democracy. Monuments recognizing the movements of peoples prior to the nineteenth century, and for all the people that had drowned at sea in the East America, South Asia, North Africa and Australia zones, were created to recognize those attempts to move to better lives. These acts were considered to be the precursors to the global free human movement.

Supraliberalism and the freeing up of borders also meant that the relevance of the nation–state declined and, following on from debates, discussions and political theories developed over many centuries, the nation–state relationship was seen as the root cause of wars, famine, and 'Remove Difference' became the *esprit de corp* and thinking of the times.

After reaching their high points in the late twenty-second century, China and the Russian Federation commenced a decline during the twenty-third century, fracturing into smaller autonomous zones and then becoming borderless in the early 2400s.

Through continuous and automated micro-financial payments, transactions and incentivation programs, the need for government controlled bureaucracies diminished dramatically. In the United States, the reformist President Julian Navarro presented the New Deal in the year 2285 that dissolved the country, and following the Lagos Agreement of 2290, all areas previously recognized as states, nation–states or countries were formally dissolved. Borders after the year 2290 were officially open for capital, labor and people movement, and the Lagos Agreement of 2290 codified what had been a *de facto* existence for around a hundred years.

The world worked towards a financial and social equilibrium and the need for official borders and governments morphed into crowd-sourced decision-making processes and areas defined by geography, rather than nation.

The final and current stage of globalization arrived through the development of biotechnology. After the world economic system was consolidated through the global free movement of capital, people and labor, a fast-tracking process of computer enhancement creating the link between electronics and biological material resulted in the development of a vast range of new technologies, most notably, the continuum, which created the nexus between computers and the biological world, and genetic recording.

The world without borders, historically, was regarded as the greatest human achievement, as it removed many of the issues that had plagued the world since time immemorial—nationalism, racism, religion, isolationism, terrorism, fanaticism—and rewarded humanity with virtually every technological asset it could think of in the field of health, education, commerce, arts, entertainment and communication. The downside was that the byproduct of these technological wonders was the biggest level of surveillance and corporate interference ever in the daily lives of people all around the world. The creation of Biocrime.

*

UNCHAIN MY HEART

A powerful advertising campaign was developed in the early 2100s, promoting the end of national and international borders and pushing forward the free movements of people to any part of the world.

It was a ninety-second visual recording that featured a montage of oppressive images of negro slaves from the southern states during the 1860s, Australian Aboriginal people held in neck chains from the 1930s, images of the torture of Chinese citizens during the Japanese invasion in Nanking in 1937, with the audio backing of 'Unchain My Heart', a song written by Bobby Sharp and sung by Ray Charles, a popular American soul, rhythm and blues musician from the mid-twentieth century.

The serious male voiceover commenced: "Man was born free, yet everywhere he is in chains. Our mission is to unchain our hearts and move towards the freedom we were all born with."

It gradually faded into a sharper montage of footage from what was considered to be the pinnacle of fascism and destruction in the world, the rise of Nazism throughout the Europe Zone during the Great War and World War of the twentieth-century, machete attacks between the Tutsi and Hutu people during the Rwanda–Burundi Wars during the 1990s, and famines in the northern parts of the Africa Zone in the mid-twenty-first century. These sequences used 'Blue Monday' as the audio backdrop, a song originally performed by New Order, a post-punk electronic dance group from the Northern Europe Zone.

Towards the end of the sequence is an orchestral version of 'Unchain My Heart', showing slow motion footage of chains being broken and adults helping children leap over barbed-wire fences, and a soft and seductive male voiceover narrating a series of sophisticated images from around the world, following the path of a sophisticatedly dressed man of Moroccan appearance travelling through a downtown part of Casablanca: "He's checking his weather on a phone made in Beijing; while riding in a cab produced in Germany; he pays for his meal with his bank account held in Zurich; he watches the football game played in New York, on a television screen made in Korea; he's a multi-national, but he's part of the one nation: the human nation".

The final scene ends with a group of families in a wide shot, with a smooth female voiceover saying: "We're moving towards a better world, towards a better future. Towards a borderless world."

The final graphic contains the two stark words: 'Remove difference'.

It fitted perfectly into the zeitgeist of the time and was the most successful advertisement in the early part of the twenty-second century.

CHAPTER 14.   RECRUITING KATCHER

"Welcome and thanks for being here: The Decline of Organized Governments—some would say governments were never organized and have always been in a state of decline. And that's why they finally died off, and to use an ancient Japanese word, we said *sayonara* to them."

Katcher started his next session at the community hub with the perfunctory jovial remark—standard Presentation 101 tactics—humor the audience to get them engaged and feel more comfortable in their own skin, almost like being the 'song-and-dance' man for the day to entertain the crowd. And he loved to use words from a dead language that meant something in the *lingua franca* of the day, English. 'Sayonara' was an old Japanese word that was used interchangeably with 'goodbye', as was the old Italian word 'ciao'. Not many words from the Teutonic languages survived the gradual cull of universal words over the centuries, but many of the words that did survive had their basis in popular culture, such as 'borgen', a word that was used interchangeably for 'castle' or large edifice of a building, after the title of a Danish television crime series from the early part of the twenty-first century.

In this session, there were forty-one participants, and as he scanned the room, he could see Banda seated close to the back. Katcher briefly thought this to be strange: her avatar—

DynaMiteMax—didn't appear on his list of confirms. He was okay with this, he didn't mind so much, it just meant he wouldn't receive any income from her attendance, but he'd much rather have interested unrecorded people come along to his sessions, rather than recoup the €5 he'd receive from an official attendee bored out of their brains.

Everyone in the room—Katcher included—never lived under a government or within a centralized control of the economy and resources. In 3034, the entire world was controlled and organized through the continuum, the world memory bank and a vast array of sophisticated crowd-sourcing apps. However, there was still a fascination and thirst for knowledge about yesteryear, the way humans used to live—not so much for a return to this life, but a bemusement and surprise for how a small section of the citizenry formed governments that were responsible for deciding allocation of resources, direction for the economy, creation of laws, and the bizarre notion of the election of officials to carry out these tasks.

As Katcher continued in the session, he outlined how some of the smaller remaining states in the world had maintained the semblance of government, holding elections and electing representatives, for the sake of historical continuity. These officials were figureheads, rather than holding any meaningful power, and the last remaining international state was the small principality of San Andorra, contained within the South Europe Zone, but it ceased being relevant—its last election was represented by less than one per cent of the citizenry and, by that stage, it resembled a small debating society, not dissimilar to Katcher's sessions at the community hub.

The session continued to run through a range of ideas about government—like a magical performer, Katcher wove the intricacies of time and space throughout history, moved from one concept to another, and produced mental gymnastics by going through a wide range of theories of knowledge. If Katcher was a performer at a circus, it would have been the equivalent of juggling balls on the high-wire trapeze, without a safety net to catch any incorrect or inadequate moves.

It was a riveting lecture and, ninety minutes later, Katcher finished speaking and concluded the session with lightscreen montage of moving images from the time of governments: the footage of President Navarro signing the end of the United States in 2285; the last election in San Andorra during 2517; footage of a range of world presidents of the twenty-second century; the Battle of Agincourt of 1415, recreated from genetic recording and lightcapture; President Mikhail Gorbachev, signing off the end of the Soviet Union in 1991.

It was an inspirational end to the session, some of the participants left the room before the final screening had completed, but there was the requisite number of participants that remained for further discussion—they could always continue these discussions through a wide range online platforms—the main ones such as Lifebook and BioEd, or the smaller more obscure ones like Tweetie, BunSwang, AliBaba or Cursory—but what better way to soak up the information than to hear the words straight from the the mouth of a former revolutionary.

It would be another twenty minutes before Katcher palmed off the final curious participant, but while he packed the materials from his presentation away, he noticed Bander approaching him. Banda had just activated the decoder apps for Katcher, so they were both now out of detection of the continuum, and Lifebook and Biocrime.

After the last meeting with Banda, he knew there was something different about her, but his immediate thought this time was the fact that she hadn't paid for her attendance today.

"You're a no-show and this time you didn't even register," Katcher said, as he put away the final material back into his bag.

"Sometimes the tech fails me," Banda said, "but I was keen to come along. I'll get you a meal to make up for it."

"Look, it's getting late, and I really must get going." Katcher noticed it was close to 16:00, but felt he could do with a coffee and a bite to eat. His body language signaled to Banda that he could be amenable but before he had time to hesitate further, she took control of the conversation.

"We won't be long—let's go. Gloria Jean's again?"

Before Katcher knew it, he was walking away from the lecture room, through the quiet atmospherics of the parkland near the community hub, and onto the bustling streets of downtown Berkeley.

On the way to Gloria Jean's, there was the idle chat between Katcher and Banda about the end of government and quaint notion of the small star chambers throughout history that decided what was best for the community when, in actual fact, most political leaders had always acted corruptly and in self-interest.

Fifteen minutes later, Katcher and Banda walked through the doors of Gloria Jean's: again, Katcher wanted to sit in a space close to other people, but Banda summoned him to the same quiet location where they sat the previous week. It was relatively foolproof—because of Banda's decoder apps, they were currently off the grid, but Banda still didn't want to attract any unwanted attention at all. On this occasion, Banda realized she could keep Katcher longer if she was eating as well, so she ordered the burger and fries; Katcher went for the pasta bolognaise. It was kitsch food and synthetic, but it was cheap and affordable.

The food was made with the usual promptness, delivered by robohelper: they were both hungry and launched into their respective meals, interrupted only by the occasional sip of the synth coffees. Banda wasn't quite sure how to bypass the intellectual and historical conversations, but half-way through her burger, she decided to stop the banter and went straight to the point of her purpose.

"John, I'm not here for the conversations, I'm here for the Movement."

Katcher had heard this before, from many others, but he related back to his thoughts about something being different about Banda. His initial intuition was that he suspected it might come to this type of point—as it usually did—but he just didn't know who Banda was. His mind raced through a range of permutations. *Is she with Biocrime? Is she a nutter? A rebel without a tribe? Or just lonely? Or is she really from the Movement?*

"Look, I'm not interested," Katcher said, "never will be. This is just fancy talk, and you know all of our conversations can be retrieved."

He knew all of the conversations he made with Banda could technically be retrieved but, nevertheless, decided to at least hear her out. Of course, he'd always be interested in discussions about the Movement but he knew his acts of deniability and refusing these overtures meant he was safe, and less likely to face any sanction from Biocrime in the event he was caught out by some citizen stalker.

"We've worked out a way of bypassing Biocrime," Banda said.

"Oh for sure, the most complicated surveillance system in history, and of all the people that have tried to bring it down over the centuries, you've managed to work this one out?"

"No, not just me," Banda said, as she ignored Katcher's put down. "We've had a team working on this—it's a decoder that interrupts genetic recording and lightcapture—"

"—look, I know my history," Katcher interrupted, not believing a word Banda had uttered. "Many subversives for the Movement have tried disruption over the centuries and they've always been caught out. Why would this one be any different?"

"Because it uses light storage itself and refraction to scatter the DNA logic. We know that some parts of the world are not part of Biocrime—like the universal penal zone—"

"—like I said," Katcher said," I know my history, that's a system used in the twenty-seven hundreds and look what happened to the people that tried to install it. Found out, captured, and their bones would now be scattered in a penal zone somewhere, after being carved up by some wild cloned animal or one of the deranged prisoners on those islands. Look, I gotta go, you know some stalker is going to pick up this conversation."

"But they won't. I'm using the decoder now. And I've linked one up to you too. My tribe from the Movement picked up on those developments in the past and it works. We've been using it for a year now, acting out our subversion on the surface, and none of us have a profile recording with Biocrime."

"Yes, but that's because Biocrime is reeling you in. You can't escape the continuum, you know that. Nice chatting, but I gotta go."

"We've also got insider information from Biocrime…"

This made Katcher pause for thought. Not for long, but enough time for him to consider it a possibility.

"You're getting information from Biocrime?—from a Technocrat?—why would they do that? That does not make sense. Biocrime data is the most restricted part of the universe. If they were leaking information, they'd create a high-level taskforce to find out what happened—they'd work out a way, like they always do."

"There's a lot of Technocrats out there that don't subscribe to all this 'new world' crap and the divide between us and them," Banda said. "You wouldn't believe how many Technocrats want this whole order of things to change and their number is growing. There's not many, but they're as fucked as any other human, infallible, they question their existence—and don't care if they're caught out."

"Well, I don't know any Technos, aside from the ones turning up to my sessions," Katcher said. "They seem reasonable, but I've always assumed the Technocrats that have anything to do with humans are spies and selling information back to Biocrime to supplement their universal income.

"I still don't trust it. How do you know it's not a plant? How do you know that you're not being reeled in? Biocrime has done that in the past with people like you."

"John, we've been using it for a year. It works. And we need you to come back to the Movement. What are you going to do, spend your life giving meaningless history lessons to a few groupies and Technocrats that want to boost their BioEd credits—the ones that you think are spies anyway? And you want to be keep being humiliated by Biocrime for the rest of your life?"

Katcher knew what Banda said was true. He wanted to come back to the Movement, but what good was it if this ended up being a sting, and he got captured and was sent away to a universal penal zone in a remote island? He's knew Banda was saying it was better to die standing up than from your knees, but this was dangerous territory. But could he also run the risk of being seen as someone who was given a chance to return to the Movement but turned his back on natural humans?

"I know you're thinking 'who is this crazy woman; she's a spy; she's a Biocrime agent'," Banda said. "But check Lifebook, check Biocrime. There's no profile on me, and there never will be while I use this decoder. Has anything registered on your profile? Search my name—Greta Banda—it's nowhere. It's a system that works, I'm telling you."

Katcher reached for his cell device, opened the Lifebook app and searched Banda's profile and history. There was no evidence of her presence at his lecture last week, or their catch-up at Gloria Jean's. On her live visual page, he could see Banda at her ground-floor apartment watching the lightscreen and reading her tablet, even though she was actually sitting in front of him. He then summoned over onto his own Lifebook profile. On his live visual page, he expected to see the images of him seated with Banda at a table in Gloria Jean's. Instead, the visual page showed him on the Line 7 autobus, probably heading back home to his apartment. There was no reference or data relating to any conversations he'd had with Banda.

It took a while for Katcher to understand what was happening, and it altered his understanding of the time–space relationship and assumptions of the continuum being the undeniable arbiter of truth and a record of everything that took place in the world.

There was the saying of the times: '*If it's not on Lifebook, it doesn't exist.*' But what he had just seen was a revelation for him—he knew human experimentation never happened in isolation. Through amorphic resonance and convergence of thinking, if decoding of genetic lightcapture was here in front of him, there would be others that knew about this technology.

"This is Biocrime technology—straight from my source at Biocrime," Banda said, in a quieter tone. "We haven't got the same resources as them, but if we've got access to the same technology as them and they don't know about it, that means we're one step ahead."

"So you say there's no genetic recording or lightcapture with this device," Katcher said, impressed but still skeptical. To be sure, he thought it might be possible for the Movement to have an informant within Biocrime—he had come to accept there could be disgruntled Technocrats in the world that would sell Biocrime secrets, but he still thought, on balance, this was an elaborate sting set up either by Biocrime, or a group of citizen stalkers that wanted to cash in on a big catch.

Conversely, that didn't make sense to Katcher either. He was a well-known former revolutionary leader—and a potentially dangerous one—but his Biocrime profile had almost no activity on it for almost a decade. He'd been under the radar for a long time, and there was no need for Biocrime to entrap him and send him off to a universal penal zone forever.

"I know this all this might seem a bit far fetched," Banda said, "but we need you back at the Movement. You're the missing link and there's a groundswell of support to end this domination by Technocrats and oppression of natural humans. Even some Technocrats want it to end."

"Well, you're right—it does sound far fetched," Katcher said. "You have to do something else to convince me. And how far are you prepared to go?"

"You'll see—"

"—well, until then, get the fuck out of my life."

*

'GLORIA JEAN'S, OUR MILLENNIA'

Gloria Jean's was a coffeehouse company founded in the North America Zone in 1979, a cheap low-end establishment that offered hot beverages and small meals. It was one of the few remaining brand names from the franchise era of the late twentieth-century period. Its name became synonymous with longevity and survival, after an endless sequence of scandals relating to exploitation of its workers and international suppliers, provision of foods that comprised high levels of sugar and fat, and relationships with extreme evangelist religious groups.

In times of corporate troubles, Gloria Jean's would rehabilitate itself through slick advertising material, and used innovation to future proof itself. In response to constant problems with underpayment of its workers, Gloria Jean's become the first company to fully mechanize its in-store staff, implementing virtual assistants, robohelpers and automated systems where all of its stores worldwide became staffless. It was also the first franchise foodstore to fully implement synthetic food and coffee.

In the year 2979, it commissioned the most expensive advertising campaign in history, to recognize its one-thousand year history.

There's a thirty-second montage of images from the past thousand years. Like most high corporate advertising, it's slick clean, highly emotive. It shows families in fun times, a fast moving train, high tech gadgetry, handshakes, and ends with a contemplative forest of tranquility.

There is no mention of coffee or food, but there is a watermark of the ubiquitous Gloria Jean's logo in the bottom right hand corner. It conveys emotion, a feeling of what the brand of Gloria Jean's is—a survivor over many years, through trials and tribulations, but it's still here, in a world of constant change and still here after over a thousand years. It ends with a fade to black with the words in stark orange and a crimson maroon edge: 'Gloria Jean's, our millennia' and in smaller type: 'since 1979'.

CHAPTER 15.   THE DEATH ZONES

Universal penal zones were the human enigmas of the time. Everyone knew of the universal penal zones but, at the same time, nothing about them; what went on there, how people got there. But they knew about the final outcome, that there was no coming back.

To fill the void of information, the understanding of universal penal zones grew within the public consciousness: that wild animals roamed these lands; it was lawless and anarchic; the criminals rendered non-citizens by Biocrime were sent there and only lived for a few days before being devoured by these wild animals, or attacked by organized gangs of violent jungle mafia, eaten for food, because supplies were scarce in the universal penal zones. Some theories were that the zones were used for scientific DNA experiments, the creation of hybrid human animals, replicating the imagined creatures of ancient Greek and Roman mythology, where a human head would be coupled with the body of a horse, or the head of a cow coupled with the body of a human.

There was an opposite school of thought that contemplated universal penal zones as inventions of Biocrime; that they were really zones of paradise, where undesirables and miscreants with no hope of living in mainstream worlds would be sent off to live the life of luxury, much like the old-style dictators from old-world republics that bargained away their incumbency for a secluded life containing all the luxuries for their lasting days. This theory had some traction, due to the belief that Biocrime depended on these types of public and counter-community figures to whip up frenzies about crime, law and order, and create the income needed to support their surveillance system. These citizens were worth more to Biocrime alive than dead.

There were two universal penal zones—southern and western. The southern penal zone was reserved after the earthquakes of in the year 2314, where the former republic of New Zealand was reduced to rubble and declared unsafe for human life, and the existing population of twelve million in this area was dispersed throughout the Asia and America zones. New Zealand had historically been an earthquake prone zone, where major earthquakes in the 1930s and the 2010s destroyed major cities, and a series of smaller and continuous earthquakes throughout the twenty-third century built up to major quakes throughout 2314, which brought down four major cities, created a series of massive tsunamis and flooded the southern coast region of the Australia Zone.

The western penal zone was created soon afterwards in the former republic of Madagascar, where a bio-viral outbreak in the year 2321 killed ninety per cent of the island's eighty-two million people—the remaining people were moved to a quarantine zone in the Western Africa Zone, inoculated and dispersed to other African zones, and the Eurasia Zone. Madagascar had developed into a sophisticated metropolis zone and a center of creative ideas for the future of humanity—the capital of the zone, Antananarivo, had become a diplomatic zone for resolving international conflicts and dilemmas, in a similar way how the city of Reykjavik in the Icelandic Zone was used to negotiate nuclear arms reductions between the

United States of America and the Soviet Union during the cold wars of the late twentieth century.

The bio-viral outbreak was mysterious, but it was widely regarded a rogue scientist entrepreneur had instigated a series of surreptitious biological experiments with exotic animals on the island, with extracted DNA from bones of animals over three million years old—from the mainland Africa Zone— and rendered the land unlivable for a period of almost two hundred years, before the zone became fully free from the virus. The virus was related to an encephalitic auto-immune disease that caused brain synapses to stop connecting with each other, and caused chemical imbalances in the relationship between acetylcholine and cholinesterase in the body muscles, creating a fast-tracked version of motor-neuron disease and causing victims to die within a matter of days. It afflicted humans and animals in a similar way, and was considered one of the greatest epidemiological crises in human history, rivaling the bubonic plague from the middle ages, and the Spanish version of influenza during 1918.

The northern part of Madagascar was retained as a quarantine zone until the remaining population of around eight million were inoculated and moved to other zones around the world. Due to the nature and unknown properties of the virus, the entire island was abandoned and monitored remotely through soil samples collected by autonomous robohelpers, but the entire island remained as an open grave site, with the rotting carcasses of millions of human and animal bodies left behind where they fell.

Aerial footage from the western penal zone acquired through drone cameras showed that through a combination of precipitation, humidity and hot temperatures, metropolis areas had naturally crumbled through weather and fast growing weeds and other arboreal matter encompassing the former cities, and remained a biohazard for many years after it was cleared of the remaining human population.

After depopulation, Biocrime initiated a process of land acquisition in the southern and western penal zones—a painstaking but relatively cheap process that was completed over a ten-year period. It was much easier in the western penal zone, as many generations of land owners had perished during the viral outbreak, but surviving landowners were happy to hand over their titles and recoup whatever they could for otherwise worthless land. Biocrime's longer term corporate strategy was to seek land masses away from the general citizen population, and instigate penal zones where it was possible to bypass the world memory bank and lightcapture systems, and contiguous land masses that were now free of populations, such as the former republics of New Zealand and Madagascar, were perfect.

The existing prison zones on mainlands were expensive to operate, manage and maintain, and zones where non-citizens could be deported to and left to fend for themselves without worry was the perfect solution for Biocrime. For Biocrime, these zones were out of sight, out of mind. And, most importantly, at little cost.

As Biocrime already had crowd authorization to do as they pleased with existing criminals, they completed the software exclusion areas to bypass the world memory bank and lightcapture, and gradually deported mainland non-citizen detainees, initially to the southern penal zone and, after the biohazard had cleared, to the western penal zone.

Of course, Biocrime kept data on the non-citizens that were deported to these universal penal zones but that was the extent of their interest. The two zones were redacted from satellite imagery and because the zones were also excluded from the continuum, very few people on the planet knew what was happening in these areas.

It was expected that with no skill in being able to survive, no access to technology, or organize themselves to escape from these zones, detainees would quickly perish.

The deportations commenced in the early 2600s and within one hundred years, all twenty-two million of the world's non-citizen criminal population had been moved to the universal penal zone, and the prisons that previously housed the non-citizens were sold off for industrial development or apartment buildings, with some prisons retained for short-term detention zones which were the stage before deportation, if it was deemed a detainee could not be rehabilitated, or was a repeat offender.

Permanent physical and electronic surveillance was maintained along the coastlines of these two universal penal zones, just on the periphery of the world memory bank exclusion area, but with only around one hundred non-citizens managing to work out a way of getting themselves off the zones each year, the physical surveillance was outsourced to thrillseeker bounty hunters, usually crowd funded to the tune of €25,000 per person, where they could fly off from the either the Australia or Africa zone in solo-propeller flight units, loaded with ammunition, and shoot the offenders dead with high range laser bullets. Even with the costs of flight units and laser bullets, and the twenty per cent commission with Biocrime, it was easy prey and possible to make a €15,000 profit, and as the escapees usually tried to escape the penal zones in groups, it was a lucrative trade.

Although the Biocrime motto was 'Do not kill. Do no evil', non-citizens were not considered remotely as human.

They had been decommissioned and deauthorised and were officially dead, so any Technocrat involved in thrillseeker bounty work that involved killing was legally covered, and was essentially killing someone that was already deemed to be dead anyway. And, besides, they were non-citizens that had tried to upend and destroy the social order of the world.

Over a four-hundred year period, Biocrime estimated that at any given time, there were around ten thousand living in each of the universal penal zones, based on the amount of non-citizens that had been deported there, around five-hundred million over four-hundred years, and the likely rate of survival of one month.

Not even Biocrime knew exactly what went on in these universal penal zones, but with the bio-viral heritage in the western penal zone, the constant structural instability of the southern penal zone and the introduction of several species of wildlife, the survival rate was very low.

CHAPTER 16.   AN EVIL PLAN

Banda knew Katcher was keen to return to the revolutionary guard, but he wasn't going to jump into a two-time chance meeting with an unknown who presented information to him that seemed far-fetched, as well as getting him caught up with Biocrime and a possible deportation, if it didn't come off.

He probably thought she was a middle-ager that was part of a young punk do-gooder society, a disorganized rabble big on talk but low on action, and when the going got tough, would retreat and only think about their universal incomes and how to protect themselves, rather than actually promoting the Movement.

Katcher was selfless—Banda thought of herself in the same way too, but she needed to carry out an act that would prove her *bona fides* to *him*. Nothing was ever officially proven, but the rumors of Katcher killing Technocrats and using incendiaries in key locations was always held in high regard within the Movement—not so much the act of killing but the fact that the revolutionary leader was prepared to lead from the front and do whatever it took to reach the goals of the revolution and achieve the social change that would matter to all people, not just the select few.

Katcher had told her to 'get the fuck' out of his life just the previous afternoon, but Banda was determined to prove to

Katcher that she was a real member of the Movement, a real revolutionary and one committed to upending the current social system.

As the morning light peered through Banda's window again, she contemplated her recent conversations with Katcher and planned her next course of actions. As usual, she awoke early, while Kransich caught up on some extra sleep next to her. Her mind fluctuated between her meetings with Katcher and the way it ended yesterday afternoon, and her relationship with Kransich, and whether it was as beneficial as she liked to think it was.

He had some new material for her—updates about the impending Anika-6 inspection and software patches for a beta surveillance program Biocrime had instigated: in return, Kransich asked for €10,000 in crypto-currency. Banda thought it was a too high, but through her personal private network, she transferred the amount while he slept. She thought about how many private lives Kransich had, and what he did with all the black-market currency he'd been provided with. He was on a decoded system, different to Banda's system, but decoded nevertheless, so she could never search and find out what he was up to—Kransich said he supported his 'biological' mother in a far away zone, but that would involve crypto-market support on the recipient side, so she wasn't sure how he could actually do this.

Banda was not sure how true his story was, as she assumed he was cloned from a central source over a thousand years old, but whether he'd been tricked in an elaborate scam or somehow engaged in military trades, she didn't really care too much about what he did with the crypto-currency. But knowing he was caring for his biological mother—even if wasn't true— meant that Kransich was emotionally closer to the Movement than most other Technocrats would be. Kransich told Banda that he actively sought his biological mother—something very few Technocrats would do—several years ago through a detailed scanning and investigative process through egg donation databanks, and became despondent to see that she was in a decrepit state in a remote zone in Europe. Banda felt Kransich knew *what it is to be human*, and even though he was a mercenary selling Biocrime secrets, she felt he was a safe bet.

She waited until Kransich left—he was annoyingly slow this morning—and she wanted to get to Anika-6 so she could announce to Weller, her grand plan to entice Katcher back to the Movement, and the sooner she went down there, the better. Kransich finally left after the two exchanged farewells, and she prepared her datacard with the new material from Biocrime.

With Kransich gone, she switched on her decoder app and, after she left the room, her Lifebook Live page departed from real-life, and transitioned into fabrication mode. The fabricated visual footage showed that she was still in her apartment, and the algorithm made subtle changes to the footage, so it didn't look like an inane loop of inactivity.

She messaged Weller about her impending arrival and slithered through the tubing to get to the underground cavern. It was a thirty-minute journey through the tunnel to get to Anika-6 and, after she travelled through the security passages and unlocked the tungsten and titanium control door, she was inside control central and greeted by the typically enthusiastic Weller.

"What have you got today?" asked Weller in his usual curt manner.

"News about the targeted inspection," Banda said. "Kransich said he couldn't get access to any clearer details—

we'll have to work out what to do about it—and some more bypass patches for Biocrime's surveillance program."

"We'll have to monitor the surface chatter ourselves—it's just that we won't know when it's likely to happen, but we have to be prepared. And Katcher?"

"He's pissed with me—thinks I'm a plant from Biocrime trying to set him up, and told me to fuck off. I think he's got an interest, but at the moment, we're no different to all the other groupies and the bullshit wannabes that have approached him over the past ten years. I've got to prove to him we're for real."

"Yeah, for sure, but what are you proposing?"

"We've got to attack a Technocrat zone," Banda said, "something big that will show our system works and can't be detected by Biocrime. And I've got to be part of it—I have to do it. It will be dangerous, but if this is what we have to do to prove to Katcher our system works, then we've got to do it."

"You mean, just like Katcher used to do—the attacks? Bombs?"

"Exactly like Katcher used to do, and the bigger, the better."

With some hesitation, Weller reached out to a lightscreen and prepared for a surface scan and within minutes, estimated one region of San Francisco about eight miles away would be suitable to let off a high-impact detonation, with minimum disruption to natural humans, and maximum damage to Technocrats.

"This one's in the East End between Richmond and Anza Vista, a high-density Technocrat zone and in this apartment block, there's access to the underground aircon system—there's very few natural humans in this area. Looks like there's lots of old digital surveillance cameras—most are broken though. It's all concrete out the back there, so less DNA material that can record anything meaningful, but you'll be on decoder, so you won't register anyway."

"How many in the apartment?"

"Looks like there's around six hundred…" Weller said the figure slowing, before repeating the number: *six hundred*. "…this is a big fucking deal, but I feel like we're being so nonchalant about killing a huge number of Technocrats—and some of our own."

"Mav, you don't have to do this," Banda said. "I can take charge. It's not a big deal to me, I don't think they're real people."

"How about Kransich? Is he real?"

"He's a mercenary, and he's using us as much as we're using him—look, don't get all moralistic on me—"

"—we can't decide this for ourselves—this is a big call, it's high risk. And we're all equal in this aren't we?"

Weller wanted to seek counsel from the other members of the revolutionary team—all supposedly equal, but some were more equal than others. Weller summoned Mike Scanlen and Maria Renalda—the two that successfully defended Katcher in his crowd trial all those years ago—from another cavern, and it took five minutes before they appeared with Weller and Banda.

Scanlen and Renalda were both in their mid-fifties, with a high level of technical, legal and analytical skills, and when wise heads were needed to prevail, they were the people you really needed to have by your side.

Scanlen was a contemporary of Katcher—although nine years older, he was a critical background part of the machinery of the revolution before Katcher was arrested and detained. While the movement was destroyed then by Biocrime, it was felt that it was just a matter of time before they regrouped and led the pathway for the Movement again. But ten years on, with technological advances in surveillance and Katcher out of the picture, they were still regrouping—they were a patient group but even this amount of time was starting to test them.

Renalda was the leader in the legal crowd-sourced case for Katcher against BioLaw, the legal behemoth that was appended to Biocrime. Although BioLaw lost the case to make Katcher a non-citizen and deport him to a universal penal zone, they were legally able to restrict what Katcher could do in his life, enabled a twenty-four-hour surveillance of him, effectively ending his position and work as a revolutionary leader of the Movement.

Scanlen and Renalda were both now 'off-the-grid'. Scanlen was now understood to be 'missing, presumed dead' within Biocrime and Lifebook—a status allocated to people not seen or sighted through the servers in the continuum after seven years, were officially listed as 'expired'.

Renalda's death was fabricated soon after the completion of Katcher's crowd trial. Being the lead legal person behind the crowd defense of Katcher didn't exactly enamour her in the public's view, and her ability to supplement her universal income was severely reduced. In combination with Scanlen, Weller and Banda, she decided the best pathway to stoking up a revolution was to 'go underground'.

Scanlen and Renalda were considered 'thinking' substitutes for the absent Katcher—*what would Jonathan Katcher do*—and they were precisely asked this when they arrived to see Weller and Banda.

"What's up?" Renalda asked, focusing her attention on Banda.

"It's pretty straight forward really," Banda said. "We need to bomb a Technocrat area to prove to Jonathan that I'm not a plant. High risk, and it's a lot of people. Mav thinks we needed a consensus if I want to proceed."

"Well, is it a high-risk plan," Renalda said, "it goes without saying. The highest order of crime is killing Technocrats—and you'll go straight to a universal penal zone, or they'll work out a way of killing you before then. That's the first point—"

"—and Katcher would always think," Scanlen added, "'what's the end game, how will this achieve our goal'. It's always based around the risk."

Banda was calm but reasoned. "Katcher's had nothing to do with the Movement for almost a decade, and we have to do something to show him we're not a Biocrime plant, and we're prepared to bring on the Movement. We've regrouped to the stage where we can go to the next step, and we need to bring him back in."

"But it's a fuckload of people," Weller interjected. "Six hundred people, including a few natural humans." The magnitude of what was proposed weighed on Weller's mind, but it was more about the protection of Anika-6 than any concern he had for Technocrats. He hated the Technocrats as much as anyone else, but killing six hundred people to prove a point to one person seemed out of kilter, as well as the prospect of Anika-6 disbanding because of one false move. It was too high a price to pay.

"The road to hell is paved with good intentions," Banda said, "which means the opposite can be true too, doesn't it?"

"If this goes ahead," Scanlen said, "there can never be any blowback to us—any of us. If you're captured in this raid, that's the end of Anika-6, and we'll have to start up all over again. And it could even mean the end for Jonathan Katcher if Biocrime can make the link between the two of you."

Weller was still reluctant and believed it was a high-risk strategy that outweighed the benefits but felt it was best to make the consensus—it wasn't the best strategy in his opinion, but was the only one on the table and they probably didn't have the time to wargame other scenarios. He was reluctant when it came to high-level decision-making anyway, but with Scanlen and Renalda at the table, he felt more secure, as well as diluting the decision across more people.

He'd hate to see Banda go down, but he was more concerned about losing Anika-6. Ten years' worth of work going down when they were so close to realizing their dreams would be a disaster.

*

Semtex was the explosive of choice for terrorists for many years. Its first usage was in the Eastern Europe Zone in the late twentieth century and gained currency for the politically disaffected because it was difficult to detect and highly explosive, even with smaller amounts. Banda could recite all the original ingredients—crystalline, styrene-butadiene, noctyl phthalate tributyl citrate, naphthylamine.

Although the original Semtex was long gone, the formula in the year 3034 was a mixture of new-wave explosives and synthetic chemicals laced with plutonium. While the original Semtex was extremely powerful, research and development over the centuries had created a formula ten times more powerful and more condensed.

Semtex was still used for construction site detonations, and clearing of geographical features such as rock faces and hills that need to be flattened out for apartment construction, but its use was highly restricted and easily detectable.

This brand of Semtex was ZJ478. The name disappeared from the public domain because of its association with terrorists acts, most notably, the destruction of a commercial aeroplane in the Northern Europe Zone in the late twentieth century. As with most reappropriated names and concepts, ZJ478 bore little semblance to the original product, but in true retro style, some features were replicated, such as the dark red synthetic color, although that had changed slightly to a deep hot pink.

Anika-6 purchased a batch of Semtex through black market crypto-currency, and with the help of Kransich's secrets from Biocrime. This batch was two years old and was obtained for this type of purpose—they didn't know it at the time how it was to be used, but every organized revolutionary cell needed to be prepared.

Banda, Weller, Scanlen and Renalda agreed on the plan: Banda would take the Semtex in a small package into the basement of the Technocrat apartment block selected by Weller. The package included a biodegradable decoder patch that shielded it from the continuum and Biocrime, which meant that both Banda and the package were undetectable.

She would leave the package in the basement of the apartment and detonate it from a viewable distance using an app created by Weller. It would be impossible to trace this back to her, or back to Anika-6.

And how would she prove the *bona fides* of the Movement to Katcher? Her plan was to record her act on a video capture button to show to Katcher, and the news of the explosion would be available everywhere through the continuum and Lifebook. It would be reported as the worst attack on Technocrats in three-hundred years.

She knew Katcher would still be skeptical when she showed him the footage—doctored and manipulated video footage made up almost seventy per cent of all material of Lifebook visual pages—but once he realized her attack was similar to the ones he organized when he was the leader, and that it was highly unlikely Biocrime would stage such a catastrophic explosion that killed six hundred of its own, just for the sake of entrapment, Banda was certain he would be convinced about the true intentions of the Movement.

If she survived—and Banda was very determined to survive—she'd also mention to Katcher that Scanlen and Renalda were waiting for him in the underground.

CHAPTER 17. THE BOMBING AT ANZA VISTA

It was a cool San Francisco morning, overcast with water-laden clouds ready to burst open. Banda had her tools of trade and she was just off the autotram, walking towards the apartment block in Geary Boulevard in the Inner Richmond East End area, eight miles away from her apartment. She had to move quickly, discretely and undetected. Her decoder app was switched on as soon as she left her apartment, and the disposable decoder patch was attached to the Semtex package in her small backpack. It was small and discrete, and she didn't want to do anything to attract attention. As she moved towards her destination, the rain commenced slowly, and then increased to a heavy fall. She made sure her video capture button was on, and she could see on her cell device the recording was stable. She occasionally took the video button off the lapel and turned it towards herself to check its operation, as if she was doing a 'selfie' or masquerading as a citizen journalist.

The apartment block was tall, a forty-story concrete edifice with artificial black and grey marble veneer, but it melded into the horizon of many other apartment blocks in the area. Banda could see the Golden Gate Bridge and the hills further beyond and, after briefly taking in some of the sights, showed some regret that her actions would spoil an otherwise excellent view.

The rain shielded Banda from the gaze of other people that were walking along the boulevard, but it was a zone where people minded their own business anyway, and she was free to carry out her work. She walked to the back of the apartment block and saw an access point for garbage collection. Although the apartment block had a sleek and fashionable design, it was a lower socio-economic Technocrat zone with few modern conveniences. On the inside of these apartments, it was almost top of the range in technology, but lacked facilities such as in-home self-recycling and garbage combustion machines. Some parts of the apartment block were old style, and portable garbage vehicles drove around to apartments like this, keeping the recyclable items, and vaporizing the rest.

At the access point to the basement, Banda could see the old-style surveillance cameras were broken—as Weller suggested to her—but there were four others inside that he told her about. She was also wearing a partial facial disguise and her decoder app meant her genetic data wouldn't be recorded, but it was best to be in there and out as quickly as possible.

Through the heavy rain, Banda went through the access point, and straight into the disposal unit area which co-ordinated all the pipes where garbage from each apartment was collated and extracted. The strong pungent smell from the disposal unit stopped Banda in her tracks but, because she only intended to be there for less than thirty seconds, she tolerated it. Just as she left the explosive package behind the extraction pipes, a garbage vehicle came through the access point and startled her—but she had enough time to slither around the side walls and through an access door, unseen by anyone.

The bag with the Semtex had been left behind and soon, it would also leave behind a scene of carnage. Banda had a clear conscience about what was just about to happen and fended away the small whisperings that pulled at her heart—many people were going to die and the amalgam of body parts left behind were too gruesome for her to consider.

She ventured towards the Anza Vista lookout—a small park just seven-hundred yards away—but Banda estimated that it was enough to avoid injury from any flying shrapnel but, importantly, close enough to record the event on her video button.

The heavy rain had subsided, reduced to a light patter of water, but the grey clouds still hung ominously, tempting to release another deluge of rain at any fickle moment. Like an arsonist disappearing from the scene of their crime but wanting to see the results of their misdemeanors, Banda positioned herself at the park bench, with a clear view of the apartment block and ready to record the event as a visual trophy. On any other day, the view would be picture perfect, but the gloom and the rain soiled the scene, appropriate for what was just about to take place.

Banda was committed and there was no going back. She retrieved her cell device and located the app that Weller developed to link the Semtex with the detonator. She pressed the button on the app, but the rain droplets interfered with the traction, so she wiped the screen and pressed the button again.

Three seconds later, a massive crashing boom was heard across the suburb. As far as a spectacle was concerned, it disappointed Banda. She expected a pyrotechnic display but after the initial boom, there was no immediate carnage and all she could see was the smashed glass panes on every level of the building and some smoke emanating from the lower levels. That changed after a few more minutes, where fires started to engulf the sides of the building.

The presence of some rain ensured the fires weren't as extreme as they could have been, but the fires had been fueled by a range of chemicals and gases that powered the building and were going to rage for sometime, irrespective of how much rain was falling, or other retardants poured onto the flames.

The fires were coming, but many were already dead. The sonic boom had already blasted the lungs of over a hundred Technocrats on the lower levels—that was just the start—and those trying to escape through the internal stairwells were taken by the flames, many burnt beyond recognition.

Banda had never killed before but, to her, pressing a button to set off a remote incendiary wasn't the same as seeing the face of a victim seconds before they died. She felt some remorse but she quickly consoled herself. '*They're not really people anyway.*'

*

The fire services in San Francisco, managed and operated by a subsidiary of Biocrime, were very effective and efficient and generated a sizeable profit. But even their skills and efficiency were no match for the fast-burning flames in the apartment block.

Fire crews assembled at the base of the apartment block within seven minutes of the blast—their task wasn't a rescue mission, but to stabilize the environment and put out the flames to ensure nearby apartments weren't affected. It was part of their job, but the fire workers also had to mask out the smell of so many burning bodies—a mixture of the aroma of burnt human meat, not dissimilar to the smell of barbequed beef and pork; the metallic-coppery smell of burning blood; and the distinct sweet perfumed muskiness of boiled cerebrospinal fluid.

BioMed staff and medical robohelpers moved rapidly to tend to any survivors from the blast—but Semtex was a type of explosive that had sharp results—survivors were also severely injured and very unlikely to live for too much longer.

The scene was one of an organized chaos—the teams of fire and health crews analyzed the likely causes of the blast, moving through the vulture-like presence of the collection of citizen journalists who recorded moving images and acquired the *mise en scene* of the blast. There was big money to be made, and if they attracted more 'likes' and 'wants' to their Lifebook profiles, it meant a higher level of supplementary income, especially if their reportage ended up screened on the large-format lightscreens throughout the city.

There was a fee for everything and everything had its price.

The fire crews weren't left behind in the financial stakes either. As soon as the blast was acknowledged through their data systems, their messaging went to a wide range of crowd sourcing outlets, requesting €12 for their work to go out and put out the fires, under the Lifebook category of 'Community Emergency Safety'.

Nor were the health and human rescue services left behind. Their task was likely to only be body retrieval at this stage, but it was €4 for their fee, under the 'Emergency Medical Service and Retrieval' category of Lifebook. The financial assets of all the deceased would be automatically accumulated by Biocrime and distributed to the service providers that exinguished the fire, the health and rescue services that retrieved the bodies, as well as contributing to the cost of rebuilding and rehousing the apartment block.

Despite the catastrophic nature of the blast, the Technocratic ethos was unemotional and pragmatic. Live was all about the living: the dead couldn't contribute to the world any further. The clean-up was fast and efficient—after the embers died out and the building was deemed safe to inspect, all bodies would be retrieved within twelve hours, and the rebuilding would commence within forty-eight hours.

Banda looked on at the ensuing calamity from her position perched atop Anza Vista, and recorded every moment. The view was now more spectacular, given the flames had more fuel to furnish them and although the fire was under control, the top of the apartment block had a bright orange glow to it, almost like a massive cigar upended and embedded into the ground, exporting its smoke and fire into the sky. And like a cigar, the smells were unusual: the gases and chemicals; the human flesh; the fire retardant sprays used by the fire crew.

It approached midday and Banda switched off her recording device and left the scene, knowing there would be no blow-back to her or any evidence that linked the blast to Anika-6 and the Movement. She headed toward the nearest autotram to return back to her apartment, the sounds of the mayhem she created diminished with each step she took away from the blast site. There was a chance she might be stopped by Biocrime for a routine inspection, as they would under these circumstances, but it didn't matter to Banda. Her job was done.

CHAPTER 18.   FRAMING A BOMBER

News of the bombing at Anza Vista quickly filtered through to Lifebook, and was accessed on many lightscreens, and displayed on messaging, news services and online hubs.

All city large-format lightscreens and holographs screened the footage of the bombing, with information that almost six-hundred citizens had been killed during a terrorism attack, and three suspects have been already arrested, and charged with multiple offences.

Of course, this was not true.

Within thirty minutes of the bombing, Biocrime data systems and the world memory bank had been scanned for events leading up to the bombing, and they couldn't detect anything at all as far as how the bombing took place and who was involved. Their data systems had tightened up dramatically since Katcher's crowd trial a decade earlier, and this was the first major incident since that time where they hadn't been able to immediately detect who was responsible.

Less than one-tenth of a per cent of all criminal matters were, on *prime face* evidence, unsolvable, but it was usually because of a minor software malfunction, or what was called in the trade, 'parallax error', where genetic data recording was not entirely conclusive and the visual record disputed the actuality of events. The issue of parallax error was used in

Katcher's crowd trial defense a decade earlier, and Biocrime corrected many of the software malfunctions to ensure that type of technicality could never happen again.

However, parallax error couldn't be reduced completely. For these cases where evidence still remained inconclusive, there was a specialist team within Biocrime that recreated and manipulated data to make evidence conclusive, a modern-day version of police verballing. Biocrime was an omnipresent edifice and was the strongest pillar of society. For it to have continued success, it needed to be seen as perfect and infallible, and in the absence of the real malefactor in the Anza Vista bombing, it allocated the crime to three other suspects—miscreants with a history of low-level violence—with reconstructed and fabricated evidence to link them to the crime, which then became available for crowd assessment.

All crimes needed to be allocated to someone—whether they were actually responsible for the crime or not—and in this case, the Anza Vista bombing was allocated to three low-level human activists. The three—now known as the 'East End Bombers'—were Eva Alvarez, Yasmin Dominian and Paulo Mascerati—small fry, but they were active enough to have the crime pinned to them.

This solution would do for the time being but, for Biocrime, this incident was different. This was a major terrorism incident where almost six hundred Technocrats were murdered: a national emergency for Biocrime, and they didn't have any evidence of who was responsible. In all other crimes where evidence slipped through the cracks because of a technical glitch or human error, such as the occasion where a Biocrime security officer forgot to back up a data from a major case before he went for a coffee break: at least that provided a reason that could be overridden or resolved through deeper datamining.

But in this case, there was no data evidence at all—Banda's decoder app made sure of this—nothing that could be retrieved from genetic recording in the world memory bank; nothing on the surviving surveillance cameras; and nothing in the public domain. Pinning the crime on someone, innocent or otherwise, wasn't the problem for Biocrime; fabrications of evidence were simple. Biocrime needed to find out why there was no record of the planting of the bomb, and they needed to find out who was behind it. Biocrime had the right people who could find out.

*

The leader of Biocrime's Unallocated Incidents Team was Don Capone, a fourth generation human clone from the Southern Europe Zone.

He was sharp, ruthless and strategic and had been provided with the task of cleaning up the Anza Vista incident and finding out what happened. He was fourth in line in the chain of command at Biocrime and, because of this, was entitled to a windowed office on the fifty-sixth floor of the Biocrime building, a location in the heart of the financial district which provided views to half of San Francisco. The president, Michelle Luanda, was in the heavily fortified sixtieth floor, and as far as the hierarchy of control was concerned, Capone was close to the top of the pyramid.

His office was spacious, and had a vast array of lightscreens and other technological devices delicately poised throughout the workspace. It was clear and open, uncluttered in any way that could stultify his thinking or act as a deterrent to strategic thinking. He was a great believer in the principals of *feng shui* and allowing for the free flow of ideas in a working environment. It was a workspace that could accommodate several security officers and support staff, but Capone liked to 'war game' by himself and, on this occasion, was alone.

He was a powerful figure that had every available crime detection resource at his disposal—forensic specialists, coders and programmers, surveillance officers, finance, auditing and actuarial experts, problem solvers and strategic thinkers.

There was also another team he had access to, a team that managed digital clean up and propaganda—a collection of programmers, visual artists, speech writers and algorithm bypassers for propagandizing and manipulation of public perception. In this case, they were the team responsible for allocating the crime of the Anza Vista bombing to the three suspects, and creating the crowd trial so citizens could determine the guilt, or otherwise, of the suspects, with a closing date of fourteen days.

And with the amount of support material this team would fabricate against the three suspects, they would be found guilty, and sent immediately to a universal penal zone: there was no question about this. A major crime like this was going to attract a large number of 'likes' and 'wants', and would pay for all the deportation work, reparations to the families of the victims of the bombing, contribute to the rebuilding—which had already commenced—and generate a massive profit for Biocrime. For Biocrime, the guilty verdict was secondary to the income stream that was likely to arise.

But revenues and a guilty verdict aside, Capone needed to determine how Biocrime failed to detect who actually planted the bomb and if citizen stalking was a better method in this case to get to the heart of the matter.

He liked to ponder and after he stared out the window to look over the long horizon of the metropolis and collected his thoughts, he moved over to stand in front of his main lightscreen and summoned a list the highest ranked citizen stalkers in the San Francisco region.

Within seconds, the lightscreen displayed the long real-time list of the top-earners in citizen stalkers, with Marine Lestre heading the list, some twenty per cent higher than her nearest rival. Capone read through a number of profiles; collating, pondering, strategizing, working out which solution he should implement, and which option provided him with the clearest pathway.

*

Lestre was in her small apartment and watched two events concurrently on her lightscreen—her usual assessment and monitoring of Biocrime profiles, and the ongoing reportage of the Anza Vista bombing in the lower right part of the screen. There was an ongoing stream of video material—citizen journalist reports and analysis: who were the East End Bombers, what was their rationale and did they have links with other natural humans, or were they lone wolves?

Of course, everyone had a theory and a rationale, but the conglomeration of opinions, facts and theories added to the circus of the event. Lestre was almost immune from the charade and sideshow—but below the rolling visual footage from Anza Vista, she noticed a small advertisement for Amore coffee, and she wondered whether it was time for her to replenish her supplies.

Lestre then summoned her Lifebook account to switch over to BioLaw, which showed a list of the current crowd trials, and the trial of the East End Bombers headed the list. She zoomed in on the trial, and it showed the details for the case against the East End Bombers: footage of the bomb planted—fabricated by Capone's team of propagandists—and Biocrime profile photographs with links to all the 'evidence' in the special part of Prosecution Zone, with the perfunctory Defense Zone for viewers who offered commentary for why they thought the bombers were innocent.

And, just like a computer-game simulation, there was a real-time bank of statistics—the current figure of 31,327,056: Guilty; 795,454: Not Guilty, with final projections and an advertising reminder for citizens to lodge their verdicts before the closing date. It was part pantomime, part revenge, part citizen jury; but for Biocrime, it was all about generating revenues. It had only been one day since the profiles of the East End Bombers went up and, at €2 per lodged verdict, Biocrime was likely to likely to recoup around €1 billion in revenue from the case alone.

On another part of Lestre's lightscreen, an incoming datacall flashed up—it was encrypted at level nine—the highest—and she could see that was a call from Biocrime. As a former employee, Lestre was known within Biocrime, but the highest level encryption she'd ever had before was a seven.

With level nine encryption, no-one could intervene or overhear the conversation, regardless of where they were. D'Souza was within earshot in the next room, but high-level noise cancelling software meant he couldn't hear the conversation, even if he was sitting next to Lestre.

Lestre summoned to accept the call, and Capone's face appeared on her lightscreen.

He was dressed in the orange and black stylized Biocrime suit: smart, clean and slightly oppressive, as if he was shielding the rest of the world from the dirty nasty work that went on behind the gated community of Biocrime.

"Marine Lestre? It's Officer Don Capone, leader of the Unallocated Incidents Team."

There wasn't a need for him to state this, as below the call display on Lestre's lightscreen was an outline of all the key details for Capone—his position, his history, and his key role in the destruction of one of the Movement's underground cells seven years ago. As well as a brief outline for the reason of his call. But basic human instinct remained intact: it was a rhetorical introduction and just plain good manners to someone he was meeting for the first time.

"It's about the Anza Vista bombing," Capone said, "and there's been a few issues that we need to get to the bottom of."

"Well, pleased to meet," Lestre said, "but there's not much to get to the bottom of. You've got your suspects, they're on crowd trial and the way things are going, they're about ninety-nine per cent guilty, and the good thing for you is Biocrime is going to make a motza. And, by the way, I hope I'm getting paid for this call."

"We can look after that later, but there's a few anomalies within the system."

"Anomolies? You do get glitches occasionally but what's up now?"

"Best that you come down to Biocrime and meet up," Capone said. "You've already got the clearance here, but best to have you in here to go through it. You've been our best stalker for the past two years, and we want you in on this project. And bring Lumbardo."

"You know of Lumbardo?"

"We know everything here, but we've psychometrically matched you with what we've got planned here, and you could probably do with his help. Have a five-minute think about it, but we want to move fast on this."

Lestre didn't need the full five minutes: she decided as soon as the encrypted call with Capone was over—she messaged Lumbardo immediately: 'High profile work with Biocrime. Anza Vista bombing. Are you in?' and within thirty seconds, she received Lumbardo's smiley-face response, with a small emoji on her screen, and also reminded her the synth coffee, Amore, was available on sale at a vendor just three minutes away, or if she was too busy to venture out, she could summons a small drone delivery to be received in just thirty minutes.

On her lightscreen, a small flashing green screen bounced up and suggested six options for meeting up with Capone at the central Biocrime building, having registered her recent interactions with him, as well the responses from Lumbardo. Capone was available tomorrow at 14:00, but at the moment, nothing was available for Lestre. She summoned away some of her regular appointments for the afternoon, and summoned away until there was a clear space for her—she wanted to move quickly too—and her scheduler calculated the timing for the autobus trips, a likely briefing session with Lumbardo at The Old Soviet, as well as the walking distance, and reallocated all of her tasks according to her previous behaviour and actions.

She knew Lumbardo would always make the time for this type of high-level activity, so she confirmed the meeting to Capone on his behalf.

*

In the corner of her eye, Lestre could see the distinct profile of Lumbardo sitting in his usual spot at The Old Soviet. It was just a another short trip again to the Biocrime headquarters from The Old Soviet and her scheduler suggested a twenty-minute timeslot for coffee, and a small snack for lunch, but only if they were quick.

Lestre entered The Old Soviet, and was keen to move fast. "Same again for you Mister Lumbardo?"

"Sure," Lumbardo said, "but we've only got twenty minutes, so we've got to be quick."

Lestre summoned for their usual 'quick snack': cheeseburgers, with Slavic gherkins on the side, and the synth latte each, delivered to their table by robohelper.

"What do you think they might be up to?" asked Lumbardo impatiently, not even waiting for Lestre to be seated.

Lestre noticed Lumbardo's shirt had its advertising zones switched off—which was a great relief to her—but showed that Lumbardo recognized the potential importance of this mission. Biocrime had a 'hands-off' approach to most of its dealings with the outside world and to bring outside people in to 'discuss' something meant a big case—and a potential big catch—was on the cards.

"It's to do with the Anza Vista bombing," Lestre said, "something about 'not quite adding up', or some 'anomolies', whatever that means."

"I've heard they may have some deeper software glitches," Lumbardo said, "but why call us in? If it's software, they've got a team of coders in there that can sort it out. And, haven't they already got their guys?"

"They have, or so they say they have, but just said there was something different about this one. Ah, gherkins! Love these…"

Lestre and Lumbardo finished their snack, and were tagged with a €13 bill each. It was quick, nourishing, and cheap. It wasn't good to go to a meeting on an empty stomach and they knew it hadn't cost the earth.

The next autobus trip after The Old Soviet was a twelve-minute ride. There was a lunch-time crowd which meant they weren't getting a seat, but to stand for the entire journey gave them a discount, so they weren't too fussed, especially Lumbardo.

The autobus neared the Biocrime headquarters, and Lestre and Lumbardo were three minutes early. They slowed their walk when they got off the autobus: it wasn't good to be early, or fashionably late—it had to be precisely 14:00.

The Biocrime building, contrary to the nature of the work that it performed, was not a hideous or overbearing building. It was a business, and the unusually welcoming features comprised sleek designs, a combination of modern silver metal styling, and a deep burnt rust orange color complementing the corporate black.

There was a lightwell at the entrance of the building, almost as though it was an enterprise that produced perfumed products or a benevolent society that provided good work and social support tasks for all citizenry.

In the lobby area, there was a collection of comfortable corporate seats and, on the wall, a large projected image of the current president of Biocrime, Michelle Luanda. The large three-dimensional Biocrime logo above the concierge was held by an invisible string, almost hanging like the sword of Damocles. Behind the concierge were the words of the company motto embossed in a sleek san-serif typeface: 'Do not kill. Do no evil'.

"Citizens Lestre and Lumbardo," the voice said from behind the desk, as they approached the concierge. "You're here for your 14:00 meeting with Officer Capone?"

It was a perfunctory personal engagement. The concierge was actually a hologram and had the details of Lestre and

Lumbardo on 'his' lightscreen as soon they walked through the entrance to the building, including the high level nature of their talks and the instruction for them to enter through the secret de-engagement zone.

"Certainly is," Lestre answered.

"For this level meeting," the concierge said, "we'll have to de-engage you, please follow our customer service officer, and she'll go through the procedure with you."

The concierge was 'George'. He had been programmed to accept around twelve million responses and could perform rudimentary tasks such as accept the arrival of attendees, and send voice and text messages to whoever needed to receive them. It was a fail-safe system, and if there was an instruction or command that 'George' couldn't understand, there was a voice autoresponder with the message: 'I'm sorry, but I can't resolve this for you right now. I've sent a message to a customer service officer, who will personally come here and deal with your issue shortly," followed by a prompt for a real person to appear to deal with more difficult problems.

Today, it was 'George', and he would be in his position for two months. Holographic assistants were the norm for many 'meet-and-greet' situations in reception areas, far cheaper than a real person, and available to perform these tasks all year round. When 'George' finished his two-month period, 'Emilia' would return. Of course, the hologram could technically change every minute of the day, but having the one hologram for several months gave the appearance of continuity and stability for Biocrime.

Being a former employee with Biocrime, Lestre had been in this building before, but not to this level. The de-engagement 'George' referred to was where visitors needed to change into the black and burnt orange vests, so none of their conversations could be recorded by the world memory bank and remained undetectable, primarily to protect Biocrime.

The customer service officer greeted Lestre and Lumbardo and led them to two small cubicles containing vests in their size, and locks matched to their genetic code. Once they stripped and changed into their vests, the customer service officer lead them to a special security zone, where they were approached by Capone, dressed in a similar type of vest, but with the extra golden badge to indicate his superiority, next to his embroidered name: 'CAPONE, D'. Impressive.

They courteously exchanged handshakes and moved into a secure room. After a minute or two of banal niceties and introduction to the synthetic cream biscuits and tea, Capone moved onto the business at hand.

"First of all, nothing discussed in this meeting happened. Never did, never will. Like everything else in this building, it's not recorded, it's outside of the realm of Biocrime and anyone else. We've only got you in here because of your history and we think you're about two-hundred per cent safe."

"And if we did say anything on the outside," Lestre said, "you've got plausible deniability. Is that right?"

"You got it. Lumbardo? I've seen you on Lifebook—you didn't come in wearing your advertising today?"

It was partially to break the ice, but Capone disliked the wearable advertising as much as Lestre.

"These seem to be important citizen matters," Lumbardo said, "and even I've got my levels of standard. But don't worry, as soon as I get back into my clothes, they're being switched on. A man's got to earn his money somehow."

Capone got the conversation back on track. "Okay, it's about the Anza Vista bombing—as we like to say: *we. have.*

a. situation. There's no data recording or evidence of who planted the bomb."

"But you've already got the guys," Lumbardo said, trying not to sound too naïve. "They're already on the crowd trial."

He knew of the stitch ups that happened in the past and some of the flaws within the Biocrime software, but they occurred because of software glitches, rather than a deliberate bypass of the system.

"We've checked all the systems, there's no record of a glitch, no software malfunction, nothing on the surveillance cameras—although the ones to the front entrance were broken—no-one saw a thing. Not one citizen. Now, the camera stuff and no-one seeing anything—it was late afternoon, and it was raining heavily—that can easily be put down to chance, but genetic recording through the continuum and the memory bank: it's infallible—or meant to be infallible."

"But we're not software people," Lestre said. "I mean, we could analyze and report—"

"—no, it's not that," Capone said. "Both of you are top-line stalkers—the best in the field, the top earners. We need top-line specialist surveillance—which you'll be rewarded well for, as well as any bounty proceeds."

"Sure," Lumbardo said. "We can do that, but what other information do you have? Any ideas of what actually went wrong?"

"The upshot is this," Capone said. "We have DNA exclusion zones, most notably, the two penal zones in the west and south, that avoid genetic capture. It's not that there's anything wrong with the DNA in those regions, we just don't want to know what goes on in the penal zones, and we don't want anyone else to know.

"A large part of our Biocrime headquarters is also outside of genetic capture, for security reasons. Somehow, details of our software program have been sold for €5 million—we know that much, but we don't know who did it. Or why.

"We had scant details about the whole thing and weren't too sure if it was real or not, but we started our 'due diligence' about six months ago. Nothing happening during this time until now, and the bombing at Anza Vista confirmed our suspicions."

"I'm not a techno," Lumbardo said, "but I thought this would be the last place on earth to be excluded from the continuum." He was trying hard to not sound too naïve, but the rumors of the Biocrime headquarters exclusion from the world memory bank, while not rife, were out there. And he certainly knew about insider corruption. But still, news on this level was a surprise.

"There's two-thousand people that work in our exclusion zones here," Capone said, "and they're all Technocrats. We've searched and found nothing so far and we're down to the last three-hundred possibilities—we had to use traditional methods, you know, sit down, talk, ask questions, where were you, that sort of thing. We're all Technocrats in here, we're not expecting this type of thing to happen."

"We can work on surveillance," Lestre said, "that's our field, but three hundred Technocrats that don't have a Biocrime profile? That's quite a bit of work."

"Since the bombing, we've fast-tracked the vetting of the remaining three-hundred. We can't raise suspicions, so it might be a slow process, but we'll get there. We'll find whoever is behind this."

CHAPTER 19.   THE NEXT MOVE

In his small apartment room, Katcher watched the rolling coverage of the Anza Vista bombing on his lightscreen. Of course, he knew about it as soon as everybody else did—this was big news—and he was entranced by the events as much as anyone else.

He occasionally switched to hologram mode for the complete interactive process but his mind was elsewhere, pondering what this meant and who could be behind it. He knew there were already suspects being crowd trialed and with the usual hysteria attached to these type of cases, they'd be found guilty, but he also knew Biocrime fabricated information about suspects and wondered if these were the real people behind the bombing.

He also wondered if this was the type of event Banda would concoct to 'prove' her credentials to him. But it was extreme behavior to destroy a building and kill six-hundred Technocrats to prove a point.

Katcher's mind wandered over to the contents of his next lecture for the next session: *Technology change, social markets and the labor reforms of the 2500s*. He was like a popstar preparing to play their best songs on a stage: this lecture subject was old, and he knew the contents backwards and forwards. He found it passé and perennially boring, but it would keep his crowd happy and could even pull in a few extra attendees on the day. And it could give him a chance to ask Banda a few questions—if she actually turned up.

*

The community hub was the usual hive of activity, the communal large format lightscreen displayed the ongoing coverage and statistics of the crowd trial of the East End Bombers. The coverage contained snippets of childhood visual footage of one of the suspects—Eva Alvarez—presumably put up by her crowd defense. For every crowd trial, there was all types of evidence put forward to convince the citizen crowd, one way or another. At the bottom of the lightscreen display, it showed the time of 13:58 and, like ants scurrying away when they've been disturbed, citizens moved off to their respective sessions, including the forty-eight destined for Katcher's lecture.

It was the standard process—at the time of 14:00, some late-comers were still entering the room. Katcher was always prepared fifteen minutes before the lectures commenced and he couldn't quite understand if he could make plans to arrive on time, why everyone else in the universe couldn't get their act together to do the same. He waited a few more minutes, drank from a small bottle of water, quietly cleared his throat before he switched on the sound and image presentation, and stood up to commence his talk.

"Welcome and thanks for being here, today we look at technological change…"

Katcher's mind drifted off while his words were coming out. His mouth was on autopilot, and he didn't even start off with the required quirky remark to engage his audience. That might get him a slight mark down from the class in his crowd ratings on BioEd, but he wasn't concerned.

He could see Banda in the back row of the seats, and wondering if there might be any further light she could shed on the Anza Vista bombings. He was thinking: *she said she'd do something to convince me. Could this be it? She said our genetic data couldn't be captured, and it hasn't been. None of our liaisons have appeared on Lifebook or my Biocrime profile. Is it true? Is she a plant? If she isn't a plant, who's behind this?*

The lecture raced through its ninety-minute allocation. Katcher knew it wasn't his greatest performance, but the sound and audio show that was part of his presentation made up for it.

He went through the motions of chit-chat with the attendees, but he didn't want to rush or look like he was agitated. It was Banda he wanted to talk to, but she would have to wait.

After the last attendee had departed, Banda approached Katcher while he packed up his lightscreen and cell device.

"Can we talk?" asked Katcher.

Banda knew Katcher was referring to the decoder app, and nodded to indicate that both of them had moved into off-grid and all of their actions from now on wouldn't be detected by Lifebook.

"It's all set," Banda said. "And I've got something to show you—but it's at my apartment."

"Well, let's get out of here."

Banda and Katcher left the community hub, and walked briskly towards the autotram stop. There was almost no exchange of words between the pair and, this time, there was no Gloria Jean's. Katcher realized something was up—some big news and possibly the link he needed to find a way back to his revolutionary path.

They boarded the autotram and, after a thirty-minute journey, alighted at South San Francisco, and near the back of the underground autotram station was a small dark pathway surrounded by rats and sewerage, leading to a slightly larger tunnel. There were good reasons why nobody used it.

They waited until there was no-one left at the station and Banda lead Katcher through to the dark pathway—it was difficult to avoid the stench of sewage, collections of rotting fruit, dead bird carcasses and rat excrement—but after fifteen minutes, they made to the underground of her apartment. They crawled through another small hole which exited into the middle of Banda's laundry bathroom, and climbed up through a small floor door.

"It's a little bit tough getting through," Banda said, "but it's the best way. Coming here on street level might have been a bit difficult. Come on, you might be interested in this."

Banda wiped her feet and instructed Katcher to do the same. They moved to the loungeroom where Banda switched on her lightscreen and displayed her appropriated Lifebook Live stream, which screened the fabricated live footage from her apartment. It showed her sitting in this same space, eating from a bowl of soba noodles, and swiping on her lightscreen. This was an extension of what Banda had shown this to him during their last meeting at Gloria Jean's, and Katcher was beginning to understand—Lifebook Live always showed live *actual* footage, but the lightscreen was showing something completely different and there was no sign of Katcher on the screen. This was the work of the decoder and emulator, the apps constructed by Weller, and Katcher was seeing the results of it.

"I told you we could bypass Biocrime—how many times do I need to tell you? I'm taking a shower—you might also be interested in this."

Banda summoned up her visual recording of the Anza Vista bombing through her private personal network and Katcher started to watch on the lightscreen, as Banda went back to the bathroom. It was a recording of the entire event, from the time Banda walked towards the apartment block in the Richmond East End in the pouring rain, positioned the Semtex explosive package in the garbage recycling unit, and walked away to view the explosion.

Katcher scanned through the footage, ignoring the stench he acquired by travelling through the tunnel—he looked at the footage forwards and backwards, and viewed it in three-sixty-degree mode—he could see a semi-disguised face, but could still make out that it was Banda. He knew this type of footage could be fabricated through enhanced computer graphics systems, but that took time and wouldn't be possible to produce unless there was a large team of coders—something Biocrime could do if they were trying to deceive him, but certainly not within a day or two.

Katcher alternated between the Banda's lightscreen and his own Lifebook Live stream on his cell device. The stream showed him in his own apartment preparing a meal in his food processor—even though he was miles away from there. Banda had bypassed the continuum and Biocrime through the decoder and emulator apps—he still wasn't a hundred per cent sure how this was happening but the proof of her claims was right in front of him.

Banda, finished her shower and came back into the room, where she saw Katcher studying the footage from the bombing and alternating between the lightscreen and checking his cell device.

"Yeah, that was me. I'm the East End Bomber, and there's no trace back to me. And there's no sign of you either on Lifebook. You're at your apartment—apparently—cooking up a meal. Convinced?"

"Well, who's behind this tribe and how is it all being operated?" asked Katcher.

"There's a team of us," Banda said, "as well as some of your old team."

"Like who?"

"Like Mike Scanlen and Maria Renalda. That's who."

Katcher was initially confused, before he recalibrated his mind to focus on those two names. The narcotic concoction hidden in his daily BanPro mixture had muddled parts of his memory matrix and he needed to concentrate fully to process this information from Banda. He hadn't seen or heard anything about Scanlen or Renalda since his crowd case over a decade ago. He further focused his memory and recalled he had assumed Scanlen had been deported to a universal penal zone and Renalda had died after being blacklisted for her work on his crowd trial.

"Mike and Maria?" said Katcher, exasperated. "But they're both dead. Aren't they? Or at least Maria is."

"Nope, both alive," said Banda. "Mike went underground, and we staged Maria's death. As I said, we're organized and we'll got highly motivated and highly active people working with us. We've got high-level tech and coding facilities available, our alternative networks, all underground. Mike and Maria are our brains trust."

Katcher was still processing the details provided by Banda, taking moments to extract memories from that hadn't been affected by the narcotics.

"I know this is hard to piece all together," said Banda, "especially with that shit Biocrime puts in your breakfast every morning."

"What shit?" asked Katcher.

"The shit Biocrime has been using to make you forget over the past ten years," said Banda, "the shit that's been frying part of your brain. They used it on a lot of people like you— mental torture, hallucinations. It's in the BanPro you have every morning."

"That sweet banana drink?"

"Laced with all sorts of crap, compliments of Biocrime— throw it down the sink. Here…" said Banda, as she threw a sachet of thin white powder towards Katcher. "Cocaine. Old millennium drugs. Use this for your habit, stop using the BanPro, and what I'm saying will be easier to comprehend."

Katcher took the sachet and hid it in his pocket. Feeling foolish and berated, he moved the conversation back to Scanlen and Renalda.

"Mike and Maria alive?" said Katcher. "This is something I did not expect. But Biocrime is supposed to be infallible, but a underground ragtag team has managed to beat the system?"

"Fuck, stop underestimated what we can do and thinking about us as 'ragtag', shouted Banda. "Biocrime's a big heavy unit, but a lot of it is based on a façade and stupid propaganda. You've seen it for yourself. Idiot Technocrat 'stalkers' trying to make ends meet by detecting useless crimes and searching for the big hit. And when Biocrime can't fit the bill, they make shit up. Like they did on Scanlen and Renalda—and the East End Bombers.

"You've seen the footage—it was me, not some low-life riff-raff—Biocrime is fallible, and we've got a way we can take it down."

Katcher was taking his time to allow this information to sink in, but the news about Scanlen and Renalda still being alive took the longest. If they really were still alive, this could be the grand opportunity to kick-start the revolution again.

"You can see Scanlen and Renalda now if you want," Banda said. She sent a message through her personal private network to Scanlen and Renalda, informing them Katcher was with her. They were as surprised as Katcher was, but they responded to say they were ready and would be in Anika-6 cavern soon.

Katcher wasn't expecting this. Two hours ago, he was presenting a lecture to a groups of revolutionary wannabes and naïve activists. But now he was back to the real thing, possibly meeting with the people that saved his life—the ones he thought were dead—and, perhaps, taking him back on the pathway to his true revolutionary redemption.

*

'Going underground', historically, had been the main metaphoric catchcry of counter-establishment movements, and any actions and activities deemed to be outside of mainstream life, subversive, or standing in the way of human progress, were usually labeled as underground movements.

Literally going underground was a lot more difficult. Even to this day, exploration under the surface of the earth—especially underwater—had been difficult; the need to drill, dig, and move large sections of rock and soil always proved to be a major deterrent for creating an existence for humans under the earth. But it was possible.

Resistance movements during times of war, usually against large scale oppressors, created underground networks where they could launch attacks, most notably, the French resistance movements during the worlds wars, and the Vietnam War in the twentieth century.

The Movement was lucky: because of the centuries of water and fuel extraction from the crust of the earth, there were many pockets of the underground that were empty caverns—soulless and airless, but still livable if the right conditions were met. There was a swathe of tunnels under the city of San Francisco, many were flooded, many were unknown, and some were still radioactive, like the ones currently used in Anika-6.

Banda and Katcher left the apartment and moved through the first part of the tunnel, in commando crawl mode, and reached the circular tunnel where they could then comfortably walk upright and be guided by Banda's lightpen.

"Bet you weren't expecting this today were you," Banda said.

"I'm still half-expecting all of this to be just a big set up. If it is, you're pretty good at it." Katcher walked his hand across the lining of the tunnel, feeling the smooth surface of the walls. "What's this made of?"

"It's lead–plutonium mixed in with a hard plaster," Banda said. "It's solid as shit, but moves with earthquake activity and can't be detected by above-ground sonar scanners. Compliments of our good friends at Biocrime."

"Through your contact? What's in it for him?"

"He's kinda going through some type of existential crisis, the 'what does it mean to be human' type of crisis. Well, has been for three years. He sees the whole point of giving me the secrets as a game, he loses if he gets caught. And he doesn't want to lose."

They were winding down through the circular tunnel, and had reached about two-hundred yards below the surface, with about another ten minutes of walking left to go. Katcher kept up with the questions: he was intrigued about this underground network and wanted to know more, but he was really more intrigued about Scanlen and Renalda. Could they really still be around after all these years? Will they really be there? Or are they now with Biocrime, trying to entrap people like him?

"Just another few more minutes to go," Banda said, as she motioned with her lightpen.

It was getting warmer as they went further down into the underground—generally, it was around fifteen degrees warmer for every mile beneath the surface. It wasn't unpleasant, but Katcher felt that he was running out of air—not quite gasping, but almost.

"Not much air down here," Katcher said. "How do you all survive down here?"

"It's a combination of thin tubing to the outside world and artificial air. Another secret from Biocrime—it's probably not as clean as their formula, but it does the job. We don't have anything in the circular tunnel, that's why you're feeling it. But behind the control door, it's all fine. There's air pressure issues and needing to come up to the surface occasionally for the sake of keeping sanity, but that's about it."

They reached the end of the tunnel and came across the thick circular control door made from tungsten and titanium. Banda deactivated the DNA lock to the door, which led them into the vestibule. After she checked the lock to the control door, Banda decoded the vestibule door and led Katcher into Anika-6 for the first time.

Katcher's first introduction to Anika-6 was spectacular. It was a large cavern with low-level light, a vast and spectacular collection of stalactites and stalagmites, and a series of white circus-tent like structures dispersed throughout the cavern floor. He couldn't see very much, but his first impressions were of high-tech sophistication, part war-room, part secret society.

The first person he saw in the cavern was Weller, the technical wunderkind.

"This is Maverick Weller," Banda said, "head of our tech team."

"Pleased to meet you," Weller said as he outstretched his hand to make the link with Katcher. "Welcome to our world—it's taken us a while to create, but it's safe and we want you to be a part of it."

"I had no idea you could do this," Katcher said. "This is where you created the decoder and all of your counter-surveillance work?"

"You got it. Piece by piece, we've put it all together. A combination of having some brilliant people down here, a bit of hard work and luck, and the materials Greta's managed to get from Biocrime."

With Banda and Weller, he moved through different tents, and came across an astonishing array of high-tech machinery and computer gadgetry, large format lightscreens, most of which were monitored and operated by the vast collection of revolutionaries Banda mentioned to Katcher, the ones that wanted to change the world and end the rule of the Technocrats.

They all knew who Katcher was: some shook his hands, and the more naïve ones, not knowing exactly what to do, saluted. They felt their commander-in-chief was now back with them—they'd been waiting for this day for a long time.

Katcher was impressed with Anika-6, with all of its technological sophistication and the collection of committed adherents. But he was getting impatient—as fantastic as this scene was, he wanted to see Scanlen and Renalda and he'd continue to hold his seeds of doubt until he was re-united with them.

He had a number of mixed emotions. He'd never been here before; he'd never met any of these people before, and it was the strangest world and most unimaginable he'd ever come across. But yet, he felt safe and secure. He felt like he was home.

*

Katcher looked at his cell device—it was just after 18:00, he hadn't eaten and he was hungry.

"I guess there's no Gloria's down here," Katcher said to Banda.

"No, I don't think so. I've organized for some food—and Scanlen and Renalda are on their way. They're just in the tents in the next cavern, but we wanted you to meet some of tribe and get an idea of what we're capable of down here."

The quality of food processors in Anika-6 wasn't as great as the ones on the surface—they used a much lower level of energy and were of a much smaller size. Banda set the food processor to prepare two bowls of goulash and the familiar hum of the machine preparing a meal commenced. The fake meat would feel rubbery, and the liquid would have the taste of a tinge of plastic. But it would still be nutritious and quite edible, even if the flavors were not quite right.

The physical features of people change over time, especially when they start to reach their older years. Sometimes, they became unrecognizable, even if their character remained the same. There were numerous theories related to how the psychiatry of the mind changed as a person aged but the consensus was: after the first seven years of life, essentially, a person remained the same, even if knowledge and experience provided them with increased levels of wisdom.

Scanlen and Renalda were in their early-forties when Katcher last saw them, and he wondered what they would look like now and how much they'd changed. He concentrated on the scattered images he had of them, certain he could still retrieve some semblance of his memory, distorted by years of swallowing the BanPro mixture provided by Biocrime.

He was recalibrating his mind to accept they were not dead, as he had believed for many years, and a realization that his political dreams could be back on track. Katcher was finishing up his meal in a larger tent with Banda when Scanlen and Renalda arrived and made their entrance.

"Jonathan?"

There is a curious and clinical moment for people that haven't seen each other for a long time when they fix eyes on each other, that momentary assessment of their respective physical features, compared with their preceding memories of those people that became fixed in time. In that instance, Katcher focused deeply and collated his memories of Scanlen and Renalda—a strong presence, both of solid build and stature, exuberant—and quickly compared with the here and now. They seemed more gaunt than they were a decade ago, Renalda now had grey hair and Scanlen had none, possibly the effects of living underground for a very long time. But their presence and character was still there.

For Scanlen and Renalda, Katcher had not changed much as all. The physical change in people from their mid-thirties to mid-forties wasn't as severe, but they'd seen Katcher televisually almost on a daily basis through his Biocrime and Lifebook profiles so, to them, the visible change wasn't as significant.

The three engaged in a group embrace, and processed the fact that they hadn't seen each other for a long time, and that Katcher assumed they were both dead. As they released the embrace, they looked at each other, the momentary comparison with decade-old memories was replaced by what they could now see in front of them with their own eyes.

"I wasn't sure about you Mike," Katcher said, still piecing together his thoughts and memories. "But I knew you were dead Maria, I saw your funeral on Lifebook."

"Well, just shows you can't believe everything you read—or see," Renalda said. "It was miserable for me up there. Being in the Movement and getting you off the crowd show trial wasn't going to work for me. So I thought it was better to go off-grid and go one step further underground."

"It wasn't exactly a show trial," Katcher responded. "I committed those crimes, but you led the defense too well. Everyone hated that, lost money on the trial, Biocrime lost out. And Mike? What happened?"

"I just decided to go away from the surface. As soon as you were arrested, we thought you were going to a penal zone for sure. By the time the crowd trial was over, and you weren't deported, we were already half-way through the underground process.

"We had links with a few off-gridders, and people like Banda, and created smaller tribe cells underground, linked with a larger tribe above ground. I just 'died' naturally. I hadn't been seen by anyone for years, no Lifebook, no continuum, no genetic recording. I was dead to the world."

"So how long has this set-up been operating for?" asked Katcher.

"We started about ten years ago, but it's been operational for about eight, and we achieved the current capacity about three years ago. The decoder was the biggest breakthrough about a year ago. Maria and I have been above ground a few times—undetected—and we think the decoder can work permanently. Not sure how you live up there. Same shitty control by the Technocrats, same day-to-day mundanity."

"Well, not sure how you live down here," Katcher said. "That goulash was terrible…"

"Funny John," Renalda snapped. "We're the ones trying to get this revolution underway, and you're complaining about the goulash? It's not too bad down here, once you get used to it. We have sunpills each day, exercise areas. If you squint a little bit and accept the food, it's almost like living on the surface."

"And if you accept the poor air quality, water leakages, the radioactive material, the damp and occasional rat," added Mike, "it's also not too bad. Anyway, let's get down to some business."

It approached 19:00 and both Banda and Katcher needed to get back to their apartments soon. The emulator app and its algorithmic bypass could keep deceiving Lifebook for a certain period of time but if the deception went for too long, it could raise suspicions. Katcher's cell device didn't work down in the underground, so he asked to look at his Lifebook profile on a lightscreen. Banda summoned up his Lifebook profile and he saw visuals of himself reading from his mini lightscreen device, eating from a bowl of Singapore noodles—one of his favorite meals. Banda assured him their decoder and emulator apps created by Weller was safe, secure and foolproof. As far as the rest of the world was concerned, Katcher was in his apartment alone, and minding his own business.

Through his many readings of historical revolutions and in-depth analysis of philosophers and theorists such as Sun Tzu, Niccolò Machiavelli, Carl von Clausewitz, Rosa Luxemburg and Paul Virilio, Katcher understood that revolutionary thought needed to have a praxis with practical actions through group activity. While overthrow of an oppressive system needed to have popular movement of the masses, the seeds of dissent needed to start small and Katcher, like many others in the Movement, subscribed to the somewhat naïve belief that only five people were needed to commence a revolution.

But which five people? He knew Scanlen and Renalda were as committed as he was, but he barely knew Banda, and he'd only met Weller a few hours before.

Katcher, Banda, Scanlen and Renalda sat at the table inside another tent, surrounded by lightscreens and links to the outside world, providing every key piece of data imaginable. Weller soon joined them and the five were ready to commence strategic talks and get Katcher up to speed with what they could do from their underground war room.

Although they felt like equals, Katcher the revolutionary leader had returned, and they felt like the collective was already greater than the sum of its parts. It couldn't work without Katcher, and now he was back. Katcher commenced the talks, and they took turns in discussing how to take back the city by strategy, interspersed with questions about how they all arrived at this point.

*

It was 23:00, but without sunlight throughout the day, it was impossible to have a feeling for the time. The melanin produced by the skin when exposed to sunlight lets the body know when daylight ends and night commences, but there was nothing down in the underground to indicate the demarcation between the two phases. The sunpills they ate provided the body with its requisite vitamin D, but that didn't help to keep their circadian rhythms flowing correctly.

All up, it was four hours of discussion about how to move the revolution forward, a range of tactics and strategies: it wasn't everything, but it was a start. Technically, it didn't really matter what time Banda and Katcher resurfaced, as far as their body clocks were concerned, but in the back of their mind was the anxiety about their return, in case of any issues with Lifebook and the off-chance of someone detecting the visual recording of Katcher on his stream was a fabrication. Banda was sure the algorithm was permanent but Katcher, being new to this system, wanted to be sure. He now had control of his decoder and emulator apps—he'd rather have a seamless decoding synchronized to his emotional responses, just like the audio speakers in his apartment, but this system created by the Movement used older technology, so he had to remember to switch the decoder app on and off.

Katcher wanted to spend one more day on the surface and back in his apartment to soak up the day and accumulate his thoughts. Afterall, returning to the surface was where they would all have to come back to if they wanted to reclaim their world.

It was an eventful day and although buzzing with the excitement from the evening's events, Katcher was tiring quickly. After the goodbyes with Renalda, Scanlen and Weller, Banda and Katcher left Anika-6, entered the vestibule and began the journey up through the circular tunnel. It was a steep incline and because of the low levels of oxygen, they had to venture slowly. Banda's lightpen guided the way, and she could feel Katcher's relief and satisfaction.

"I told you it would work out," Banda said smugly.

"I had to be careful. I didn't know who you were, and I've had similar approaches before from 'groupies'."

"So I'm a groupie? Gosh, I thought I presented myself as a self-respecting revolutionary intellectual."

"I sensed you were different but how was I to know? All those people that come to my lectures? They're deluded inner-city street rat wannabes that want to see themselves close to some kinda sub-culture and revolution, so they can tell their friends. They've just got no idea about the world."

"So why did you keep doing it?"

"I had to maintain my intellectual interests, but had to lay low—for a long time. I was waiting for the right time—and the right people—to start up again. Sometimes, just when you look at the horizon and see nothing—and keep seeing nothing—there's something that comes up when you don't expect it—like now."

"As they say, all good things come to those that wait," Banda said. "This is the time, and I'm glad I proved it to you."

"It's just a pity you have to kill six-hundred people to prove a point—"

"—they're not people to me. Sounds harsh—some of my best friends are Technocrats you know—but some of them are like the walking dead. Just follow orders, do this, do that. No wonder they want to fuck us over."

"Well, we've got a chance to change that. Who knows when, but this is a start."

Eventually, they reached the top of the circular tunnel. The quality of air had improved at this level and felt like there was more of it, but the steep incline had taken its toll and Banda and Katcher were both exhausted.

The next step was back through the thin tubing. It wasn't as steep as the circular tunnel, but it was another crouching commando walk back to the back of the Banda's apartment. As they came closer to the end, the stench of sewerage returned, with the added bonus of freshly laid rat faeces. It had been raining on the surface and some of it had seeped through the tubing.

"You can keep going that way," Banda said, pointing to the continuation of the tunnel through to the autotram station, "or you can come back to my apartment—you might need to freshen up."

"It's getting late but I probably should get cleaned up. And maybe a synth to wake me up."

They reach up through the base of Banda's apartment and into the laundry room.

"The bathroom's over there," says Banda, motioning to the left side of her apartment. "Throw your clothes through the door, and I'll put them through the autoclean."

Katcher moved into the bathroom, and threw his clothes just outside the door. He'd rather clean his clothing himself, but Banda offered and he now had a few minutes to collect his thoughts. The day started off like most others over the past ten years—flying under the radar, keeping to himself, like a bear in hibernation, waiting for the cold dark winter to be over, and spring to arrive. Now, he'd been reunited with his old revolutionary colleagues, and showering in the apartment of the woman that killed six hundred citizens just to get his attention. But she was also the woman that created the pathway for the revolution to recommence after a ten-year hiatus.

Banda collected Katcher's clothes and put them in the autoclean. It had been a long time since she'd put any man's clothing in the autoclean and, normally, she'd refuse to do it, but she made an exception on this occasion. The cycle commenced and the autoclean sprayed a jet of soap water throughout all the clothing, rinsed a second time with clean recycled water, and passed through a layer of intense heat lamps, through an ironing flatboard and folded through the side tray. It was all over in five minutes.

She felt Katcher's clothing—soft and supple, it belied the look and feel of the man that wore them. Katcher was a strong and big man, but his soft clothing smoothed his hard edges. She left his clothing in a neat pile next to the bathroom.

*

"The coffee's on, should be ready in a few minutes," Banda said.

Katcher was out of the bathroom and in his replenished clothing, and Banda moved into the shower. The fresh aroma of coffee already had the effect of a wake-up call for Katcher, but he upped the caffeine level on Banda's food processor. It was just past midnight and he needed to keep awake for at least another hour. He was too tired to think sexually, but wanted to be alert for his trip back to his apartment.

While Banda was in the shower, he scanned around the apartment—it was nothing unusual, quite a common looking apartment: clean, white walls, fake wooden floorboards, a space well utilized. There was a selection of smaller lightscreens on the walls displaying different photographs from yesteryear: Banda as a child with what seemed to be her parents; another photograph of the same people at a protest march with the Biocrime headquarters in the background; a moving slidescreen of old-fashioned paintings from the late-twentieth century: Mondrian, Kandinsky, Pollack.

Banda came out of the shower and saw Katcher looking at the slidescreen.

"Interesting?" asked Banda.

"I like these ones," Katcher said, pointing to the paintings. "Reminds me about what real art is."

"Well, they're only electronic replicas, who knows what the originals look like—they wouldn't have survived a thousand years I wouldn't think."

"Probably not. Probably mashed up by some idiot Technocrat that knew the price of everything but the value of nothing. Pulped or collecting dust somewhere. We could look it up through the world memory bank."

"Could, but who's got the time and money for that? At least we've got the memories of them. Anyway, a copy is as good as the original, right?"

"Not if you're a Technocrat. That's what this is all about isn't it?"

The food processor finished humming and the coffees were ready as they moved to relax on the lounge couch.

"That's your parents on the screens?" asked Katcher. "They look like you."

"Yes, they were in the Movement, but now both gone. They could have lived longer but I'm pretty sure Biocrime fixed things up so they couldn't get nanopills or other medicines that could keep them alive. Always harassed by Biocrime agents, always under surveillance. Quite often, I thought it was just to give those fuckers something to do, something to supplement their universal income.

"After my parents died, I wanted to continue their work. But it's hard to do without support and getting a whole team of people to work against the tide has taken a long time."

"We'll get there, but it will take some more time," Katcher said.

"But we have to start moving quickly," Banda said. "We've got everything pretty much in place—all our tech and coding material, our counter-propaganda units—we were just waiting for you to return at the right time. And this is the right time."

Katcher finished his coffee and signaled that it was time for him to go. He was putatively number one, and Banda was his number two. He was impressed, but there was still a lot of work to do. He had an urge to stay but felt the need to return to his apartment.

"I've got clean clothes, freshly washed, and now I've got to back through the sewer to get back to the autotram," Katcher said, as he got up to leave.

"Take this," Banda said, as she reached from a pouch under the lounge couch and threw a small packet of plastic ponchos towards him. "Compliments of Biocrime. They're like overalls, keeps out the stench, keeps you clean and biodegrades five minutes after you take it off and throw it away."

"You couldn't have thought about using these before?" asked Katcher.

"Maybe. But then you wouldn't have got to use my bathroom and look around my apartment."

Katcher wasn't sure what to think about Banda's comment, but they embraced and gave each other a soft kiss. He also wasn't sure if they should continue the embrace but thought it was best to leave matters uncomplicated. He pulled on one of the ponchos Banda had given to him and lowered himself to exit through the floor door in the laundry.

"I'll see you tomorrow."

*

Katcher walked through the city streets, and true to Banda's word, the full-body poncho had kept him clean and the phantom smells that would normally reside after a closed-in walk through sewerage, garbage and animal excrement, were not present. The rain had subsided but there was still the light drizzle refracting the glowing lights of street fair and human activity. It was after one in the morning but this was a city that never slept. He wasn't too concerned, but he wore his hoodie top to conceal his identity as much as he could. He was anonymous in this cityscape at this time of night, and he wanted to keep it that way.

He reached into his pocket to switch off the decoder app: he was close enough to home for the bypass algorithms of the emulator to meld between the fabricated vision on Lifebook Live to his real-life position now. As soon as he switched off the decoder app, the fabricated Lifebook Live stream reanimated to show Katcher in his apartment getting dressed into exactly the same clothes that he was wearing right now, exiting his apartment and moving towards his current location.

In five minutes, the Lifebook Live stream merged seamlessly from the fabricated footage to his actual location. Anyone who had been watching Katcher on Lifebook Live would have never known about his escape down to the underground, and neither would the data be recorded through the world memory bank. The decoder and emulator apps were Maverick Weller's best coding inventions, created through the theft of technological secrets from Biocrime.

Katcher walked to the front of his apartment, the door automatically unlocked and opened when his hand touched the door. He was back in his apartment and no-one on the surface would ever know what he'd been up to over the past ten hours.

He undressed, threw his clothing onto the floor and climbed into his bed. As the autowarmer scanned his body temperature and adjusted the heating in his room, Katcher lay on his bed and stared up at the ceiling. He was thinking about Banda; about Scanlen and Renalda; about the wunderkind Weller and his technical brilliance. But he was especially thinking about Banda.

He was alert and wide awake. The extra strong coffee he had at Banda's apartment had made sure about that. He was tired but he was satisfied. He would doze off soon enough, as he dreamt through all the possibilities that could be just around the corner. These were early hours of the next stage in his life, but the Revolution Five was now complete. It had been a good day.

***

A GRAND OLD DAY

'It's a Grand Old Day' was an advertising hit in the early 3020s, sung to the song of 'You're a Grand Old Flag', a patriotic American song from the early twentieth century, and strongly associated with conservative politics. The advertisement was a feel-good campaign created by the Retail Food Group company, and promoted interchangeable food and beverage products, including the popular synth coffee, Amore. Its popularity peaked around 3024, around the same time of Katcher's crowd trial, a trial that gave Biocrime the strong belief that this revolutionary figure would be sent to a universal penal zone and publicly seen just a few more times before his final demise.

It was a combination of nostalgic images from the past fifty years—contemporary nostalgia—produced to promote feelings of allure, sophistication and enlightenment. One of the few advertisements to successfully use 'smellorama' technology, it was thirty seconds of pure visual delight, and on constant rotation on all major public lightscreens at that time.

It ended with the sound of teenage giggling the words 'that's Amore', and image of a smiling princess and a discount code for purchases within the next two minutes.

It was the number one advertisement played during Katcher's crowd trial, and the memory of the tune played havoc with his mental wellbeing. It was popular and still distributed publicly but the sound of it was like a dagger being plunged straight into the middle of Katcher's heart.

BOOK 3. A CITY RISES

"Those who fight with monsters might take care, lest they thereby become a monster. And if you gaze for long into an abyss, the abyss gazes also into you."

—Friedrich Nietzsche

CHAPTER 20.   A NEW DAY

It was six in the morning and Jonathan Katcher woke up to go to the bathroom. He calculated he'd only slept for about three hours, and the strong coffee that kept him up for most of the night was still pushing up his adrenaline levels. His body was tired, but he didn't feel it.

These were going to be his last few hours on the surface before he went back to the Anika-6 underground. He set his food processor to create his daily breakfast of BanPro—the textured sweet protein and banana paste drink monitored and manipulated by Biocrime—and his regular synth coffee, and jumped into the shower.

He was certain about Greta Banda, now that Mike Scanlen and Maria Renalda were around and part of the scene, but he was never sure about who was acting behind some of the other players underground. It was part of his thinking to never trust anyone at all and to hold a healthy dose of cynicism and skepticism, but all it took was for the wrong move, a wrong calculation or the wrong word said at the wrong time, and any cell or structure could be taken down. How often did the underground workers from Anika-6 go back to the surface? Were there any Biocrime plants or spies in Anika-6? If Banda had someone from Biocrime providing secrets to her, could someone else in Anika-6 be offering information the other way back to Biocrime? *It's always a possibility*, thought Katcher, laying a seed of doubt in his own mind. But an opportunity had arisen, and the risks were outweighed by the possibilities and resulting benefits to the Movement, so he decided it had to be seized with both hands.

Banda told him there were 'thousands' in the underground, and the existence of some Technocrats who wanted change, but there were different levels of commitment to any cause, ranging from the hardliners—like the Revolution Five, who were prepared to do anything for the Movement—to wannabe activists that just came along for the ride because they didn't have anything better to do. When the going got tough and the hard work had to be done, these were the people that usually dropped off like flies. How many were really committed to the Movement?

Katcher reached into his food processor to retrieve the processed BanPro, poured it down the kitchen sink and then reclined on his lounge couch to sip his synth coffee. He methodically opened the sachet of cocaine Banda gave to him, and snuffed a small portion into each of his nostrils. It would take a while for the euphoria from this batch of cocaine to set in, but as soon as he felt more energized, he swigged the final mouthful of his synth coffee, and got up to pack his laser gun and cell device. He visually scanned his apartment to assess whether there was anything else he needed to take with him—he wasn't nostalgic, but this had been his home for the past decade. He wasn't likely to come back to this apartment ever again, but he wanted to reflect on what it had represented to him over the years—lost opportunities, a long period languishing in the doldrums, a wasting away of his life.

He took some small mementos with him—an earring from his mother, a small urn containing the ashes of his father, and a stained post-card size cover of Tolstoy's *War and Peace*, one of the last books to be printed in the 2400s. He was dressed just like he was on any other day—there was nothing in his limited wardrobe that would raise any suspicions anyway, but he made sure he was wearing his most standard attire. He knew this was not a normal day, but the outside world needed to see that it was no different to any other.

He messaged Banda on his newly created personal private network to let her know he was on his way. He flicked on his decoder app and turned his head to have one final look at his apartment. He opened the front door of his apartment and, after exiting, he made sure the door was secure. He was never coming back here again, but no-one needed to know.

*

The early morning autotram trip to Banda's apartment had a motley collection of stragglers from the night before, reeking of alcohol and vapored e-cigarettes, office workers scanning their personal cell screens, and people on universal income just starting the long process of filling out the day to stave off boredom. Katcher's day was the first in the transition from an old life to new, one which opens up many possibilities for what he believed would be the start of a new direction for humanity, and correcting a broad range of historical imbalances and inequities. He wasn't naïve about it—far from it—but the world never changed in an instant, and only in smaller increments—the Movement had adopted the philosophy of the 'snowflake effect', the one snowflake that created the avalanche of change—but it needed to start somewhere and major movements throughout world history had always commenced through a convergence of smaller acts, moved along faster by bigger global events, just like the ones that he was planning to lead.

He imagined a different world, one that existed in equilibrium, and a balance between citizens, where natural humans co-existed equally with Technocrats, instead of this constant oppression and their rights downplayed, and the unbridled pursuit of technological change and consumerism.

He knew he woudn't be the beneficiary of this change, but he always thought *if only people started off this process years ago, we wouldn't be in this position now*. He had the dichotomy of thought though—he wanted social change but for whom was he enacting this change? Was the social change for his benefit and for the few people like him? Was he implementing change for people like Banda, or for the memory of his parents and all people in the Movement before him? Was he acting for all of humanity, even for the people that didn't want change or couldn't care less about it, happy with their lot and a desire to keep to the *status quo*?

He looked around the autotram where some of the riff-raff late-nighters, the ones with the strong aroma of synthetic alcohol and ingested nicotine, were aggressively harassing some of the office workers minding their own business. It was their alcohol doing their talking but they would be marked off by Biocrime at some stage, either through the creation of a Biocrime profile, or detained if they became serial offenders.

Was the revolution Katcher wanted to instigate for the benefit of these people? Or for the people that just travel around all day long because they've got nothing better to do than keeping themselves amused with sightseeing and ongoing entertainment through their lightscreens?

He wasn't confused: he knew his path and it was the right one. The path had to be universal and he couldn't choose who should benefit from social change and equity. He wasn't disturbed by his counter-thoughts—he knew there needed to be questions of doubt and cynicism for any movement or process, otherwise it would be taken over by the mindless and naïve, and social change was too important to leave to the ignorant.

The place of God and religion within the world also went through a period of solid questioning and doubt, and this resulted—over time—in the disintegration of religions as mass movements. And this satisfied Katcher—the thousands of years of knowledge and existence based on superstitious beliefs, in his opinion, held back humanity and had inflicted much human suffering throughout history, through wars, enforced famines, and ethnic cleansing. But, for Katcher, perhaps this disintegration of beliefs and superstitions had gone too far—not that he wanted religion and superstitious beliefs to ever return, but the pendulum had swung to another extreme. Humanity needed to reclaim *what it is to be human*, and that was the driving force behind his actions.

The autotram approached the South San Francisco station and, after alighting, he walked to the point where he could access the tunnel passage to Banda's apartment. He pulled on another Biocrime poncho Banda had given to him, effective in protecting him from the dirt and the smell of the tunnel sewerage. He slowly walked past the sewer and the rats scrimmaging through rubbish, found the correct access point, and slithered across to the apartment. Banda was prepared by the time Katcher arrived, they departed her apartment and continued the descent back down to Anika-6.

CHAPTER 21.   A MYSTERIOUS DISAPPEARANCE

Marine Lestre had a habit of working around the clock and tonight was no exception. It was two o'clock and the aura of the soft green light from the lava lamp matched the early hours of the morning, although the noises from the streets below reminded her that there wasn't too much downtime in this city.

She occasionally glanced across to the incubator kits housing the three developing fetuses, the lightscreen displays comforting her with the information that everything was functioning normally, and there were no concerns about the impending inceptions. She had almost filled herself to the brim with synth coffee, which at least guarded her from the sleep she so desperately needed but also kept her brainwaves ticking over.

And she had much to think about. She had been given a new and important task but was bemused by the approach by Biocrime and laughed internally at the prospect of resolving the same type of case—the theft of secrets—that she herself was accused of.

Her watch list of Biocrime profiles had two-hundred-and-fifty names to scan through and her mind fluctuated between the need to assess all the potential fugitives on her list, and why Biocrime tried to frame an act of espionage on her.

Several years before, Lestre was accused within Biocrime of acquiring corporate and technology research data and trading this in a range of black market spheres. Glitches had occurred within the development of this new technology and Biocrime, rather than adopting the correct protocols to determine exactly what occurred, allocated the cause of the incident to Lestre. Once the legal mechanics from BioLaw were installed, it was difficult to backtrack from the web of legalities and Lestre almost ended up being sent to a universal penal zone, before the case against her was suddenly retracted and dismissed.

No explanation was offered at the time, and Lestre never found out who retracted the case against her but, eventually, she could no longer work within the confines of Biocrime and remade herself as a citizen stalker, and became one of the best in the field. The most difficult part for Lestre was the accusation of an egregious crime—and accusations once made, stick forever.

She pondered the inaccurate application of law from the perspectives of the innocent and the guilty. BioLaw had incorrectly accused her of a serious criminal event; she was innocent, yet she was almost incarcerated and suffered the indignity of having her name smeared. Lestre recalled the case against Jonathan Katcher from a decade ago, where, as far as she was concerned, he was guilty of every shocking crime he was alleged to have committed. He retained his freedom, albeit with very strict controls, because of a range of legal loopholes exploited by Katcher's team and Biocrime incompetence. It was a conundrum Lestre had difficulty reconciling, but it was also a driving force behind her quest to eliminate crime wherever she could. Injustice of the kind she suffered could either leave the victim with life-long scars, but Lestre decided a long time ago that to burn up on the inside was counterproductive and would only inflict more damage upon herself.

Lestre continued to scan through her watch list and checked each one of the two-hundred-and-fifty, as she cultivated her mind to create mental links between the people that could have caused the East End Bombings and possible links back to Biocrime. Her lightscreen also used interpretive software to match any possible links between her searches and Lifebook activity, but no obvious links appeared. She checked the profiles of all the most likely, but there was no activity or register on any of them.

She finally came around to checking Katcher's Biocrime profile and it came up with surprising results. Not only was there no negative activity, but there was *no* activity at all from over the past four days. She scanned deeper through the world memory bank data, and couldn't see Katcher anywhere. She called up the Lifebook Live function, which could retrieve the most recent visual recording and activity and he couldn't be seen in his apartment, he wasn't out and about on the nearby streets, and he wasn't at the community hub. *Has he died?* she wondered. She delved deeper into the world memory bank and there was no DNA or genetic connection for Katcher anywhere. It was a costly exercise to extract deeper data from the world memory bank through the continuum but she decided it was worth it, if it led to the big catch she was after.

Using data analytics software for her deeper delve, Lestre also saw there was no link for Katcher within any form of travel or death data. Even after death, the process of genetic capture continued, but with Katcher it was like he had completed disappeared.

It was late at night, but Lestre sent a message to Lumbardo through her personal private network, asking for any details he had about the fallibility of genetic capture and the world memory bank through the continuum. She wasn't expecting a reply until daylight, but Lumbardo also had night owl tendencies and responded with a short précis which outlined what he had heard about glitches in the system before, and where hacktivists had deceived Biocrime into accessing alternative genetic data as a diversion, but he had not heard of the genetic recording of a person becoming untrackable. He added that glitches didn't happen very often, but they did happen. Sometimes it was a maintenance glitch, but self-repair software usually resolved the problem quickly and efficiently.

After receiving the information from Lumbardo, Lestre decided to place an investigative task through Lifebook, actions that were usually taken on by prospective bounty hunters, and of great value. Lestre would more than likely have to pay for most of the crowd fees, but there were always a few citizens willing to crowd fund a task like this, even if it was only for personal curiosity.

She collected her thoughts momentarily and summoned her lightscreen to create the new investigative task on Lifebook.

"Whereabouts of Jonathan Katcher," Lestre said and after she spoke these words, an auto-fill voice completed the description:

Query about sighting of Jonathan Katcher in San Francisco region. Unlinked to world memory bank and Biocrime profiles for three days. Possibly a glitch but confirmation is required.

Course of action: Report and verifiable confirmation of sighting.

Crowd pledge: €1

Bounty payment: €50 + 50% of crowd fund. Half-fee only, if no sighting.

She glanced at the screen and, after she checked the details and felt confident of its contents, she summoned the task to automatically appear through a wide range of crowd source options through the continuum and onto Lifebook.

Lifebook then allocated Lestre's post to a number of different crowd source locations, including Tasker, Uber and WorkOn, the more common platforms. The response was swift, but that was expected, as Jonathan Katcher was on most people's watch list. Even though it now approached three in the morning, within an hour, over four-hundred citizens had pledged €1 each—a good result for someone with low Biocrime activity on their profile over the past ten years. Soon, a bounty hunter called 'RoboPhile' accepted the task—a few hundred ucas wasn't too bad for just checking up on someone, and receiving half of that even if they didn't end up seeing Katcher at all.

*

RoboPhile was an experienced surveillance stalker and did her inspective work in the morning, just around 9:00; she checked around at the community hub, and then made the long trek back to the environs of Katcher's apartment. She was a rather non-descript middle-aged Technocrat—perfect for this type of task—and asked questions with some local people and enquired at nearby businesses, but there were no sightings by anyone, and no-one had seen Katcher for almost a week. Katcher did keep a low profile, but it was unusual that he hadn't been seen by anyone, and even more unusual that there was no genetic data available to determine his whereabouts.

RoboPhile went to Katcher's ground floor apartment and peered through the back windows. Although she couldn't really tell if Katcher hadn't been there recently, she peered through every crack in the windows she could find, and there was no evidence of him inside. Everything in the apartment seemed neat and tidy, almost as though he could walk in through the doorway at any time. But the fact was, he wasn't there.

After several hours, RoboPhile decided to confirm there was no sighting of Katcher to Lestre, and received her payment of €150. It wasn't as much as a confirmed sighting but, nevertheless, it was still money for jam.

It was late morning by the time Lestre received the report, after managing to snatch a few hours of sleep. She scrolled through the information and visual recordings submitted by RoboPhile and decided to keep the new information to herself, without updating Katcher's Biocrime profile. She needed to find out what was going on first and she knew that any reports she added would alert other watch lists and more interest than it warranted.

CHAPTER 22.   THE PROPAGANDA MACHINE

"Synth?" asked Katcher. Banda nodded with approval and the familiar sound of the food processing machine created the coffees that would start the day with a boost of caffeine.

Katcher was in his new surroundings in Anika-6, still acquiring what this new world meant to him and the Movement. But, just like a sports tactician and strategist, he couldn't think too far ahead, and kept repeating in his mind that he had to take one step at a time, and to think too far into the future meant there was always the chance the present could evaporate in a flash.

The 'ding' from the food processor triggered a Pavlovian response for Katcher, and he rose to collect the coffees and sat next to Banda. Katcher and Banda were in the 'strategy tent' in Anika-6, a high tech zone that contained all the communication devices they'd ever need. Soon after, Renalda, Scanlen and Weller entered the tent, exchanged pleasantries, and the Revolution Five were ready to continue with their business.

"This is pretty impressive stuff," Katcher said, as his eyes scanned the vast array of technology and gadgetry. "How did you get it all down here?"

"It's been a long process," Scanlen said. "There's different access points to this bank of caverns, but we couldn't bring anything that was too big or cumbersome. We brought in most of the equipment piece by piece and assembled it down here…"

"…and you can see that everything is small scale," Renalda said. "The lightscreens, food processors, lighting, energy storage. We just had to think small and agile, and the ability to move quickly at short notice. Small and agile, but we've actually got more tech power than anything on the surface, thanks to Mav, our technical genius."

"Well, I can't take credit for all of it," Weller said, with a touch of rare modesty. "But taking most of it will do."

Katcher continued to scan the collection of lightscreens and devices in the tent, which showed a range of surveillance points on the surface in a range of cities from different zones around the world, key data and information of temperature, and inputs into Lifebook and Biocrime profiling.

"Our plan is," Banda said, "to hack the continuum, insert our own viral videos to all systems on the surface: Lifebook, Biocrime, public lightscreens, broadcasts, narrowcasts—large scale disruption, create havoc and confusion, activate radicals on the surface.

"We've completed most of the visuals—but we needed to record you and your call to arms, and insert you into our messaging and videos. Propaganda, you know, like pirate TV. We smash the continuum, and we control information.

"After we've hacked Biocrime, the viral messaging and videos will be up for at least a few weeks—that's how long it would take Biocrime to work out what's going on and to recode, and stop our attacks. But it would be too late for them."

"But what about arms?" asked Katcher. "What are people going to do—just roam the streets and shout out they've had enough and want change? That's a revolution that's not going to last long."

"We wanted some sort of peaceful change," Banda said, oblivious to the irony of expecting a smooth transition, just after she had murdered almost six-hundred Technocrats. "If we can—"

"—but you know throughout history, that has rarely happened," Katcher responded. "Power has to be taken by force."

"Everyone's got a laser gun, right?" Weller interjected, "with stun and kill modes, but the kill mode is controlled by Biocrime and we know less than one per cent of the population has access to that. Our hacking can unlock the kill mode on the laser guns, instantly turning them into killing machines. We can exclude Technocrats from the unlock and disable their laser guns completely—no stun or kill modes. Sure, an unfair advantage, but desperate times call for desperate measures. Could be a blood bath if they try to resist."

"We war-gamed this many times," Banda said. "It will work, our technology is set up and we could finally get the plan underway within a few days. We'll finish adding your agitprop and then send it out."

"But surely it can't be so simple," Katcher said. "And besides, if it's already to go, why haven't you already set it up?" Katcher knew the answer, but he wanted to hear it from the others.

"Having you as part of it," Renalda said, "is the icing on the cake. If we tried to do this while you're still under virtual house arrest, it wouldn't have had the same meaning, the same value. But if the world can see that Jonathan Katcher has escaped house arrest, that's a big coup for us all and the Movement."

"And," Banda added, "if citizens can see Jonathan Katcher leading from the front, it gives them more reason to rise with the Movement."

Katcher had the demeanor and aura of inclusiveness, deferring credit to others—he wanted all to share in the spoils of victory. But he was as ruthless and self-centered as any other political leader.

People gravitate to the centers of power and control, and Katcher wanted to be at the center of that power. He knew he was an important figure but for the past decade, he'd been engulfed by a sea of irrelevance, where he'd offered his considerable skill and intellect to young wannabes that didn't know anything at all about struggle, and probably not even interested in the struggle.

He felt he was almost back at the center of the universe: it was an opportunity that he thought had slipped away and he could see that he could just be several weeks away from seizing the power he'd been craving for most of his lifetime. He knew it was also the work of many people in the underground over the past decade. For the many natural humans that had risked their lives for the Movement—some deported to universal penal zones and never to return—they had all worked towards revolutionary change and had waited for the day of reckoning to arrive. Katcher was the figurehead of this movement and, as Banda suggested, he was the icing on the cake. He was wanted, he was needed, and he was needed right now.

*

It was time to move quickly. Katcher and Weller had moved to another tent, known as the 'communications center'. Like many of the other tents in Anika-6, this one was high-tech, and had all the tools of trade for visual and holographic production, voice manipulation, editing and projection.

Essentially, they were recording and creating a series of viral propaganda and news messages: announcements that Katcher was free and back with the Movement, the oppression by the Technocrats was going to end soon, the uprising had commenced and laser guns could be used for protection, aggression and self-defense.

The viral videos were short and sharp—there would be a series of thirty-second, one-minute and two-minute visuals, advertisement-style propaganda that would incite the masses. The storyboards on the larger lightscreens were simple and sharp, which opened with the key message: 'Jonathan Katcher is Free'; 'The oppression ends, the revolution starts now'; with images of Katcher being arrested in 3024; the crowd trial; images of maltreatment of natural humans by Technocrats; scenes of revolutionary moments throughout history, teamed up with emotionally-charged inspirational music. And the key message at the end was that laser guns were now fully unlocked.

The hacktivists in Anika-6 had also created a new predictive algorithm that would hack into holographic billboards and lightscreens, overriding the existing video streaming information, insert their own propaganda material, while predicting which actions Biocrime's detection software would implement to try and counter their actions, creating realtime recoding to bypass their message in a continuous loop. Even with its immediate response, it would take some time for Biocrime to set up its own recoding program and resume normal transmission, and the hacktivists estimated they could keep the viral propaganda videos online for at least a fortnight.

It meant Katcher's viral videos would appear in homes on lightscreens, and public billboards where normal advertising material usually appeared. Natural humans would then hear about Katcher's return to the Movement, and seeing his videos on their screens and public places, would rise up against Biocrime and the system of the Technocrats.

They were underground in Anika-6 for now, but they were moving quickly towards the key release day to hack and undermine the continuum, Lifebook and Biocrime, when all worlds would change. They were confident in their work and they were sure they were on their way towards the revolutionary change they had craved for a very long time.

CHAPTER 23. DEATH IN THE UNDERGROUND

Monday, June 7. Biocrime had four targeted assessments scheduled for the day, including the one that was due to take place four-hundred yards above Anika-6. The Biocrime underground surveillance and monitoring vehicle had returned, with its group of five specialist underground officers. They were early risers, with the first dig taking place at five in the morning, and it was now pushing nine o'clock.

Georgia the Biocrime security manager parked the USM vehicle close to their previous inspection point, the marks of their tube drilling still visible. It was their second targeted assessment today, but they were running behind their schedule.

The five, led by Georgia the security manager, quickly extracted themselves from the vehicle and swung into their trained actions, and prepared the groundwork for this deep excavation.

"It's touch and go for this one," Georgia said, pointing to the lightscreen on the side paneling of the USM. "It's a bit more complicated with that branch of crevices. I reckon we just send down a camera for this one."

"But we got the guys in the back with us, they're hungry for more action," her deputy said. "I think we should take all of us down, just have a quick look and report back—there's more crowd pay for us, and should improve our record with Biocrime."

"Fuck," Georgia said. "If we take too much time here, we'll have to rush the other two that we gotta do today. I don't want to be working until midnight."

"Think of the overtime Georgia," her deputy said. "We'll do this one now, you get the double fee for tonight, and have a day off next week. It's working half the time for the same amount. Think about that while you go down underground."

Georgia the security manager agreed—she was only half-joking about not going down—she was as greedy as any other Technocrat and she'd do anything to earn more money, while working less. And, besides, it was partially a test to see what her deputy would say—if he agreed not to go down, he'd be out of his job and replaced with someone else.

"What's the report for downstairs?" asked Georgia.

"Stable, obsidian rock. Start our drilling now, we'll be able to start our descent in about half an hour."

"Okay then. Set up, start it up. I'll let the guys know we'll go down in thirty. Synth for you?"

Georgia the security manager swiveled around to the mobile food processor, a small machine that was a lower quality compared to in-home processors, but still made excellent coffees and more-than-acceptable food. She selected five coffees and a tray of cookies: to be ready in five minutes, and the food processor started its usual hum.

Her deputy positioned the USM vehicle in its correct position and the portable deep speed tube driller slowly extricated itself on the other side of the vehicle, ready to commence its action. The driller was solid boron nitride, with sharpened diamond cutters. It was the toughest known substance in the universe and, when combined with the acid lubricant, it could cut through anything in the earth's crust at the rate of half-a-yard per second. Its diameter was three-feet wide, which left a hole with enough room for an officer to move comfortable down, and its central extraction pipe sucked out the softened earth and rock.

Georgia calculated the softened earth and rock extraction would take up a mound of about three yards high and about twenty yards square. They would concrete and mesh the top of the hole when they'd finished, just like a plug hole, and having the tunnel there would make future targeted assessments a great deal easier. A crowd-funded dirt mechanic would come by in a few days time to take away the softened earth and rock and, after a week or two, all evidence of any groundwork would disappear, and no-one would notice any difference.

The officers positioned the extraction tube in the right location to commence drilling: its noisy mechanism started to spew out the results of the drilling, and gradually moved downwards as the size of the mound increased. It was noisy with a deeply pungent aroma, but they were hungry and no-one missed the barely audible ring from the food processor, which announced their coffees and cookies were ready for consumption.

"These cookies taste like shit," one of the specialist officers said, biting into one of the freshly made treats.

"Well, the coffee more than makes up for it," Georgia said. "You can't expect the best when you're out in the field."

"It can't be any worse that the stuff coming out from the driller," the officer said. "That's where the real shit smell is coming from."

But it wasn't the smell of excrement: it was the earthly smell of thousands of year of compacted, composted, rained-on dirt and rock. It was like lancing an old pus boil and it wasn't anything that anybody wanted to see—or smell. Another twenty-five minutes and a coffee or two, and they would commence their descent.

*

Weller was near the front tent in Anika-6, working with a hacktivist on the final parts of their viral propaganda videos for release to the world. It was bright inside this tent, especially compared to the low-light outside the tent, kept dark to further minimize an already slim chance of detection.

They had moved fast and he was pleased with the work—Katcher's viral material and political messaging had been completed, and it was moving onto the simulation testing phase. In his estimation, another day or two and they'd be ready to start their surface revolution. As far as Weller was concerned, it all worked in theory, they just needed to test it in practice and all would be ready to go. Weller leaned over one of hacktivist and checked a portion of the coding.

"What else is needed to complete this part," Weller asked, pointing to the lightscreen.

"Nothing Mav," said the hacktivist, "this is complete. I've run through all the coding and all of the tests. I've checked on the parallel systems, done a thorough test. We're ready to go. We should probably do the practical test, but that's perfunctory. We're ready."

"And the back-up?"

"I've checked. This system goes down, the next one takes over. I've done the simulation—even if every system gets blown up, there's the central system that's on auto, and will start off the messaging on the surface. It's all ready. Just waiting for the practical tests—if you want them—and the word from Katcher to go."

Weller was taking all of this in—he already knew everything the hacktivist mentioned to him, but a part of his processes was to affirm and re-affirm as often as possible. It was all routine, but he needed to be assured more than a hundred per cent that everything was going according to plan.

They had developed a fail-save system, and were almost ready to implement it. But something else was distracting Weller. He could hear a low level hum—similar to the sound of a food processor—but this sound was all encompassing. It was coming from the roof of the cavern and gradually becoming louder. It didn't take him long to work out what was happening—drilling from the surface—and he frantically messaged Banda and Katcher, further down in Anika-6.

"Greta? Can you hear that?" shouted Weller into his cell device. "It's fucking drilling."

"What?" said Banda. "We didn't pick up any chatter about this at all."

"I think we've been set up," Weller said. He was usually calm in a crisis but only when he was in control. "It's a targeted assessment and someone's going to be down soon."

"Fuck. Fuck. *Fuck*!" said Banda, looking towards Katcher, who was unclear about what was happening. "This is a fuck-up. How did we fucking miss this? Fuck. Let's get to Weller."

Banda and Katcher grabbed their laser guns and quickly left the lower cavern. The humming was now at an excruciating level, and added to their confusion. Weller was outside his tent and becoming more agitated from the sound, which was getting louder and louder. The sound triggered something inside his head and he plugged his fingers into his earholes— his pain would end soon, but not in the way he would have expected it to.

The boron nitride diamond bit was nearing the end of its work and a few yards before it reached the roof of the cavern in Anika-6, a large wedge of shale rock broke off and landed over Weller, crushing him. Banda and Katcher rushed over to him among the rocks and dust, they moved him from under the rubble but it was too late. His body had been crushed and his face bloodied: Weller was killed instantly and they'd lost the main man behind their plan.

Banda shone her lightpen at the roof of the cavern. There was a hole in the top of the cavern, with a three-feet-wide tube-drill poking out of the hole. It was an ugly tool; its diamond teeth staring into the abyss like an alien being from another solar system. Its sensors knew this was the point where it needed to stop drilling and its mechanisms flicked over into a reverse direction and commenced the ascent back to the surface. Banda and Katcher had never seen one of these before but they knew that it could only mean one thing—Biocrime was at the surface and they would be down into Anika-6 soon.

*

The deep speed tube driller was a wonderful invention. As well as the drilling tube containing the hardest substance in the universe, its piping mechanism and suction capabilities enabled fast-speed drilling in most locations. It was originally developed in the 2200s in response to the final fuel crisis of that era, where all the major oil reserves were depleted, leaving only smaller pockets of oil areas that could be accessed with small-scale drilling. The original tube-drillers contained hard titanium drill bits that were effective, but with diminishing supplies of oil only being available in remote and geographically complex drilling zones, more sophisticated and direct systems of access had to be developed.

The 'peak-oil' theory was first developed by the geologist M. King Hubbert in 1956, and subscribed to the notion that when the maximum rate of petroleum resources in the world was reached, it would enter a period of permanent decline, and when the peak supply was achieved, other sources of sustainable and affordable energy needed to be developed.

Although the dates peak-oil would be reached varied, estimates at the time ranged between the years 2000–2050, with the expectation that oil on a commercially viable basis would be fully depleted between the years 2090–2150.

However, those predictions underestimated the nature of humankind in its quest for commercial exploitation and fear in the face of an impending crisis. Like rats crawling through obscure parts of sewers to find the last remnants of barely edible food, a new wave of small-scale oil entrepreneurs flourished during the 2200s, extracting whatever petroleum resources existed in the world, and the tube driller was one of the vast range of technologies developed to exploit oil as an energy resource.

Although the peak-oil community was constantly dismissed by larger business interests over many centuries, mainly accused as conspiracy theorists, radical environmental 'Marxists' that were only intent of destroying the capitalist system, and rooted in the world of fantasy, the theory of peak-oil and oil depletion eventually became a reality.

All organically-produced fossil oil was officially depleted in the early 2500s, and while synthetic oil was produced for almost a century, solar-nitrate plutonium power became more efficient and prevalent from the early 2600s onwards.

With the advent of solar-nitrate plutonium power and the depletion of traditional petroleum, the deep speed tube driller became an obsolete technology and remained dormant until Biocrime acquired the patent rights cheaply, when they realized underground surveillance was a potential revenue source.

*

Georgia the security manager instructed her deputy and underling officer to move the extraction pipe away from the dirt mound created by the tube drilling, and she used her lightpen to estimate the volume of the mound.

"Twelve-hundred and six cubes," Georgia said, as she looked towards the large pile of sand, crushed rock and sludge the deep speed tube drill had extracted. "Not bad. I was only two cubic feet out."

Georgia the security manager was competitive, even when she was competing against herself. She was always in the race against the clock, trying to beat her 'personal best', and testing to see how accurate her calculations of dirt extraction were. She motioned to the others—it was time to go down the recently created tunnel hole, and they needed to do their regular equipment checks: oxygen, light-helmet, lightpen, titanium boots, gloves.

"And laser guns?" asked Georgia. "Maybe we'll just take the one. Not expecting anything down there, but you've always got to be prepared."

"I think the most dangerous thing down there," her deputy said, "is going to be a large rare scorpion, or some kinda lost rat. We'll be fine."

"Do we all have to go down?" the underling officer said.

"If you don't go down, you don't get the pay," Georgia said. "Let's go."

From another part of the USM vehicle appeared a coil of thin tungsten rope, one-tenth of an inch thick, but strong enough to hold two tons of weight. They had a lightpen attached to the end, and the five took turns to harness themselves to the rungs in the tungsten rope, lowered slightly into the gaping hole in the earth for each officer, until all five were attached to the tungsten rope, and descended at the rate of four feet per second. It was a small tight and claustrophobic hole.

The five looked like slimmed-down astronauts, and they communicated with each other through their miked-up helmets. The descent would only take around five minutes—there wasn't too much to say between the five, and the only voice they heard was from the auto-depth detector, announcing they'd passed two-hundred yards, with another two-hundred yards to go.

They could peer down to see the dark hole continuing if they wanted to but the process was routine and automated. If there was any danger or obstruction, the sensors on their lightpens would communicate the impending issue to the motor generator above the surface and stop the tungsten rope descending further. Like many other contemporary inventions, it was a foolproof system. They were informed by the auto-depth voice they'd be at their destination soon.

*

Banda and Katcher moved Weller's body away from under the hole, into a tent, and left him with the other hacktivists. Renalda and Scanlen were back in the action with Banda and Katcher and they all had to think quickly about their next steps—Weller was close and emotionally attached to them, but this was not the time for sentiment—they had to think quick, think smart, and work strategically. Just like their computer and data systems, already, another hacktivist, Silas Newton, a twenty-five year old technology genius, filled the breach left by Weller, took control, and knew what needed to be done.

"Kransich's reports say they usually come down in teams of four or five," Banda said, "usually armed and takes about ten-to-fifteen minutes to travel down."

"Well, did Kransich get this date wrong?—what else do you reckon he's got wrong?" asked Renalda. "Whatever's coming down, we got to stop it from going back up."

"That's not so easy," Banda said. "They're all in communication, and if they see anything that's not quite right, they can communicate quickly to Biocrime."

"We'll have to take them out when they come down," Katcher said. "Make sure they're all down, and then take them out. That will give us maybe a couple of hours, we can trigger our systems, and then get out of here. We'll take positions, all lights out, and we'll wait for them to come down."

*

"*Depth: Three-hundred fifty yards. Destination: Fifty yards,*" the auto-depth detector said. It was a crystal clear sound, audible in each of the five officer's helmets, through tiny wafer-thin audio speakers, and they expected to be in the cavern in about one minute. So far, it was like any other targeted inspection. Slow. Boring. Tedious. But by the end of the inspection, they would have clocked up some seriously good income. Just like all the other targeted inspections they were planning to perform on this day.

Georgia the security manager peered down from her cramped position, and her lightpen showed the end of their tunnel and exposed an entrance into a deeper black void. She was sure she could smell coffee, but decided that it must be some type of underground chemical or a phantom smell playing with her olfactory senses. She convinced herself there was not going to be anything down in this cavern, but her confidence about this would soon add to her demise.

She had moved through the end of the tunnel and was dangling from the roof of the cavern, and scanned around with her lightpen to assess whether there was anything of interest. Her device lit up the cavern to show the beauty of the stalactites holding from the roof, almost a cathedral-like presence. She looked further afield and unsure if her eyes were playing tricks on her, could see in the distance, some kind of cloth-like material and, out of curiosity, decided to investigate further.

"Just wanted to check on something guys," Georgia said, speaking through her radio microphone. "Not sure what it is, but we're down here, so we may as well have a look."

"We're *all* getting off to look?" her deputy asked. "It will take up extra time—Biocrime won't be too happy to fork out the bill if it ends up being just a group of foraging rats making a home for themselves."

"Rats don't build homes, you fuckwit! That's what bowerbirds do, and I don't think we'll find any down here. Who's up on top?"

Agent Jack was the least experienced officer and should have been lower in this chain of five, but they needed one officer to remain in the hole, so it was Agent Jack that confirmed his position to Georgia the security manager. He managed to pull out his cell device and called up a Sudoku number puzzle to bide his time, certain that nothing was to come of this targeted inspection, safe, secure and comfortable in his harness.

The lights were out in Anika-6. Banda and Katcher were below the hole in the roof of the cavern and could hear the muffled sound of conversation between radio microphones but couldn't make out what was being said. But they were certain these people were coming down to look around and would report back to Biocrime as soon as they could, if they saw anything of interest.

Among the jagged and refracting rays of lightpens moving around from the officers, they saw four Biocrime suits appearing out from the hole in the roof—the number suggested by Kransich—and decided to take them all out when the timing was right. It was dark, so they would be guided by the lightpens from the Biocrime officers, making precision difficult and the risk of error high.

Georgia the security manager and the three others lowered themselves to the floor of the cavern and as they came closer to the cloth material, they realized they were actually a series of tents.

"Well, I'll be," Georgia said, while switching on her visual recorder. "There's fucking people down here. What the…"

"We'll take evidence and report back to Biocrime," her deputy said. "This might be big."

Georgia the security manager checked her cell device—there was no coverage, and no link to the surface. She could see the device was trying to connect to some kind of wireless networking but it was not something she'd ever seen before.

"Yep, I think this is big. Get as much data as you can and let's get—"

There was a flash of red and the sound of shattered glass. Banda laser gunned Georgia the security manager with a direct hit to the head. The laser entered her brain through her eye socket and the shards of glass scattered into her face. If the laser didn't kill her, the shards certainly would have finished her off.

Her deputy was more lucky: he had the one and only laser gun on his side, and started firing randomly in the direction where he suspected the original attack came from. He tried to switch off his lightpen, but Katcher fired his laser into the deputy's arm and leg. The deputy put up something of a struggle, but he was a sitting duck—Katcher fired away again—it was too dark to see accurately—but his laser bullets hit the deputy in the stomach and the heart. He was dead too.

Agent Jack heard the commotion through his radio microphone and the remaining officers shouted for him to leave them behind and get back to the surface as quickly as possible. Stunned after focusing solely on his losing Sudoku puzzle, he switched on his device to haul the tungsten rope—and him—back up to the surface.

"There's another one in the tunnel," Katcher shouted. "We've got to stop him too."

The other two officers were defenseless and Banda, without any emotion, clinically laser gunned them dead. Katcher moved to the hole in the roof of the cavern, but Agent Jack had already commenced his ascent back to the surface—it wasn't as quick as the descent, but he was moving back up at a rapid pace. Katcher pointed his laser gun through the tunnel and shot randomly.

The light was limited and Katcher couldn't see where or what he was shooting at. The best could do was to continue shooting up the tunnel and hope that he managed to take down the remaining agent. The tungsten rope continued to pull up Agent Jack to the surface but Katcher didn't know whether he was dead or alive.

*

"We have to release it *now*."

Banda was pressuring Katcher, Renalda and Scanlen to release the viral videos and the hack—it had been tested internally and worked, in theory, but they weren't one hundred per cent sure in practice.

"We don't know whether that officer will make to the top alive or not," Banda said. "If he does, we've got about an hour before we have to get out of here. If he's dead—someone will find him soon enough—so we maybe have two or three hours. I say we release the viral videos now."

They were all in agreement without uttering another word, but Weller wasn't here to advise. He was the technical genius and his replacement, Silas Newton, wasn't as sharp or as confident.

"I advised Mav the entire virus hack was ready to go," Newton said. "We did all the internal tests, but he wanted to do a prac test just to be two-hundred per cent sure. Mav was always like that."

"Then, let's go with it," Banda said. "Set up the system on auto—once it's in place, it won't stop for a couple of weeks. It's earlier than we planned, and we haven't done the final check that Weller wanted, but the time is now. Let's do it. And then we have to get back up to the surface."

They took their cell devices and laser guns. Newton activated the hacking and viral videos to cut out into Biocrime and Lifebook through the continuum, to be intercepted with the political messages of Jonathan Katcher and his call for an uprising against the world of Technocrats.

Soon, Katcher, Banda, Renalda and Scanlen worked their way through the tunnel and up to the surface. The team of hacktivists staggered their departures until only half of them remained in the underground, ensuring the system was activated correctly, and those that remained, operated Anika-6 on a basic level, unconcerned about their own safety.

*

Agent Jack reached the surface. His legs were badly sliced and cut by the light bullets coming from Katcher's laser gun. He scrolled through his cell device and saw there were a number of visual recordings from Georgia the security manager and the deputy, showing the underground cavern and the tent-structures underground. Before they were killed, the other officers also managed to visually record some of the technology down there. He scanned through some of the footage and set up a datacard transfer back to Biocrime. If he could transfer the data, it would alert Biocrime of his location and provide them a good deal of information about what was going on underground in Anika-6.

He rolled over onto his back and looked up at the blue sky. His injuries were far worse than he imagined: some of the laser bullets went through his legs, through his groin and into his stomach and upper organs. He was losing too much blood and his vision of the stunning blue sky gradually faded to white. He was losing control of his thought processes and there was a stunning and rapid montage of key thoughts and events from his life: the incubation hospital where he and his two children were created; sports trophies from a range of baseball competitions he won as a child; a range of dinner dates with his wife; his work as a Biocrime agent, and the final descent into the deep dark tunnel into Anika-6.

Agent Jack didn't make it.

CHAPTER 24.   THE RISE OF THE REVOLUTION

Marine Lestre was on her lightscreen, working through her morning watch list, while D'Souza lit up a bong—he was old school when it came to his recreational drugs of choice and the manner he ingested them—but he could always take a downer—or an upper, depending on which drugs he'd taken—if anything came up.

She was overseeing a list of reports and self-managing bots producing a range of scenarios and focused on likely suspects of the taker of secrets at Biocrime. In the corner of her screen was a rolling update on Katcher's whereabouts.

"Any sign of Katcher?" asked d'Souza, surrounded by a halo of hash smoke. Like most substances, it was artificial, but guaranteed to be as good, if not better, than the real thing. He didn't feel stoned, but it was all relative: he inhaled artificial hashish for most of the day, so his body and mind were used to it now.

"Nope. He hasn't been seen for four days and his digital house arrest report hasn't been made for six days. He's the only one on the watchlist that I can't match up. It's gone beyond the point of being a glitch—nothing on any hospital or death lists. Surprising. Look, I gotta take a pee—watch the lightscreen and see if anything changes?"

Lestre took off for the bathroom. She knew she'd only be a few minutes and she'd be able to backtrack on her lightscreen monitoring, but her instruction was partially to keep D'Souza on his toes and, if anything did change, he'd shout out to her, so she could immediately know.

She was thinking what Katcher's absence could mean—she knew he'd been a revolutionary leader but surely ten years away from the limelight couldn't rekindle an interest in an instance. If it wasn't a glitch, what was it? People didn't disappear and drop off completely from the continuum just like that.

Lestre left the bathroom and was on her way back to her lightscreen, and could hear the music from the Amore advertisement, and that song—'It's a Grand Old Flag'—streaming down the corridor.

She passed D'Souza zoned out on the couch, and expecting to see the Amore advertisement on her lightscreen, she got the shock of her life.

"What the fuck is this!" shouted Lestre. d'Souza, startled, zoned back in and saw Lestre standing in front of the lightscreen, with what he recognized to be the face of Jonathan Katcher talking directly to the audience. D'Souza took an upper pill and the effects of the hashish wore off within a few seconds. He was annoyed that he had just wasted a good batch of hashish, but he was now alert enough to realize something was wrong, and possibly seriously wrong.

"You stupid cunt! You were meant to monitor this," Lestre screamed.

"Well, fuck, it's not like one minute is going to make a difference—"

"—well, in this case, one minute could mean everything."

Lestre toggled between screens and called up different light channels and systems, but it was all the same. The voice and face of Katcher was on every screen, every channel, and she couldn't access anything else on her system. She looked at her cell device hoping for some relief, but it was the same. Her communications were down.

"What about your cell," Lestre asked, still in a furious mood. "Anything on it?"

"Just the same as yours—looks like we've been hacked—I can bypass and go onto the PPN."

Katcher's face was onscreen, and his voice outlined a series of short pithy statements.

"Friends, I'm Jonathan Katcher, and I've escaped from my virtual arrest and ready to continue the fight against our oppression against Biocrime and the Technocrats. Remember when your mother disappeared? Or you father? Or your sister, or your brother. That was the work of Biocrime and the Technocrats."

"This revolutionary crap," Lestre said, dismissively. "It's for babies! We've got to find out what's going on. I can't access anything, except for Katcher's face onscreen. So *that's* what the fucker's been up to."

Katchers' messages were short, slick and stylish, almost indistinguishable from any other modern advertising. Key graphics and key points flashed up on the screen, outlining the terrible history for natural humans since Technocratic control. The messages were on a loop, followed by documentary-style footage of terrible acts perpetrated by the Technocrats, and then another thirty-second message from Katcher.

"Friends, we've had centuries of oppression from the Technocrats. I am now free to lead our uprising against Biocrime. And with your help, our battle starts today."

And at the bottom of the screen was the graphic that guns belonging to natural humans have been unlocked to 'kill' mode, for the sake of self-protection and advancing the uprise.

"Have you got the PPN working yet?" shouted Lestre.

"No, this looks like it's a serious hack," D'Souza said. "I can't get anything in or out. What's happening outside?"

Lestre looked through the window of the apartment, and the large billboard lightscreen was not showing the usual advertising or news material, but Katchers' closeup face, and the superimposition: 'the Movement is coming now!'

"Fuck. It's on the billboard too, same as what's appearing on my lightscreen. If this is showing everywhere, we're fucked."

There was a knock on the door of the apartment. Unsure of what this meant, Lestre and D'Souza took their laser guns. Lestre looked through the peephole and could see an agitated Lumbardo, and she opened the door to let him in.

"You've seen the visuals?" asked Lumbardo. "This could be big. I can't get to Biocrime, nothing through the continuum, no contact. Nothing!"

"We don't know what this means yet. Could be big. Could be small. But Biocrime will be onto it. It's only been thirty minutes so far."

And, indeed, Biocrime was onto it, but there was little they could do at this stage. Their counter-hacking unit commenced their work within a minute of Katcher's viral videos appearing, but this hack was going to be a difficult one to stop. The counter-hacking unit was mainly a collection of sophisticated auto-bots assessing hacking and viruses, attempting real-time solutions, and engaging in speed coding to catch up and overtake the interventionist hacking.

But, after his death, Weller's coding was creating havoc and was the most advanced viral hack ever created. The beauty of Weller's algorithm was its reactive nature, and once it was ahead of the field, it could react to whatever coding was put in its way to destroy it, and in theory, could be infinite, unless Biocrime's system were clever enough or advanced enough to break the code. And until they could do this, Katcher's viral videos would be on infinite loop—on every visual device and in every location around the world.

*

In a twenty-four hour free-market city like San Francisco, there was no difference between night and day. Business and social activity was constant, the only change was the faces: different people that came in at different times, according to their body rhythms, lifestyles and personal choice, moving along to the rhythm and cycle of the city. Contemporary life was so dependent on technology that it was almost impossible to exist without it: work, eating, entertainment, surveillance, security. Through the continuum and Lifebook, everyone was born into technology, so they lived through it, and died through it.

It was late-morning when Katcher's viral videos appeared on every lightscreen, billboard and personal cell device and, initially, there was great confusion in the community. The messaging sounded like advertising—it was slick, professional, and used the jingle from the famous Amore advertisement. It wasn't selling anything, but was a call to arms and for natural humans to uprise against Technocrats. Most citizens were annoyed because they couldn't access Lifebook and the vast range of mindless visual and digital material that was available to them through the continuum. The assumption was that this was an unusual glitch and an expectation that normal transmission would resume soon, but Katcher's voice and image kept on appearing on lightscreens and would keep appearing for some time.

It took a while amid the confusion, but citizens realized that if Lifebook and Biocrime couldn't be accessed, Lifebook and Biocrime couldn't access them. Without access to Lifebook and technology rendered useless, there was nothing to do in their apartments, citizens started to leave their buildings—with their laser guns for protection—and massed onto the street, checking each other's cell screens to confirm what they were seen on their own screens. In every location and on every screen, there was Katcher's face and his revolutionary videos.

In times like this, there are many critical points that need to concatenate for a social upheaval and mass movement to commence, and the pieces started to fall into place. For many citizens, especially those in the Movement, this was the moment they'd been waiting for, the one they'd been told about for many years. For others, they were furious but not sure who was at fault and who to blame: like addicts to the drug, they wanted their access to technology returned, access to Lifebook, surveillance of other citizens and, most importantly, to supplement their universal income. The pissant on the screen—Jonathan Katcher—was talking about an uprising and revolution, but was this what they wanted as well?

There is an incredibly fine line between human order and chaos, and societies are held together by insidious control through a manufactured consent—a consent where citizens are amused and entertained through the mundane and meaningless, while being controlled by others. History has shown how human order can quickly descend into a destructive chaos, even when the possibility seems distant on the horizon, but once the manufactured consent had been removed, an uprising seemed the most inevitable conclusion.

Like a young dog trained to perform tricks for its master, the collective mind of a community reacts quickly to changing events, and returns to basic self-protective instincts. Without external control, social systems fall away very quickly, and the streets of San Francisco began to unravel.

In the midst of this confusion, many citizens were waiting for the next moment, unsure about what awaited them. Some were waiting for the 'glitch' to recede, so they could continue accessing the continuum: others, unable to make contact with anyone, went down to the streets, enquiring if anyone knew what was happening and when it would all return to normal.

Some of the more technically inclined, tried to access personal private networks—many weren't working, but some did, and scant and sketchy details moved slowly across the city, mixed in with the whispers of rumor and unreality: *Jonathan Katcher has returned; the Movement is coming; Lifebook is broken; the unhackable system has been hacked; Biocrime can't watch us anymore; revolution is coming, people will die.*

War.

The street crowds grew larger with every minute, and the combination of confusion, self-interest and basic instinct created a sense of impending pandemonium, much like aimless wandering of the streets after a fire alert.

Coinciding with the release of the viral videos and the confusion on the streets, Katcher, Banda, Scanlen and Renalda reached the surface and mingled with the developing crowd. Some in the crowd recognized Katcher; others made the correlation between his face and the face on the billboard lightscreens. There was no time to react though, no-one really knew what to do anyway, and it was best to continue with self-preservation.

Scanlen and Renalda were still adjusting to being in the outside world again, but Katcher was reveling in what was an uncertain time. This was his moment, but it was also the first part of what he hoped would be the start of a brave new world. Banda was agitated and impatient: even though the crowd was building up, she wanted action now.

"You should be leading from the front," Banda said, pointing to a point further in the crowd.

"There is no front," Katcher responded. "This is happening all over the city. When the time is right, we'll intercept the lightscreens and livecast from wherever we happen to be."

By early afternoon, there were tens of thousands of citizens on the streets—relatively small when compared with the city's population of thirty million—with Katcher's viral messages on all lightscreen billboards in the background. Many were caught up in the groundswell of group think and action: they disliked the Technocrats but everyone else was here, so they should as well. Many had their unlocked laser guns with them, about to become untethered and sophisticated killing machines.

The Technocrats—even the ones supportive of the Movement—watched from their apartment buildings. They outnumbered the natural humans by a large ratio, but because their laser guns were now inoperable, it was best to keep the distance. No-one was sure how this was going to work out and the rumors from restricted personal private networks kept coming: *a revolution is taking place, Lifebook and Biocrime are gone, danger for Technocrats*.

Katcher knew a breakdown in communications meant that very little real news would come out and, in a news-filled world, there was every chance the void would be filled with whatever news became available, even if it was far from the truth. So far, it was working out exactly in the way he anticipated.

Initially, this was a controlled mayhem—Technocrats were hiding away, and some natural humans looked on in bemusement—but there was a wave of low-level street crime and vandalism that threatened to break out into violence at any moment.

Biocrime had been blindsided. It had the mechanisms available to it to suppress such an intervention, but this was the biggest systems hack in human history. Whatever machinery and human resources it could use to intervene were as good as rusted iron without the technology to co-ordinate and manage it all.

A groundswell of support started from more citizens. There was now a larger group of humans rallying in the streets, and there were others in different parts of the city that were also taking up the cause. It was difficult to think about safety: something that seemed innocuous a few hours ago had turned into a hazardous and out-of-control event. The streaming masses were building on the many streets of San Francisco; the visuals and sounds of Katcher on the large lightscreen billboards seemed to become more omnipotent. On empty streets or any other average day, the visuals wouldn't mean much, but the look on Katcher's face became more menacing with the groundswell of action at the coalface.

There were now hundreds of thousands on the streets: Scanlen and Renalda had fallen off the pace, but there was a larger number now following and supporting Katcher and Banda, chanting with ongoing monotony: *"Kat-cher! Kat-cher! Kat-cher! Kat-cher! Kat-cher!"*

It was partially a release of pent-up energy, partially hooliganism, but mainly an opportunity to change the social structure. Katcher, with the larger support of people behind him, decided it was now the best time to livecast through the continuum—they had complete control and access to it—a short sharp speech and when completed, with great agility, move to another location or, disappear completely.

They were in a lower part of Visitacion Valley—and Katcher positioned himself in an area surrounded by trees and low-level buildings. Although laser guns had been disabled for Technocrats, he didn't want to take any chances. It was old school—a classic off-the-stump rallying cry: he was standing on top of an old stone wall, about three feet above the ground. Banda activated her cell device and, using an auto-live cast software app called 'Live!AppTV', which collated key points from the spoken word to create a ticker-tape of scrolling text at the bottom of the screen, she prepared for a livecast of Katcher's speech.

The visual messages on the lightscreens were interrupted by the live footage from Banda's cell device. It was high resolution vision, a little like hand-held *cinema verité*, and a jumbled image before final zooming in on Katcher's face.

The graphic from the auto-program superimposed the words: 'Jonathan Katcher to make public statement at 13:15'.

Katcher was nervous, but people that are so sure about the changes they wanted to make in the world, force themselves to reach into the right personal zone. It reached 13:15 and for Katcher, it was time to act. He spoke forcefully—although Bander's cell device would track his voice perfectly and clearly, the crowd noise was overwhelming.

"Friends, we made this decision today to act upon the injustices that have been taking place against us for many years."

The crowds throughout San Francisco settled somewhat in anticipation of Katcher's announcement. Many had been expecting this for some time, but they were also bemused, unsure of what would happen next.

"We've been brutalized for many years by the Technocrats, made into second-class citizens, false arrests by Biocrime, spied on, watched over and had our way of life destroyed.

"We've had our body parts and pieces of us sold for a song, exploited and misused by Technocrats, blamed for every ill in the world, surveilled and, if we ever supposedly do the wrong thing, sent off to far away penal zones to be devoured by wild animals.

"This can no longer happen. No-one will touch you again!"

The crowds started to cheer and applaud, somewhat placated, and the Katcher chant rose up again, and increased in crescendo.

"Kat-cher! Kat-cher! Kat-cher! Kat-cher! Kat-cher!…"

"I stand here today and I promise you this one thing…" … Katcher was speaking loudly, but the volume of the crowd had become too extreme, and Katcher's voice was drowned out by the increasing cacophony.

Behind where Katcher spoke was another group of people. They were disaffected dissidents, but couldn't care less about Katcher and his musings. They were new wave radical decadent nihilists, mainly interested in access to the continuum, lightscreens and the easy way of life. They started to pitch found objects at Katcher's supporters, and knocked several over.

Katcher had the look of confusion on his face. He hoped his message about the injustices caused by the Technocrats would have prominence, but there were other actions here at play. Had he overestimated the support for the Movement, or underestimated the resistance that might exist among natural humans? Any kind of social movement had a number of different factions, in some cases, diametrically opposed to the values and objectives of the movement, but new wave nihilists? That was another matter entirely.

One of the found objects—a shard of broken concrete—was heading towards Katcher. He saw it coming towards him in the last split second, too late to avoid it completely, but the shard hit him just above the eyebrow. He was momentarily stunned and assessed the damage that revealed a cut and a lump, and a small amount of blood streamed onto his fingers.

Banda switched off her visual recorder and the datacasting reverted to Katcher's viral propaganda videos.

"Fuck," Banda shouted, amongst the backdrop of rising crowd violence. "We'll have to get out of here."

"Where are Scanlen and Renalda?" asked Katcher.

"They must have fallen back into the crowd. They might still be adjusting to being on the surface again, but we can track them through our PPN."

"We'll find them on the way—we gotta get back underground."

"But we can't go back down," Banda said, "we'll be sitting ducks."

"Any other suggestions? This is getting out of control, it's our best bet."

Soon, there were other radicals joining in the action, the group-think had caught on and shops started being vandalized. The nihilists weren't exactly sure about what they wanted, but whatever it was, they wanted it now. They were disenchanted and with every passing moment they acted with impunity, they were encouraged to increase their violence, which soon escalated into a major fracas.

A band of radical members from the Movement—the useless punks and street rats Katcher complained about to Banda—threw a brick through a shop window. It was actually a shop managed by a group of natural humans, but the radicals weren't bothered by this. They had pent-up anger, and directed it at anyone, regardless of who it was. Their tribe was speaking and they wanted everyone to listen. Just yesterday, they were a ragtag collection of nobodies but now, they were taking their place in the sun. As far as they were concerned, their putative leader had returned and had spoken, and now they were armed and dangerous.

In all revolutions and civil uprisings, there is the one moment that crystalizes the movement and escalates events to another level, and this one moment in Katcher's revolution was just about to happen.

One of the radical street rat punkers, Gavin Pinkston, was shouting anti-establishment slogans with his tribe. He was in his mid-twenties, loud, big, angry and, with his unlocked gun, he was dangerous and lethal. He looked menacing with his spiked Mohawk green hair, his graffiti-designed leather jacket with studs, and black t-shirt with 'FUCK YOU' in a thick hot pink typeface.

He was the classic supraliberal, where he could do whatever he wanted, whenever he wanted, because it was his freewill that commanded him. He was surrounded by citizens, surrounded by the noise of shouting and chanting, his mind filled with words from Katcher's voice, and the amphetamines he took this morning.

Pinkston realized that with the swelling and moving crowd, he had arrived into a Technocrat area, and he could see many Technocrats peering through their apartment windows, and some that watched the events on the streets from their small balconies. The Technocrats were unsure about what to do or what to think. Some were recording the events on their cell devices, others were monitoring their lightscreens, and tried a number of software patches and fixes to bypass the Jonathan Katcher that relentlessly appeared on their screens. For them, while there was an unpredictable mass of people on the streets, it was too dangerous to go down there, and they were still expecting some type of response from Biocrime.

But Biocrime didn't respond. Their systems had been blocked too—they were receiving the same Katcher-ite messages that everyone else was, and they were working hard to determine what had happened, and how to decode and recode their systems. In the meantime, the outrage on the streets of San Francisco continued.

Pinkston's mind was racing, his heart was pumping. He was caught up in the moment: the high-energy of street protest, the realization the time had come and this was to be a big moment in history. He pointed his laser gun towards an apartment balcony—he didn't care who he hit, or whether he hit anyone at all—but he wanted to shoot. He could see two men half-hiding on the balcony and his years of pent-up anger was just about to be released. When he pulled the trigger on his laser gun, a series of laser bullets reached the men and penetrated their neck and chest muscles. They were direct hits and both men were down and dying.

There was a flurry of action, where other Technocrats in the apartment pulled in the dying men away to safety. Pinkston took aim at them too, and the tracer bullets ricochet into their bodies, taking them out. In all, Pinkston killed two men, two women and a child. It wouldn't be immediate, but the Technocrats would retaliate as soon as they had the chance.

Someone else's actions might have followed the same process, but Pinkston was the first and his unwise actions had started the war. And it would be difficult to stop.

CHAPTER 25.   BIOCRIME RETALIATES

The mid-afternoon shadows were seeping through Don Capone's window on the fifty-sixth floor, and the golden glow of the sun disturbed his thinking about the events taking place below him on the streets.

This was a serious incident, and the top ten floors of Biocrime were in lock-down, and groups of security officers were war-gaming their operations through their internally protected system. Through their lightscreens, they too could see what was happening in the outside world, and their collection of coding teams were rapidly working on a solution, to be implemented as soon as possible. The last major incident like this occurred sixty years ago in 2974, when a group of hacktivists created a viral loop that took out the continuum and Lifebook systems for a few hours—and resolved within the day—but this disruption was more severe and would involve more than just a bit of patchwork and digital cement work.

Biocrime worked quickly, and within thirty minutes, Capone was assigned a team of twelve security officers, headed by Officer Janet Dyson, a high-level tech-head who was charged with co-ordinating the campaign to stitch up some of the networks of surveillance so, at least, they could receive some close-up action of what was happening on the streets. The old-style surveillance available to them—high-powered telephoto lens—could tell them there was mayhem out there, but they needed to have a clearer view of faces, the people involved, and any way of being able to identify them.

"This is a pure shitstorm Janet," Capone said. "Pure and simple. The President is not going to be happy."

"Not happy?" said Officer Dyson, her eyerolls confirming the understatement. "She'll be fucking furious, but we'll deal with that later. We've got the coders working on creating a network of surveillance through the existing cameras on the streets. There were quite a few that were malfunctioning—old technology."

"Shows you what happens when we don't pay to get those maintained and fixed up," Capone said. "Trying to save a few million over the years is probably now going to cost us billions. How long before we can at least get that system sorted?"

"That should take a few hours, hopefully before sunset," Officer Dyson said. "We can try to link all the working cameras, and create the algorithm that predicts all the movement in between. Not a hundred per cent, but pretty close. That will give a better look at the ground action."

"From up here, it's not good. A fucking disaster."

Capone was using his high-powered telephoto lens to zoom around the different parts of the city that he could see from his vantage point. The imagery was fuzzy, but in one zoom, he could see several bodies slumped in the corner of an apartment's balcony—he assumed they were Technocrats— and in another zoom, he saw a group of street-rat punks punching a middle-aged man, and laser gunning his head. He saw other Technocrats using the laser guns to stun, but these were just temporary barriers to further harm—without access to the full features of the laser guns, they were just sitting ducks against the rampaging and out-of-control street-rat punks.

"No-one's in communication at the moment, Don. And we can't do anything with robocops, because they're all synchronized and activated throught the continuum. We'll have to set up several private networks and see who's going to scan into it. It will take time, but just through crowd and peer networking, we should be able to get some counter-action on the ground."

"But it's a massacre down there," Capone said. "And will continue for as long as Biocrime's not on the ground. My course of action is: set up the private networks; instruct our people to switch on their personal visual recorders so we can start scanning at the street level. Offer payments for their recordings."

"Yes, Don, I agree—there's a few other things we could add, but let's take it upstairs."

Capone and Dyson were due for the emergency session in the Biocrime President's chambers; they packed their cell devices and datacards and moved to the elevators to take them up to level sixty—the President's penthouse—the entire floor with three-sixty-degree views of the city, rooms with all mod cons and food supplies to last a year, and a massive conferencing meeting room, with monitors, devices and a team of tech-heads summoning up a range of different screens, deep in soft discussion with others about what key data meant and how to extrapolate the information.

When they entered the conferencing room, there were twenty key Biocrime officers of different ranks—all the important ones—and they deferred to the President of Biocrime, Michelle Luanda, simply know as 'El', as in *el presidente.*

Michelle Luanda was someone who moved up the ranks with Biocrime, now in her late-fifties, a grand accumulator of wealth through a range of Biocrime crowd-sourcing financing schemes, ones that grafted small percentages of monies from unsuspecting Lifebook accounts, and a mastermind of a range of different criminal detection systems that created large sums of income for Biocrime. Her presence was large: six-feet-four, short-ish dark hair, and the commanding look of strength that suggested she could easily knock down anyone that stepped in her way. Like almost everyone that reached this station in life, she was a ruthless sociopath, and virtually destroyed everyone in her pathway to become the most powerful person in the world. But her driving force was the continuous accumulation of money, and if this was at risk, her position as President was also at risk.

"Capone, Dyson, please be seated," Luanda said sternly. She tried to be professional but barely disguised her anger about the events on the ground. "These are trying times, but we'll sort this out."

"As always, El, as always," Capone said. He needed to exude a high level of confidence that he had the ability to end the troubles on the streets, but this time around, Capone was not so sure about what exactly needed to be done. This was unknown territory and no-one really knew what they were going to do to resolve it.

"I think we're ready to start," Luanda said, seated at the head of the large conference table, assured, and in control. "As you're already aware, Biocrime, Lifebook, all of our surveillance is out and, from what I've been told, is not likely to come back in a hurry. And it looks like we're on the verge of civil war on the streets. We can stop this, but we have to act strategically, and we have to act quick, get this shit off our screens, and find Katcher.

"It will cost us the big bucks, but that's not the aim right now. We have to stop, stabilize, and then we can get Katcher, and find out how he slipped through the net—supposedly fail-proof."

"It's not so easy, El," Capone said, "it will—"

"—look, don't fucking tell me it won't be easy," Luanda said, furiously. "I fucking know that. But we've got to fucking act fast and fucking stop the massacre that's happening on the street. In the spirit of acting fast, I'm going to try to stop being pissed—but I am—we've supposedly got the best systems in the world—we are the best and only—but couldn't stop Katcher from sneaking away from under our noses, hacking our systems so badly—and we didn't even know about it? Fuck me..."

"It's best if we go through—"

"—*shut the fuck up*—you're number five in this place, Capone, let's listen to the number two."

Cowered, Capone stopped talking and retracted his thoughts: 'El' was angry and in these circumstances, it was best not to intervene. The Deputy Brian Kasprovich—on level fifty-nine, and second in the hierarchy—took over proceedings and summoned up the lightscreen, which displayed a number of points of action to reclaim the streets of San Francisco and restore order.

Kasprovich spoke directly to the points on the screen, displayed in a stark presentation: solid black for the key points, shaded charcoal for the lesser points, and the estimated budget cost of implementing these actions at the bottom of the screen.

"What we know so far through our private networks," Kasprovich said, "is that this is a worldwide event—we can tell that it hasn't been anywhere near as effective in other zones, so we can safely say that it's focused in the San Francisco region—"

"—well," Luanda interjected, "we do like to think of San Francisco as the center of the universe."

The table broke out into laughter, much in the way underlings humor the boss after they've uttered an insipid joke, but the humor had resonance and broke the ice somewhat. The rivalry between San Francisco, Los Angeles, New York and Chicago had existed for over a millennium, with each city trading places in the jockeying for grand supremacy, but it was San Francisco that had reached the pinnacle after Biocrime headquartered in the city four hundred years ago and seemed to keep an unassailable lead over all the other major cities in the world.

"We're just lucky this didn't happen in New York," Kasprovich said as the mirth started to die down. "But the longer it goes on, the more likely it is to spread to other regions to the same level.

"It seems that Katcher's viral videos and hacking—wherever it came from—sophisticated as it is, was released prematurely, without final testing—which explains why it hasn't taken off as well in other regions—some of their systems operate on different bandwidths, meaning that it didn't hack too much of Biocrime and Lifebook in other areas—there was enough critical mass that remained to either stymie any counter-social activity."

"So, this is some good news so far," Luanda said, thinking out aloud. "If we know that it was released prematurely, they—whoever they are—were probably startled and decided to release now. And if it's working so well in San Francisco— it's where Katcher lives—it probably started here. What about other parts of the America Zone? How have they been affected?"

"From what we can tell," Kasprovich continued, "it's virtually all of the America Zone, anywhere that operates on the same bandwidth, and within a contiguous geographic space. Los Angeles has had a series of riots—usual street rat and sub-culture stuff—you know, face masks, petrol bombs, upturned vehicles—people trying to be the modern-day Che Guevara. New York is always on its own tangent, but the same as many other places—low-level violence, street marches showing their 'unhappiness'—whoopee do. New York's a money hub—it's like Shanghai in the Asia Zone, citizens just want to make money and live their lives—even the natural humans.

"There's been a few street marches in London and Sheffield in the Europe Zone—the usual stuff they have over there, you know, those guys with anonymous masks—several thousand of them, but easily dismantled."

"How many have been killed?" asked Luanda.

"Our reports say maybe ten thousand world wide," Kasprovich said, "not counting what's happening in San Fran. Coders in other parts of the world managed to stop the hack before it went viral through the systems, and deactivated all laser guns. Katcher's hack is meant to be self-replicating, and keep one-step ahead of any attempts to recode to destabilize the virus.

"I must say, it's a beautiful piece of coding work—we managed to stop it in its tracks in other parts of the world—other zones, like L.A. and New York are manageable, but the real problem is here in San Francisco. The virus is out of control, and so is the city."

"Okay, what I've heard so far has calmed me down somewhat," Luanda said. "Don, what's our course of instruction?"

"San Fran is still dire and very serious," Capone said. "I'd say other parts of the world can manage themselves. Our reports through the private networks add up to about thirty-thousand dead—that's in about six hours—our intel from up here is that it's mainly street rat and no-hoper punks that have taken up the cause, and other citizens have bought into it—mainly because their systems are down, and they've swallowed all the propaganda streaming everywhere. It's not only Technocrats that have been killed, but natural humans too. Seems like Technocrats are doing the killing too. There are no political activists or political strategists—they're people that have been licenced to kill, and have the means to do it.

"So, the best way to act first?" Capone continued. "We remove their means of killing—all of our efforts now have to be decoding the laser guns—not just the killing mode, but the stun mode as well—completely."

"Well, that's a good start," says Luanda. "But then what? We've still got mayhem on the streets—albeit without the guns—we've got to get back Biocrime and Lifebook—and get Katcher's crap off the screen. What sort of timeframe are we talking about?"

"We'd have to talk to tech to confirm," Capone said, "but we'd have to code to get ahead of the virus—it's like a hamster in the treadmill—we have to keep coding just to keep up, but then do a super batch of code just to leap ahead. And then keep coding. Then we can bypass the first part of the code and disarm all laser guns. That might take a day or two—"

"—a day or two!" interrupted Luanda. "That will result in a million deaths! We'll have to work faster than that."

"We will," Capone said, "but it's all dependent on whether Katcher's team is still coding and adding, and whether there's others around the world that are coding as well. It's quite a sophisticated code—if we put all of our resources into disarming the laser guns—and that's fucking important, let me tell you—reactivating Biocrime and Lifebook will take longer."

"We'll make these fuckers pay," Luanda said, "but we got to get things in place first. Stop the guns, get back Biocrime online. Okay, continue with your work, let's meet again in a few hours."

The meeting ceased and the officers dispersed to their respective duties. The sixtieth floor was a hive of activity and the buzz of soft communications between staff and sounds of the scenario-acting from the war game room highlighted the urgency of the task ahead in this high-stakes game.

Luanda took Capone aside into one of the antechambers of the penthouse. "Sorry about the personal abuse Don, I gotta show them who's boss and you're my best fall guy."

"It's okay El," Capone said, unsure of where exactly he stood with Luanda and who in the upper echelons she was trying to play him off against. "We gotta work fast though, we'll get through this."

*

It was nightfall and a scan across the skyline of San Francisco showed a stream of fires burning in apartment blocks. It was twelve hours since Katcher's viral videos and hack were released, and the murder and mayhem on the streets continued on the streets, unabated.

It was strenuous for the team at Biocrime to continue working at a rapid pace, knowing every minute away from finding a solution was causing numerous deaths and they couldn't do anything to stop this—for now—except for continuing to code and work out different permutations to stop the viral attack. Their team of five hundred programmers and coders were de-hacking and de-activating lines of codes that kept diverting and replicating themselves. It was furious hand-coding and installation of bugs and apps that multiplied reams of anti-codes and data tasks, and collectively trying to determine the best point to commence dismantling code that had destroyed the continuum. The most essential part of their work was to deactivate all the laser guns, and they were coding as quickly as they could.

From his vantage point on level fifty-six, Capone could see the violence on the street and, at this stage, there was little he could do about it. Because it was nightfall, the wave of attacks continued, and the twenty-four-hour activity of the city continued the endless loop of terror, looting and murder, as if there was never enough energy that could be expended on the lust of revenge, blood and larceny.

"What's the estimation now," Capone asked, looking over at Officer Dyson's lightscreen.

"The best estimate we have," Officer Dyson responded, "is that we can end this by four o'clock tomorrow afternoon. But there's a lot of things that have to fall into place for us to achieve that. It's a unique virus that keeps replicating— whatever counterhacks we put into it, it puts up another defense and recodes to put itself ahead of ours. We have to get ahead of it, once we're there, we can disarm the laser guns. But we have to get there first."

"And I guess there's no point in sending out any Biocrime supports or armored tanks?"

"Nope. They'll just be butchered by lasers. Sure, we've got our own, but there's just too many on the streets. Stop the guns first and—if we can do that—and then we can close down the streets."

It was difficult to shut down a city of thirty million, but that's what Capone had to do. In the heat of confusion, there was always a fight-or-flight instinct that engulfed most behaviors and responses, and there were many Technocrats—and some natural humans—that were beginning to leave the city behind, unsure of where to go, or what to do. But anywhere, no matter how difficult it would be to get there, would be preferable to the terror that had reached the streets of the city.

Through his high-powered telephoto lens, Capone saw these people leaving the city. Scanning through other parts of the city, he could see that in some areas, the violence was not severe, almost as though the initial part of the uprising was to release tension from the assortment of social misfits and deviants and let the rest of the world know what they thought—but other parts of the city seemed to have more intense action continuing. Capone assumed it was the more hardline element and probably the off-grid street rats aligned with the Movement—people who would latch onto any bandwagon that was coming through and they had nothing to lose. This was their time, and they would lap it up as much as they could.

While he was scanning through other parts of the city, Capone received a message from Luanda, requesting his presence in the penthouse.

"Janet, I gotta call from El, asking me upstairs."

"Well, off you go then. I'll just save the city myself."

"Don't worry, I'll give you a medal once we're done, and maybe a move up to level fifty-seven."

"Wow, closer to the President's drinks cabinet. Can hardly wait." Capone loved Officer Dyson's cynicism and gave her a mock-general's salute while he collected his datacard and his thoughts, and moved towards the elevator.

Capone elevated up to Luanda's penthouse, and upon entering the room, could see she was enthused about something. He'd been one of Luanda's favorites for some time—she enjoyed his humor, his laid-back nature, his professional approach to matters, while keeping his team engaged with his level-headedness. He was the fifth in line at Biocrime, but wasn't as crusty and serious as the others, certainly not like Brian Kasprovich.

"Check this out," Luanda said, motioning Capone to her lightscreen for a close-up scan of four people. "I haven't shown the others yet, but who do you think this is?" she said, as she pointed to slightly blurred disheveled face.

"It's Jonathan Katcher! How did you get this?"

"He made that live speech a few hours ago," Luanda said. "He was only live for about a minute, but we got some shots on the ground through our patched up surveillances. Some techno sent it through on her PPN—she'll get her reward later—we can get some imagery from the ground, and it's not a real-time set up, but we should be able to locate him—once we get past the viral code."

"And there's Scanlen and Renalda there too," Capone said, looking at the image. "I thought they were both dead."

"Scanlen, no. He disappeared—we assumed he was dead, but just didn't have any proof. Renalda, yes—well, she was supposedly dead, I remember the funeral from years ago. Maybe they set up a sophisticated hack on Lifebook. Who knows, but it doesn't matter now. We'll be able to get their approximate locations and try to find them once Biocrime is back online."

"And who's this one?" asked Capone, zooming in on Banda's partially obscured face on the lightscreen.

"Could be anyone, but it's hard to make out. But if she's with Katcher, Scanlen and Renalda, she's probably someone that's important to the Movement. Or Katcher's fuck buddy? She looks cute."

"We'll scan her through the Biocrime back-up," Capone said, "and find her profile. Unless she's one those off-gridders, then it's anyone's guess."

*

Katcher and Banda were on the streets, a cool San Franciscan evening, moving against the crowd, swathing through back lanes and alleys, trying to get back to autotram station that could take them back to Anika-6. Many hours had passed since Katcher's viral videos commenced and, like many other people, they'd been trying to get back to wherever their safety zone might be—for Katcher and Banda, they decided their best chances were to return to the underground. There was likely to only be a few people back at Anika-6 but they had to get back—above ground was not safe for them.

The mania from the hours before had subsided—there were still sporadic groups roaming the streets, instigating mindless attacks and pilfering. These were the people they needed to keep away from, not because these people were politically inspired or intellectually motivated, but bands of bored drugged-crazed lunatics that trawled the streets for an opportunity for more plundering and killing. The social contract that had been patched through the continuum had been broken, and would remain broken until its main tool of order and control, Lifebook, went back online. Until then, the disorder and chaos would continue.

Many of the large billboard lightscreens on the sides of apartment buildings had been vandalized—some had their screens damaged so only a quarter of the pixels were displayed; some had their loudspeakers broken off; others had their power supply cut off; others had been completely ripped off the sides of large office buildings—no mean feat, as some of these lightscreens were almost three-hundred feet tall.

Katcher was in two minds: the uprising that he'd been after for a long time had kick-started, but he felt like he'd abandoned the people that he encouraged to rise up. But he started to think that it wasn't the Movement the people supported, just the chance to engage in payback brutality and an orgy of killing. For Katcher, violence could be a means to an end, especially as he had practiced it in the past himself but, in this case, he wasn't so sure.

"Any sign of Scanlen and Renalda on the PPN?" asked Katcher.

"They're just further up," Banda said as her eyes gleaned over her cell device to show two blue dots on a basic map, indicating Scanlen and Renalda were about five-hundred yards away, in a location near the autotram station. "But it seems they haven't moved in a while, so they've probably holed up somewhere."

Along the way on the main streets, they saw smashed windows, graffitied buildings with 'Fuck Biocrime' sprayed onto them, some with 'Fuck Katcher', and others with the standard tagging and scribbles that had dominated cityscapes for over a thousand years. They passed some bodies on the streets, but could also see in the apartments above, the scrapings of laser bullets on walls, and the spray of blood on many balcony walls. This had become a movement not of revolutionaries who were trying to make the world a better place, but a world of nihilistic and anarchic revolt, one that damaged as much as possible in its path.

They were moving closer to the personal private network signal for Scanlen and Renalda, but this area had an even greater scene of carnage. It was the aftermath and the masses had come and gone: the main apartment block was on fire, and several vehicles had been overturned and blasted. The personal private network signal led them towards the back of an overturned vehicle and they were overcome by the putrid smell of burnt bodies. There, amongst several other bodies and strewn debris were Scanlen and Renalda, both with laser bullet marks at the back of their heads and through their upper bodies.

"Fuck. Fuck! They're gone. Any signs of their decoders?" asked Katcher, as he leaned closer to the bodies of Scanlen and Renalda.

"No, gone," Banda said, scanning the bodies with her cell device. "Nothing. All gone. Killed by the people they were trying to save."

Trying to save. These were three words that momentarily grated Katcher. There was something sanctimonious and condescending about how the words sounded and they way they came out, as if Banda was on a mission to create the world in her own image, rather than comprehending a diverse world of different perspectives.

Katcher didn't have time to deeply analyze his thoughts—correlating the awful stench of burnt human flesh with the fact that it was coming from people he knew well, as well as the need to find a safer location underground, clouded his mind.

"Maybe these people don't want to be saved," Katcher said. "Let's go. Get back to the underground."

They were distressed but had to check their emotions until they got to safety. Scanlen and Renalda were close to the Movement, but they were now gone and it was best for Banda and Katcher to retreat and plan their next moves. This was a revolution, but not in the way they had planned or had expected. Banda and Katcher were angling through the backstreets and alleys, still surrounded by the continuous viral videos of Katcher promising an end to oppression and overrule by Technocrats and Biocrime.

The streets were dangerous, but it wasn't a case of being killed on sight—it was easier to move through at night—but Banda and Katcher needed to be careful. The support for the Movement among the citizenry was strong but, like many revolutionaries, they were trying to defy classic human behavior—one of self-interest—and the fact that, in reality, even if popular support was strong for a special cause, not many citizens were prepared to participate, and action was usually implemented by the few adherents and hard-liners.

In their case, it wasn't so much a miscalculation of strategy and action, but a miscalculation of the good will of humankind. Self-interest usually won out, collective groups followed patterns of human thought that directly benefit them, and the ancient Roman charade of 'bread and circuses' was needed to keep the populace occupied.

Just as Katcher and Banda were moving to leave the site, a skirmish developed just around the corner of their location. A group of laser gun wielding youths were scanning the apartments to see if there was any movement on balconies, or through any other rooms—kitchens, loungerooms, silhouettes in bathrooms. It was too late to hide or retreat: they caught a glimpse of Katcher and Banda and fired away, laser bullets hitting the metal of the vehicles.

One of the light bullets caught Katcher in his left shoulder— it was a sharp hot pain, but pumped up by adrenalin and the need to get away, he kept running. And running. Banda was shooting behind her, keeping some of the group at bay, but they kept chasing, advantaged by the fuel of amphetamines and the smell of blood.

Katcher and Banda could feel the laser bullets whizzing past them and reached a small access point into an underground shop. Just as they reached this point, another band of drug-crazed youths, attracted by the sound of the chase, appeared on the other corner and start firing their laser guns at the first group. This was a welcome distraction, but they'd have to get out of this safe spot at some point. They scanned the location and saw an exit point in the back of the shop, and they moved through this into another alleyway. They were safe for now, but the danger would be evident until they returned to Anika-6.

They continued to slither through the backstreets and the smaller crowds for another hour and moved towards the South San Francisco autotram station which gave them access back to the underground. Katcher's left shoulder was throbbing and, although it was manageable, he also had a splitting headache from the rock lump on his head.

There were some people that sought refuge at the autotram station but this was not a safe area and there was some evidence of attacks, with laser bullet shimmering on the roof and walls of the autotram station, and, although there were no bodies in the station, there were trails of blood on the platforms of the station. Too tired and injured to worry about anyone following them down to Anika-6, they moved towards the tunnel access point.

It took them a while to come back down to Anika-6—exhausted, overwhelmed and emotionally drained after the loss of their two partners—Scanlen and Renalda—and they were unsure about what their next steps should be and what the unfolding events on the surface meant. Katcher was injured, and they weren't as careful to cover their tracks on the way back down to Anika-6.

Despite the uncertainty, as least the descent to the underground offered respite and a temporary sanctuary—but it was a question of how long. Once the mayhem on the streets dissipated, Biocrime would instigate a clean-up operation, retrieve as many of their own as they could, and look for Katcher. He knew that would be the only option available to them now, and they'd be looking for retribution.

Banda unlocked the thick tungsten and titanium control door with a hand scan and they straggled through the antechamber and slammed the door shut behind them. Once in, they were greeted by Weller's replacement, Silas Newton, one of the five remaining hacktivists in Anika-6.

Newtown moved seamlessly into taking on superior responsibilities after Weller was killed when the cavern roof collapsed during the Biocrime drilling, and was doing whatever he could to fill the breech. He'd been monitoring the events from the surface through the personal private network and although he saw the failure of the uprising, he was a dedicated member of the Movement and decided to remain underground.

"You're hurt Jonathan," Newton said. "We'll get some food into you and get some nanos for the shoulder. And you Greta, all okay?"

"If you think a total fuck-up and everything is disarray is okay," Banda said, "sure, things are okay."

"Hasn't turned out as planned, has it," Katcher responded, ignoring Banda's sarcasm.

"Nope," Newton said. "Mav was sure it would all work out, but maybe we should have done the final testing after all."

"Maybe, there's always a maybe," Katcher said. "We had to act when we had to. What's the assessment from the surface?"

"Our viral videos are still appearing," Newton said, "but you probably would have seen that most of the billboard lightscreens have been vandalized or deactivated. It's still up on personal lightscreens, but it seems like most people are using off-line systems, game playing, old news, old visuals."

"How long before Lifebook comes back online?" asked Katcher.

"Probably a few more days. Mav had a secondary system that he was going to instigate after this first intervention… something more permanent. It was only theoretical, but something he said he could do once this algorithm had reached a certain time and frequency.

"He's the only one that had the knowledge and information about it—I mean, it's all here encrypted in this datacard, and who knows what it all means."

"It means that we now know we can defeat Biocrime and close down its systems," Katcher said. "That's the important thing. It didn't work this time, but this adds to the future. Even if we're captured, there's other people that have access to this data material. Is that right?"

"Sure," Newton said, "some of the other units we have around the world that have access to this data can understand where we went wrong."

Katcher was tired, hurt and needed sleep. Newton handed him a nanopill, which he swallowed and waited for the drugs to start working on his head and left shoulder.

This had been a disaster, but he felt some consolation that it was possible to defeat Biocrime, albeit for only a few days. Others in the Movement now had the knowledge and the know-how to take this path to the next step. He thought about how different life would be today if others had taken this path three or four hundred years ago, how much easier their next step would be.

He was defeated for now, but still, this was a good result in the long-term desire to change the world for natural humans.

He looked over and saw Banda lying down on the mattress, but she was already asleep. He lay down next to her, but almost as soon as he was horizontal, he'd fallen asleep too. The nanopills started to do their work.

*

It was late evening in the Biocrime headquarters, and Don Capone flicked through reports and monitored the assessments coming in from Officer Dyson. He was tired, it was late, but even though there wasn't much for him to do practically, he needed to be at the headquarters and be seen to be doing things. He was playing a high-level difficulty game of chess against Deep Blue—the number one interactive chess app—but he was sharp as a tack and fluctuated between the critical parts of his chess game and the real world when he needed to. Like the baseball player in between pitched balls, he psychologically switched off when he wanted to, but switched back on when any new details or information came to hand.

He was half-thinking about strategies and 'what-if' scenarios for the action on the ground, and his next move against Deep

Blue, contemplating whether he needed to defend his game using the Budapest Gambit. He was keeping his mind active while he waited to digest and interpret the next round of analysis from Officer Dyson.

"You want some pizza, Don?" asked Officer Dyson, struggling in the Sudoku game she had just commenced.

"Sure," Capone said, thinking about how many hours it had been since the last time he had eaten anything. "Just the usual margarita, if that's available—something up?"

"No, not really. We're progressing as planned—I'm getting all the data from downstairs that they're on track to disable all guns in the region at sixteen-hundred hours tomorrow, but there's probably a bit of C.Y.A. going on down there."

"Cover your ass?"

"Yep. They'll say sixteen-hundred, but that's probably a case of under-promising and over-delivering. I hope that's the case, and they can close off gun access by about midday. People are still being cut up down there."

"They're doing what they can," Capone said. "I know fuck all about coding and hacking, but I'm sure they know how to stop this virus."

"Well, you probably know more about it than the guys upstairs. What do they do up there anyway?"

"They're like the partners of Biocrime," Capone said, "the 'think tank', with Luanda at the top. They work out ways of generating more income for Biocrime, partnerships with different larger-scale businesses that work for the populace— you know, BioMed, BioEd, universal income.

"They're not really concerned about the human factor here, or the killings—this will cost them the big bucks, but now they're trying to work our ways of minimizing the damage— like retrieving all the universal income accounts from the people that have been killed, or new ways to crowd fund the clean up, or getting the costs of cleaning up the virus."

"Sounds boring. Just as well I'm just responsible for coding. So, there's the four of them up there and their team. Why aren't you up there too?"

"Because I'm the strategist. Strategy, that's what I'm all about. I'm not interested in the games of money, or the games of thrones up there. Luanda's been the *el presidente* for about four years, and the others are scheming to take her job. She knows that I'm not interested in being a partner, but she uses me as a buffer and support against the others. It's just standard political games, which don't interest me."

"But you want to be at the top, don't you?" asked Officer Dyson, anticipating their pizzas would be ready soon.

"Yeah, sure," Capone said, "just not in the way they do it. I want it be on my own merits."

"Well, you'll be waiting a long time," Officer Dyson said, raising her eyes cynically. "What if we can't end this virus. What happens then?"

"No-one really knows. I guess that's why they've got all their team and staff up there, go through all the 'what ifs' and actuaries looking at how it affects the bottom line in the long term, break-even points and that type of shit. I guess we're interested in the 'what ifs' to end the crisis, they're just interested in the money side."

"You had a scan of Katcher," Officer Dyson said, "I saw the scans on the internals this evening. He's out there. It will take a while, but we'll catch him."

"Sure, but then it's a question of what we do with him when we find him. We've got high-profile stalkers that were working on insiders leaking secrets to others in the Movement, and they'll work on finding Katcher, once we get these systems back on line.

"Pizza?"

*

It was the crack of dawn, and Officer Dyson was in front of her lightscreen; her team had been methodically analyzing and assessing incoming data and material, through a combination of data aggregators, apps and data-bots. The large room they worked in had that aroma of all-night human activity, the combination of perspiration, bad breath, suppressed flatulence, and stale pizzas and synth coffee. Many people had fluctuated between Capone's office and the floors above but Capone and Officer Dyson were the constant presence throughout the early morning.

Capone had caught up on some sleep through mini-naps, alternating between monitoring assessments and his moves against Deep Blue, and sips of strong synth coffee, not so much to keep him awake, but to keep him alert while he was awake.

"Good news Don," Officer Dyson said, moving over to Capone's desk with her synth coffee. "The team downstairs have cracked the coding for the guns, and say they'll have them deactivated by nine. And that's precise. The coding has been calculated and formulated to round up at nine-hundred hours."

"That's the under-promising and over-achieving in action, right?" Capone asked. "And what's the bad?"

"The carnage on the streets is severe," Officer Dyson said. "Still going—we've estimated maybe about a hundred thousand dead—natural humans and Technocrats—and continuing until we complete the first stage of closing off the guns."

"Fuck, oh fuck. One-hundred-thousand. Let's see."

Officer Dyson summoned basic live visual footage from the streets, and while power supplies was still functioning, every frame they viewed had a similar scene of death and destruction; the common factors of fire, and bodies strewn on the ground. In other scenes, areas were completely untouched—like the wildfires that burn large areas to cinders, but inexplicably leave small pockets alone, as if to indicate their ferocious appetite for destruction had limits—a strange sight, where apartment blocks in Technocrat zones were operating as though nothing had happened, while just five-hundred yards away, a scene of total calamity and disaster.

One-hundred-thousand deaths from a city population of thirty million people was less than half a per cent, but it was still a large volume—Technocrats and natural humans—and it had all been instigated in less than a day.

"So, another three hours of this," Capone said, as he contemplated the visuals on Officer Dyson's lightscreen. "But at least we're getting to the end of it."

*

Gavin Pinkston and his assorted gang had been on an eight-hour killing rampage, fueled by amphetamines and the constant smell of blood. His gang was one of the many that had filled the streets, leaving a path of destruction behind them. His loose alliance of a gang grew to a peak of sixty-six, but was now about half of this number; many were attacked by other gangs—attacks usually based on just their looks— but, more typically, because they happened to be in the way of another whirlwind of destruction.

Pinkston's actions weren't political, or looking to address any historical antecedents of his forbearers. It wasn't intellectual, or even based on revenge. It was pure nihilism, wanton killing and destruction. He had no cause to follow, no history, and no desire about the wellbeing of humanity. He was the lead killer, and had randomly mown down around five-hundred people—humans and Technocrats alike. Like many others, he was addicted to a cocktail of his drugs of choice and the mindless war games he played through Lifebook. Once Lifebook came crashing down and with it, his endless access to online war games, he needed to find something to replace it, and once he had full access to a lethal laser gun, there was no stopping him. He wasn't yet one of the one-hundred-thousand dead that Officer Dyson had documented, but he soon would be.

It was one minute before nine-hundred hours. Pinkston's last drug-fuelled and maniacal attack—this time, an eight-year-old girl that had lost her way and was separated from her family. He had reached the peak levels of his hallucination and he imagined the girl was an alien being with thin two-feet long spikes surrounding her body, and razor-sharp teeth as large as an alligator's.

Like many of his other victims, he killed her by aiming at the skull, and shot her straight through the head. She was only eight years old, but his drug-induced mind told him he had to kill her before she killed him. He looked like a death warrior, with specks of blood spray covering most of his jacket.

He rested momentarily, before continuing on his killing spree. He lined up another group of targets: this time, there was a group of six people that, in his mind, had massive claws like the talons of an eagle, each with a dragon's head and the body of a gorilla dressed in military fatigues. He tried to shoot from his laser gun, but there was nothing. Pinkston didn't know this, but it had just ticked over to nine o'clock, the expected time that all laser guns would be deactivated. He kept trying to shoot and realizing that nothing was changing, he tried to run away from his own hallucination.

He ran and turned back behind him to see he was still being chased by his imaginary dragons. The fires that he was surrounded by and his hallucinations led him to run over a tall bridge, and confident that he was jumping into water, he leapt over the railing, hoping to find the comfort of cold calming liquid. But it wasn't water. Pinkston had jumped over the railings to a four-hundred-feet drop, and landed directly onto flat concrete, his skulled shattered, internal organs ruptured and most of his two-hundred-and-six bones broken.

The killing spree for Pinkston had ended, as it soon would for the many others still rampaging the streets. The guns had been silenced, and there was still a great number of deaths that would soon follow in the aftermath but, at least the biggest impediment to restoring order had been removed.

It was the prompt for Biocrime to reclaim the streets.

*

'Guns don't kill people; people kill people'. This was the fashionable catchcry of the National Rifle Association for around three hundred years from the end of the twentieth century. It was the classic disprovable 'chicken-or-egg' argument: guns don't have the free will to kill, people do; but if the guns weren't there in the first place, the killings wouldn't take place. But then the next corollary: if the guns were already there, other people would need guns to protect themselves, a form of half-way thinking between an escalation of arms and mutually-assured destruction.

Eventually, it was the National Rifle Association that won out in this public debate, with legislative changes by the US Congress in the year 2238 to remove restrictions on all guns and weapons, and citizens were guided by free will to obtain whichever weaponry was available to them.

Through crowd-decisions and the limits that became socially and publicly acceptable, and through many technological changes, the CX-44 laser gun became the common form of personal defense weapon—the two-mode gun with stun and kill features—controlled and authorized by Biocrime and with the kill functions that were available to less than one per cent of the population.

Drug-fueled street rats like Gavin Pinkston were social catastrophes in-the-waiting—access to guns for these people made them lethal killing machines and once they smelled the blood of their victims, there was no turning back.

At 9:00 hours, when all guns were deactivated, there was still no let up. To be sure, the guns were silenced, but the combination of drugs, hallucinations, vengeance and the knowledge of being able to act with impunity, was still a destructive force.

Pinkston was dead, but there were many others that were picking up where he left off, appropriating any weapons they could find: wooden pickets, iron bars, sharp objects, knives and, if they could lift them, broken concrete slabs and rocks.

There was still a large danger on the streets but, without access to guns, the balance of power shifted to a more even keel. Technocrats could now defend themselves again, and take out the more destructive elements surrounding them. And without guns on the streets, Biocrime could now activate their retrieval services and reclaim San Francisco, street by street.

Within an hour of the guns falling silent and through their personal private networks, Biocrime headquarters had authorized the release of their tank services from their barracks on the outskirts of San Francisco—these were the most expensive services Biocrime had, and all partakers and contributors to the clean-up would be paid in arrears, once the streets had been cleared up and Lifebook was back on line.

There were four hundred and seventy security tanks available to Biocrime, each with around fifteen service officers and robocops—a task force of over seven thousand—and all were navigating their way through the city, beginning from the perimeters and working a pathway through to the center. They couldn't be a match for the million or so citizens on the streets armed with laser guns, but now the gun threat had been entirely removed, violent miscreants and street rats were easy pickings for these large tanks.

They positioned themselves on the outskirts of the city and moved through in a web-like structure. Each tank monitored hot spots throughout the city and their surveillance sensors pushed the other four hundred and sixty-nine tanks into a different direction all over the city, to the next available problem spot. It was a massive co-ordination process, and while most of their actions were *ultra vires*—they killed with impunity—they had a job to do and had to restore order as quickly as possible.

All of the actions of the security officers and robocops were visually recorded as they went ahead with their work— they had to if they wanted to recoup the massive costs of this operation through crowd-funding—and beamed back to Biocrime headquarters.

Looking out from his level fifty-six vantage point, Don Capone inspected the street damage with his high-powered telephoto lenses, and there were more access points appearing on his large lightscreen, where he could call up visuals from any of the four hundred and seventy tanks on the streets.

It wasn't pretty: he motioned up one screen from Tank 386, in the heart of downtown San Francisco—there were thirteen Biocrime agents rounding up a team of street punks. They disarmed all thirteen of their appropriated weapons and shot them on the spot, moved their bodies to the side of the street, and moved on to the next location. So much for the 'do not kill' motto of Biocrime.

In essence, Biocrime's actions now were to stop the violence, and clean up the streets, but it was also a message to others that the uprising had failed and there were consequences if they didn't desist, disassemble and go back home to their apartments.

While he was viewing incidents from the streets on his large lightscreen, Capone summoned up research documents published several centuries ago by the medical journal, *Lancet*, relating to the psychological affects of universal income levels on the citizenry, income differentiation and collective punishment and crime. He was working on new strategies to implement after the uprising was put down—he didn't want to get ahead of himself, but he was confident by the end of the week, this would be all be over, Lifebook would be back online, and the clean-up operations and rebuilding of the social system could commence.

He was also confident because he could tell through the global Biocrime intel, that the uprising was almost non-existent in many other parts of the world, and the few hotspots were it did flourish in Los Angeles, New York and London had been quelled, mainly through a loss of interest from the populace, and stronger security presence in the field.

He looked over to Officer Dyson—it was early afternoon and she hasn't slept for thirty-six hours. He'd had his power naps, topped up with synth coffee, but she was the real trooper.

"You're not tired?" asked Capone.

"Of course I am," Officer Dyson responded, eyes glued to her lightscreen. "Wouldn't you if you hadn't slept for almost two days? I'll take a nap when the time is right."

"Any updates? I've got the vision coming through from our tanks in the field. It's hard to watch, but since the guns went down, we've made a lot of progress."

"Well, I've got nothing that you haven't got on screen. I've just got a summary of what's happening on the ground—one-hundred and fifty-K dead, Biocrime doing their sweep through now—probably another ten thousand dead from that action. We're still working on getting Lifebook back—probably three or four more days for that."

"And any updates on Katcher?"

"No, he's disappeared, the cowardly cunt," Officer Dyson said nonchalantly. "He might have been killed but we're not sure. We've picked up an I.D. on the location of Scanlen and Renalda—nothing on them in our archive—as we expected—but they're gone. Dead. I'll get the scans up for you."

The cowardly cunt. Capone focused on those words—he didn't need a supreme genius to realize that was the Biocrime propaganda campaign against Katcher in a nutshell. Not exactly those words, but the sentiment. If Katcher was still alive, and they captured him, he'd be set up as a traitor who left his cause, left the battle to others to fight on his behalf, and scurried off like a rat in the ranks. He spoke to rally his troops for all of one minute and, when the going got tough, he sought shelter, rather than fight from the front. It wasn't the real story, but it would become a brilliant entrée into the propaganda war against Katcher.

If Katcher was still alive, once the crowd-trials were set up, Capone could see massive revenues coming in for Biocrime and a high rating in the verdict. And, for Capone, a possible move to level fifty-seven, or even higher.

"I've got this report almost completed," Capone said. "Let's go up and see Luanda in about thirty minutes and after that, you can have a nap. And that's an order."

"Okay, captain. I'll get my work ready and we'll shoot on up."

The elevator up to the penthouse was a steely cubical, no frills, and a basic design. It was only another four levels up but Capone noticed the streamlined look of the steel and the platinum finishes. He rarely took notice of the details, but today he felt was on the verge of a grand achievement, and challenged himself to appreciate the finer points of the interiors. These were all common features of modern architecture—sleek finishes to streamline thought processes and productivity. Neutral colors to avoid influence of thinking and workflow in any way: an extension of the *feng shui* in his own office, the type of thinking Biocrime wanted. Clear and pure results without interference.

Luanda greeted Capone and Officer Dyson once they came out of the elevator: she was a lot more satisfied than yesterday and the pathway to a solution was much clearer today, even though there was still a massive amount of work that needed to be completed before she could claim success.

"It's looking much better than yesterday," Luanda said. "I'm up to speed on all the facts, but let's hear what our next steps are straight from the horse's mouth."

"The guns have been deactivated," Officer Dyson responded. "That was a big step—ahead of time at nine o'clock this morning. We estimate there'll be up to two-hundred-thousand killed on the streets—because the guns had high killing rates, there won't be too many serious injuries on top of that, so there'll be lower follow-up medical costs—that's an issue for BioMed anyway."

"Lifebook—that's the big one—when's that coming back on?" asked Luanda.

"We estimate three more days—the big issue was getting the guns deactivated, and we've now got all the tanks from the outskirts of the city into field. That's pretty much stabilized the situation, but it will take a few more days to clear out the riff-raff."

"And the other big one—Katcher—any sign of him?"

"No, not yet. No sign of him dead or alive. If he's dead, we'll locate his body when Lifebook comes back online. If he's still alive, that's something we'll have to work out later."

"Don, what about that surveillance stalker you had on the case—Lestre?"

"She's our best," Capone said. "But, like everyone else, she can't do much until Lifebook comes back online."

"Well, authorize her to make a posting for the capture of Katcher—if he's still alive. And money, what about the money?"

"We'll work out the strategy—which we'll test through a confidential focal group—but the essence of it is to depict Katcher as the deserter, the useless cunt that tried to set up a revolution the second time around, couldn't his act together and, when the going got tough, he fled."

"Anything else?" asked Luanda.

"Another recommendation is to tithe the universal income for natural humans in the San Francisco region—it's collective punishment for Katcher's actions, destroy his legacy, and incite hatred for Katcher among humans and Technocrats too—the guy who failed the revolution, has now caused their living standards and income to drop, as well causing the destruction of half of the city. It's an argument we can't lose."

"And the other major issue—the leaker in our own ranks?"

"Lestre and her team will be onto that as well—we were down to checking our last fifty security officers, but that was before the uprising. These will be big crowd-trials, but if we can get the source of the trade of secrets, this will be the biggest ever—the source of revenue will more than pay for the destruction on the streets, and a handsome windfall for Biocrime."

"And maybe a windfall for Captain Capone and Officer Dyson," Luanda said. "Thank you for your work. It's not quite time to start measuring up curtains in the upstairs floor, but there's always the possibility of a move."

*

Banda and Katcher slept for as long as they needed to, but Katcher was the last one to arise and he groggily woke up to see Banda seated at the end of her mattress, sipping on a synth coffee.

"How's your shoulder?"

"Still hurting and burning," Katcher said. "Much better than last night, but still hurting."

"How many nanomeds did you take?"

"The three high-powered ones, two for the shoulder, one for the lump."

"You might need a bit more to top you up. A synth for you?"

Katcher nodded. He needed an upper after the drowsiness caused by the nanomeds. The pills he took were the more advanced onset nanomeds, the strongest form available. They were a concoction of narcotics to ease the pain, but also relaxed the body so all of its energy went into tissue repair. While Katcher slept, the nanobots in the pills travelled through his bloodstream, working on his injured shoulder and facial lump.

The facial lump was left alone—that would heal itself over time, and localized pain killers and disinfectants were released to stabilize the wound. The shoulder was where the main damage was, and the nanobots inspected and repaired the internal damage. Luckily for Katcher, it was mainly muscle damage and because the laser bullets he received were ricocheted, they only went two inches into body.

While he slept, and once the nanobots had completed their internal repair and diagnostics, they sent a laser signal to a small medical robot in the Anika-6 medical room to start up and patch up the external work. About the size of a child's hand, the medical robot resembled a wafer-thin metallic spider, similar to a large cellar spider. It walked along the ground, climbed onto Katcher's sleeping body, positioned itself on his left shoulder and started to perform the needlework required to close up the wound.

The sutures surrounding the wound were precise and perfectly formed, a total of eight stitches. His shoulder would be sore for a few more days, but the nanopills ensured that he'd make a full recovery.

The small leftover team at Anika-6 was setting up the links between their private data systems and the outside world— they only had the remnants of the Biocrime surveillance system through their personal private network, but it was enough to let them know the uprising and their actions to implement it had failed.

Banda brought the synth coffee over to Katcher's resting place and sat down next to him, her body language suggesting a half-way point between defeated disappointment and delusion.

"We acted too soon," Banda said. "Too soon."

"You can't just keep waiting for the right moment," says Katcher, "you have to act when you can."

Banda rightly felt like it was the end of the world but Katcher tried to enthuse her with the same words he used with Newton the night before.

"Every revolution has its time and place Greta. This might have been fucked up this time around, but see it as a testing ground. The work that we've done will make it easier for the next group of people. And the next people after that.

"We're just a passing part of this, just like all the people before us over the past thousand years. Our time will come."

"But we won't be part of it," Banda said. "I wanted to see this happen, and I wanted to see it happen now."

"Well, just imagine if there was a group of people three hundred years ago that achieved what we have today," Katcher said, "our role would be so much easier. Consider it a gift to our future generations."

"If there is a future generation," Banda said. "If Biocrime catch us, that's it, we're mincemeat. Off to that fucking stupid island in New Zealand."

"It might not get to that. We've got a few more days here; let's recover, recuperate and work out our next steps."

Katcher let his thoughts drift. Always the optimist, he saw the actions over the past few days as a victory, and would continue to do this. It was partially the effects of the narcotics from the nanopills, combined with the synthetic coffee, that were giving Katcher the ability to think clearly, but he felt powerful, even if this power was buoyed up by opiates and self-delusion. He would ponder and think for several hours before fading back into a deep sleep. He would also recuperate, for sure, but there was another series of dramas to follow, just around the corner.

***

BOOK 4. END OF MEMORY

"We are the offspring of metropolitan annihilation and destruction, of the war of all against all, of the conflict of each individual with every other individual, of a system governed by fear."

—Ulrike Meinhof

CHAPTER 26.   TAKING BACK SAN FRANCISCO

Don Capone looked out over the San Franciscan horizon, a sight he could never get sick of. It was day five of the uprising, but as the on-ground surveillance became more complete and more sophisticated, he could see the progress of the operations. It wasn't quite time to instigate the clean-up: the first task was to restore order on the streets, and while there were still many skirmishes on the streets, San Francisco was a city of thirty million and to reach this level of progress within five days was still quite an achievement.

"We've got to update Luanda in about forty minutes," Capone said to Officer Dyson. "Progress on Lifebook? Still a few days away?"

"You've got it," Officer Dyson replied. "This has been the fastest development of apps, bots, algorithms, hand coding—you name it—I've ever seen."

"You'd hope so. How many thousand people are working on it?"

"The hack damaged quite a lot in Lifebook and Biocrime, including back-ups. And back-ups of the back-ups. All this predictive stuff, binary and trinary code. We're doing well, but still a few more days to go."

"How many more days do we have to listen to Katcher's shit for?" asked Capone. "At least we can bypass a lot of it up here. Down there? I'd be ripping up a few of those screens too. It must be like waterboarding torture."

"It goes hand in hand," Officer Dyson said. "When we get Lifebook back up, that's when Katcher's stuff comes down as well. And then we can start work on finding him, who's behind this, and finding the mole within Biocrime—that's if it's just the one."

Capone and Officer Dyson collated their data, and hurried up the elevator up to Luanda's penthouse office. They exited the elevator into a full meeting with all the 'second-in-charges', support staff, tacticians, strategists—Luanda, as usual, was heading the table and, by now, there were around forty people in the conference room.

"Friends," Luanda started, "we're starting to get on top of this crisis, the biggest to hit our city, and the world, in over forty years. We hope to have Lifebook and Biocrime profiling back online within two days, the streets have been stabilized and then the clean-up operation begins. And, of course, the small task of finding Jonathan Katcher, and all the people behind the uprising.

"There will be a massive cost involved in rebuilding and restoring confidence in the systems, but I will now ask Brian Kasprovich to outline the details for this. Brian…"

Kasprovich commenced his outline of all the details— reducing universal income for natural humans by ten per cent as collective punishment—which would create some problems for the economy, but it was more important to implement this punishment than concerns about fiscal rectitude and fiduciary responsibilities—amortising costs over twenty-five years, by which time the local economy would grow to a level of three point nine per cent of gross zonal product…

Capone started to glaze over all of the facts, figures and key data that was appearing on the large lightscreen, and Kasprovich was someone who liked to read verbatim from a presentation, rather than extemporizing—so it made for a boring presentation, and it was material which Capone would synthesize at a later time. For all of the years of technological civilization and advancement, Capone couldn't understand why many presenters of this type of material felt it necessary to read word-for-word what the rest of the world could see in front of them, as though he was some kind of three-year-old child that needed every single word thrown back at them.

The points outlined by Kasprovich were all Capone's—good ones of course—after all, as chief strategist, he was the one that devised all the points of order. But, it was the same age-old system: The underlings produced all the work and created all of the ideas, only for those further up the production chain claiming all the credit.

In a nutshell—and according to Capone, it could have been wrapped up in about five minutes—Kasprovich outlined the damage to the community and infrastructure was great; many people had lost their lives; the uprising had been neutered; Biocrime was securing the streets; Lifebook would be back online in a few day's time; the full clean up would commence after that; the cost would be great, and recouped over many years, and the natural humans were going to pay for it, as collective punishment.

But Kasprovich carried on, squeezing out all interest of the discussion by laboriously outlining each issue—it might have been of interest to others, but Capone knew the plan in microscopic detail.

The meeting dragged on for eighty-three minutes, all spoken conversation was recorded and translated into text, and all documents tables were scanned and available for future reference. Luanda took back control of the conference meeting after Kasprovich ended, and prepared the group for a special announcement.

"Thank you all for being here," Luanda said, "I think we've got a plan to implement order back to the streets of San Francisco and I thank you all for your great efforts.

"I'm very honored to invite Richard Framton to speak to you, one of our most creative and influential entrepreneurs—you all know who he is, and he is a great friend of Biocrime. Richard…"

*

NOTHING GOES TO WASTE

Richard Framton was a free-wheeling entrepreneur, on the look out for marketing and money-making opportunities. He was a Technocrat of the highest order, and San Francisco's wealthiest man through his company, Origin, and being the wealthiest man in San Francisco also meant he was the wealthiest man in the world.

But he didn't become the city's wealthiest man with a do-nothing, clean approach to life. He was corrupt, had his enforcers, and would crawl into any deep hole or up a rat sewer to find a source of income.

He pulled deals together fast, used psychological games and tricks to implement his deals, and exploited any situation for personal and private gain. The uprising created a grand opportunity for him and his business interests. Although there had been great mayhem on the streets, he was cocooned from it within his fortressed compound and personal security detail.

Before arriving to the meeting, he was in his personal visuals production suite, with a team of image and sound designers, putting the finishing touches to a series of visual advertisements and billboard messaging for his new product of a range of premium pet foods, including 'Canine Pure', 'Sassy Treats', 'Royal Organic Black Hawk', and 'Paw Paw Premium'.

His team of musicians created the voiceovers and soundtrack for these advertisements—sophisticated inspirational ambient music, with deep soothing female voices, enticing the audience towards these new premium products: "Your pet is your best friend: She deserves the best". The visuals were sophisticated montages, with a sleek black cat, walking perfectly over the rooftops at midnight during a full moon.

Within the space of forty-eight hours after the uprising commenced, Framton had stitched up a lucrative five-way deal between Origin, Biocrime, BioMed, BioLaw and BioCycle, a niche waste management company.

The deal involved the immediate clean-up of the streets of all human bodies and left-over body parts—including any animals that may have been caught in the cross-fire during the uprising. All bodies would be removed of all clothing and any personal effects, and recycled through resale, or re-manufacturing.

The bodies would be sanitized through BioMed products, which removed rotted flesh and any organic content that contained unwanted bacteria not fit for animal consumption.

Suitable meat and bone would be crushed and processed into a wide range of products, including sausages, steaks and cat biscuits. These are premium and boutique pet food products catering for the more affluent families and pet owners around the world and, as it contained real meat, would command a price roughly around ten times the price of comparable synthetic food products.

Biocrime and BioLaw provided the legal groundwork and establishing precedents for this clean-up and commercial operation. Framton was part of the winner's circle and this was a victory for unbridled commercialism and capitalism. This was a world where nothing goes to waste.

Framton made his presentation to the Biocrime executive team: his plan was accepted in full and the session ended with hearty applause and a standing ovation.

CHAPTER 27.   LIFEBOOK COMES BACK TO LIFE

It was a race against time for Don Capone. The meeting with the upper echelons was perfunctory, and he was back in his level fifty-six office with Officer Dyson, the space where he felt more comfortable and free of the political and bureaucratic distractions. He'd been in the Briocrime headquarters for the past six days, and while he had his ensuite with all the personal accoutrements, he rarely left his desk—except for the briefings with Luanda upstairs, or to lounge across to collect yet another slice of pizza from the food processor.

All the plans for the immediate clean up of the city to remove bodies and other organic matter were ready to go, but the longer the plan to instigate was delayed, the more likely the city would start to move towards a biological health hazard, and while the citizenry was still dealing with the shock of what had taken place over the past six days, there was always the chance the next wave of violence could start up, unless the central lifeblood of Lifebook returned online.

Biocrime tanks had stabilized the city, but was there another batch of hacking to come that they didn't know about, one that could reactivate the guns again, and ready to arouse another bout of violence? This was Capone's main concern, that there was a litany of unknowables that could be anywhere, and could appear at any time. His world, and the world of many others, was based on knowing what the near future looked like and, at the present, no-one was quite sure.

"What's the latest Janet?" asked Capone, crunching on another piece of old dry pizza.

Officer Dyson was glancing up and down on her lightscreen, summoning and swiping different key data around the lightscreen, checking on her coding team downstairs, with real-time updates.

"It's hard to say," Officer Dyson responded. "Like I keep telling you, it's a sophisticated hack, almost like a perpetual motion machine that just keeps going. It's not impossible to stop, but solving it is a bit like a creative thought—the solution might appear in a few minutes, or it might take a few months. Or a few years."

"You know we haven't got that amount of time," Capone snapped, knowing Officer Dyson wasn't too serious about the solution taking that long. "Upstairs is worried about the money and lost revenues, and that type of thing. And then there's the health hazard on the ground. I can almost smell it from up here."

"Well, that's not possible—we're too high up and we're in a bubble. Your olfactory senses are playing with your mind and you're imagining it."

"Maybe. Maybe it's the smell of stale pizza that's getting to me. Or it could be—"

"—oh, fuck! Fuck!"

Officer Dyson's lightscreen momentarily flashed up her Lifebook account. It was only up for several seconds, but she noted that it was in exactly at the same state as she left it before the uprising started, and then tinkered over to some of her other profiles, and then Lifebook blacked out, and reverted to the ongoing Jonathan Katcher broadcasts.

"We've got some movement happening," Officer Dyson said. "Lifebook was only up for a few seconds, but I think the team might be on the verge of defeating the hack."

"Who's responsible?" asked Capone. "They'll deserve a medal if they crack this. Call him up on the screen."

Officer Dyson summoned up Officer Paul Jurgen on her lightscreen, the leader of the anti-hacking team, into a three-way visual conversation, and they waited for him to accept the datacall.

After a few seconds, a beady looking unshaven face appeared on the lightscreen, through the internal network. It was Officer Jurgen. He was antisocial, and taciturn, but could talk the leg off a chair when it came to coding, hacking, computers, and anything remotely related to technology.

"Janet, we've cracked the code," Officer Jurgen said. "I must say, I was very impressed. It was a combination of ancient codes like Woda and XML—stuff that we hadn't seen for centuries, mixed up with different systems. It would have taken a few geniuses to create this but, luckily, we've got more than a few geniuses here. We'll have to keep the team running it for a while, but with the apps and bots doing their work, we probably won't need as many coders on the case—they can take a rest."

"What stage is it at," asked Capone, "and where do we go from here?"

"The first step is to cut out Katcher's viral videos. The flash of Lightbook you saw on your screen was us circumventing his code, and seeing how long we can run it for. As always, it's still theoretical, but we'll fully put in our code in about an hour—it should remove Katcher and put back our systems in place.

"It's taken a while, but it was like mixing Pythagorean theory, ten cryptic crosswords, three-D Scrabble, and then throwing in a few diabolical Sudoku puzzles all into the mix, and doing that at a hundred miles an hour with one hand behind your back."

Capone didn't fully comprehend the analogy Officer Jurgen presented—perhaps if he'd mentioned a chess reference in a grand play-off between Gary Kasparov and Magnus Carlsen, two players regarded as the best ever in history, he might have understood—but, at the least, he recognized the amount of human resource that had gone into resolving the problem.

"Well, I appreciate your efforts," Officer Dyson said, as he signed off and motioned down the datacall.

"What's the verdict?" asked Capone.

"First, they'll get rid of Katcher on the screen," Officer Dyson said, "and then our code will do its work—scrub out the hack, disinfect systems, and reinstall Lifebook. According to Jurgen, the hack was a brilliant piece of work—closely resembling our work here. I guess that's what the leaker was getting up to, providing secrets about our coding plans for the future. Ripping us off, probably selling it on the black cryto-market, and fucking us over."

"Don't worry," Capone said. "When we catch whoever's responsible, they'll burn. And then we'll get Katcher and his team, and they'll burn too. It's what they deserve."

*

Modern apartments, for most people, were designed for minimal engagement. Most were used for sleep and personal entertainment—small, secure, and laden with small technological gadgets and personal cell devices. The action of the civil world took place outside of the apartment blocks and on the streets of life—commerce, fitness, leisure, intellectual stimulus, eating, dining and wining.

Except for the people like Marine Lestre, whose life was taken up with surveillance and her new special assignment to find the people that were leaking secret material to the Movement and, if she was lucky, finding Jonathan Katcher.

Since the uprising, like so many other people, she'd been holed up in her apartment for safety, but without any technology—except for the constant droning of Jonathan Katcher's revolutionary ramblings—there was not much more to do except for be fearful and wait for the next steps to take place. The incubators containing the three fetuses were unaffected and still functioning normally, despite the calamity in the outside world, and Lestre had more time to think about a future beyond the uprising and whether life would ever return to a semblance of normality.

The apartment she shared with D'Souza faced away from the streets, so she hadn't felt the brunt of the attacks or the laser bullets that had afflicted other parts of this apartment compound. The front of the building had bullet marks and the signs of several spot fires that were easily put out by residents. No-one had been killed in her apartment compound but, then again, it wasn't at the center of the major uprising and had been spared.

Lestre was like a restless tiger—no physical activity, no lightscreen time, no interaction with the outside world, except for basic text updates from Don Capone through her personal private network. She had more information, albeit sparse, than anyone else in her region—it wasn't much, but gave her more reason for hope than others. She received one important piece of information: a brief text message from Capone that the hack was close to being successfully defeated—without knowing the timeframes, she was confident she'd be able to get back to work on her cases soon.

D'Souza had been stoned for six days, following an unrelenting digestion and inhalation of a wide range of low-level drugs and old-style hashish, just to pass the time. Asleep on the couch, he wasn't fully aware of what was going on around him, but he decided days ago that if the world was going to end, he wanted it to be a happy ending, an artificial joy aided and abetted by his constant drug taking.

Lestre glanced through her back window, and saw a Biocrime tank slowly moving down the backstreet, with security agents scanning the perimeter, using their laser scanners to assess damage, and record any casualties. It was mainly a show of strength from Biocrime but to also provide the citizenry with a sense of confidence that life would soon return back to normal.

This area was a Technocrat stronghold, so the damage was minimal, but Lestre noticed as the tank and security agents passed through the backstreet and disappeared to the next zone, the large billboard lightscreen that had been playing the Jonathan Katcher messages over the past few days blanked out for several minutes, followed by an advertisement for Amore synth coffee.

She moved back inside and summoned her lightscreen to reboot, the system NextGen icon appeared, followed by the 'Life is Lifebook' start-up screen, and the lightscreen set up Lestre had before the uprising commenced, exactly as it appeared six days ago.

Within a minute, there was an incoming level nine datacall coming through—from Biocrime—which meant it could only from one person.

She accepted the datacall to reveal the disheveled, unshaven face of Don Capone.

"Marine? I guess you know what this call is all about."

"You've defeated the hack and Lifebook is back?"

"Well, that's stating the obvious, but yes, we've done it," Capone said. "We did some pre-testing and put it back online about twenty minutes ago. Biocrime profiling is back too. You would have noticed through my updates on your PPN, that there's been a lot of death and damage, but we've stabilized the streets, and the clean up will commence soon."

"And the cases? To be continued?"

"Oh yes, most definitely. We had a few other stalkers working on finding the leaker at Biocrime, but they've been killed—our resources in the field are down a bit, but yep. Finding Katcher is the top priority, but finding the leaker might lead us to Katcher, so I guess you know what needs to be done. And when we find them, off to the penal zone they go. I'll send through the authorization to lodge a post for Katcher—if it comes off, big bucks for you, and a few less people to worry about."

"It's all good Don," Lestre said.

She knew Capone was a busy man, and it wasn't the time for any small talk, but she signed off from the datacall, and started scanning through her lightscreen. Even after only six days, a endless habit took time to rekindle, but Lestre took only a few moments to refamiliarize herself with her tasks, and slowly reorganized her workspace.

She had work to do.

*

The blue Origin vehicles travelled down every street of San Francisco, looking out for every dead body they could find— not that it was difficult. Many bodies just lay where they fell, some had been there for almost a week, collecting flies, ants, rats—anything that could find its way to the feast of flesh.

By now, the rotting bodies had become a biohazard, and no amount of public deodorizer could cancel out the stench that was permeating through several sectors of the city.

But, encouraged by the profit drive, Origin proceeded efficiently and effectively. There was great money to be made in the clean up, with the added bonus of recycling organic matter, and making a healthy profit there too.

The process was very clean and very efficient. Origin officers and robohelpers scanned DNA samples from each body they came across to confirm identities and, now that Lifebook was back online, automatically notified the next of kin that all financial and physical assets of their dead relatives were to be acquired by Biocrime, with percentages instantly distributed to Origin and all other providers in the clean-up operations.

The Origin vehicles could transport up to forty bodies at a time, and with a bounty fee of €5,000, each vehicle would generate €200,000 by the time it returned to the processing unit on the outskirts of the city. The vehicles were multi-function but were usually used to transport frozen foods and medical supplies around the city and on this occasion, the full fleet of one-thousand vehicles would be used for the clean up, meaning the removal of all dead bodies from the streets would take around two days, with a gross income of almost one-billion ucas, and that was before any of the organic recycling commenced.

Each vehicle filled with bodies collected from around the city arrived at the processing center, a facility normally reserved for animal waste product processing. The facility had the same stench as an abattoir, with some alleviation through public deodorant so at least it wasn't as overwhelming as it could have been, and could be tolerated for a certain period of time.

The processing center was as clean and efficient as the collection of the body parts from the street: there was a long conveyer belt, where bodies and body parts were placed on the belt, and whatever clothing that could be removed, was removed by a team of robotic arms and some manual human workers, assessing whether the clothing could be sold and, if so, the likely value.

Most of the personal effects from the bodies had already been pilfered on the streets, but there were still some smaller items found in pockets, such as small rings, personal visual recorders and, in some cases, personal cell devices.

After everything of value was removed, the bodies moved through the processing unit's central conveyor belt, initially sprayed with hair removal liquid, a primary jet spray wash, and then sanitized with a range of BioMed products—the end result would only be animal food, so it wasn't the premium disinfectant, but the inexpensive budget product which disinfected anything that could be hazardous, even for an animal, and removed any bacterium and toxins that may have built up in the body.

The next stage involved the crushing of the bodies into meat—everything went in, including skin, bones, organs, teeth—and then distributed into eight different vats, each with their specialist synthetic flavors: traditional chicken, fish, lamb, beef and pork, and some lesser novelty flavors, with the inclusion of vegetables such as potato, pumpkin and carrots, with apple essence.

From here, there were distribution points, channeling the meat into dry and wet areas: dry, where meats were rolled out and cookie-cut into small bite-size shapes, and dried under heat lamps; wet, where the meat was inserted into small plastic sachets, and shrink-wrapped.

The end result was a collection of packaged products in sleek black, fashionable plastic packaging and meat packs that would be sold in premium locations around the world. These were long life products, to be kept in cold storage, in a remote warehouse that was linked into sophisticated supply chain logistics. At the end of this process, there would be over twenty-million individual pet meat products for sale, and at an average retail price of €50 per item, the sale value was around one-billion ucas. The work was nasty, but somebody had to do it and, for a good price, Richard Framton and his Origin company were the ones to do it.

All up, the value of the clean up, just of the body parts, was two billion ucas—and most of this would end up in the coffers of Origin. Some would go back in graft to Biocrime, as well anyone else that needed to have their palms greased to get this job done, provided in one of the more obscure crypto-currencies.

It was the way business had always been performed but, in the modern world, it was just a few swipes at a lightscreen, as well as a few datacalls with the right contacts, and it was a done deal.

CHAPTER 28.   THE SEARCH FOR KATCHER

It was a good day for Marine Lestre. She'd just been authorized to complete the task of finding Jonathan Katcher and, if she was successful, it could possibly net her the greatest crowd-funded bounty ever. But, first, she needed to plan out her strategy—Katcher could be anywhere, cloaked by decoders and in a remote location undetectable by Biocrime scanners.

She roused Marlon D'Souza from his drug-induced stupor to work on this case too—her skills were brilliant but more analytical, while D'Souza's input tended to be more lateral and more radical, a style of thinking aided by his drug habits.

While the city was being cleaned up rapidly—two-hundred-thousand dead was a great number—the return to technology proceeded at a much slower pace.

Lifebook was just coming back online but the local citizens were slow to go back to their addiction. Lestre decided it was best to create the crowd-fund posting for Katcher early and get the ball rolling—for such a big case, whatever she created would first need to be approved by Biocrime, as they had to be certain to avoid the mistakes from a decade before, when Katcher eluded their net.

Lestre created a new entry through the Biocrime profiling and spoke into her cell device.

"Capture and trial of fugitive Jonathan Katcher."

As with all of her other postings, an auto-fill voice completed the description:

Jonathan Katcher was the sole cause of the recent revolutionary and counter-social upheaval in San Francisco, caused the deaths of 200,000 citizens, widespread destruction of community property, and undermined the safety and security of all citizens.

In keeping with his cowardly mindset, Katcher has retreated to an unknown location, and we are working towards his capture and trial, and to ensure these types of actions cannot continue into the future. Detecting his location and his capture will enable us to find and delete others who have been supporting this counter-social upheaval, to further protect the citizenry and the community from further harm.

Course of action: Arrest, detention, trial and deportation.

Crowd pledge: €10

Below the main screen, Lestre collated a series of visual montages, depicting scenes of the aftermath of destruction, actuality footage of wild street gangs shooting their laser bullets at unarmed Technocrats in their apartments, hyperlinks to Katcher's history, and a series of articles about the technicalities from his previous trial in 3024, and how it was highly unjust that Katcher avoided capture and deportation at that time. It was a highly emotive posting and framed Katcher as the sole architect of the upheaval. Satisfied with her work, she needed an audience of support before she delivered it to Biocrime for their approval.

"Marlon? Come and check this out before I send it to Capone."

D'Souza dragged himself over to check the posting on the screen, nodding his approval.

"It's fine," D'Souza said. "Biocrime will want to add their part to it too, change a few words here and there. It's good. But the key is how are you going to find Katcher? He could be anywhere—he could even be dead."

"Well, if he's dead," Lestre said, "that would be great for the community, but not good for us or for Biocrime—no money for his capture, no show trial, no deportation. We need to find him alive. Where would you start?"

"At Biocrime itself," said D'Souza. "There was a suspicion of those agents that were handing secrets to the Movement. It was down to the last fifteen wasn't it?"

"It was, but they couldn't be sure about all the others either. It was old-style policing work—where were you, why and all that sort of questioning. They're no good at that psychological interrogation anyway, but then the upheaval started. They had other priorities."

"Biocrime is outside of the lightcapture system, right? Why not bring it into the system, just for a few days and see what happens?"

"Fuck, don't you think they would have already thought about that?"

"Maybe. But they haven't done it—"

"—no, but it's not like they can just flick a switch and that's it. Plus all the security and hacking issues. They just wouldn't do it."

Lestre liked D'Souza for his ability to think outside the square and come up with ideas that nobody else would think of but this one seemed too far outside the square. She sent through her proposed posting for the capture of Jonathan Katcher to Capone and pondered D'Souza's suggestion to temporarily include Biocrime within lightcapture and genetic recording—she didn't think it would be accepted, but would try.

One hour later, Lestre's lightscreen lit up with an incoming datacall—it was Don Capone and, as D'Souza suggested, there was a series of minor changes to the text of the posting, as well as the addition of more visual footage and historical material and information about Katcher—all negative, of course.

"Marine? We've removed the embargo on the posting and it's ready to go—our legals also changed the Biocrime revenue percentages from fifty to sixty-two per cent. I can't do much about that—nor can you—but they want to extract as revenue as possible to support the clean up. I hope you understand."

Lestre wasn't in a position to do anything about the change in revenue percentages but a big case like this, if solved, would lead to untold personal revenue. She wasn't fussed.

"If I complain, no-one's going to listen," Lestre said, "so what's the point? I'll make the posting go live in a few minutes. One other thing Don—is it possible to include Biocrime within lightcapture and the world memory bank, even temporarily?"

"Of course it is," Capone said, "but why would we want to do that? Every hacker and scammer would be into us as soon as we opened it up. Is this about finding our leaker?"

"Yes," Lestre said, "I've been thinking through every option and possibility, but finding our leaker will lead us to Katcher. Even we can get a rough location—or can find out if Katcher is still in San Fran—it would be a big help."

"We thought about that option, but the security risks to Biocrime are too great. We've already asked our data officers if there are any options along these lines, but everything leads back to security issues that we can really budge on."

"Okay," Lestre said, accepting that it was a stupid idea in the first place. "Can you send me the details of the remaining fifteen officers that we need to check? I'll do some psycho-testing on them."

"Sure, but you'll have to come into Biocrime for these ones. This stuff never leaves our domain."

Lestre wanted to move on this quickly and prepared herself to go to the Biocrime headquarters—she allocated her approved posting and let it sink into Katcher's Biocrime profile. The posting was distributed through the continuum and allocated to GoFunder.

Soon after Lestre allocated her posting, Katcher's Biocrime profile was prompted on watch lists all around the world. While Lestre prepared for her visit to Biocrime headquarters, she monitored her lightscreen, and within several minutes, the GoFunder crowd pledge to find Katcher increased to €3,000. As she exited her apartment door, Lestre glanced over to the lightscreen and the figure increased to €8,000 and by the time she arrived at Biocrime headquarters—just over forty minutes later—the bounty had increased to €125,000.

If Lestre could find Katcher, she would crack the jackpot.

*

"How's your shoulder feeling now?" asked Greta Banda, rousing Katcher from his deep slumber.

Katcher awoke and gained his bearings, unsure how long he'd slept for. He momentarily had a blank mind before he remembered the events of the preceding days and composed himself for about twenty seconds before responding to Banda.

"Still painful but it could have been worse. I'd forgotten how painful those laser bullets are."

"They're not used for fun. They're meant to hurt."

Banda's response annoyed Katcher, and he wondered whether she fully understood the events of the past few days and the gravity of the new situation.

"We were lucky to get out of there alive," Katcher said, "but we won't be able to stay here for much longer. Once they've got their systems back online, they'll be looking for me."

"They're already back online," Banda said, "while you were sleeping. Our work is down, and Lifebook is back up. Silas?"

Banda summoned Silas Newton from his workstation to bring a cell device to show Katcher how far things had moved above ground.

"Lifebook is back online, Biocrime profiles have just started up too," Silas said. "You might be interested in this profile Jonathan. Looks like they're after some special kind of renegade…"

Katcher glanced at the cell device, which depicted his full profile and posting outlining his bounty and capture, the large flurry of digital crowd data streaming down the screen, so rapid that it was almost indecipherable. But there were enough key words streaming down the screen for Katcher to understand the general nature of the animosity towards him, something that always been simmering under the surface, but unleashed through the posting released by Marine Lestre: *'traitor to the Movement'*; *'kill the cunt!'*; *'to the penal zone now!'*; *'death too kind to this fukker'*; *'get the coward!'*

"Four million ucas already… that's some bounty," Katcher said, scanning through his profile on the cell device. "You guys aren't thinking of turning me in are you?"

"We've got more than that in our third rate crypto accounts," Newton said. "But if you don't behave…"

It was all gallows humor. Katcher knew his situation was dire, the Movement had taken a huge step backwards, and he was responsible. He always held the belief that actions needed to be instigated whenever the fine slither of opportunity arose, not endlessly waiting for the perfect occasion that never arrived, or situations determined by others. He was firm in his philosophy of working tirelessly for the future of the Movement, even if it took another millennia of time and effort to achieve its final goal.

He thought of the antiquated idea of the return to Zion for Jewish people and how that, essentially, was a one-thousand-year idea that only gained traction in middle of the nineteenth century. It developed into a major international flashpoint in the Middle East for around three centuries and was only resolved after the role of China in international diplomacy superseded the role of the United States of America towards the end of the twenty-second century. It took time, but it was one issue that was resolved after the great effort by many.

He recalled other instances. Large edifices throughout human history took centuries to crumble—ancient empires, Rome, Britain, the Soviet Union, America, Russia, China—they all dissipated, even when least expected. The modern age was all based around entropy, and with the downfall of empire and religion, language and difference, issues like the Israel–Palestine conflict seemed to fall into insignificance, and age-old enmities were wiped away through an age of economic freedom and opportunity.

Would Biocrime fall by the wayside in the same way? For Katcher, it was a culmination of all the problems of empire: competitive nationalisms, corruption, propaganda, greed, all wrapped into one major problem for society. And all implemented and managed by heartless Technocrats that wanted to exploit the human condition and the tendency for human societies to gravitate towards fascism when faced with fear.

How would Biocrime fall, and what would take its place? When would this happen? What would happen between the Technocrats and natural humans? Would they all manage to live happily ever after, just like the Jews and Palestinians did in the twenty-second century, after the sands of time washed away their differences?

Katcher was unsure of the answers. A part of him wanted to remain in Anika-6 and secure everything they had here for others to take the Movement through to the next step. He knew Banda wanted to return to the surface and fight, but was that really the right answer?

He felt the Movement was not so much a political or economic struggle, but a biological one, and he was fueling his own doubts about whether he was the right person to take the next step. Was he the coward the citizen crowd was calling him, or was he positioning the Movement for a future that might not be resolved for another thousand years? His introspection was interrupted by Banda's impatience and her desire to get things moving again, even through she was unsure about what this should be.

"We have to get Biocrime intel on what their next actions are going to be," Banda said. "Secure our data, and then get away from here."

"But then what," Katcher asked. "We've got our decoders, but how long before Biocrime reprograms. We'd be sitting ducks above ground."

"We still need to find out how much time we have. I'll make the call to Kransich."

"Kransich? You don't think Biocrime might be clamping down a bit and maybe doing a bit more monitoring?"

"We've had secure conversations and data for three years through our PPN—I'll make a deal with him and see what he can do for us. He's a sucker and a risk taker. He'll do it."

*

Banda swung into action quickly and, after she secured her personal private network, she could see she still had a clear communication available directly though to Kransich. Katcher was correct in suggesting Biocrime were in the process of clamping down their security and monitoring their internal officers, but that would take additional time and resources from Biocrime, and until this work was completed, Banda and Kransich could continue with their secret liaisons.

She sent a request for a datacall to Kransich and after several denials of service and unconnected calls, she finally made contact.

"Michael? We've got another deal."

"Greta, I can't do it," Michael warned. "It's too risky after the upheaval—it always is after any sort of drama, and this is the biggest event in over fifty years. I can't."

"What about five-hundred thousand ucas?"

"It's not the money, it's the security risk and the chances of being caught."

"You don't think after all this time we would have been caught before? Our systems are secure and will be for as long as Biocrime is outside the lightcapture system."

"Biocrime is mainly concerned about the clean-up," Kransich said, "and how it's going to recoup costs over the next twenty years. That's probably what its priority is. I'd say that it will keep the crowd profile for Katcher for as long as possible, to retrieve more income. It's got other things to concentrate on—the clean up—Katcher can wait. That's what I think—"

"—that's what you think, but what do you know? We need to find out how much time we have before Biocrime can realistically find us. We just need everything you can give us about Biocrime's plans."

"Look," Kransich explained, "it's going to be really risky and I'll need some time. I could stay past my regular times today. How about two-fifty thousand for trying, and seven-hundred if I get the data?"

"One-hundred for trying, eight-hundred for the real data. But we'll need the data quickly."

"Mmm. High risk, more money. I'll get what I can and meet you at the apartment. It's a deal."

CHAPTER 29.   THE END OF A DOUBLE AGENT

In Biocrime's headquarters, Lestre moved past the concierge and changed into her security vest. After this, she met Capone in the security zone, greeted by his outstretched arm.

"Greetings to you, good to see you in person again," Capone said, firmly shaking Lestre's hand.

"And to you Don. Looks like I've got a bit of work to get on with."

"You certainly have," Capone said, as he summoned Lestre to follow him into another security room, filled with lightscreens and several Biocrime data researchers.

"Here are the files on the fifteen final officers—that's not to say that any of our other officers have been fully excluded, but we've done as much testing as possible on those. What we have been able to do is exclude the possibility of collusion, so we think it's just a lone wolf, operating on their own."

"And all of the final fifteen have full access to all Biocrime data and material?" Lestre asked.

"Yes. They're some of our top agents—everyone here is vetted before they start for skill level, psychological tests, character, loyalty—all scored a hundred per cent."

"Well, let's see what we can find," Lestre said, as she moved closer to the large lightscreen. She scanned her finger over the lightscreen which recognized her genetic match with Biocrime data and permitted her to read through the profiles.

"Anderson, Browning, Courtney… mmm, not very interesting names," Lestre said, continuing through the list. "Ah, an interesting name at last—Kransich—how long has he been around for?"

"He's been with Biocrime for some time," Capone said. "Seems like a bit of loner, keeps to himself. Why did you single him out?"

"No reason. Different name, different to the rest. Good looker. Let's surveil him, just to see what he gets up to. Can we do anything with his decoding serum?"

"No, but even if we could he'd know in a flash that it wasn't working."

"Well, let's do something really old fashioned and prehistoric. I'll tail him and see what he gets up to."

"But that could take forever. And if it's not him—what next?"

"We move onto the next one… Lienstein, Mitchell, Nitshcke, O'Brien, Smith—there's always a 'Smith' isn't there?—Thyssen… we just keep going. In the old days, it was called 'going undercover'. Fancy a bit of old-school police work?"

Capone agreed. Biocrime had considered options outside of the computer systems, but anything that didn't use technology was deemed to be useless and primitive, beneath the modern life of Technocrats. If it couldn't be resolved with technology and gadgetry, it wasn't worth resolving.

"Given the timing, there'll be nothing like starting right now," Lestre said. "I'll set up a PPN as a recruitment zone for the people I need—Lumbardo and Marlon are already a part of it. Agreed?"

"D'Souza?" asked Capone. "He's not too drug-fucked is he? You think he'll be secure?"

"Sure, he takes his drugs," Lestre said, "but he knows when he needs to be on the 'up' and when he needs to be on the 'down'. He's the lateral thinker—I'm the 'yin' and he's the 'yang'. Lumbardo's the real enforcer, he'll put him into line."

Lestre scanned the lightscreen and picked up the Biocrime profile for Michael Kransich. She had virtually selected him randomly, but had a hunch about him. If he wasn't good for a lead to Katcher, she felt he'd be good for something else.

"This will get the ball rolling," Lestre said. "Interesting profile for Mister Kransich, I'd say. Loner, keeps to himself. Very good looking. Where is he today?"

"He logged on at eight-fifty this morning. Because he's one of the ones with decoding serum, we don't know where he is. But we know he's in the building."

"And after he leaves the building?"

"He's decoded—that's the whole point. We don't know where he goes, or what he does. Like the others, he's a combined security officer, spy, enforcer—he's like a 'five eyes' for Biocrime. Like the others, he was highly regulated, passed his regular security ops, flies under the radar. Just like any other good security officer."

"It's the good ones that usually turn bad isn't it?" said Lestre. "I can see he's got a reasonable income here, not great but not too bad. Does he seem greedy? Probably not. Maybe he's one of those Technocrats that gets into all that 'meaning of life' crap and *what it is to be human*. It happens. Has it happened to you?"

"Of course," Capone said. "Everyone contemplates their purpose in life and existentialism—"

"—no," Lestre interrupted, "I don't mean that, I mean all the 'where did I come from', 'what is it to be human, 'why am I a Technocrat'. All that stuff."

"Sure, I think about it, but I never question it. This is the right way—emotions get in the way of the choices that we have to make, that's why the humans are failures and Technocrats are in control. Why question when you're the biggest beneficiary?"

"Maybe Kransich—or whoever it is—started asking the big questions, the type of questions that have destroyed civilizations in the past."

"Maybe. But I guess that's why you're here, to get the answers to these hypotheticals."

"That's right. And I better get going."

Lestre scanned Kransich's profile and extracted everything she needed—profile images, genetic data, and the times he usually left the Biocrime headquarters. It was 15:30 and she'd worked out that she needed to wait in the Biocrime foyer between 16:48 and 18:25. Kransich had never left the office outside of these hours.

*

The foyer at Biocrime was a busy place at the end of the day, with scores of people leaving the building at this time. The auto exit register was not such an important facility—Biocrime wasn't so concerned about people leaving the building, but it did want to register that someone who entered the building had eventually departed. Entering the building was a different matter: authorized personnel were auto scanned and matched up to their iris data. Unauthorized personnel couldn't proceed at all.

The entrance and exit points in the foyer of Biocrime for high-level authorized personnel were a series of three-yard-wide holographic barriers. Visually, they had the same appearance as airport security doors, except there was no physical material. The holographic barrier impaired entry for everyone, except for those with iris clearance. Clearance was provided instantly and the hologram disappeared to allow the person through but, for other non-authorized people, the barrier was impossible to get through. It comprised a gradient of electrical amps through its three yards of holography—initially, a small shock of voltage as a warning, through to over three-thousand volts at the end of the three yard hologram. It was an effective deterrent and no-one had ever got past the two-yard point of the hologram.

Lestre sat in the concierge area of the foyer, her personal device was in the scanning mode, and switched to a small scale app version of the mainstream exit scanner, known within Biocrime as DataEx. She created a link between her device and Kransich's iris data, from the material provided by Capone. It was coming up to 18:25 and there was still no sign of Kransich. She checked his profile again, to confirm his regular departure times, just to make sure—18:25—it seemed unusual that for the decade he'd been working at Biocrime, he had an exit window of only ninety-seven minutes.

It was 18:59, and it was at this point that Lestre started to query whether her app was functioning or correctly set up, and whether Kransich had another device that could bypass the Biocrime's exit system and, if he did, what the reasons would be to do this. The amount of workers leaving Biocrime was now sparse and Lestre moved outside the doors of the building. It clocked over to 19:45 and she was on the verge of making a datacall to Capone, when the soft ping of her device altered her to an iris match. She followed the lightscreen on her device and looked across to see Kransich in his civilian attire as he walked through the auto exit register, attractive and confident, busy and business-like. It was 19:46 and he was out of there, but Lestre kept thinking: he was in Biocrime for eighty-one minutes outside his decade-long record. Why today?

Lestre needed to keep visual track of Kransich, casually and not too officiously in case he suspected her actions, but she decided keeping fifty yards away from Kransich was a reasonable distance. He headed for the autotram that took him to the southern part of San Francisco, the opposite direction to where he lived. *No need for concern*, Lestre thought. The city was recovering from an uprising, and there were parts of the city that were difficult to access, but there were still many areas that were operating as though nothing had happened.

Late night shopping, a dinner date, the gym—there were many reasons why people didn't go straight home—but in such a segmented city like San Francisco, they would at least go somewhere nearby their residence. Kransich was going somewhere completely different.

She followed Kransich onto the autotram—she didn't need to be completely incognito, but she didn't want to raise any suspicions and needed to keep her distance. As the autotram approached the autostop in South San Francisco, Kransich moved to exit, and Lestre moved with him—but there was a rush to get off the autotram and through the crowds of people, Lestre momentarily lost sight of Kransich but then picked up that he was moving towards a smaller village area, complete with eateries, street hawkers and old-style markets. It was dark now, and Kransich was wearing darker civilian attire, so it was easier for him to blend in with his surroundings. He didn't look out of place and neither did he feel the need to glance behind or suspect anything unusual.

It was a heavily populated area and like many other parts of San Francisco, it was hard to find some peace and quiet, but it was easy to find anonymity. It was getting harder to keep up and follow in the dark, but she continued to follow Kransich for another ten minutes through a convoluted route, until he walked down a smaller side street, towards a smaller block of apartments, just around the corner from the main streets. Lestre realized the circuitous route was Kransich wanting to remove any suspicions of his activities, and probably took a different pathway each time he ventured to this location, to avoid familiarity with any of the people that might have ever noticed him.

It was an obscured part of the apartment, unusually dark, and Lestre saw through the small fraction of vision she had from one-hundred yards away, Kransich knocking gently on the door. It was a quaint old-fashioned sight as, generally, people were automatically authorized to enter approved dwellings, until Lestre remembered Kransich had no recordable DNA and probably still used datacards or even keys to get into his own apartment.

Her views were still largely obscured but a door opened, followed by an exchange of indecipherable words, and the closure of a door after Kransich entered the apartment.

Lestre's thoughts wandered: Kransich has a lover in a human zone? It wasn't unheard of, but it could raise some suspicions for a Technocrat. Perhaps, but one of her best friends and crime-busting colleague was Lumbardo, and that relationship had never caused her any problems. But Lumbardo lived in a Technocrat area, and this area was human central.

It was hard to be nonchalant when her main purpose was surveillance, and Lestre wasn't exactly wearing the type of clothing that could fit into the surroundings, but she waited—it had been twenty minutes since Kransich entered the apartment block. Not that anyone would have cared, but she made herself look occupied by scanning her cell device, and called up 3D-WWF, a three-dimensional word game, based on the ancient board game of Scrabble. She had never played the game before, but she mindlessly swiped and swatted the screen, while she kept one eye on the apartment.

Her thinking continued to wander: should she move closer to the apartment? Should she try and peer through the window—after all, it was on the ground floor—would they be having sex? Would they be eating? Or just talking?

Lestre decided to stay where she was—she had a location and that, at the least, would give her something to work on. Time was important, but she needed to play a longer game. Forty-five minutes later and Kransich left the apartment block, walked and straightened himself up, an indication to Lestre that this had been some type of assignation, but she wasn't sure if it meant anything else.

Lestre kept her distance and, as she predicted, Kransich walked an alternative route away from the apartment, this time through a different part of the busy streets and markets. She continued her discretion, feigning interest in the wide range of wares offered by the street hawkers in the market, and waited until Kransich walked past and let him continue, and assumed he was going back to the autotram, probably on his way back home.

Wherever Kransich went now was not such a big issue for Lestre: she had some material and some information—Kransich had got off the autotram in the south—a natural humans stronghold, which raised a new set of questions and paths of investigation. Why did Kransich get off in the south of the city? Who did he know there? It wasn't a crime to go to a different zone, but in a city as big as San Francisco—and especially after the recent upheaval—everything that anyone ever needed was in their own patch. And why did he spend an extra eighty-one minutes inside Biocrime earlier today?

Was this venture just a friendly fuck for Kransich, or was he engaged in some risky business? Was he reaching his mid-life crisis where he started to ask *what does it mean to be human?* Who was in that apartment block? Female? Male? Lestre decided to walk back down the street towards the apartment and visually record whatever she could. The apartment was not exactly boarded up and secretive, and although she was now just a few yards away, it was hard to see what was happening inside, other than the silhouette of what appeared to be a woman appearing through the curtains.

Lestre tried to match up this location with Lifebook Live and any existing Biocrime profiles. She called up the location on her lightscreen and accessed the part of Lifebook that could show her what was going on inside the apartment, but the imagery showed an empty apartment, even though Lestre could see movement from her vantage point. A glitch? Some kind of data blockage? She decided that it was best to record some visual data and moved towards the window and planted a miniature light recorder at the window where there was a slight gap in the curtains, just so she could see who was inside. She moved away back to a distance of about fifty yards, and monitored the visual recording of the interior of apartment.

It was nothing spectacular: but she could see a basic loungeroom, very similar to the display that she saw through Lifebook—except in her live vision, there was an attractive woman sitting on the couch, finishing off a bowl of fried rice, and placed down next to another empty bowl. Was it dinner? Sex and dinner? Talk? Or was it all of these reasons? Whatever the case was, Lestre now had high-definition images of the woman in the apartment, and she could use her skills to try and find out who the identity of the woman. Would it lead to anything? Perhaps. But the apartment seemed to be off-grid and it raised many more questions than answers.

*

The trip back home from the south seemed to move quickly. Lestre thought through all the possibilities about Kransich and what he might be up to: a lover in the south, money, dare and risk, opportunity… or perhaps just plain company and a rice dish for dinner? And with a woman who was off-grid?

Lestre reached her autotram stop, still with some visual remnants of the recent uprising, but at this stage it was mainly Biocrime assessment vehicles and, as there had been little damage in her area, these vehicles moved through the site quickly.

She moved up through her apartment block, still pondering the different options and possibilities presented by Kransich. Upon entering her apartment, she moved past D'Souza spread-eagled over the couch—another late night marijuana-fueled session while viewing mindless pop-culture visuals—and moved into her workroom.

It had just ticked over to 23:00 and she transferred the high resolution images to her lightscreen and attempted a range of simple image matches and searches but came up with nothing. Lestre realized the woman in the apartment was an off-gridder, but what is she and who is she? She scanned through Lifebook and a range of Biocrime profiles using deep search tools and software scanners but still couldn't find anything. She then switched over to DNA mode in her search tools to access the world memory bank and, still, nothing appeared. She summoned to a different part of the lightscreen and entered a datacall to Lumbardo—it was late at night, but Lumbardo was always switched on and ready to go, almost like a human 'no-wait-state'.

Lumbardo accepted the datacall but, as with most things involving Lumbardo, a short Amore message appeared, informing Lestre her local specials were still available, but only if she approached her local store before 23:59 tonight. She tried to swipe it away, but it was up for another another eight seconds before the message disappeared. Lumbardo had collected his five ucas for the message appearing, and Lestre was left wondering whether he would still promote these banal messages for the sake of a few ucas, even if the world was facing doom with a fired inferno ball heading towards it.

"Ah, Gordon," Lestre said, "just the man I want to see. Remember those deep DNA search tools you've got?"

"Uh ha. What about them?" asked Lumbardo. "They were beta tools and not fully tested, but for a small fee you could use them if you want."

"If I *what?* Fuck Lumbardo, just send them through—I need them. Urgently."

"Well, what are you trying to do? They might not be the right tools."

"I need to get some interpretive DNA and predictive lightcapture sampling. I've found someone that doesn't exist—"

"—this I'd like to see," Lumbardo interrupted. "You've found someone that doesn't exist. You've solved the eternal philosophical paradox of all time. *I exist, therefore I'm not*, the absence of presence, all in one fell swoop—"

"—look, don't be a stupid fuck. You know what I mean. I've come across someone that doesn't exist on Lifebook or Biocrime."

"That's probably just someone off-grid—could be just a low-life human," Lumbardo said.

"Sure, I realize that, I wasn't born yesterday," Lestre responded. "But if a Biocrime security officer meets up with them, I think it could be a lot more than that, don't you?"

"Oh. It's not the Kransich guy you were talking about?"

"That's the one."

"I'll send the tools through the PPN—I'll be over in five."

The tools Lestre wanted were straight from the beta testing lab at Biocrime, which Lumbardo purchased with black crypto-currency. He knew Biocrime officers sometimes sold internal materials on the dark net, but they were usually items of commercial interest: he'd not heard of operational matters being leaked out before. The beta software, codenamed Karl-499, was created to fill in lightcapture gaps in case of technical glitches, and detect attempts to circumvent Lifebook and Biocrime profiling, including Biocrime's own decoder and lightcapture cloaking system.

The software was still in its rudimentary and developmental state, but would complete the holy grail of full and permanent lightcapture—predicting and suggesting DNA evidence and light, in those cases where it had been removed or destroyed. It was still another decade or so before it could be completed, but it would then fully enable Biocrime to surveil any part of the surface world, even if the DNA evidence didn't exist.

Karl-499 could only provide small samples of information, but tried to match up any data or information—such as from

Lifebook—and provided clues or samples for actions that may have taken place in the past.

The rap on the door was not as loud as Lestre expected, and she barely heard it, but it could only be Lumbardo at this time of night and she eagerly opened the door to let him in, replete with his advertising banners and messaging, even at this late hour.

"I think you've got something, very promising. Is he up to speed on this too?" Lumbardo asked, glancing over towards D'Souza.

"He's on all sorts of things at the moment," Lestre said. "Best to let him sleep. This needs some literal thinking, not the spark in the sky or some obtuse thought patterns. Check this out."

Lestre moved the lightscreen towards Lumbardo—she'd already activated Karl-499 and accessed key data material from Katcher from over the past three months.

"Look," Lestre said, pointing to several snippets of visual footage on the lightscreen. "This is during the time the viral code was first released—Katcher at the community hub, finishing up his stupid lecture, and then walking on his way home. Fast forward: the autotram, his apartment, cooking, watching his lightscreen. But then, check this out."

Lestre pointed to another piece of visual footage on the lightscreen. It started off exactly at the same point as the recorded light data, but then had some variations where Katcher was walking somewhere else, and with another person in tow. The footage was not very clear, but they could definitely see Katcher and a woman, walking off towards the food area nearby.

"Check all the Lifebook data for Katcher's lecture on that day," Lumbardo said. "Now, let's see. Thirty-one arrived on the day, looks like there's five off-gridders, and there was one newbie on the day—DynaMiteMax. That's odd—DynaMiteMax enrolled to go to six sessions, but didn't attend one of them."

"Hang on," Lestre said. "I'll upload the visuals from Biocrime from the uprising—Karl-499 can predict obscured images of people? We've got a few citizen images from the day Katcher made that speech last week—"

"—if you think a one-minute speech is a speech," Lumbardo interrupts, "then go ahead…"

Lestre admonished Lumbardo with a roll of her eyes, but continued. "My high res photos from the apartment and the photo of the speech—compare them."

Lumbardo loaded the photographs into Karl-499 and within twenty seconds, completed the complex algorithms and produced the results on screen.

"We've got a few affirmatives," Lumbardo said. "It's confirming Katcher, Scanlen and Renalda, but also confirming the other woman in the photo, and the woman that accompanied Katcher after his lecture, and the woman you took a photo of a few hours ago are the same person. I'd say DynaMiteMax is the woman you saw in the apartment a few hours ago. And I'd say that she also receiving the materials from Kransich, and providing Biocrime secrets to the Movement. Well done, Marine. I think you've cracked the first part of the job."

CHAPTER 30.   MEMORY EXTRACTION

Don Capone's face when it appeared on a lightscreen was one of those faces that appeared more surreal televisually. His jaw seemed more jutted than it did in real life, and it made him look less animated. Still, his enthusiasm couldn't be masked when he accepted the datacall from Lestre and she explained what she saw and how she thought Kransich was implicated in the uprising.

"So, Kransich is the leaker," Capone said, almost with a nonchalance that suggested he'd seen this type of act over the years, if not to this level. "He was pure when he was first enlisted, but I guess it's a bit like those religious priests from yesteryear—you know, close to a non-existent God, being the model of excellence to everyone in the community, yet, behind the scenes, fucking married women, abusing young children, taking drugs and pilfering the coffers of the church."

"You don't seem surprised," Lestre said. "Were you aware of Kransich or any others?"

"Kransich does surprise me," Capone said, "and I didn't suspect. But it sometimes happens to security officers after a while—they're highly intelligent—but that's when they start getting into personal philosophy, query their existence, all those questions—'why was I born in an incubator, not inside a mother', 'why me, not them'. And the good old one—'what does it mean to be human'. I'm sick of all that bullshit. Why not just do your job and not worry about those sort of existential things?"

"Perhaps you might be the next one to crack, Don. How long have you been at Biocrime? Fifteen, twenty years? So close to the top of the food chain, and you'll crack—that's what will happen."

"Unlikely. I've not had one scintilla of questioning or a sniff of the existential crisis. I'll be in this job until the grave, not wasting my time thinking about whether it was better to have monkeys as my ancestors, or born into the hospital incubator."

"So, what's the next step," asked Lestre. "Detain Kransich, shine the light above his head, waterboarding, play some loud pop music, psycho-torture?…"

"You love the old-school practices, don't you," Capone said. "So I don't think I'm going to disappoint you. We start off with the easy way. Offer up all sorts of inducements for information exchange—promotions, say that their actions have resulted in Biocrime being able to make arrests and deportations, they're being moved to a special undercover Biocrime unit that trades secrets with the Movement. They're always surprised to hear about this—which they should be, because it doesn't exist—and begin to believe their actions are part of their expected work. That preps them for the next stage, which I have to admit is on the verge of torture. Give them a batch of hallucinogenic drugs which plunges them between near death and the afterlife and they'll just about cough up anything. We can only do it once, because it fries their brains, but we usually get the information we need."

*

In the early morning hum of the Biocrime office environment, Kransich was scanning for any other data he could provide to Banda when the message came through on his lightscreen.

Michael, there are new opportunities within Biocrime and wanted to hold a quick meeting to gauge your interest. Meeting can be held at 13:00. Signal Y to attend, N for another time.

Thank you, Mikhalia: People and Resources.

Kransich started to panic. 'Mikhalia' was a synthetic bot, and these were routine messages sent through occasionally, whenever Biocrime had vacancies for superior work, or additional tasks in times of crisis, such as the recent uprising. Kransich refused offers over the past three years, and assumed the people and resources unit had given up on any work promotions for him and had pushed him out of the information loop.

Why now? Had they suspected something? He read through the message again—there was no 'out'—there was no option to say 'yes, he was interested' or 'no, he was not': it was only an option of when to have the meeting—now, or later. It was 10:44 and Kransich needed a few more minutes to collect his thoughts. *Do they have anything on me? Is this just routine? Is it to enlist more people after the uprising? If I select 'N for another time', does it suggest to Biocrime that I'm stalling?*

Kransich summoned his lightscreen to respond, sent a 'Y' to 'Mikhalia', and received an immediate confirmation.

Meeting confirmed for 13:00 in Surveillance and Operations, Zone 43-X. In attendance: Officer Capone.

Thank you, Mikhalia: People and Resources.

*

Kransich had sweated for several hours before he managed to compose himself, and he arrived at Zone 43-X in the Biocrime building at 12:58. As he entered through the door, he was greeted by 'Ramona', a holographic assistant who confirmed his approach and attendance.

"Michael Kransich, thank you for attending the meeting today. Mister Capone is waiting for you inside. You're a few minutes early, but you can go straight through."

Although she was a hologram, 'Ramona' was discrete and professional, and always a welcoming sight to all that ventured into this office.

"Thank you Ramona," Kransich said, as he entered the antechamber of the room where Capone was seated. Capone summoned Kransich to come forward, without making eye contact with him.

"Sit," Capone said as he pointed, and Kransich dutifully proceeded to seat himself in the comfortable recliner, unable to determine whether Capone was being naturally curt, or because he had suspicions about him.

Capone shuffled around on his lightscreen, reading data and moving back and forth between his lightscreen and his cell device. Occasionally, he put up his finger to indicate 'one more minute' but Kransich knew this routine. It was to put the guest on edge for that extra period of time, pushed up their anxiety levels, and lowered their resistance so they'd provide more open answers to questions. As well as increasing the chances of becoming severely impatient and annoyed.

It was an entire seven minutes before Capone finally got down to business, but for Kransich, it felt like seven hours.

"I'm sorry about that Michael, but there's always things on the go," Capone said. "Pleased to see you again, it's been a while."

"Yes, it certainly has," Kransich responded. "Good to see you too, and hope I can be useful."

'Useful'. It was a word Capone focused upon in his mind. *Fucking useful.* In front of him was someone on the inside who had traded Biocrime secrets, probably amassed a personal fortune, aided and abetted a revolutionary cause that had killed almost two hundred thousand people and caused untold damage to the city of San Francisco. And he wanted to be 'useful'? Capone pondered for an extra minute or two. If he could reach out with his bare hands and throttle Kransich, he would, but there was a process that had to be followed and, besides, they hadn't received full confirmation of his actions.

"Stating the obvious here," Capone said, "but there's been quite a lot of mayhem in the outside world, and it seems like Jonathan Katcher has been one up on Biocrime, and we don't know why. As you can understand, we need to cut this off at the head, and we've decided to create a new team to directly deal with the Movement—like an undercover team—and we wanted to include our best agents in this team. Of course, the main part is to capture Jonathan Katcher, but we need to get back to being one step ahead of the Movement, not the other way around. We're just gauging your interest—higher grade, higher responsibilities, higher income."

Kransich wasn't sure what to expect, but he arrived at this meeting with his best poker-face to cover any secretion of guilt and other misdemeanors. Unknown to Kransich, behind the walls of the room in Zone 43-X was Marine Lestre and a small team of behavioral scientists and psychoanalysts, assessing every single move on Kransich's face through remote visuals, analyzing every skin fold and muscle twitch.

"Of course, I'm available to work on the capture of Jonathan Katcher," Kransich replied. "Nothing would give me greater pleasure. I could start working on an immediate plan."

"But," Capone said, "before we can introduce agents to this deeper level of work, we need to know everything about them—any crypto-work, trading secrets, spying—just so we can get a handle of what we're dealing with. As you know, Biocrime itself is a zone free of its own lightcapture technology and exists outside the continuum—you and me can get up to anything we like. It's a system based on trust, and that's how we make this whole system work. Is there anything we need to know about you?"

"Like what," asked Kransich. "I'm clean, always have been, always will be."

"Look, we all dabble in some sort of illegal activity," Capone said, "something we might not be proud about, and live to regret it. Even me, I was short of a little bit of money, the universal income wasn't working for me, nor was the salary I was getting from Biocrime—I just wanted that little bit more. So, I traded some Biocrime patents on the black cryto-market—no-one ever knew, and look at me now, five levels from being the boss of Biocrime. And you? Anything of that nature?"

"No," Kransich said, "nothing of that nature."

"If there is, you know, we can make things 'go away'," Capone said, moving his hands up and giving his words air quotes. "Just to have that level of trust—we all do it, but we're friends here. We can scrap any of that, and ignore it, we have the means to do that. But this is like an amnesty—because you'd never be able to do any of that when you move to the next level. And this would be the only chance to expunge these details. If we find out later on though, well, you're fucked."

Kransich was unsure whether Capone was telling him the truth. A high-level security officer close to the top at Biocrime engaged in illegal actions? Unlikely. Was Capone bluffing him so he would reveals his misdemeanors? He imagined any trading of secrets would be severely punished, not through death, but something close—deportation to a universal penal zone.

Did Capone know what he'd been up to? Kransich believed it was impossible because of his decoding—he was invisible to Biocrime on the inside, but he was also invisible on the outside. He correctly assumed Capone was bluffing, and quickly synthesized his answer into a clear succinct response.

"No, there's nothing that I've ever done that's illegal or counter to Biocrime's intentions," Kransich said. "Nothing whatsoever. I'd be happy to move to the uncover unit."

"Fantastic," Capone said. "I'll just confirm the psych-ops and then we'll take to you to the next level of approval."

Capone moved out of Zone 43-X, and into the room behind, where he greeted Bronwyn Cargill, the lead psychoanalyst for Biocrime, and head of the behavioral science team. Her smallish and demure appearance hid the fact that she was one of the best analysts in San Francisco, and was able to determine the veracity of people's inner thoughts.

Capone was keen to put Kransich through direct memory extraction, where receptors were inserted directly into the brain and could extract individual memories, going back all the way to inception and beyond. It was an extreme measure, and was only used in extreme cases. Direct memory extraction plunged the recipient into a half-way zone between death and afterlife, could only be done once, and left the recipient psychologically damaged for the rest of their life. And the process needed a special authorization from Bronwyn Cargill, backed up with evidence.

"What do you think, Bron?" asked Capone. "I think we've got our man, but it's all circumstantial. One of our freelancers sighted him off in the southern San Francisco zone, heart of the natural humans. It's a smoking gun—without the smoke."

"Yeah, I like that Don," Cargill said. "A smoking gun without the smoke. Where do you get these dumbs phrases from?"

"From the heart of my ass, I'd say. You like the way I said I was engaged in trading secrets, illegal activities? You think he believed it?"

"Of course not, you think he's a fool?" said Cargill. "But he's lying through his teeth. Look at this." Cargill zoomed into a part of her lightscreen that showed visual footage of Kransich's iris and then his eyebrows, to show minute eyebrow twitching, a slight dilation of pupils and a glowing iris. "He'd be great at poker, but he's in denial mode. The question is why."

"I'm not so concerned about the why," Capone said, "but whether we should take him to the next stage of interrogation. He's lying, but everyone tells lies. I'd think we have enough on him but, don't forget, this isn't petty. It's Jonathan Katcher we're after."

"We see this in a lot of Technocrats of his age," Cargill said. "It's unusual for Biocrime officers, but it does happen. Life's questions: 'where are we', 'what are we', 'who are we', and 'why'. They might mix with natural humans and they see a world they could never have imagined. Existential thought. Meaning. Emotions and feelings. The ones that fall for it start to think that it's a better world, or a better way of life.

Some get over it, some don't. That's where Kransich is at the moment. He's a lost cause for us now."

Cargill moved back over to her lightscreen, and brought up Kransich's profile.

"He was one of Biocrime's best officers," Cargill said. "But over the past three years, he's done nothing of note— no ambition, hasn't put up his hand for any promotion, or superior duties. It's like he stopped working three years ago."

"So, in your professional assessment," Capone said, showing the alacrity of a small dog reluctant to release a newly found bone, "we can proceed with direct memory extraction?"

"You know that I'm always reluctant to sign off on these processes," Cargill said with a cautioned look on her face. "I'm never a hundred per cent sure, and there's always the risk of getting it wrong."

"But have you ever been wrong before?"

"No, but that's because I've always exercised extreme caution, and try and get to as close to a hundred per cent as possible. I'm always worried about these things, but I'll give you your approval."

Cargill moved towards the lightscreen and looked at Kransich's profile, and the live visual footage from the room where he was seated. She didn't know Kransich, and had never met him. He was fidgeting on his cell device and she summoned the controller to zoom onto his face. It wasn't obvious on the surface but she saw a confused man, caught between two worlds, and struggling with his personal demons, wanting to do the right thing for both of those worlds, but succumbing to the age-old human flaw of corruption.

Cargill had a small glint of sorrow, but she needed to do what needed to be done. She called up another screen with a series of menus, and scrolled down to a list of procedural options, which included 'Direct Memory Extraction'. She linked the option with Kransich's profile and had one more glance at Kransich through the visual screen, then summoned the approval button, and quickly swiped the three steps of the 'Are you sure' options on the screen.

Soon, Kransich wouldn't be a part of either of the two worlds he tried to live in.

*

Kransich waited in the room in Zone 43-X, and scanned his cell device for world news and some scientific material from *Science Today*, one of the more popular sources for research. The latest headline detailed the clinical tests of pyscho-codeine on ants and how the benefits on insects could be transferred to humans to improve awareness and intelligence levels. Showing disinterest in whatever these benefits could be, he swiped across to the old ancient favorite, Scrabble, for a quick word challenge, just to fill in the time for whatever administrative tasks Biocrime needed to complete before he moved into his new undercover world.

He called up his current game, played against 'Marguerite', a player with an average game score of three-hundred and eighty-two, and a high score of six-seventy. He had a poor collection of letters, including 'Q', three 'Y's, two 'B's and one 'G', but before he could assess his digital board, two Biocrime agents stormed into the room, apprehended him and applied digital handcuffs before he had even the thought of being able to struggle away, and was whisked into an adjoining room, simply known as 'The Memory Room'.

Before he had time to work out what was going on, the Biocrime agents strapped him down horizontally, and injected a powerful sedative, *nicomorphenite*, a new age hallucinogen, combining phencyclidine and dextromethorphan, with traces of herbal elements, salvia divinorum, psilocybin and mescaline. On its own, it could result in a deep trip and likely death, but the Biocrime agents inserted electrodes into the side of Kransich's head and connected to a small lightscreen, which enabled Bronwyn Cargill to mix and match the way the drug would manipulate his memory synapses.

Within seconds, Kransich was meandering between his reality and misty-eyed memories. He fluctuated between his in-body and out-of-body experiences: his incubation thirty-five years ago, his first words, not only from himself, but all of his previous iterations, like a montage of his previous lives mixed into the one experience. His images and memories fluctuated from those of five minutes ago, to those from over a thousand years ago: his recent handshake with Don Capone in Zone 43-X, offering him a new career within Biocrime; on the fields during the Battle of Kosovo in Eastern Europe during 1389, where he was evading capture by the Turks and travelling through a field of impaled military prisoners.

His memory took him back three years, to when he first met Greta Banda, the many meetings and the sexual encounters, his feelings for her and the overwhelming sensation of engaging in deeper emotions for the first time, hearing the stories of natural humans and empathy, the first time Banda asked him to provide information and secrets from Biocrime.

His memory finished up with his most recent meeting with Banda, where he provided his final batch of Biocrime data files and material, leaving Banda's ground floor apartment, and discretely reappearing at the southern autotram station.

Kransich had gone back and forth between every memory of every one of his cloned iterations, going back to the thirteen-hundreds but, all up, the elapsed real time had been just over three seconds.

Cargill collated the visual data from Kransich's memory batch, called up the data on her lightscreen, and created a share zone with Capone and Lestre. Lestre was the one who would now move forward with the data, with Capone's oversight. Few words were interchanged between the trio, but Lestre was extracting the information she needed to proceed with her work for finding Jonathan Katcher, and Biocrime now had every piece of evidence they needed to detain Kransich, and apprehend his accomplice.

"We have what we need," Cargill said through her lightscreen, as she summoned the Biocrime agents to remove the electrodes from the side of Kransich's head and move him to the rehabilitation zone, where he'd recuperate in time for his crowd trial, and likely deportation to a universal penal zone.

Cargill retrieved some of the recent visual material from the data extracted from Kransich's memory and, together with Capone and Lestre, viewed the interactions between Kransich and Banda on her lightscreen.

"So, we have a name now," Capone said. "Greta Banda. Some kind of off-grid revolutionary. Good work Bron. It's difficult work, but it's what we had to do. We've got all the evidence we need against Kransich and this Banda woman, and then we'll find Katcher. We're getting closer."

The memory extraction was a very clinical process, but Kransich staggered after he was lifted up by the Biocrime agents and moved into rehabilitation. He would never be the same person again, but his recovery was essential to generate revenues through his Biocrime crowd trial. A feeble and defeated Kransich might gain some sympathy, but a resolute and defiant Kransich was likely to fuel animosity, resulting in a higher guilty verdict and higher crowd-sourced revenue.

Lestre moved to another part of the lightscreen, and accessed the history of Greta Banda. She'd been off-grid for twenty years, but Lestre secured her DNA details and created a new Biocrime profile, placing Banda back into the continuum. She entered the secure Biocrime profile zone, created a new task entry and spoke into her tablet.

"Apprehending Greta Banda, key fugitive in recent revolution and theft of Biocrime classified material."

The auto-fill voice completed the description:

Greta Banda has been stealing highly sensitive and classified material from Biocrime for three years, and providing this material to key members of the Movement. She was a leading figure behind the recent street revolution in San Francisco and her apprehension will lead to the capture of Jonathan Katcher.

She is off-grid and was last seen in the apartments of Miller Avenue, South San Francisco, believed to be her residence. Can be lethal, approach with caution, needs to be alive to extract key data and generate high revenues.

Course of action: Arrest, detention, leading to crowd trial

Bounty payment: €500,000

Lestre checked the text and approved the posting, and Lifebook allocated the task to the usual tasking and crowd funding systems. She felt she was getting closer.

CHAPTER 31.   AN UNTIMELY END

"I'm not a fool." It was one of Banda's favorite saying, wheeled out whenever someone stated the obvious to her, partially a defense mechanism whenever she felt she was being undermined. She felt her relationship with Kransich had been coming to an end; it was only a matter of time before Biocrime either caught up with him—or her—and she wanted to extract as much material from him as possible before this happened.

Initially, she thought the ruse with Kransich might last for a few months, but three years of receiving top level security files from the heart of Biocrime was about as good as it could get. Kransich was a sucker but he was well remunerated for his part within this Faustian pact. Banda never knew how Kransich spent his accumulated black crypto-currencies, but she really didn't need to know, nor could she care less. She always pondered about Kransich's motivations—whether it was the money, the dare, the risk of living dangerously—but, ultimately, she received what she wanted, and he was rewarded handsomely.

Every time they met—and it must have numbered in the hundreds over the past three years—the risk of being found out increased and, as time progressed, he seemed less concerned about ever being caught. For all of this time, had anyone seen

Kransich and his approaches to Banda's apartment? Did anyone care? It wasn't easy to be completely anonymous in this day and age and Kransich's decoder serum removed those concerns, each visit adding that extra level of dare and extra level of risk.

But everything had changed. Since the failed uprising, Biocrime was on additional alert, and Banda decided it would be the last time she'd make contact with Kransich—he had been used for as much as possible, he was expendable, and it was time to move on. And it was the last time she'd return to her apartment.

Like an advanced chess player, Banda tried to keep one step ahead of her opponents: although she wasn't aware of Lestre's surveillance the previous night, Banda had a subconscious hunch that she had to leave her apartment behind, not just for herself, but for anyone else, and decided to destroy her apartment and the pathway down to Anika-6. But pressure and a change in circumstances play on the human mind, and Banda was thinking on her feet, clouded in her judgments. It would have been best to advise someone in Anika-6 about her intentions but, like a failing gambler or someone knowing the odds are stacked against them, she behaved erratically and without strategy.

Banda secured a patch of Semtex to the base on her apartment, just next to the hatchdoor that led to the smaller tube tunnel down to Anika-6. Because of the lead-plutonium plaster lining, her app link wouldn't be able to detonate the Semtex package, so she had to improvise and used an old-fashioned technique—a countdown timer on a small cell device, linked to the explosives and set to destroy the building in seventy-five minutes—more than enough time for her to get down to Anika-6, seal the main door, and return to Katcher.

Banda knew Semtex was a powerful explosive, and she also realized the package would not only destroy her apartment, but also the one-hundred and forty-three others in the block—as well as killing anyone who happened to be inside at the time. But it would also block off access to Anika-6, and any evidence leading that way: for her, that was the most important factor.

She collected the data she'd received from Kransich the night before, and slithered down through the tube tunnel for the last time, crawling through the larger exit point and then to the circular chamber going down to Anika-6. Banda was clear and methodical, and used her lightpen to guide her way down to the control door. As she approached the control door to Anika-6, her timer showed there were forty minutes to go before detonation. She reached out to the genetic lock to open the control door, but it remained firm. Confused, she waved her hand over the lock, and then moved her body closer to the lock, but still it held firm. The genetic lock was synched to Biocrime profiling and as soon as Marine Lestre activated Banda's genetic coding through the continuum, her ability to access the genetic lock into Anika-6 was rescinded.

Banda thumped the door, but it was no use—the thickness of the door meant nothing could be heard behind the barrier. She accessed her cell device, but the signals couldn't penetrate the wall either. Someone—Katcher, Newton, or another underling—might be able to see her from their lightscreen in the one of the tents inside Anika-6, but no-one was expecting her right now and they all would have assumed Banda could let herself in through the control door. Banda weighed up the risk of either waiting for a chanced glance at the surveillance screens from someone on the inside—and who knew how long that would take—or moving back to the surface as fast as she could.

If she stayed there and waited, she'd suffocate from the dust coming through the tunnel from the explosion. She started to panic and looked down at her timer—thirty-eight minutes before the Semtex exploded and if she was to survive, she would have to reach her apartment in less time than it took for her to come down—going back uphill—and disarm the timing mechanism.

Realizing she didn't have time to waste, Banda started running back up the circular tunnel—it was hot, the air was sparse, and she wasn't clear about whether she'd be able to make it back in time. There were now thirty-three minutes left, and Banda needed to balance her timing, the air, and her ability to run—if she ran too quickly and exhausted herself, she would faint.

Twenty-three minutes. Banda was panting, breathing heavily and sweating profusely. Her lightpen reflected light from the walls of the circular tunnel, but the non-descript nature of the walls gave her no clues for how close, or how far she was from safety.

Fifteen minutes—Banda was sure she was getting closer, but that was based on a feeling, rather that any empirical evidence that might have mentally collated in her mind over the years. She'd been up this tunnel hundreds of times but she always travelled at a much slower pace and on this occasion, she was racing against a finite amount of time and space.

Banda came across the small part of the entrance tunnel, back to her apartment. Her timer indicated nine minutes before detonation and she was certain she could make it back in six minutes—but the stress of dealing with the life or death circumstance had left her totally exhausted and drained of energy, and unable to clearly think through the few strategies available to her. She was already committed and couldn't go back down or stop now—she just had to push through to survive.

She pushed and pushed, and pulled in as much air as possible to gain an extra level of energy. It took longer than she expected and her timer was down to two minutes but, at this stage, she didn't want to waste time by looking down at her timer to see how much time was left. She finally reached her destination but struggled through the hatchdoor of her apartment to the point where she was just seconds away from the Semtex package and the detonator. She could see the detonator and reached out to deactivate it, but time had run out.

Death came quickly for Banda and much faster than the many citizens killed in the East End Bombing. She didn't have the benefit of her life moments flashing in front of her for those final seconds: her birth, her life as a child, or the time she spent with her parents, who motivated her and inspired her towards a revolutionary life. There was no chance of reliving her moments with the Movement, or with Jonathan Katcher or Michael Kransich, or the short experience of the failed San Francisco uprising.

Her home of the past decade had blown up, along with the other one-hundred-and-forty-three apartments in the building. It was early afternoon, so not as many natural humans were home but, all up, fifty-four people were killed. There would be times in the future where Banda would be idolized by the next generation of activists for her contributions to the Movement but, for now, her body parts were strewn about in the basement of her apartment, and covered by seven levels of concrete and apartment rubble.

*

Even though San Francisco was still cleaning up its streets and rebuilding after the aftermath of the uprising, the news of the blast at Banda's apartment travelled fast. The datastream on Lestre's lightscreen flashed with a news alert—a citizen's report and story timeline about the bombing of an apartment block in southern San Francisco. Just like the East End Bombing several months ago, this was a big news event, with streams of citizen journalists recording the event, narrowcasting and broadcasting from the site.

Lestre had been scanning the area for further clues since the time she recently created a Biocrime profile for Greta Banda, but as she delved further into the typographical display and scanned through the topographical data, she calculated the bombing she saw in the news reports was in the same apartment block she saw Kransich enter the previous night. She switched into the DNA reading mode on her lightscreen, narrowed it down to the bombing scene and links to Banda's profile. But instead of the DNA coding depicting one location, the lightscreen picked up a number of readings, scattered over three hundred yards. Lestre quickly realized Banda was in the blast, and her body parts had been spread over the site, as well as remnants from the other fifty-four people that died in the blast.

"Fuck!" said Lestre, crunching her fist onto her table. She'd just lost access to a crowd-fund of €500,000 but, more importantly, she had lost what she thought was the main lead to finding Jonathan Katcher.

"What's up?" asked D'Souza, as he roused from the loungeroom couch.

"The woman I was hoping would lead us to Jonathan Katcher is dead. And I've lost the bounty fee."

"Just add it to the bounty for Jonathan Katcher," D'Souza said. "It will all add up in the long run."

"Sure, but I have to fork out the ten per cent for people that have already signed up in the search for Greta Banda."

"Greta who?"

"Greta Banda. She's the one who was receiving Biocrime secrets from Michael Kransich. And probably the one who was passing them on to the Movement. The one in the photo with Jonathan Katcher during the uprising. And now she's fucking dead."

"Call up the data from the East End Bombing," D'Souza said, thinking quickly. This wasn't a case of D'Souza thinking outside the box, but it was an obvious connection. Blasts of any nature were not a frequent occurrence in San Francisco, and the East End Bombing was the most recent one.

"What's your thinking?" asked Lestre, as she called up the key data from the East End Bombing, and placed it side by side with the data from Banda's apartment.

"Two blasts, almost same results," D'Souza said. "Large apartment blocks, many people dead. Look at the aerial shots—ground floor area explodes out, the rest of the building implodes. What was the explosive used in the East End Bombing? Semtex? Analyze the new bombing."

Lestre summoned a deeper delve on the data from Banda's apartment. She extracted sampling data and compared it with the Semtex coding from the East End Bombings. The screen showed a nine-eight per cent match between the Semtex from the two locations, close enough to suggest it was from the same batch.

"It's the same Semtex, but doesn't mean that it came from the same person, or the same location," Lestre said.

"It's not like there's a box of Semtex on every corner of the streets of San Francisco. Of course it's the same!"

"But East End is a Technocrat area," Lestre said, "this area is human. Why would Banda want to blow up an area she lives in?"

"Could be any reason. Could have been an accident, a mistake. Could have been trying to hide evidence, or hide a link. Or she might have found out we were on her case."

"But to kill yourself for the Movement?" said Lestre. "Plausible but unlikely. That's what underlings would do. Being part of the leadership is fulfilling your ego, part of the mode to not only change the world, but be part of that change when it happens. I'd say it was an accident, or she was trying to get back to her apartment for some reason."

"Have you searched the area around Banda's apartment block? There's bound to be something suspicious nearby."

"Since yesterday," Lestre said, "we've searched around the apartment in a five-hundred-yard area, just through the drone and mini-satellite. We could expand a little."

"Zoom out and call up the comparison software," D'Souza said. "Go incremental for topographical changes and any large features."

Lestre entered the comparison mode on her lightscreen and created two inset screens: the screen on the left was a still from current mini-satellite data, and the screen on the right was the same image and ratio, and she commenced an incremental back-dating of the image, a slow-motion time lapse of two seconds per twelve-hour period. The lightscreen image showed an area of about three square miles, and the only changes that had occurred showed the aerial movement of people and vehicles, and the transition from daytime to night.

D'Souza studied the changing screens and after it came up to almost five minutes, he was just about to give up on his brainwave of thought and move onto another idea. But then in the top left section of the screen, there was something that caught his eye.

"Look! There! Slow down and zoom in."

Lestre followed his instruction and zoomed in closer to the image and detected a change in the topography. It was a scan from over a week ago, just before the uprising commenced. They compared the two aerial scans, one from June 6, the other from June 7.

"Zoom in on that part just there," D'Souza said, pointing to an area that appeared to be a large mound of dirt, "and toggle between the two days. "See. It's there on that day, but not the day before."

"I'm sure it's just routine Biocrime work," Lestre said, "just doing the underground surveillance work they routinely do."

"Sure, but zoom in—looks like it hasn't been cleaned up or cleared yet, but take a closer look."

Lestre switched over to live mode and zoomed further to the ground. She could see a mound of dirt, and the three-feet hole extracted by the universal service and monitoring vehicle. Lestre surmised it could have been left behind during the uprising and there hadn't been enough time to clear it up—Biocrime had other priorities—but she scanned around the vehicle and zoomed in further to reveal the body of Agent Jack. His body showed the signs of a week of decay out in the elements, and an extreme zoom revealed his sunken face. It had been pecked at by various birds of prey and smaller insects and, trying to deflect the macabre image, Lestre scanned further until she noticed a datacard next to the body.

She zoomed in on the datacard, and called up the serial code—GT-4536-2517-XY—and matched it up through the continuum. The code was linked into the Biocrime system but when she tried to access the data remotely, it was heavily encrypted and inaccessible. But in the world of crypto-technology and sophisticated coding, anything could be hacked for anyone prepared to pay the right fee. Lestre summoned up another panel on her lightscreen to create a task post, and entered an insecure deep portal within the continuum where all kinds of illicit activities and services were available for hire. Even for Lestre, this was a dangerous zone to access, and the end result that she was trying to achieve might not provide her with immunity, but she needed to act swiftly and urgently.

She spoke gently into the lightscreen—"Urgent decryption service required for visual recording"—prompting an auto-fill function which completed the rest of her post. It wasn't a usual course of action for her, so she carefully checked the predictive text on her screen.

Visual recording, coded GT-4536-2517-XY, heavily encrypted, require open access to datacard and visual material.

Course of action: Password and release of visual material

Payment: Time-based incremental fee of €500 per minute, maximum €10,000, minimum €1,000.

It was like a reverse auction, as well as a race against time, where the sooner the decryption occurred, the closer the task payment matched the maximum €10,000 fee.

It was a high fee, but it was an incentive to have the decryption completed as soon as possible and, within thirty seconds of lodging the task, Lestre's lightscreen showed six hackers had taken up the job, each of which was hoping to attract the maximum fee.

While she waited for the decryption task to be completed, Lestre returned to the original post she created for Greta Banda, and summoned a cancellation. The lightscreen responded:

Cancellation fee: €50,000. Do you wish to proceed?

Lestre agreed and the €50,000 was extracted instantly from her income account and distributed to the eighteen people that had already started working on the case to capture Banda. It was a hefty amount but Banda was dead and there wasn't much she could do about it now. For Lestre, cracking the case of finding Jonathan Katcher was the bigger picture and €50,000 would be a relatively small amount compared to the large bounty she would receive if she was the one that found him.

A few minutes later, a data message appeared on her screen—from Grandmaster Ratte', a reformed hacktivist and data groper—the hack was completed in twelve minutes, for a total of €4,000. Lestre scanned through the message and retrieved the data keys, loaded Agent Jack's datacard and extracted the ninety-two minutes of visual recording instantly into her lightscreen. Satisfied with the results, she agreed to the release of the funds to Grandmaster Ratte', and he signed off with the iconic cowskull ACSII-styled artwork that had been fashionable for over a thousand years. It had been an expensive day—€54,000 already but Lestre felt it was a necessary expense and she was getting closer to finding the elusive Katcher.

"Well, that's expensive footage," D'Souza said. "It'd better be worth it."

"It's more than a hunch," Lestre said, "but I've got a good feeling about this. It could be our lucky day."

They both moved towards the lightscreen display and Lestre activated the data. The visual recording from Agent Jack was slow to begin with. It was a multi-cam recording showing simultaneous screens from all six agents that were down in Anika-6, almost like a self-referential loop of visual activity.

Lestre and D'Souza were impatient at first—it was mundane and tedious, and Lestre scanned forward until the agents were shuttling down through the drilled hole and down to the underground. It was dark with the occasional glimpse of a headlamp—Lestre fast-forwarded another ten minutes of footage until it appeared to show the agents had reached the end of the drilled hole and entering into an underground cavern.

She picked up snippets of scratchy lo-fi audio from the agents: *"Not sure what it is… we may as well have a look"*. There was the panning of the lightpen to reveal different parts of the cavern, one section that looked like tents in an underground city. The last grab of audio she picked up was *"there's fucking people down here… What the…"* and *"Get as much data as you can,"* interrupted by red flashes and the sounds of laser gun fire.

Several multi-cam images stopped moving, which Lestre assumed were the cameras from the fallen agents, and she scanned through the visual recording in slow motion. The lighting was not good, but she scanned through and zoomed in on one figure which revealed the face of Jonathan Katcher. She toggled back and forth, zoomed in and out to reveal his possession of a laser gun, and then over to another figure, which seemed to match up with the profile of Greta Banda.

The rest of the footage was a confused red and orange lightshow of laser bullets, but enough for Lestre to determine five of the agents had been killed. The visual footage became a solid black, intercepted with the audio of the tungsten rope retracting, scrapings of Agent Jack resurfacing through the drilled hole, and the sounds of gasping for air. The footage continued until Agent Jack completed his ascent back to the surface, struggled out of the drilled tube, passed out and died, when the auto-record function ceased.

Lestre closed down the visual recording and sat with D'Souza in silence for a minute, a time she needed to compose her thoughts. Although the footage was low quality and difficult to see clearly, it was documentary evidence of the killing of several Biocrime officers, and a definitive link of where Katcher was likely to be found.

"Our new public enemy number one," Lestre said, "has now been placed further up on the perch, and he might be there for some time. Inciting public disorder, revolution and now murder. Not any old murder, but Biocrime officers and there's six of them."

"So, that's the link," D'Souza said. "Banda's apartment—just one mile away—linked up somehow. There'd have to be a tunnel from Banda to this underground cavern and Katcher. But he was up on the surface for the revolution—would he still be down there?"

"There's only one way to find out."

Lestre returned to the lightscreen and checked the GoFunder crowd fund for the capture of Katcher—it had ticked over to €24 million and would continue to rise. She wasn't sure if was best to continue with the public bounty, or close it off to registered Biocrime agents, but she decided it was best to have specialist speleology skills for the final capture—either way, the bounty would be a large portion of the total crowd fund, and Lestre wanted the job completed as efficiently and quickly as possible.

She created another internal task post on the Biocrime profiling system, requesting the services of twenty commandoes with excavation and caving expertize. As usual, it was urgent, and there was a high bounty fee for this difficult assignment. Lestre was sure her man was still alive and down in that deep hole, and she was going to get him.

CHAPTER 32.   CLOSING IN

The final intelligence material from Kransich never made it down to Anika-6: the digital data was destroyed in Banda's apartment, along with her remains. In his haste, Kransich copied whatever data he could and gave it to Banda but, as he had suggested, it confirmed Biocrime's priority was to clean up the streets of San Francisco and restore stability to the community. Their assessment was the people behind the uprising, especially Jonathan Katcher, would be caught in due time but, for now, they weren't the highest priority.

Katcher had recuperated from his injuries but still moved about gingerly in Anika-6, in a state of confusion and insecurity, and he had become impatient with the time it was taking for Banda to return from the surface. No-one knew what the next move should be but Katcher's instinct was they should be on the move, because being on the move meant they were in control: staying still meant other people were pulling the levers.

"No sign of Greta yet," Katcher said to Newton.

"No. She's been gone too long. Something's up. I've tried her on the PPN, but there's no signal. There was some seismological movement above ground, but we've got someone looking at it."

"I think we should move," Katcher said, "close up the systems and get out of here. Scan the tunnel and see what's happening out there."

"Getting all of us out quickly is ambitious," Newton said. "We could access the other supply tunnels, but that's about five miles and would take forever to get through."

Newton summoned his lightscreen to show the view on the other side of the thick control door, but the usual pristine view was cloudy, almost like a thick pea-soup fog. He scanned further up the tunnel and the closer he scanned to the tube tunnel leading up to Banda's apartment, the thicker it became.

"Looks like there's been some kind of disruption or explosion above ground," Newton said to Katcher. "Dust all the way from Greta's tube access to the control door just outside here."

"Switch to surface surveillance, just above Getchen's apartment—I think something's happened to her."

Newton's datastream switched to the surface to show an aerial view but instead of seeing the expected sight of Banda's apartment block, there was a pile of collapsed rubble. He flicked over to the news datacast and there were several incoming citizen reports on the collapse of the apartment block, the amount of deaths and casualties, and the similarities with the East End Bombing.

"Fuck, oh fuck. She's not coming back," Katcher said looking at the news datacast on Newton's lightscreen. "Move to shutdown, and destroy all material. It's time to evactuate."

Newton signaled to the others to start erasure of all data—their key data and material was backed up through their underground cells in other parts of the world, so the process of digitally and physically erasing their local presence commenced. They sprayed fine particles of acid into the datacells of each of the seventy-five lightscreens and to the central data storage, and packed whatever basic food, laser guns and medicines they could find. They were minutes away from commencing evacuation through the five-mile supply links in the other direction when a massive light flare illuminated the entire cavern, followed by several lachrymator capsules, which released plumes of colored smoke and tear gas.

They reached for their laser guns, but the smoke and gas was overpowering. Coming down the drilled hole from the surface were the twenty Biocrime commandoes that accepted Lestre's task request. These agents were more prepared than the last ones that made the descent; their gas masks and impenetrable helmets and jackets made sure of that. They were also equipped with a far superior technological advantage, immune from any smoke or laser bullets, and had anti-glare and smoke receptors in their helmets. While everyone else in Anika-6 was confused by the colored smoke and tear gas, the commandoes could see as clear as day, and proceeded to shoot down the underlings of the underground operations, almost like a turkey shoot, and quickly overpowered and shackled the leaders—Katcher and Newton, and four other data controllers.

It was an operation that ran with the efficiency of an Austrian clock from the fourteen-hundreds—twenty had been killed with precision shooting: Katcher was detained, along with five others from the Movement, and these captures would work wonders for propaganda purposes and increase the crowd funding revenues when it came to the crowd trials. Six crowd trials for these detainees from the Movement, especially the one for Kransich, were going to provide a large financial windfall for Biocrime.

Katcher looked at the face of the commando, a threatening shiny dark charcoal colored mask made out of tungsten. Katcher was sure there was a person somewhere behind the veneer, but the outfit was designed to defy any form of humanity that might exist behind it. The gas had subsided, but Katcher's face was red and puffed up, his eyes welled up and dirty. He looked over to Newton and without saying a word, they both knew it was all over, and the Movement had been set back for a long time. And, as for their punishment, they didn't have the time to consider it, but they both knew the likely outcome.

*

Marine Lestre surveyed the rubble of Banda's apartment, and watched a team of Biocrime contractors removing pieces of glass and concrete, and placing them into a waste removal and recycling vehicle. Another contractor scanned the site for any evidence of life but confirmed the initial reports of fifty-four deaths, and gave the thumbs up for a larger excavation tool to come through and remove the rubble quickly, including human remains. There was nothing left to retrieve and the unsentimental nature of this type of clean-up meant everything was removed quickly.

Another contractor was positioned next to the lateral driller attached to a USM vehicle, a handy machine for enlarging smaller underground cavities, and after several hours of lateral and flexible drilling, the tube canal that previous led from Banda's apartment to the main access tunnel in Anika-6 had become an eight-feet square tunnel.

"Marine! You've got your man."

Lestre turned to her right to see Don Capone and his entourage arrive, Capone's extended hand was a comforting sign that her mission was almost over.

"Not yet," Lestre said, "he's still down there until we finish off this tunnel. He's just sitting down there with enough time to think about what his future might be."

"It's all been confirmed? It's him?"

Lestre held up her cell device and summoned a series of visual recordings and static images and thrust it towards Capone's face.

"The commandoes sent up some images from below," Lestre said. "It's hard getting the data out, but they've bypassed some of the controls the Movement set up down there. The images are very clear."

Lestre swiped through a range of images on the cell device—close-ups of Katcher's face, the digital handcuffs and footcuffs; images of the other five revolutionaries that had been captured; wide-shots of the damage to the data equipment and revealing some of the dead humans; selfie shots of some of the commandoes drinking the second-rate synth coffee while they waited for the escape tunnel to be completed.

"Looks like him," Capone said, "but we can't be a hundred per cent sure until he's back up on the surface."

"What's another hour or so if we've been waiting so long to stitch this guy up," Lestre said. "What are the plans for the rest of the cavern?"

"We have to retrieve the bodies of our guys stuck down there, and then fill it with flexible concrete."

"Not worry about the other bodies or trying to access any data?"

"No, they can all stay down there as far as I'm concerned," Capone said. "I don't even want to retrieve them for pet meat.

As for the data, we've got reports it's all been acidified, except for one lightscreen—it might be useful, but probably only for evidence against Katcher—not that we need anything more—but we haven't got any another data. That's why we'll concrete the cavern so it can be never used again."

Lestre and Capone moved from one area of the site to another, not so much to scan for any other details or evidence, but to pass the time while they waited for Katcher to resurface with his commando escort.

"It was you that got me off those Biocrime charges, wasn't it," Lestre said.

"What makes you think that?" asked Capone.

"It all adds up. The case against me suddenly dropped. I honed my skills on the outside, just doing fine. But then you needed an insider on the outside, someone who knew the logic of Biocrime, someone you could trust who knew what they were doing."

"Biocrime fucked up," Capone admitted, "and it was my fuck up. You know how it is in there—once something is put in place, it's hard to stop. I pulled the investigation when I realized that it couldn't have been you selling those secrets, but it was too late. I had to intervene with Luanda, and she reluctantly pulled the plug too."

"But that was years ago," said Lestre. "Luanda had only just started as *el president*, hadn't she?"

"That's why she didn't want to pull the plug," Capone said. "A back-down at that stage wasn't a good look for a new president, but I managed to get it. I argued that we needed good people onside in the future, rather than sent off to a universal penal zone by mistake. Turned out to be right."

Lestre checked her cell device again, and the status of her crowd funding—a total of €29 million—the biggest crowd fund in history. Around sixty-five per cent would be distributed to Biocrime and the commandoes that finally captured Katcher but, nevertheless, it was a hefty reward for Lestre.

"And getting me on the case?" asked Lestre. "There were hundreds of others you could have chosen, but you chose me. Why."

"Business my dear friend," Capone said. "We needed the best to solve the case, and get the revenues flowing in from it. Assuaging my guilt over my own fuck up? It wasn't intended but it's a bonus."

At the site, there was a growing group of citizen journalists capturing the action on their cell devices, and offering ongoing commentary to whoever and wherever their viewers were through the continuum and Lifebook Live. It was a busy scene, with the droning sound of excavators, rubble and glass lifted into the backs of empty removal and recycling vehicles, the buzz of an expected happening, and the murmuring of citizen journalists filing their stories to their audiences.

Capone checked his cell device and could see the visuals of the hole at the top of the tunnel being secured, and all but six of the commandoes had exited Anika-6 through this top hole. Capone and his entourage were now at the exit point to what was Banda's tunnel: the zone had been cleared and there was now a clear exit point from the Anika-6 underground, back up to the surface.

The first of the commandoes appeared with one of the shackled hacktivists—a no-name that no-one was interested in, but it was the build up to the main event of showing Katcher to the world that was the real plan here. It was the media event that was now of interest to Biocrime, and a graphics and visual production team in the main headquarters prepared a series of stills that would be superimposed over the visual images that were coming out from this live event, to be screened on Lifebook, public billboards and any other visual access point.

They comprised the standard clear televisual graphics that showed the mugshot of each person, name, age and alleged crimes, with the usual text embellishment: *terrorist, fugitive, crimes against community, a member of the Movement, supporter of the uprising.*

Capone summoned Lestre to come closer, so she could see the fruits of her work and to be one of the first to see Katcher when he surfaced from the tunnel. Four of captives had come out, then followed by Silas Newton. After a short five-minute delay to add to the pandemonium, Jonathan Katcher appeared, pushed forward by the lead commando.

Katcher was disheveled, unshaven, cuffed with titanium bracelets, and had the look of confusion, understandable considering he was coming from a dark underground location into the bright midday sun, surrounded by the spectacle of machinery and hoards of people wanting to catch a glimpse. There was an air of expectation as he walked past Capone and Lestre. He grimaced and nodded with a sense that his quest was now over, and then a nod to Capone and Lestre. He'd never met them before but he knew from their stance who they were and the roles they played in his capture.

"And so," Katcher said, glancing at Lestre, "it has come to this."

"You've always had that philosophical bent to you, haven't you," Lestre said, knowing although it wasn't a crime, it was best not to speak to the arrested and apprehended.

"Without philosophy, what is life? My journey ends, but others will take up the Movement. It might take twenty years, it might take a thousand. But it will come."

"Well, this part of your journey is definitely over," Capone said, "Most definitely. I won't be around in a thousand years, but good luck if you can make it." Capone motioned to the commando to continue taking Katcher away.

The six were led forward to a waiting Biocrime vehicle; this vehicle was an orange color, with the obligatory Biocrime logo on the sides. The orange color for these vehicles was used to signify the presumption of innocence, but for all intents and purposes, they were all guilty of their crimes and Biocrime would ensure with all of its tools of propaganda, a high guilty rate would be achieved through the subsequent crowd trial.

The commandoes ensured Katcher was at the front of this queue and had the maximum exposure to the waiting pack of citizen journalists. No-one had ever heard of Silas Newtown or the other four that have been captured, but everyone knew who Jonathan Katcher was, and he was the one that everyone wanted to see. The others were led into the Biocrime vehicle and secured.

It was an ignominious end to Katcher's public life, ushered into an orange van and driven off to a detention center to be processed, and then sent off to a remote island somewhere in the Pacific. Biocrime had everything needed to convict Katcher and every possible piece of evidence they could retrieve for his crowd trial.

It was over. Katcher felt dead even before he got to the Biocrime detention center.

CHAPTER 33.   ARREST AND PROCESSING

The orange vehicle sped quickly through the streets of San Francisco on its way to the Biocrime detention center, a location not part of the headquarters, but in a fortified location at San Quentin. Katcher sat in the back of the vehicle, wondering about the speed of his delivery to incarceration. He pondered about why humans, contrary to the infinite patience of the universe, always acted in haste to get things done—he'd been captured, he wasn't going to somehow escape, and speeding to save what could end up being twenty or so minutes seemed pointless to Katcher.

Although the vehicle travelled at a rapid speed, the journey seemed to go on forever—not that Katcher was too concerned, as every delay was advantageous to him and postponed the inevitable dispatch to a universal penal zone. Eventually, Katcher and the four hacktivists arrived at the Biocrime detention center, dressed in their personalized orange and black detention overalls, and taken to different parts of the location for processing.

Once he was inside, Katcher didn't mind the detention center too much: he'd been there before but noticed it had changed since the last time he was detained in 3024. He knew in keeping with the 'do not kill' principle of Biocrime, even though it was largely a façade, he would be treated relatively well. It was the other part—'do no evil'—that troubled him most, as he knew this motto paid lip service to an ethic that didn't exist.

His waiting room was almost like a triage cubicle at an emergency hospital—a small room with five seats, and a protected window to a small room housing what seemed to be a Biocrime bureaucrat processing new arrivals. It was safe for both: Katcher was shackled and the bureaucrat was protected by a clear shielded glass. A large lightscreen attached to the wall showed the televisuals of his capture, and a smaller screen in the corner depicting rapidly changing and advancing numbers. Katcher had that short reflective moment where he realized he was the one on the wall screen and, although it took him a while to work it out, it was the beginning of his crowd trial on Lifebook.

Even though it was only a few hours since he was captured at Anika-6, his crowd trial had already commenced and the legal documentation was fully available through the continuum and Lifebook—unlike his trial from a decade ago, in this case, there was no prosecution or defense team: just an outcome manufactured online decided by the crowd, and a simply mathematical choice: fifty per cent, plus one, meant a guilty verdict and anything less than that guaranteed freedom.

An update on the wall screen flashed up an unsavory criminal mugshot of Katcher, with the current crowd trial numbers, key graphs and pendulum graphics. Although it was early, the figures were not good for Katcher: there were two columns of figures: Guilty, showing a total of 967,456, and Not Guilty, a total of 87,112, a percentage of 91.7. The next graphic provided a reminder for all citizens to cast their vote through Lifebook within the next six hours, before the closure of the crowd trial, and then returned to the televisuals of his capture, the destruction on the streets of San Francisco, and further propagandizing against the Movement.

Katcher's crowd trial was the main event, but trials of the others captured at Anika-6 were held concurrently and, after a few minutes of watching his own image on the wall screen, the profile of Silas Newton appeared. His figures were just as damning as Katcher's, and the other four hacktivists—names that Katcher didn't even know: Angela Prizmic; Julian Brogden; Sidartha Amarpu; Marcus Azzapardi—followed in a cycle after Newton, before the visuals returned to Katcher. He expected to see the name of Greta Banda appear for one of the crowd trials, just as a confirmation that she was alive, or had evaded capture, but it was a name that never appeared.

Assuming that he would be waiting for another six hours before his crowd trial was determined—and he wasn't expecting anything other than a verdict of guilty—Katcher tried to move his mind into a meditative state to help pass the time, when another image of another crowd trial appeared on the wall screen, a mugshot with the name below: Michael Kransich.

Katcher had never met Kransich, but in the photograph on the wall screen, his glazed eyes appeared to sink inside his head, a consequence of the memory extraction a few days earlier. There was a list of his purported crimes, along with the causal explanation of the link between each of his acts and the devastation of San Francisco.

A special treatment would be reserved for Kransich. Because he was a Technocrat, he was presented as a traitor—which he was—for revealing Biocrime secrets to the Movement, and instigating a massive risk to the citizenry, an act of foolishness that resulted in deaths and instability for the community. Biocrime never missed an opportunity to reveal and shame one of their own to deter others. Biocrime had already recreated a visual recording of his misdemeanors: his meetings with Banda, the explosions at Anza Vista that killed over six-hundred Technocrats, Kransich shackled and processed at the detention center.

The voiceover as part of the visual imagery kept referring to Banda in the past tense, which raised Katcher's concern about what had happened to her, until the final section of Kransich's video segment confirmed what he had expected: the voiceover explained how Kransich was under suspicion and underwent memory extraction to reveal all of his trading of Biocrime secrets to the Movement, and in an unrelated act, Banda had been killed in the explosion in the apartment block.

Katcher felt sorrow, but not shock. He had only known Banda for a short time and although she was a part of the plot to reclaim the world for the Movement, he felt no deeper emotional attachment to her. So much had happened in such a short period and time continued in a compressed state; but defeat and loss had few friends, and Katcher was quick to detach himself psychologically from the recent past. He'd always been a loner: the Revolution Five was short-lived and provided him with some succor for a future he could believe in but, from this group, it was only he and Silas Newton left, a person he barely knew.

The large lightscreen on the wall continued with the visuals from Kransich's crowd trial, played over and again, before it returned to Katcher's material again: the constant voiceover and the confusion of numbers, figures, statistics and graphs provided the opportunity for Katcher to retrieve the meditative state he was after, and he slowly descended into a sleep, something that helped him pass the next six hours quickly.

*

Katcher thought he was in Anika-6 when he awoke, but he was reminded of his place when he tried to move out of his chair in the waiting room and realized he was still cuffed with titanium bracelets. This was one of the few items that had stubbornly resisted the waves of massive technological change—it was still the best way to fully restrict a prisoner and ensure they weren't able to go anywhere. Digital products such as virtual ankle bracelets and detection mechanisms were tried over the years, and were frequently used to detain prisoners, but the cuffs were still considered the best and most effective, as well as maintaining a historical link with penal societies from millennia ago. Although the cuffs automatically registered the name and details of the person they were attached to, detention officers still preferred to go through the motion of verifying the identity of the prisoner.

The Biocrime security officer stood over Katcher, firmly roused him from his slumber and, in one quick action, lifted him into an upright position. Katcher felt the force was unnecessary but wasn't foolish enough to engage in futile resistance—there was nothing he could do and the forces against him were too great to allow him to engage in a fracas with this security officer and manufacture an unlikely escape.

As Katcher was led away from the waiting room and into a processing unit, he noticed more surveillance screens, more Biocrime security officers and subtle changes to uniform compared to the last time he was inside. The black and orange outfits were still the same, but stylized differently—clean and neat, with a small Biocrime logo on the front—and Katcher was impressed with the professional look. But the business here was to confirm his deportation to a universal penal zone, and he knew this was the only outcome when he was forced to sit down in front of the Biocrime processing officer, who quickly started the administrative work to decommission Katcher's existence in the world.

"Name?" asked the processing officer, sternly and officiously.

"You know my name—"

"—name?"

"Okay. Jonathan Katcher."

As the voice recorded details were converted to text and appeared on the processing officer's lightscreen, Katcher noticed the identity on the officer's shirt: 'Clinton Forster 4465'. *Clinton…* Katcher thought about whether Clinton had just been given a random name at the incubation hospital, or whether he'd taken the name of the human that had supplied their DNA so another Technocrat could be created.

He also thought about which was the worse proposition: Clinton, the Technocrat in front of him who was just about to process the end of his life, or the natural human who sold his DNA for a song, so Clinton could be created? Was Katcher's revolutionary life concerned about the lives of all natural humans, even the one's selling their DNA who contributed to the modern Technocratic life, or should he have just been saving his kind, people like Banda who was now gone, or Newton, who was also going to suffer the same fate as him?

"Is it 'For-ster' or 'Fost-er'?" asked Katcher. "And do you know who your mother is?"

Katcher liked to talk and he tried to engage in at least some banter with Office Forster but, to Katcher, he seemed like the standard Technocrat: do the required work—and not much more. Anything that was superfluous to the task at hand used up energy and reduced efficiency. For Office Forster, his task was to process Katcher, not to answer irrelevant questions.

It took a few minutes for all of Katcher's details, profile and crowd-fund results to appear on Officer Forster's screen.

"Jonathan Katcher," Officer Forster announced, "we now have your crowd trial and profile results through Lifebook, and I'm obliged to read them out to you. Your alleged actions are Community Subversion, Community Treason, Counter-Establishment, Terrorism. The crowd results show 39,404,767 affirm, 230,188 deny."

"Only two-hundred and thirty thousand deny?" asked Katcher. "That's a real slap in the face."

Unhumored, Officer Forster continued. "Ninety-nine point four-one per cent of crowd citizens confirm your alleged actions, and you are found by Biocrime to be guilty."

Katcher repeated the 99.41 figure in his mind. He knew he'd be found guilty but 99.41? The figures must have been fabricated but it didn't matter. These were level seven actions, the highest level of crime, and the crowd had decided he was guilty. But *99.41?*

"As a result," Officer Forster said, "you will be transported to a universal penal zone vessel and taken to the next available position in a universal penal zone."

"Which one?" Not that it mattered to Katcher. He still tried to be talkative and engage with Officer Forster. He'd just pissed up his whole life against the wall and was trying to manage his emotions and make light of it.

"Which ever one is next," Officer Forster said. "Biocrime doesn't choose, it's random. You know it will be one of two, West Zone or South Zone."

The banality of bureaucracy thought Katcher. The end of life as he knew it, cut down at the age of forty-four. How would he be remembered? Would there be another Revolution Five in the future? Would other natural humans take up the Movement, or was this the end of it?

"This way, please," Officer Forster said, pointing in the direction of yet another processing room, "this way, Jonathan Katcher."

The more he heard the name 'Jonathan Katcher', the more irrelevant it sounded. *Who is Jonathan Katcher* he thought. *Who was Jonathan Katcher?*

Officer Forster led Katcher into the final processing room where, officially at least, Katcher would be terminated. Katcher's bracelet was scanned and his details appeared on another lightscreen, this one attached to a dye sublimation printing machine and two sockets, one to insert his left arm into, the other for his left leg.

Although printing technology largely disappeared many centuries ago, Biocrime was the receptacle for all kinds of old-fashioned machines, the sublimator being one of them.

Officer Forster was decommissioning Katcher, linking the Biocrime crowd-funded adjudication with his main Biocrime profile. There were several sections on the lightscreen he had to go through to terminate Katcher's account, with final verification after he went through four more prompts. There would be an archival process for historical interest and future investigative work by Biocrime, but after physically linking to Katcher's body, all DNA data and light recording from this point on would cease.

"Jonathan Katcher," Officer Forster said, almost like the voice of an automatum. "Please insert your left arm in the top socket, and your left leg into the bottom socket."

The sublimator was a large white metallic box resembling a horizontal freezer, shoulder height when someone was seated, and had the surface area of a large table. The two sockets were to the right side of the sublimator; Katcher sat down, rolled up his arm sleeve and trouser leg, and placed his arm and leg into the available spaces, rubbered straps automatically secured both his limbs, and he was unable to move.

Officer Forster activated the sublimator and Katcher felt a sharp pain on his left forearm and just above his left ankle, and then the smell of a medical disinfectant. The hum of the sublimator printer continued, and two sublimated sticker sheets were printed and appeared in a side tray.

The rubber straps were released, Katcher extracted his arm and leg, and looked at the back of this forearm, which was etched with a barcode and the alpha-numeric SANFRA-56187261-JK. Katcher worked out the obvious—'SANFRA' was the world code for San Francisco, the numbers were his universal income code and the final characters were his initials.

Officer Forster peeled the sublimated sheets, and stuck one on the front of Kester's shirt, the other sheet on his back. The sheets contained his summary details:

Jonathan Katcher
SANFRA-56187261-JK
Natural human

Community Subversion
Community Treason
Counter-Establishment
Terrorism
Murder
Affirmation: 99.41

BIRTH 1.4.2990
TERMINATION 7.5.3034
SOUTHERN PENAL ZONE

The processing unit had completed its work. Katcher was now officially dead to the world.

CHAPTER 34. DEPORTATION

Katcher assumed it was morning, as he had just woken up in his single cell cubicle, but there was no way of knowing. He had been taken from one location to another the previous night and while the interior of the cubicle depressed him, at least it offered some respite from the constant moving around. The Biocrime detention center was sunless, windowless, almost airless, and possibly the most stark environment on the globe. Aside from its corporate mantras and loglines placed sporadically on the walls in large lettering—'do no evil' the most prominent—there was little else of note.

He wasn't sure when he would be moved on to the next stage of this process but scant information was part of the mindgames Biocrime loved to play on its detainees. No-one told him what to expect from now on, but Katcher felt that whatever it was, it was going to happen sooner rather than later. After a basic synth breakfast of poached eggs on sourdough with a coffee—which was quite good and nourishing in Katcher's opinion—he was moved on from his cubicle by two Biocrime security guards.

In a journey reminiscent of the travel down the circular tunnel into Anika-6, he was taken endlessly down until they reached what he assumed was the basement of the building, with the doors opening up to show a large window-less vehicle—it was predominantly red, but also contained the Biocrime orange and black corporate coloring on its side paneling, a white logo of two stylized people, with a thick arrow pointing towards an icon of a container ship, and then the large white letters 'UPZ'. Logo-wise, Katcher thought it was well designed, and typical of how well a cynical and slick style could hide the actions and intentions of a malevolent corporation.

Katcher was bundled into the back of the red vehicle, in with twelve others, all dressed in their personalized orange overalls and all with the printed termination sheets on their fronts and backs. He could see on some exposed arms and ankles, the same sublimated tattooed barcode markings as his. And all of them, like Katcher, were officially dead.

He could see the face of Silas Newton, which he expected—after all, the two had been arrested at the same time—but he was surprised to see the face of Michael Kransich, who he'd assume would have been withheld for further propaganda purposes but, perhaps, Biocrime had recorded everything they needed and decided to cut costs by sending all terminations over to the universal penal zone at the same time. Besides, if Biocrime needed any further vision for propaganda, it was relatively easy to manufacture and manipulate the footage they'd already recorded of Kransich.

As the door to the large red vehicle closed and started off to wherever they were going—Katcher assumed they were being taken to an airport or straight to the universal penal zone vessel somewhere near the docks—he moved closer to Newton. As far as Biocrime and the rest of the world was concerned, they didn't exist anymore.

"That's it, it's the end," Katcher said.

"We fucked up," Newton said, "totally, fucked, up."

"It's okay Silas, it's just a part of it," Katcher said. "Others will take up the Movement and we did what we could. Remember the Jews? Just like them, it might take us another few hundred years or a millennia, but we'll get there."

"Yeah, the Promised Land," Newton said, his expression suggesting he wasn't as sanguine as Katcher. "More like the murdering fields. Took them a thousand years to get back there, and then fucked it up for another thousand years."

History was littered with many failed causes over the years, and many that ebbed and flowed, and glowed with hope, only to be cut down when the mistakes were made, the wrong strategy used, or the wrong people involved.

Kransich sat in the opposite section of the vehicle, unemotional and totally disengaged with his surroundings. His mind had been zapped by the memory extraction but he still had the power of thought and recollections. *Was all the gambling, alcohol, all that fucking worth it? Was it worth it to live like a real human and end up shamed, humiliated?* He wasn't fully aware he was surrounded by other fugitives in the back part of the red vehicle but his awareness would gradually improve on the long boat trip to the universal penal zone. As intended by Biocrime, he'd certainly have the time to relive his mistakes and ponder where he went wrong.

Katcher quickly scanned around to the others in the vehicle, and focused on a face he recognized—it was Radhika Romanov, the off-grid woman Biocrime chased down several months ago and entered her back into the continuum. He also recognized some of the others from Anika-6, and other unfamiliar faces, their origins unknown to him. They'd all been sanitized with mextractodine administered by Biocrime, an amalgam of morphine and artificial endorphine. It was used to gain intelligence from off-the-grid citizens—a substance that stopped the body from passing out and magnified levels of pain. They were all officially dead to the world, but they physically looked dead too—they would survive the cargo vessel trip to the universal penal zone but, even if they did, they would probably be the first ones to perish after that.

Katcher could see on their sublimated sheets, they were guilty of the same crimes as he and Newton, and also had crowd affirmation rates of close to a hundred per cent. He gave a queried look over to Newton to assess any recognition of the others in the vehicle.

"I don't know them," Newton said, "but they would have been part of the underground. Tortured, the information Biocrime wanted extracted from them, and sent them off with us to finally die."

"That means they'll find the underground tribe and the others in the Movement?" asked Katcher.

"Yeah, probably, but they'll only send off the leaders to a penal zone. People like us, maybe a few others like these guys, and 're-educate' the others, maybe detain them for a week or two. Get them to work as spies, the weak ones. It's all broken."

"There'll be others though," Katcher said.

"Maybe."

"We managed to break the Biocrime system," Katcher said. "We didn't break into it for long, but we managed to break it. And it might not be us in the future, but someone will break into Biocrime again."

CHAPTER 35.   ARRIVAL AT THE PORT OF AUCKLAND

The supply-chain logistics behind the transportation was quite sophisticated, with a network of large red vehicles, just like the one Katcher was imprisoned in, travelling in the larger cities around the world, and taking their human cargo to their local docklands, almost like a livestock animal trade.

The Motor Vessel *Nova Tampa* was one of the larger ships used for human transportation, an imposing purpose-built container ship of a length of almost nine-hundred feet, and width of around a hundred feet. There were many of these around the world that were destined for one of the two universal penal zones and the MV *Nova Tampa* floated patiently at its dock in the Port of Oakland, waiting for its new arrivals.

It was a technologically advanced vessel that was painted in the ubiquitous orange, and the large black Biocrime lettering on its side gave a clear indication of ownership and intent. Although this vessel was only thirty-three years old, the name of MV *Nova Tampa* originated from a similar container vessel—the MV *Tampa*—that rescued almost five-hundred refugees and asylum seekers in the early part of the twenty-first century in torrid ocean waters near the South Asia Zone and, after this point, the 'Tampa' name was used to signify any kind of vessel that transported human cargo.

The red vehicle drove towards the docklands and through a large anonymous gated area, and then onto a small bridge that connected the base of the dock to the innards of the MV *Nova Tampa*. It was predominantly an automated experience, with scanning devices at each checkpoint automatically accessing the barcode printed on the ankles of each occupant in the red vehicle, and asserting all twelve detainees were still present as it reached its destination inside the vessel.

Inside the red vehicle, there weren't many exchanges of words, just the occasional glance around from each of the occupants, as if to confirm this event was really taking place and grasping to a forlorn hope that there could be a final part of redemption, and their lives could continue just like before.

Once the red vehicle securely reached inside the MV *Nova Tampa*, the engines stopped and, with due efficiency, the back doors swung open and a team of black-masked security officers and robocops took each of the twelve occupants out and scanned their ankle barcodes, a process which synchronized their details to a unique fingerprint code and would allow them to access a specially provided cabin. The twelve would join the other four-hundred-and-forty-eight detainees already on the vessel, and each of them would be solitarily confined to their cabins for the duration of the journey.

Katcher assessed his surroundings inside the cavernous hull and, as he expected, it resembled a multi-storey prison block. He didn't care too much about which universal penal zone he was going to but whatever was at the end of this journey, he wanted the process to be over and done with as quickly as possible. It was a wordless experience, but he was led by one of the Biocrime security officers and a robocop up the stairwell and past a series of other rooms until he came to a room with a light-emitting-diode display above the door, indicating his name, and the destination of the Port of Auckland.

The Port of Auckland was in the heart of the southern penal zone and Katcher estimated the journey would take around twenty days in good weather conditions, a decision that he found favorable, as it assured him he was ever so slightly in control of his circumstances.

The Biocrime security officer instructed Katcher to access the door with his fingerprint, pushed him in and slammed the door shut. The room was about twenty-five feet long and about ten feet wide, a size Katcher considered to be reasonable: a basic room, but it contained a sleeping area, and table and a small food processor, what looked like an area for doing exercise sit-ups and push-ups, and a washing area with a narrow shower, laundry and toilet.

His room was one of the few with a porthole, and Katcher looked through it to take in his last views of San Francisco. His room was slightly higher up than the others, and he seemed to be about thirty feet above the ground. It afforded him a view of parts of the Port of Oakland and revealed the industry of a port devoid of human activity; a series of driverless cranes lifted container crates into even larger ships; remote trucks assembled boxes of organic materials; robotic sweepers picked up debris in their efforts to keep the ports clean. The MV *Nova Tampa* itself was a captain-less vessel, a large ship controlled remotely from the Biocrime headquarters, the only staff on board was a collection of one-hundred robocops and seventy well-armed and well-paid security officers whose job it was to secure the passage of the four-hundred-and-sixty detainees to the southern penal zone.

It was a room that would be his home for the next twenty days and, like the other detainees, he wouldn't be leaving the room until they arrived in the Port of Auckland. Katcher lay down on the small sleeping area, a thin ground-level rubber mattress that he found surprisingly comfortable. From this vantage point, he saw a grey barcoded bag made from hemp material stashed under the table, and he leaned over to open the contents. He was surprised to see the top of the bag contained some items of his clothing, which he assumed Biocrime retrieved from his apartment and decided that a man destined to die must have at least some memories and personal artifacts from his life. He quickly took off his orange overalls, momentarily studied the barcode on his left arm, and changed into his personal clothing.

He looked further into the grey hemp bag and retrieved the remaining items: the earing from his mother, the small urn containing the ashes of his father, the post-card size cover of Tolstoy's *War and Peace*, and a wrapped small thick package. It was a poignant moment, and Katcher had no idea about how these items were brought here, or who retrieved them. As far as he knew, he had taken his personal items down to Anika-6 and they would have been destroyed or discarded once Biocrime came across them.

He opened the small wrapped package and inside was a printed book from the year 2390 titled 'Kirsten Chamber's War *and Peace*', one of the last books ever printed. He checked the inside pages and the text was actually the original words written by Leo Tolstoy, but he remembered that in keeping with the level of appropriation that had taken place throughout history, Kirsten Chambers must have purchased the right to publish *War and Peace* in her own name. Katcher had only read the novel on a lightscreen some years ago and, he'd almost forgotten how to read a printed book, but he turned a few pages past the frontispiece and commenced reading. He only read several pages before he lost focus and his concentration, and fell into dark and deep sleep.

*

The days and nights merged through the eternal boredom of solitary confinement and Katcher had lost count of the days he had been on this vessel. Each day was only slightly discernable from the previous one and it was difficult to either keep the count or be reminded of the mental signposts that provided any clues to him. He had fallen asleep while the vessel was docked in the Port of Oakland: he was tired and overwhelmed with the proceedings and the next time he awoke and looked through the porthole in his room, it was pitch black outside and there was nothing that could give an offering to what his bearings could be.

Over the following days, he exercised whenever he could in the restricted exercise area and interchanged his clothing between his own and the orange Biocrime overalls so he could wash his clothes several times each day, just to pass the time. For amusement, he produced a low humming noise to mimic and synchronize with the sounds of the engines of the vessel coming from deep below, and, like a child, he played a range of Scrabble games in his mind with imaginary friends.

Katcher also kept himself occupied by playing games within his book; deciding which part of *War and Peace* was the best, and fluctuating between the endless number of characters within the story. He became obsessed with the name of Kirsten Chambers and, although her name only appeared on the cover of the printed book and several times within the frontispiece, he etched her name out with his fingernails and, failing to find any type of utensil to write with, he used leftover synth coffee and his index finger to scrawl a capital 'T'—for Tolstoy—in her place.

He tried to recount parts of *War and Peace* as a mental exercise, and read aloud certain key moments that enthused him; or counted votes in his internal competition to decide upon the best extract from the book, before agreeing on the scene where Prince Andrew was hit in the head with a bludgeon in the field of battle, chiding himself for not appreciating the vast blue sky above him as he lay on the battleground looking towards the heavens, half-way between life and death.

Inspired by this passage of prose, Katcher looked out the porthole, wanting to see a magnificent vista of the blue sky melding into the splendid shades of aquamarine, but all he saw was grey clouded skies, and an endless depressing dark steel blue ocean that resembled a flat plain of concrete, rather than a panorama of hues that inspired the imagination.

Although it was painful to recollect, his mind jumped from thinking about the failed revolution, his meetings with Banda, and the death that consumed his good friends, Scanlen and Renalda. He also thought about why he was given a printed copy of *War and Peace*, as well as the small amount of personal belongings. Was it for Biocrime to offer some kind of homage to the person they had captured and assuage the institutional guilt of sending people off to their likely death? Was it Biocrime again paying lip service to their motto of 'do no evil', providing mementoes as last rites to prisoners before their *de facto* execution?

Katcher again looked out the porthole and decided it must be day fifteen of this journey. He thought that whatever awaited him and his fellow travellers when they arrived at the southern penal zone would be simple, compared to this interminable and insufferable boredom. He used his powers of concentration to imagine a clear blue sky but the view outside remained stubbornly attached to a deep wet grey. Katcher was right: it was day fifteen of this journey, which meant there were five more days of internal introspection, literary competitions, mental games with imaginary friends and the inane repetitive washing of clothes.

*

The final day of the journey to the southern penal zone was marred by inclement weather, heavy rain and winds at the speed of a hundred and thirty miles per hour, and a rising swell rocked the MV *Nova Tampa*. It was still around two hundred miles away from its destination, and the vessel barely moved at seventeen knots per hour and, perhaps, still another ten hours of the journey to go.

It was three o'clock in the morning and Katcher couldn't sleep. He'd exhausted all permutations for amusing himself and biding his time, and even sleeping couldn't keep the infinitesimal tedium at bay. The rocking of the vessel and the pounding of the restless waves against the side walls made sleep difficult, but Katcher had almost reached his mental point of oblivion and it was unclear to him whether another escape into the nocturnal zone would make any difference. He matched his circadian rhythms with the rolling of the vessel and this helped to close his mind and moved him into a hallucinogenic state that made the time move faster.

Several hours later, the encroaching sunlight through the porthole made Katcher more alert to his environment and he surmised the vessel was closer to land. The roaring sounds of the rough seas had been replaced with a serene flat expanse of water and the vessel cut through the waves cleanly and efficiently. He peered out of the porthole and the aftermath of the storm had left a cold cloudy veneer of steam above the water, almost as though they were travelling through a discarded haunted cemetery in the dead of night. He could see flashes of land and trees through the cold clouds of water vapor but could not make out whether the vessel was closer to a mainland, or whether these were some kind of disparate islands playing tricks on his mind.

All of a sudden, his door was unlocked and two plastic-masked Biocrime security guards barged in officiously, followed by three robocops, and instructed Katcher to collect his items and place them in the grey hemp bag, and then cuffed his hands. He was moved out of his room and, through the corridor, he could see all the other detainees moving upwards in unison. It was perversely quiet and Katcher felt the anxiety building up deep into his throat, as he imagined the feelings of Jeanne d'Arc, the heroine from the French Zone during the Hundred Years' war in the fourteen hundreds, just before she was burnt at the stake. And the feelings of the scores of people throughout the Europe Zone that were led to their extermination during the world war of the 1940s: the Jews, Romani, Russians, Poles; the gay men and lesbians; the mentally and physically disabled; all the people from history Katcher identified with. Katcher and all the detainees were moved from their cells and, eventually, all four-hundred-and-sixty were huddled at the open top deck of the vessel, resembling pockets of penguins jostling for the best view from the icepack.

The views from the open top deck of the vessel were impressive and showed a large island leading into the port, but it was difficult to discern fully what lay beyond, as the vapor above the cold waters partially obscured the view. The vessel moved closer towards the Port of Auckland, and a group of

Biocrime security officers and robocops advanced in a small dinghy to activate two tug boats that would help navigate the MV *Nova Tampa* into the port.

Katcher could see on either side of the water, a solid titanium picketed fence of around a hundred feet high that seemed to go on as far as the eye could see. There was a pungent smell, not overwhelming, but constant—a combination of decaying food and meat, sewerage, excrement and an odd industrial chemical stench.

The two heads of the port were surrounded by lush forest, but there were instances where Katcher could see the rubble of what seemed to be a series of old dwellings. In the distance, there was a collection of taller skyscrapers and apartment buildings, but instead of seeing the clean and stylized concrete designs, these were covered with green moss, lichen and overgrown foliage. From what he could see, many of the building structures had crumbled and were decrepit, a modern-day version of the ruins of the ancient Colosseum in the Southern Europe zone. It was a confusing sight, almost like coming across a forgotten and broken city in the middle of a cold savannah; lush, seductive and mysterious, but not in a clever or benevolent manner.

It was relatively peaceful, until Katcher heard the sound of some kind of animal that screeched in the distance, followed by other unusual guttural noises, and he could hear the sound of water and waves lapping the foreshore. It was gentle and serene, but it was an awkward silence. In the aftermath of the storm, the skies were still a deep dark gray, and a light drizzling rain began to fall.

Through the crowd of detainees on the top deck, Katcher could see familiar faces: Newton, Kransich and, further along, Radhika Romanov. It was like an unintended collective act of silence, and the use for words had expired, a suggestion there was no further need for them.

As the crisp breeze flushed through the top deck and onto Katcher's face, he optimistically reminded himself about the doubts of what lay exactly within the confines of the universal penal zone—doubts which were just about to be removed. Every citizen knew about the universal penal zone: most were fearful, but there were cynics who believed that like all propaganda, these zones were just a fanciful idea to deter the citizen population from illegal behavior and anti-community activities. The cynics believed the opposite of the common version—far from being a place of dread and horrible deaths, it was actually a utopian haven of plenty: a type of Faustian bargain for activists to give up the errors of their ways in the common land, never to return, but live the life of pleasure in a remote area. The universal penal zone was outside of the continuum and no-one could see what went on there, so any absurd or fanciful theory could be entertained.

The vessel arrived closer to the docks in the Port of Auckland. There was a well-serviced embarking ramp and jetty but beyond that, it was decrepit, aged and rusted. Further beyond the jetty through the lush forest, Katcher could see small pockets of activity through the canopy. It looked partially like a human zoo, partially like a wildlife enclosure and had the feel of an apocalypse, a forgotten world from a thousand years ago.

In the distance, Katcher could see what looked a disheveled bearded man masturbating, mimicking the actions of a chimpanzee, gesticulating wildly. His eyes scanned to another part of the forest, and he saw a tiger for the first time in his life, but it seemed about twice the size he expected it to be and was feasting on the carcass of what he assumed to be a woman. Further along, he could see a smaller group of upright animals that had a human appearance, but were crushing the head of some kind of beast with a large stone. Katcher had never seen these kinds of creatures before, but they reminded him of *homo naledi*, a species of primitive hominin humans that roamed the world about 350,000 years ago.

There were other animals that ventured close to the docks to gain a closer look at the incoming vessel, as though they were curiously expecting an incoming treat and a fresh delivery of sustenance, and they seemed to suggest their approval. It was hard to discern but many had human similarities and all had consistent features—hollow faces and emaciated bodies, an indicator of a lack of food and resources in this universal penal zone.

Katcher could feel the dread enveloping his insides, and felt a strong tension inside his stomach, as well as the feeling of nausea created by the stench. The glimpses of life that he saw at the Port of Auckland confirmed the many fears he held of the universal penal zone and now, he was going to witness it for himself and suffer his demise.

DID YOU ENJOY THE BOOK? YOU CAN MAKE A BIG DIFFERENCE TO THIS INDEPENDENT WRITER!

Reviews are the best way for independent authors to receive attention for their books, and to help them write even more material in the future! In the indie world, we don't have the same resources and large marketing teams the established publishers have to run large-scale advertising or heavy the bookstores into stocking their best-seller titles. It's us against the machine.

But what can we do in this continuous battle with the giants of the publishing world?

Easy. Ask for reviews from our readers!

Reviews of my books help to bring them to the attention of other readers.

I'd be very grateful if you could spend just a short amount of time to leave a review from the online location where you obtained this book—it doesn't matter how long the review is: a few choice words, a short pithy statement, or a long paragraph; it all makes a difference.

Thank you!

ABOUT THE AUTHOR

 Erik Tabain is a future fiction writer and is the author of *The Biocrime Spectrum* series. He occasionally dabbles in crime writing and horror stories. He has lived in many parts of the world—including the United Kingdom, Eastern Europe, North America and Australia—but his online home is: www.eriktabain.com
You can connect with Erik Tabain on **Facebook** and **Twitter**.

BOOKS BY ERIK TABAIN

The Biocrime Spectrum series.

The next installment of *The Biocrime Spectrum* will appear towards the end of 2019.

www.ingramcontent.com/pod-product-compliance
Lightning Source LLC
Chambersburg PA
CBHW071147100726

47908CB00002B/275